The Kingdom of Haven Series

The Order of the Wolf
Stenson Blues
The Eastern Factor

THE EASTERN FACTOR

FREDDIE SILVA

Wolf
Jape

MAP

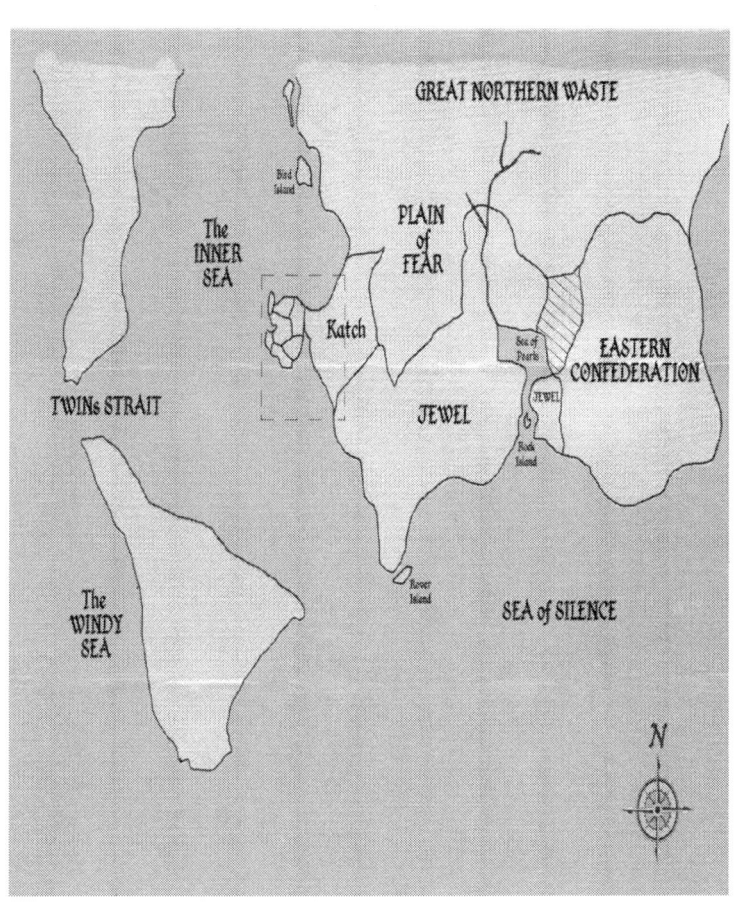

CHAPTER 1: THE ENDLESS SEA

I couldn't get the vision out of my head: the flash of a dagger, a spray of crimson blood, and Tessa's face gone stark white. When I reached her side, she asked, "Why are you crying?" Her voice was bewildered, as if she didn't know that I loved her—or couldn't understand that she was dying.

Tessa of the night-dark hair and scarred visage—she had been the love of my life. Yet she had died calling out to her long-dead husband and child, as if I had never lived in her heart. And she was lost because of my stupidity.

Tears came, hot and fast. I thought they had dried up for good.

"Master Olaf." A familiar voice called from over my shoulder.

I gripped the sterncastle rail, shifting my gaze to sea and pretending not to hear. I was on a voyage to the Eastern Confederation—running away, really, from that flashing dagger and the realization that my ladylove had greeted another in the Halls of the Dead.

The ship lurched and I caught myself against the rail.

"Master Olaf." Gabriele's voice grew closer. "Will you take your meal?"

The sea breeze dried my tears, leaving my face feeling brittle from the salt. I spun around to glare at my maid. She stood taller than I, because of my twisted right leg. It irked me every time I looked up at her. She wore a blue woolen dress and white cap with strands of her fair-colored hair peeking out around the edges. Gabriele was pretty, but could not compare to the imperfect beauty that had been Tessa.

Gabriele's presence was an unintended consequence of making her brother, Bren, my valet. For some reason, I had inherited his entire family when I took him into my service. His mother served as

1

my housekeeper, his sister Gabriele as my maid, and his youngest sister—I had no idea what she did.

I looked past Gabriele to spy my valet on the main deck below. Bren stood out among the barely clad sailors in my crew, with his Stenson blue trousers and coat. His normal, impeccable appearance was marred only by his lack of shoes; he had decided to leave them off in imitation of the crew. Seeing him barefoot reminded me of our time together in the stables at Stenson House.

Bren had been one of the few servants who had not treated me like an outcast. Of course, it's hard to look down on someone when you're both ankle-deep in horse shit. When my fortunes reversed, I granted him his greatest wish. He had always wanted to go to sea. I named him my valet so he could experience the sea voyage.

His sister Gabriele was the issue. She was sixteen, a few years younger than me, and of a prime age to marry. She liked me, and her mother had made it known that she was available. I had known Gabriele as long as her brother. Under different circumstances, I might have … but she wasn't Tessa.

I wanted to close my eyes and make it all go away, the sea, the maiden before me. But I was afraid of the flashing dagger waiting behind my eyelids.

"Olaf." Now she stood beside me. "I know you heard me. Will you have your meal?"

"I am not hungry."

Gabriele pursed her lips as if preparing to scold me and then shook her head instead. "Mother will come, if you don't eat." She flashed me a satisfied looked before turning to make her way toward the shelter at the back of the sterncastle.

This was no idle threat. Gabriele's mother, Ursala, *would* come. She would berate me into eating, or use my guilt, depending on her mood. I wasn't sure which tactic I preferred, but she was a master at both. I had no doubt that her late husband had left for the Halls of the Dead to avoid her tongue.

I sighed and followed Gabriele to the shelter.

A tent of sorts was set up at the rear of the sterncastle. It was no more than a swath of canvas stretched overhead, but it kept the sun at bay during the heat of the day. A food-laden wooden table was attached to the deck in its shadow, where my housekeeper and her two daughters stood quietly, awaiting my arrival. The ship's captain was less patient. He loomed next to the lunch table and shifted from foot to foot, rewarding me with a scowl as I approached.

"Master Olaf, shall we eat now?"

Captain Gregor had ignored me as much as possible on the voyage. My family owned the ship, and therefore owned him—and the captain hated to be reminded of the fact. He was a short, balding man with an unruly gray beard. Even though he was entitled to wear a coat of Stenson blue, as captain of the ship, he opted for a sweat-stained grey tunic that nearly matched his beard. His only other clothing was a wide leather belt that didn't quite hold his paunch in place, but from which hung a wooden staff and the key to the weapons locker. The staff, which was about the length of his forearm, was both a symbol of his office and a tool he used to dispense justice aboard ship.

When I nodded, the captain lunged toward the food on the table. I stood and waited as he filled a plate and almost laughed at the looks Ursala gave him. I shook my head at her. She bit her lip and waited for him to finish serving himself.

When Captain Gregor was done heaping his plate, he turned and strolled past me with his sailor's rolling gait and a satisfied smirk on his face. I didn't blame him for his behavior. He had reasons to feel put out by my presence: he'd been forced to relinquish his small cabin under the sterncastle for my use on this voyage. I had tried to compensate by inviting him to share in my meals. It was the only time he acknowledged my presence.

"Would you like me to prepare a plate, Master Stenson?" Ursala asked, loudly enough for the captain to hear. Her use of the title was inappropriate. Only the head of our family could use the Stenson title. Yes, I was a Stenson—and my Uncle Olaf's namesake and closest relative—but the title belonged solely to him.

I nodded as I held back a sigh. Ursala had been at odds with the captain since we stepped aboard the ship, although they probably would have made a good couple. Both were going gray. Both were a bit stout around the middle, and they had similar dispositions. Ursala, however, wore her new Stenson blue dress with pride.

I stood patiently as Ursala prepared a plate for me. She insisted that I should not serve myself. She handed the plate to Gabriele to bring to me.

As I stood waiting, it dawned on me that somehow, Ursala had taken charge of my life. I glanced over my shoulder at the line that had formed at my back, waiting patiently to be served. Besides Ursala's brood, there were Moshe and Mehki, a pair of Wolf guards assigned by my uncle to keep me safe. They were brothers and stood out because of their short stature, long Katchian tunics covered with mail, and full beards cropped short in the military fashion. They shadowed me, even aboard ship, their presence so constant that I hardly noticed them now.

Behind them stood my contingent of Stenson guardsmen in their blue coats, about half a dozen, waiting for me—for Ursala really—to call them forward.

"Your food, Master Olaf."

As I took the plate from Gabriele, she gave me a shy smile. Not long ago, she would have treated me more like a brother, but she had been acting skittish since leaving Kartoba—since Tessa had died.

I felt the anger rise within me like a sudden windstorm. Gabriele had chosen the worst time to decide she had feelings for me. I clenched my jaw to avoid lashing out at her, but then spied Ursala over her shoulder, giving me an encouraging nod. That broke my control.

My anger flashed white-hot as I struck the plate out of Gabriele's hand, shouting, "I don't need your pity!" The pottery plate shattered when it hit the deck. The pain on Gabriele's face sent me reeling away, and as I stumbled back to the ship's rail, my anger vanished as suddenly as it had come. My ears burned hot from embarrassment.

I wanted to close my eyes and catch my breath, but I couldn't. Since Tessa's death, it felt as though I couldn't think straight. My anger consumed me, and when it didn't, I felt nothing but loss. I gripped the rail and stared again at the green sea, trying to lose myself in its expanse.

Before I could escape, I felt a tug on the hem of my tunic. I knew who it was; only one person aboard ship was that short. I looked down into the face of Ursala's youngest daughter, Sofie.

"Mama says you have to eat." She held a plate out to me.

Ursala didn't play fair. She sent the one person she knew I wouldn't attack. I took the plate with shaking hands and said, "Thank you."

Sofie gave me a fake smile—a smirk, really—but stayed by the rail instead of going back to her mother. Sofie's hair was dark and unruly. She ran around the ship in a dirty tunic that barely covered her knees, and looked more like a street beggar than one of Ursala's children. I often wondered if she was truly Ursala's daughter.

"She's not really my mama, you know."

"What?" I was shocked that her words mirrored my thoughts.

"Ursala—she's not my real mama." Sofie smiled at me, as if inviting conversation. Instead I looked her over more closely. I could never tell ages well, but she seemed to be about fourteen—or at least, she acted that age. She was probably too old to be running around with her knees showing. She was thicker than Bren or Gabriele, who had long, thin frames. Add in her darker hair, and I could see how she could be from another mother, or father.

I didn't know much about Sofie. She had never come to work at Stenson House, where I grew up, and Bren hadn't talked about her. I wondered if she was telling the truth now or spinning me a tale. "Who is your mother then?" I asked.

She shrugged. "Ursala took me in so she can make me work."

I had yet to see Sofie do anything besides get in people's way. I decided she was spinning a yarn to avoid going back to her mother. "If that's the case, why aren't you working now?"

Sofie gave me a bright smile that seemed so genuine, I almost returned it. "My job is to cheer you up."

I fought to put a scowl on my face instead. "Well, you're not doing a very good job of it."

"Not true," she snapped back and then laughed. "You almost smiled."

Her laugh was one that made you want to join in, and I couldn't help but soften my expression.

She squinted and reached out to tug on my coat sleeve. "Ursala thinks you'll marry Gabriele once you get happy again, but I know you'll marry me instead."

I sputtered. "What?"

She laughed again and gave me a wide-eyed look that made me wonder if she had been serious or not. "Mama will be yelling soon." She twirled around and skipped back to the food table without a backward glance.

I watched her go. Sofie was nothing like her siblings. Bren was stiff and proper at most times. Gabriele had a sense of adventure, but she had gone shy around me. Sofie, in contrast, seemed to not have a care in the world. I would have said that she didn't want to grow up, except for her sudden marriage ambitions. I shook my head to clear the thought away and started picking at the plate of food I had forgotten I held.

It didn't take long for Sofie to leave my mind, along with everything else in the world but the rolling waves surrounding the ship. I couldn't even say how much food I ate, or who came to take the plate away.

Those long days on the ocean, I watched the sea during the day and the cabin ceiling above me at night. I couldn't sleep. Whenever I closed my eyes, the flashing dagger waited for me, and I would jolt awake to avoid reliving what came next.

CHAPTER 2: SEA WOLVES

I felt numb from lack of sleep as I stood at the sterncastle rail, staring at nothing.

I had begun to hallucinate, strange creatures peeking at me from beneath the water. When a ship appeared before me, I assumed it was just another fevered vision. But it was a birlinn—a Kail vessel. The sail was down, and I could just barely make out the oars churning the water on either side as it raced toward us. It took a long moment before I realized it was real.

I turned to shout the alarm. Luther, the captain of my small contingent of Stenson guards, stood so close that I jumped in surprise. I had not even realized he was near.

"You picked a poor time to rejoin the living," he said. His friendly tone reminded me of another guard captain. Captain Roland had befriended me in my uncle's kingdom of Haven. In reality, Captain Roland and Luther were friends, which is why I had picked Luther to lead my guards. You know what they say: "A friend of a friend ..." Thinking of Captain Roland made me reach for my sword, which had been a gift from Roland, and then recall that it was down in my cabin.

Guard Captain Luther shook his head. "No need for a sword, Master Olaf. They have us surrounded."

He sounded so calm that I thought he was joking—until I turned in a circle. Two other Kail ships were bearing down on us from bow and stern.

"We only have two choices," he continued in the same matter-of-fact tone. "We can make a run for shore—abandon the ship to them and hope they let us escape—or wait and see if they'll let us keep the ship and our lives." He raised one eyebrow as if wondering my opinion. "Either way, a sword will do you no good."

That really left us only one option. Our ship was named the *Sea Cow*. It was a jennet, a trade vessel belonging to the Stenson family. Jennets carried heavy loads but were not known for their speed. We would never outrun the Kail birlinn.

Captain Gregor was close enough to hear. "I won't abandon my ship to those wolves," he called across the deck. Then he bellowed out to his crew. "Prepare to repel boarders!" He headed toward the weapons locker that stood at the front of the sterncastle.

"No, Captain!" A guardsman stepped out to confront the captain. Even though he was dressed in a guardsman's blue coat, Ivan was not really a Stenson guardsman. He had been one of Uncle Olaf's spies in Kartoba and had come along on the journey to keep me out of trouble—or so I figured.

Ivan approached the Captain quickly. With his greasy blonde hair pulled up in a ponytail, he had a knack for looking as if he had just awakened from a drunk—but he was a dangerous man, all the same. He had been a mercenary in the past, one of my uncle's old mates.

Gregor's men were all on the main deck below, but the ship's captain didn't hesitate. He turned to confront Ivan, gripping his captain's staff as if ready to use it.

Ivan kept his hand away from his sword as he growled, "We will not fight the Kail." The Kail were known to wipe out whole ship's crews if they resisted.

The captain sized him up, clenching his staff.

Ivan stopped just outside of his reach. "I understand your concern for the ship, Captain, but Master Olaf's life is more important." He turned and pointed to the nearest approaching vessel, now easily identifiable as a birlinn. "You know they will kill us all if we resist."

I watched the birlinn. The Kail ships were smaller than ours, but they were fast and sleek, made for raiding. They boasted many more oars, and each carried probably twice as many fighting men as our entire ship's company. With three birlinn bearing down on us, the Kail outnumbered us at least six to one. Ivan was right in thinking we had no chance of winning.

Captain Gregor knew it, too. He released a sudden sigh and let his vicious-looking staff drop back to his belt. "Take the women below, to the cabin," he grumbled. He shook his head and rubbed at the balding spot on top. "No use tempting the pirates any more than we have to." The Kail were famous for selling everything they stole, including captives.

In moments, the sails had been lowered and the crew had assembled on the main deck. Ivan said to Captain Gregor, "Put on your Stenson coat." The captain grimaced but nodded. Ivan turned to me. "Take *your* coat off and try to look less ... pitiful."

My coat was much fancier in appearance than the coats of the guards, and I was well-advised to remove it. Ivan glanced at my two Wolf guards, who had continued to wear their mail, even at sea, and then shrugged. He knew they would refuse to disarm, and he didn't have the time to argue.

By the time the first Kail ship came alongside, a transformed Captain Gregor waited on the main deck to greet them. My servants were all safely tucked inside the small cabin under the sterncastle. I stood on the sterncastle in the midst of the Stenson guards, barely able to see past their blue-clad shoulders.

Ivan stood next to the sterncastle rail watching the Kail ship approach. "Let's see if they'll be reasonable," I heard him mutter.

As I waited among my guardsmen for our ship to be boarded, I remembered my Kail tutor. At Stenson House, all members of the family were given an education. We were taught numbers. We learned to write and to understand the various languages used in trade. Our lessons usually took place in the main hall in the evening, after we were finished with our daily chores.

My instructor, Seisyll, had been old and going on fat—at least he seemed old to me at the time—but he dressed as a Kail and wore his hair short, as the Kails did. As far as I knew, he *was* a Kail, but I had my doubts. While he taught us the Kail language and culture, he never had a kind word to say about his people. I always had the impression that he hated them. He found their practice of sea piracy to be especially deplorable.

I remembered the evening he stood before us and shook with anger as he described the raiding tactics of the Kail sea-wolves: "They never hunt alone," he said. "You will never see a Kail ship alone on the water." He paced before us, rubbing at his short, spiked hair. He always rubbed his hair when he was agitated, as if trying to wipe away the tell-tale sign of his heritage.

He stopped pacing and stared at us with unseeing eyes. "When you see them approaching, gliding through the sea, oars dipping in rhythmic unison, it is already too late." His eyes focused and he shook himself to clear away whatever vision had gripped him. "Remember this—when the Kail go raiding on the sea, they are not your friends. If you cannot outrun them, you might as well slit your own throat."

The memory sent a shiver down my back now, and I deeply regretted not retrieving my sword from the cabin. Fighting was not a strong point for me, but I had no desire to be butchered without a fight. I had little time to fret about it, though. The ship trembled as the first birlinn pulled up alongside, its wooden planks screeching into contact with the side of my ship.

From the sterncastle, even surrounded by my guards, I could see the mass of men on the deck of the birlinn. They were a riot of color in their various costumes, as only Kail could be, but they looked uniformly deadly. A handful of men on the Kail vessel reached out with long, hooked poles to pull the ships together, and several warriors scrambled aboard our vessel.

Captain Gregor showed great fortitude by standing his ground as they boarded his ship. His own sailors slunk away from him as the leading Kail approached.

"You are wise to greet us unarmed," the Kail leader said, his words heavily accented. He stood out, even among his kind, because of his size and because his head was completely shaved. The average Kail was typically shorter than men from my homeland, but their captain stood taller by a head than everyone else on the deck below.

As if his size was not intimidating enough, a huge scar ran across the top of his head, from his right eye to the back of his left ear. It looked as though someone had tried unsuccessfully to slice his head open like a melon. The effect was so off-putting that even Captain Gregor took a step back as the monster approached him. It probably didn't help that the Kail leader carried a huge axe, which looked like it could cut the captain in half with a single swing.

"We have nothing of value," Captain Gregor stammered.

The scarred Kail barked out a laugh. "Let's just see." He waved his axe, and his men split up to search our vessel while he headed toward the ladder to the sterncastle.

My stomach clenched as the leader's scarred head appeared at the ladder way. He frowned when his eyes cleared the deck and he spied the group of armed men waiting for him.

Up close, the man was even more frightening. His arms were the size of most men's thighs, and his own thighs looked like tree trunks. All four limbs were spotted with elaborate blue tattoos of various sizes and shapes. He wore a plain woolen tunic, which made him stand out even more among his colorfully clothed companions, and a huge golden torc hung around his neck.

He stood before us for a moment, taking in our strength. His eyes lingered on the wolf guards flanking me, and then he nodded at the group in general and asked, "Who's the cripple?" The nasty smile he threw my way didn't help settle my stomach.

Ivan had backed away from the rail as the tattooed giant ascended the ladder and now stood among the Stenson guards.

Guard captain Luther stepped forward to answer. "We have no quarrel with you as long as you allow us to continue our journey unharmed."

The giant threw back his head and laughed. "Why should we let you go?" He pointed toward me. "Is he worth a ransom, or should I just kill him?"

Moshe and Mehki, my pair of Wolf guards, stepped forward.

The scarred giant nodded. "So, a ransom it is." Now he looked directly at me. "Will you come along quietly, or shall I kill *them* first?"

I heard Mehki snort, and both he and his more taciturn brother raised their axes. The elite Wolf guards—who had been assigned to guard Uncle Olaf and his family—generally preferred long-handled axes. It had something to do with my uncle and his time as a mercenary. They were very adamant about this weapon choice and trained with the things constantly.

The Stenson guardsmen stepped back to make room. They had seen the Wolf guards in action and knew enough to get out of the way.

The giant smiled and gripped his own axe in anticipation.

"Carrog!" A voice called from the deck below. "Come see what we found."

The words had been in Kailish. I couldn't see the deck below, but I could hear Ursala cursing her captors.

Carrog glanced over the rail. "Keep them all. The old one is fat, but that means she can probably cook, right?"

The Kail all laughed, but my people remained silent. Most of them probably didn't speak Kailish and had no idea what the giant had said.

I strained to look over the rail for Bren. He had stayed with his family in the cabin to protect them, and I feared the worst when he did not appear. "Where is my valet?" I demanded of Carrog.

His eyes snapped back to me. "So you can speak."

"Yes. What have your men done with my valet?"

"Valet?" The big man shrugged. "What do I care? You still haven't answered my question." He gestured with his axe toward the men surrounding me. "Shall I kill them, or will you come along on your own?"

My Wolf guards still stood before me, axes at the ready. At my command, they would surge to the attack. I had no doubt, no matter his size or skill, they would kill Carrog. I considered giving the order. Why not? I had nothing to lose that I had not already lost. Tessa was gone. My homeland, the Seven Kingdoms, was doomed. Why should I care if we survived the fight?

But I did care. Damn my uncle and his precious Seven Kingdoms! My mission was to find allies in the east. Even with Tessa gone and that ever-present, nightmarish vision of her death haunting me, I realized that I cared about my uncle and my homeland. Damn it all! I cared, and I didn't dare give the order that would stop my mission in its tracks.

I reached out and put a hand on each of my Wolf guard's shoulders, and they instinctively lowered their axes. "I will come," I said, flashing Carrog a disarming smile of my own, "as soon as we come to terms." No matter the bad feeling I harbored for my family, I was still a Stenson, and haggling was in my blood.

Carrog was caught off-guard. He looked perplexed. "Terms?" he bellowed. " What do you mean, *terms?*" He gestured with his arm to indicate the ship around us. "Do you have more men hiding in the bilge?"

Even though I had decided to live—to attempt to go forward with my uncle's designs for me in the east—I hadn't completely shaken off my dark mood. If I could not complete my uncle's mission, what did it matter if I lived? If I couldn't find a way to continue on to the Eastern Confederation, then why not perish now and relieve my misery? My willingness to die gave me a crazy kind of courage.

I laughed at the giant man's words. "I don't need more men," I explained. "I just need to tell these two to kill you." I smiled with all the confidence I could put into it. "That is my offer: our freedom for your life."

Carrog eyed the Wolf guards before me as if judging their skill. What he could tell by just looking, I had no idea. He twirled his axe once as he looked about the sterncastle deck. He was outnumbered, for the moment. The two Kail at his back carried only shields and short spears. They seemed to be readying themselves for a fight as Carrog shifted his footing in preparation to attack.

"There is no need for either of us to die here," I explained. "But if I cannot continue my journey, then that is the only option for me. You can take whatever else you want. Just leave me the ship and my people—or die this hour."

"If you planned to die, then why didn't you just fight to begin with?" Carrog looked angry enough to hurl himself at us and damn the consequences. He let out a roar and swung his axe at the nearest Wolf guard.

Mehki sidestepped the blow as Moshe charged forward. One of Carrog's henchmen managed to get his shield up in time to deflect Moshe's blow. I felt hands on my shoulder, and suddenly I was surrounded by Stenson guardsmen determined to keep me safe.

I heard Carrog roar again, and then the sound of an axe hitting a shield. The Kail on the deck below began to shout. I imagined them swarming the ladder.

One voice rose above the rest. "Carrog!"

The sound of combat suddenly ceased, and the guardsman in front of me shifted enough for me to see again. Carrog had backed away, along with his one companion that was still standing. The other Kail warrior lay on the deck with Moshe standing over him.

Moshe had been ready to dispatch the downed warrior, but he shifted his weight, and the axe thunked into the deck instead.

"Carrog, have they not already surrendered?" The high voice, which spoke in the Kail language, belonged to a woman. As I looked below to the main deck, I realized that I knew her.

There was no mistaking the dark hair and green tunic. The last time I had seen her, she had agreed to take my friend Talon to Kailand for a rather hefty sum.

I stepped toward the rail to see her more clearly, and she turned her face upward and let out a sudden gasp of recognition. "It's you!"

I was surprised that she recognized me.

"Carrog, let him be," she called to the giant. "I know that man."

CHAPTER 3: A CHANCE MEETING

I had no idea why the Kail woman would remember me, unless ... "Is Talon with you?" I called down to her. Most likely, he was in Kailand on his mission for the Seven Kingdoms, but I hoped that somehow, he would be with her.

She grinned up at me just as my friend appeared on the deck beside her. He looked different than the last time I saw him. He had swapped his mail shirt for a leather jacket and his golden hair had grown long enough to make him stand out next to the short-haired Kail warriors. He looked up at me and then shook his head. "Olaf! What have you gotten yourself into this time?"

"He doesn't know his place," Carrog growled down to him.

Talon smiled up at the giant. "The last time I saw Olaf, he was knee-deep in shit. Now here he is with, I'm guessing, his own ship. I don't think I would try my luck against his, Carrog."

"What are you doing here?" the woman called up to me. I knew she commanded one of the Kail ships, from our last meeting—but I had no idea if she led the other two as well. Carrog still held his position on the sterncastle deck and didn't look as though he planned to leave it. Would he listen to her?

I didn't want to blurt out my mission in front of so many ears. For all I knew, the Kail could have an alliance with our enemy, the Empire of Jewel. The fact that Talon was with them was a good sign, but I was still cautious. Options raced through my head as I hesitated to answer. Finally, I decided to give them the official story and hope for the best.

"I'm the new Stenson factor to the Eastern Confederation."
Talon whistled in appreciation. "That's some promotion.
I'm guessing your uncle had something to do with it?"

I nodded. "He leads the Stenson family now."

Talon turned to the woman. "His uncle is the Baron of
Haven. He is one of the rulers of the Seven Kingdoms."

Talon was a member of the Order of the Dog, one of the
mercenary companies that helped defend the Seven Kingdoms.
He had been sent on a mission to the Kailand several months
earlier. Hearing his voice lifted a weight from my chest that I
hadn't realized was there.

"Neasa, he is mine to deal with," Carrog interrupted,
recognizing that the situation was slipping out of his grasp. "He
agreed to give me everything but the ship and his people."

Neasa, the female captain, looked to me to answer his
assertion, but Carrog had spoken in the Kail tongue, and I
hesitated to speak. After a long moment of silence, I sighed and
answered in Kail: "I made the offer, but he did not accept it."

"An offer made ..." Carrog began.

"Means nothing, if not accepted," Neasa finished. "Come
down, Carrog. Let me talk to them."

Carrog scowled at me but directed his still-standing
henchman to help the injured one to his feet. They made their
way back to the main deck. Then Neasa and Talon climbed the
ladder up to us.

Talon rushed forward as if to enfold me in an enthusiastic
hug, but my Wolf guards stopped him short. He contented
himself with a welcoming smile instead. "You have no idea
how happy I am to see you!"

I felt the same way, but felt the pressure of the Kails' eyes
upon me. "You seem to be friendly with the lady." When we
had parted on the docks of Kartoba months past, he had
boasted that he would win her over.

He grinned. "I told you I would be. And how is your lady?"

His words struck me like a blow. "She's ..." I suddenly had
no words. I hadn't spoken to anyone about Tessa since she
died, and I didn't have it in me to do so with Talon, either.

17

The smile died on Talon's face and he reached out to grasp my shoulders. "I'm sorry, Olaf …"

I shook free of him and tried to keep a level tone, but my heart ached at the sudden reminder. "We need to talk, Talon," I said quietly. "Will your friends let me go on my way?"

Neasa stepped forward. "What's in it for me, if I let you continue?"

"What agreement do you have with Talon?" I countered.

When Neasa smiled, it reminded me of the first time I had seen her, several months ago, on the docks of Kartoba. I had accompanied Talon to find passage to Kailand. We had just had a run-in with another Kail ship's crew, and Neasa had come along to see what the ruckus was about. She had the same calculating smile on her face then. I remembered trying not to stare at the tattoo of a raven on her left breast. Her green tunic still didn't hide much, and I couldn't resist the temptation to look down as she stood before me now.

She laughed when my eyes moved to her chest. "So you do remember me, Olaf Stenson? Do you have a desire to come to an agreement with the ravens?"

I remembered her ship flew the black raven banner of the Macha clan. It was the most-feared clan among the Kail. The way she said it made me think about the raven on her chest though, which in turn made me wonder if her right breast was similarly decorated.

"What agreement do you have with Talon?" I repeated, resisting the urge to look at her other breast.

She shrugged. "We will talk once we reach Gwyr." Eyes gleaming, she turned and headed toward the ladder. Talon looked torn, but finally sighed and turned to follow her.

"Will you let me complete my journey?" I called out.

She turned back at the top of the ladder and said, "We will talk in Gwyr. In the meantime, Carrog will command this ship."

With a toss of her black braids, she turned and headed down the ladder.

I stepped to the sterncastle rail and watched her progress across the main deck, Talon in tow like a faithful hound. She said something to Carrog in passing, and he turned to look up at me.

"Hah! It looks like we get to finish haggling our *terms*." He gave me a satisfied smirk and then walked over to where Captain Gregor stood before his sailors.

"First of all," Carrog called to me as he gripped Gregor's collar in his huge hands, "a ship only has one captain." He lifted Captain Gregor as if he weighed nothing and then, with a swift motion, heaved him into the sea, just past the adjacent birlinn.

The ship's crew paused in stunned silence, letting out a collective sigh of relief only when the captain surfaced, sputtering water.

Carrog looked back up at me and let out a great guffaw of laughter. "Don't worry!" he called. "They'll haul him in." He turned to the sailors, who were still knotted together in stunned silence. "Well then," he growled, "let's get this tub moving."

As a group, the sailors turned their faces toward me.

It had all happened so fast—but at least we were still alive, and apparently headed for the Kail's stronghold in Gwyr. I nodded down to them. "You heard Captain Carrog," I said.

When the sailors scurried to their tasks, I suddenly remembered my valet and headed for the ladder to the main deck.

"Wait!" Ivan grabbed my left arm to hold me back.

I hadn't even realized he stood next to me.

As I turned, he pulled me so close that I thought he might kiss me. His breath smelled of bad whiskey, but his eyes looked clear and calculating. "You should stay on the sterncastle where we can keep you safe until we arrive at Gwyr."

What he said made sense—except that my valet was still missing. "I have to check on Bren," I said, adding as an afterthought, "and retrieve my sword." Still I recognized the wisdom of his counsel.

I searched out Captain Luther's face in the crowd of blue jackets. "It would be wise to keep control of the sterncastle during the journey, though." When he nodded, I shook loose of Ivan's grip and turned back to the ladder.

Ivan blew out an exasperated breath as I turned away, but he didn't say another word. Moshe somehow managed to arrive at the ladder before me and preceded me to the main deck. I didn't have to look back to know that his older brother, Mehki, followed behind us.

As I stepped down onto the main deck, Carrog still stood in the center, shouting orders to the crew. He watched us out of the corner of his eye.

The women stood in a clump to my right, just outside the cabin, still too shocked to move. The Kail warriors, who had remained on board with Carrog, lingered along the starboard rail, where they had helped push the birlinn away from the hull. They looked like men taking their leisure, watching Carrog and the crew with half-lidded eyes—but I could see that their hands rested on their weapons and they looked ready to pounce at a moment's notice. There were not many men, but they were enough to cow the crew.

"Where is my valet?" I asked the men who slumped at the rail. I spoke in their tongue, Kailish.

The one closest to me shrugged. "If you mean the pretty boy in the cabin, he's still there." He wore a single garment of bright orange—not quite a tunic, more a swath of fabric wrapped around his waist and across one shoulder. He made a stabbing motion toward the cabin with his spear. His companions laughed as I turned and hurried to the cabin.

Ursala gathered her daughters and met us as we headed for the doorway. "He tried to fight, my Bren," Ursala said as she stopped at the edge of the sterncastle deck. The deck above served as a roof. The space underneath was used to store cargo and food, with just the one small cabin along the port side.

As I stepped into the area, it reminded me of the trading square in Kartoba with its myriad of smells. The smell of dried fish was pungent, but the strong smell of pickled cabbage fought for a place next to it, as well as a hint of smoke from the salted pork haunches.

The cabin door stood ajar, but I hesitated among the hanging meat and food barrels for fear of what I might find. Moshe took the lead and walked into the cabin. A moment later, he stepped back outside and motioned for me to enter.

The lattice on the cabin bulkhead allowed dappled sunlight to play across the cabin deck. Bren lay in the middle of the floor, face-down and motionless. My sword lay close to hand, as though he had tried to wield it. I was relieved to see no blood staining the deck around him.

Ursala let out a low moan and pushed her way past me to kneel by her son. She gently rolled him over and he groaned and grimaced in pain. I peered into the cabin, but the space was limited. The captain's bed, consisting of a large wooden frame built into the aft wall, took up half the cabin. With a small table and stool on the opposite wall under the window, there was little space between for us to maneuver.

Sofie slipped under my arm and dropped down next to her mother, and then Gabriele crowed at my back, just in the doorway.

As soon as I could see that Bren still breathed, I turned sideways to let Gabriele past. "He lives," I said to her. She was so close that I could smell her scent—musky, with a hint of lavender. I tried to step back and banged into the door frame. "I'll let you tend to your brother."

Her mouth turned up at the corner. "I won't bite," she whispered as she brushed past me into the cabin.

I felt my face burn. I had been avoiding Gabriele, and the sudden close quarters left me flustered.

Carrog, who now stood just past the shade of the overhanging deck, grinned at me. "The valet lives, yes?"

Moshe and Mehki stood between us, their bodies tensed.

I nodded. "So far."

Carrog snorted at me. "Tell him next time to leave the fighting to the warriors." He turned his head to glare at my wolf guards from his single eye. "Plenty of ocean between here and Gwyr. We'll have time to finish what we started."

He headed back to the center of the deck and I made a hasty retreat up the sterncastle ladder. Carrog scared me. I had hoped he would leave us in peace until we reached our destination.

As I arrived on the sterncastle deck, Ivan sidled up next to me and searched my face with his eyes.

"Bren lives," I said, "but is being tended by his family."

Ivan glanced sideways at my hip, raising one eyebrow as he asked, "Did you forget something?"

I dropped my hand to my belt and then realized that I had failed to retrieve my sword. Below me, on the main deck, Carrog's massive form was pacing like a caged panther. Now that I knew that Bren lived, my earlier bravado melted away. I suddenly trembled at the thought of going anywhere near the tattooed giant.

I shrugged at Ivan. "It doesn't matter."

Ivan scratched at his chin. He always had a day's growth on his face—a perpetual goatee in the making—but I had never seen him shave, nor did his whiskers seem to grow any longer. He finally tossed his head and said, "At least stay up here for the time being."

Even in his Stenson guardsman outfit, Ivan reminded me of a beggar from the streets of Kartoba. Despite his appearance, he had proven to be resourceful—and my uncle trusted him. I had only known Ivan for a few months, but for some reason, I found his presence comforting.

"Thank you, Ivan," I said. "I shall stay put for the time being." As if I would go anywhere near the one-eyed giant below. I could camp out for as long as it took, if it meant staying away from Carrog. But that thought spawned a question. "Ivan, how long until we reach Gwyr?"

The ex-mercenary-turned-spy just chuckled at me. "Long enough to wish you had a bed."

Later that day, before the sun dropped below the horizon, I stood in my normal spot at the rail watching the nearest birlinn glide across the water, shadowing our progress. I felt something poke my back, making me spin around. Sofie stood before me with my sword tossed up on her shoulder. She gave me a big grin and said, "You'd better take this back. It might get Bren killed, otherwise." She presented the sword to me and then went skipping across the deck to pester the guardsmen on the other side.

As I belted on my sword, I spied Bren making his way across the deck, supported on each side by his mother and Gabriele. He still looked worse for wear, with a bruise just beginning to purple on the side of his forehead, but at least he was awake and moving.

"How do you feel?" I called to him.

His eyes were downcast. "I will live," he replied. The words came out uncharacteristically terse for Bren. He took his job as valet very seriously and usually had only polite conversation for me.

His demeanor rubbed me wrong. "Good, then you can resume your duties soon," I called, half in jest.

Ursala shot me a dark look, but Bren shrugged her off and pushed his way toward me. He still clung to Gabriele for support. "You are right, Olaf," he snarled.

I had seen him angry before—I'd even been the brunt of his anger in the past—but he hadn't used this tone since I'd elevated him to valet. "I shall live, this time," he continued. "And I'll resume my duty of watching you pine away at that rail. But I will never feel helpless again."

I raised an eyebrow at him. This was not the Bren I had grown up with, who had always seemed content to serve my family.

"I will train with the guardsmen and learn how to fight," Bren declared. He wobbled on his feet, but stared hard at me, as if daring me to deny him. "Where we are going, you will need someone with a level head and a strong arm to keep you safe."

Maybe I had misjudged Bren. Had his failure against the Kail warriors scared him, or made him more determined than ever to serve—or perhaps both? Still, he was no warrior, and I didn't want to see him get hurt. "I have Mehki and Moshe to protect me, and Captain Luther and his men."

"Those are all your uncle's men," he said. "Who do you have that is dedicated to you alone, if not your valet?"

Valets, in theory, were supposed to be dedicated to their masters. I thought back to the brief time when I had been valet to Aldo Kaufmann in Kartoba. I'd served him only as a means to further my uncle's interests. Looking into Bren's determined face now and understanding his sense of duty, I knew his motive was much purer than mine had been. A sudden pang of guilt shot through me at the thought, and I nodded my agreement.

Bren's eyes lit up as if I had done him a favor and he reached out to his mother once again. Ursala grabbed his arm and, together with Gabriele, helped him across the deck.

As I watched them settle him onto the deck, I wondered if I would come to regret my decision.

CHAPTER 4: A PENNY FOR YOUR SERVICE

Carrog left me in peace on the sterncastle for several days. He took up residence in the cabin below and ignored our presence on the deck above. Just when I thought he might have forgotten his threat, he called up to me on the third day: "Stenson, are you ready to finish this?"

My heart raced at his sudden interest. I walked to the rail and looked down at the massive Kail warrior. To avoid seeing the nasty scar on the top of his head, I tried to look him in his one good eye; the ruined one had been sewn shut. My uncle had told me once that, to truly know an enemy, you must look him in the eye. To my surprise, Carrog's eye appeared full of friendly mischief instead of animosity.

"Time to stop hiding. Come down to finish our *negotiations*."

His smile made me think of a shark, although I was pretty sure he was trying to look friendly. What choice did I have? He commanded the ship, and I had to believe that he would refrain from harming me for Neasa's sake.

"Don't promise him anything," Ivan murmured at my side as I contemplated Carrog's invitation. I turned toward the scruffy spy and he leaned in close to me. "The woman, Neasa, holds the power here. Don't promise him anything."

"She's not here right now," I said.

"Exactly!" Ivan scratched at the patchy whiskers on his chin. "He'll try to get something out of you before we can talk to Neasa. Kail raiders are like a pack of wolves. The strongest rules—but only as long as he remains the strongest. If he can beat her to you, he will."

"Then why did she leave him in charge?" It made no sense to me. She should have either taken over the ship herself, or carried me over to her birlinn.

He shrugged. "How much do you know about this woman?"

We'd had this conversation already, and my answer hadn't changed since the last time.

"She's the captain of the Kail ship that I paid to take Talon to Kailand. I know she is a member of the Macha clan. She has a tattoo of a raven on her breast." That last I would have kept to myself, but Ivan had emphasized the need to know every detail in our previous conversations.

He scowled at my answers, as he had the last time. "Then she left him in charge as a test."

"She's testing Carrog?"

He shook his head and flashed a lopsided smile. "She knows what he will do. It is a test for *you*."

Great! I thought, scowling. What did I have to do to pass her test? Did she expect me to be cautious or bold? Did she expect bribery, or pleading, or a cold-hearted detachment? I knew so little about the woman, and now she held my mission in her hands.

"Are you coming down?" Carrog called.

Maybe this was my chance to find out more. I waved to him and headed to the ladder along with my usual shadows, Mehki and Moshe, and my newest shadow—Bren. His resolve to be my protector had hardened, and even though he hadn't completely recovered from being knocked on the head, he had already started training with the guardsmen. He'd even procured one of their spare swords. Now he followed in our wake, armed and determined.

I knew Bren well enough to realize that it would be useless to tell him to stay behind. Instead, I hoped he would have a change of heart if I just ignored him. We reached the main deck and stepped over to where Carrog stood, in the shade of the sterncastle.

Carrog leaned against the bulkhead with his arms crossed, watching us approach. "I see you brought your best fighters," Carrog mocked, his eyes flicking from Mehki to Moshe and back.

"They follow me everywhere."

His eyes finally slid over to Bren. "And now you have a third?" To my surprise, he seemed to take Bren seriously.

"My valet—yes."

Now completely serious, he said, "Now I see why you worried over him."

I glanced at Bren. His determination was obvious, true, but the bruise on his head seemed proof that he lacked the required skills.

"Okay, then," Carrog said abruptly, interrupting my thoughts. "Will you join me in my cabin?"

The room was tiny. The thought of being alone with this brute, in such close quarters, made my skin crawl.

"You can inspect it first if you're afraid I have men hidden under the bed," he said as we made our way to the cabin. His face wore the hint of a smile. We both knew the bed sat on a built-in cabinet with drawers too small for a man to fit within. We also knew Carrog wouldn't need any help, if he chose to assault me.

What game was he playing? I doubted that he would attack me. Neasa had made it plain that she wanted to talk once we reached Gwyr, and she had left him in charge of our ship. Did he plan to intimidate me? Frighten me into promising him something?

I realized the only way to find out was to go along with him. I motioned for my guards to wait outside and followed Carrog into the cabin.

The instant we entered, he spun around and shoved me up against the door, slamming it shut in the process. He moved so fast, I had no time to react. My chest tightened. My whole body was telling me to run, but he had my arms pinned to the door.

27

Carrog stared at me, stone-faced, as if waiting for me to struggle or cry for help. His expression now was such a sharp contrast to his friendly manner of a few moments earlier that I froze. My mind ran through my options and came up with nothing. So I took a deep breath and waited. Years of putting up with Cousin Jarad's bullying had taught me not to react to threats.

"I can see you're going to be a hard negotiator," he said at last, releasing me. He stepped back and settled his bulk on the single stool. "So much for intimidation. Let's get down to it, then." He frowned. "I really expected you to call for help."

I took a moment to straighten out the sleeves of my coat but stayed in place next to the cabin door. Carrog's looks were frightening, but his split-second mood changes unnerved me even more. I tried to keep my face composed as I pulled my jumbled thoughts together. Finally, when I could trust my voice to remain calm, I managed to ask, "What do you want?"

His mischievous smile returned. "I hear your uncle is a hard man, and that he is rich."

It was true. I had been in my uncle's strong room. He had more gold than I could spend in a lifetime, and that was before he inherited the Stenson family business. He was probably the richest man in the Seven Kingdoms. At last, I knew what Carrog was after—the simplest motivation of all.

"You're after gold?"

Carrog chortled. "Who isn't?"

"You'll never live to spend it if you cross my Uncle Olaf."

"Who said anything about crossing him?" Carrog asked. "I can help him."

He pushed himself off the stool. Carrog was a man of action. Watching him from the sterncastle, I had noticed that he paced the main deck like a caged animal. He looked as though he wanted to pace now, but the cabin was too small. He plopped back down on the stool and scowled at me. "Your uncle needs men—warriors that aren't afraid to go against Jewel, yes?"

I nodded.

"How much?"

"Pardon?"

"How much does he need them—and how much is he willing to pay?"

This was not what I'd expected. I had thought Carrog might threaten me, or tell me I owed him the ship and its contents. He was so big and scary that I had envisioned his negotiations to be more terrifying. I hadn't expected him to ask for a job.

Was the man truly that simple? I doubted it. But even if he wasn't a big thinker, Carrog was physically imposing. I knew he must be a formidable fighter. That meant my uncle could use him—and I could use him. I didn't trust this man, but to command such a beast seemed a golden opportunity. Why not try? "I am my uncle's representative in the east and his closest relative. If you ensure that I and my companions reach our destination, I will pay you enough to make it worth your while."

"That is not for me to decide," Carrog said as his shark smile slipped. "Neasa commands the flock. She decides whether you go or stay." Among the Kail, the Macha clan ruled the seas. They controlled all the captains that came out of Kailand, and because they were the raven clan, a group of birlinn raiding together was called a flock.

"I control my uncle's riches," I explained. "If you help me, I will make you rich."

He scowled back at me. "A dead man cannot spend the silver. I will not cross the Macha. If Neasa says you go, then you go." His eyes pierced mine. "If she says you die, then you die."

The Macha clan had a dangerous reputation. I had assumed Carrog was from that clan as well, but his words now made me think otherwise. I didn't want to ask him and show my ignorance, but I finally realized that I was in no danger from Carrog—at least until we reached Gwyr. His fear of Neasa and the Macha clan would keep him from harming me.

"Okay, then," I said. "How many men can you get for my uncle?"

"If he has the silver, I'll get the men." Some of Carrog's enthusiasm returned.

It was my turn to give him my best shark smile. "He has the silver. But first, you have to get me to the Eastern Confederation."

He slammed his hand down on the table. "You don't listen! Neasa decides!"

I leaned in and spoke slowly. "Then I suggest you do everything in *your* power to ensure she decides to let me go to the east." I paused, wondering if I dare pump him for information about her. "And tell me how I can make that happen."

He eyed me suspiciously. "Fifty silver pennies."

"What?" With fifty silver pennies, I could hire ten men for a month—and equip and feed them too.

"For fifty silver pennies—Stenson silver—I will convince Neasa to let you go. But I will go along to ensure you pay up," Carrog said. He added the last as though he regretted the necessity of accompanying me, but I recognized his ploy. His goal had always been to come along, to find a way into my uncle's service.

The Stenson family dominated the trade throughout the Seven Kingdoms and Kailand. Silver pennies minted by my family were the most reliable coin and the standard for trade throughout the Inner Sea. "Ten," I replied.

His eyes lit up. "Forty is barely enough for my trouble. She is a hard woman to convince."

The Kail loved to haggle. There is a story about haggling with a Kail. He will take your last copper and claim to be the poorer man. Of course, we Stensons had a reputation for bartering as well.

The negotiations went back and forth until we settled at twenty silver pennies. The sum was more than he deserved for what little he would do for me. In essence, I was agreeing to pay him if Neasa decided to let me continue my journey—and if she didn't, he would lose nothing. Still, it seemed a bargain if it gave me some leverage among the Kail—or if it eventually helped to cement a Kail alliance with my uncle's kingdom. And now I knew one sure way to keep Carrog interested.

"Then we are agreed," I said. I turned and opened the door as if to leave, and then paused and turned back. Reaching for the purse at my belt, I lifted it up and weighed it in my hand before tossing it across the cabin.

Carrog's eyes widened as he caught the purse. It held twenty-five Stenson silver pennies—more than our agreed-upon price, and enough to ensure Carrog stayed friendly.

I could see the calculations in his eyes as I left the cabin. Negotiating with a man like Carrog was like feeding the pigs back home: they followed whoever held the slop bucket.

CHAPTER 5: PASSAGE TO GWYR

My trio of guards waited for me, but only Bren looked anxious. Mehki, the older of the two Wolf-guard brothers, was typically the more talkative. He also had a sense of humor. As we headed back to the sterncastle ladder, he asked, "Are we going to have to kill him?"

It was sometimes hard to recognize Mehki's sense of humor, but I was pretty sure he was joking with me. I glanced at his brother Moshe—who flashed me his standard, no-nonsense, let-me-kill-something look—and reconsidered. I chose my words carefully. "I don't think we need to kill Carrog right now."

Mehki laughed, confirming it had been joke, and even Moshe gave me a brief smile as he passed to precede me up the ladder. "Maybe later," Moshe said, just loud enough for me to hear.

Even though they laughed, I knew they would attack the big Kail warrior if I ordered it. The Wolf guards were just a bit too fanatical for my taste, especially the ones from Katch. I had heard the story of how my uncle's mercenary company was wiped out, and how he had taken the Katchian survivors into his service as his Wolf-guard.

There was a blood-oath involved—or maybe it was Katchian pride that drove them. Either way, I knew they would die for me for my uncle's sake. Their single-minded devotion was a heavy responsibility for a man who had been herding pigs a year ago. Back then, no one would have stood up to Cousin Jarad for my sake, let alone given their life.

I hadn't thought of Jarad for months, and it surprised me that the thought of him had so little effect on me. Vain and proud, he had been my tormentor throughout most of our childhood. We had gone to my uncle's kingdom in Haven together, and he was probably still there, galloping around with his horsemen and making a nuisance of himself.

I no longer cared. Jarad was just a dim memory of my life before Tessa died.

"Olaf?" Mehki called softly from over my shoulder, bringing me back to the present. Despite their ruthlessness as fighters, the brothers treated me well. They had been with me in Kartoba when Tessa died. They understood my pain and were more patient than one might expect.

I realized that I stood before the ladder and that he and Bren were waiting for me to ascend. I shook my head at the memories and headed up the ladder.

Ivan met me at the top, his stone face indicating his desire to talk. Some people are hard to read, and Ivan was one of them. His expression rarely changed, but I had noticed that his expression grew even more mysterious when he was preparing himself for a battle of wills.

I nodded for him to follow me to my normal perch at the starboard rail.

"What did he want?" Even Ivan's voice sounded flat, like his whole body was tightly controlled.

"Stenson silver," I replied.

Ivan waiting for more.

I couldn't help smiling. "I paid him twenty-five silver to get Neasa to let us go," I quickly explained before he could respond. "I doubt that she'll listen to him, but he wants to work for Uncle Olaf and become rich in the process. I figured it was enough to get him on the hook. We'll see where it leads us."

Ivan nodded his approval. "Anything else?" He would prod and prompt me until he got every piece of information he could.

"I don't think he's from the Macha clan, by the way he talked."

His eyes gleamed, but his face remained passive as he prompted me to continue. "Tell me."

I repeated the whole conversation with Carrog multiple times that afternoon. Each time, Ivan asked different questions, as if trying to confuse me or catch me in a lie. Talking to Ivan was like slogging through a swamp. It was a long afternoon.

The Kail ships ruined my mood. No longer could I lose myself by staring out to sea. I felt like I had awakened from a bad dream, but I knew I wasn't sleeping. Tessa was still dead, and I still saw that dagger whenever my eyes closed. Even worse, now I had no way to hide from Gabriele mooning over me when she served my meals.

Gabriele and her mother were constantly hovering nearby—Gabriele watching me with her hooded-yet-hopeful eyes and Ursala espousing her daughter's virtues. That, along with Bren's grim determination, made me wish I had left the family in Kartoba. Sofie was the exception. She would occasionally appear in the background to make fun of her family. She made exaggerated moon eyes at me behind Gabriele's back, and she mimicked Ursala so well, I found myself struggling not to laugh.

At first, her antics cheered me up. The girl was different, running around in her too-small tunic, avoiding work and acting like a child. But then a day came when she sashayed behind Gabriele, mockingly swaying her hips in imitation of her older sister. I noticed her tunic rode higher up on her thigh than it should have—and then I noticed that some of the guardsmen watched her as well. How old was she, really?

Her dark hair reminded me of Tessa. No! She looked nothing like Tessa. I rubbed at my eyes, trying to get my thoughts back on track. She caught my eye and smiled, not like a little girl at all. I quickly turned back to the sea. She was

34

Bren's little sister! I felt my hands shake as I gripped the rail. Lack of sleep was playing tricks with me. I recognized that my mind wasn't quite right and resolved to ignore Sofie going forward.

Our ship had been hugging the coast, and we finally reached the Cape of Andamar. The cape, which consisted of rocky cliffs that jutted out from the mainland, served to divide the Inner Sea to the west and the Sea of Silence in the east. It was also the point where the empire of Jewel claimed control of the sea. That claim was tenuous, at best, because just off the cape stood Rover Island—the stronghold of the Macha sea raiders and the location of their capital city, Gwyr.

The Macha clan had once controlled all of Kailand in the west and had ruled the rest of the clans. Then came the Clan Rebellion, where the clans succeeded in driving the Macha back to their ancestral home on the east coast of Kailand. The Macha clan had taken to the sea, and their birlinn now controlled much of the Inner Sea that stretched between Kailand in the west and Rover Island in the east.

The Seven Kingdoms were right in the middle of that domain, and were the Kail's strongest trading partners. That was why it was important to gain their cooperation against the Empire of Jewel. Only the Kail raiders were strong enough to stop an empire fleet from landing on our shores.

Now we were heading into their stronghold in the east. I worried about the strength of their ties with Jewel.

Rover Island looked just as imposing as the cliffs of nearby Andamar, except for the cove that was Gwyr on the southwest corner of the island. A strong western wind had blown us to the cove, but we had to lower the sails and row into the isolated harbor. We followed the first birlinn through the entrance, notably slow and cumbersome in comparison because of our four oars. A Jennet wasn't made to be rowed a long distance, unlike the maneuverable birlinn.

Carrog paced the deck below, spitting curses at the struggling sailors.

The entrance was only wide enough for a single ship, and a pair of wooden forts guarded the entrance from the headlands that overlooked the strait. As we passed through, the forts were close enough that I could make out the faces of individual guards watching our progress.

Once we had gotten through the strait, I could see that the town dominated the harbor and flowed into the surrounding hills. It was early evening, and firelight dotted the hills around the town, reminding me of how small my uncle's kingdom of Haven truly was. But I knew that the fate of the entire Seven Kingdoms was at stake—not just my uncle's tiny, upstart kingdom.

A pair of birlinn held position just past the harbor entrance. Carrog waved to them as we lumbered past. Several more birlinn were tied to a wooden wharf that stretched across the opposite shore. I was surprised that I saw no other types of ships in the cove.

I turned to Ivan, who stood to my right. "Where are the other captured ships?"

I could tell Ivan thought it was a stupid question by the look on his face, but he refrained from saying so. Instead he answered, "The Kail have no use for our ships. They either collect a toll from a passing ship or they take everything and sink it."

That didn't sound right. "Why wouldn't they sell the captured ships?"

Now Ivan did roll his eyes. "They claim to be merchants, and they deny attacking other ships. How would it look if they started selling foreign-made vessels?"

"But everyone knows …"

Ivan shrugged. "They have a funny way of looking at things." He nodded down toward where Carrog still paced the deck below us. "They claim to be merchants, but everyone knows they are pirates."

Looking at the scarred giant, I had a hard time envisioning him as a meek trader. Then again, for the moment, he was captain of my trading ship.

Ivan caught my eyes, his face serious. "They're about to decide our fate. Make sure you give them a reason to help us." He paused for emphasis. "The likes of Carrog are easily swayed by Stenson silver, but I'm guessing Neasa and her clan are after something more. You will need to find out what that is—if any of us are to make it off this island again."

The intensity of his stare made me nervous. Ivan usually came across as a sloppy drunk, at least to those who didn't know him. When he got serious, it set me on edge.

The thump of the ship contacting the wharf distracted me. I saw Neasa and Talon waiting on the dock.

Carrog called up to me. "Grab your gear and let's go."

His sudden order caught me off-guard. "I need some time to get my people ready."

Carrog shook his head. "They stay here, and you go alone." His men were already lowering a plank to the dock.

"Go," Ivan hissed in my ear before he faded back into the crowd of Stenson guardsmen.

What should I take with me? My mind spun with the sudden need to decide. Fresh clothes? The letter of appointment from my uncle? I moved toward the ladder, realizing that I had no possessions that would convince Neasa to let me go. Why bother grabbing extra clothes, when I didn't how long they would keep me?

The only thing I brought was my sword, because it hadn't left my hip since Carrog came aboard. Moshe and Mehki shadowed me, as usual—and so did Bren, who hadn't given up on his insistence to guard me. When we reached the plank, Carrog was already on the dock talking to Neasa.

"No guards," he called to me, just as Moshe took a step towards the plank.

Moshe stepped back and gave me a questioning look. He and Mehki would not hesitate to fight in that moment—to the death—if I commanded it.

I shook my head. "I'll go alone."

The Wolf guards shared a quick look and then Mehki said, "Do not die, Olaf. Your uncle would never forgive us." His face did not show any signs of humor, and I still wasn't sure if he joked or not.

"I'll try not to."

They faded back as I stepped up to the plank, but Bren had beaten me to it. He called out to the Kail on the dock, "I am not a guard. I'm his valet. You don't expect Master Olaf to go without his valet?"

As he spoke, I noticed that he carried my pack—which held the clothes I had decided to leave behind. He also carried the borrowed sword he had worn since the Kail came aboard. I wondered if his sword would be a problem.

Carrog leaned in to speak with Neasa. She waved him off and said, "Bring the servant if you like, Olaf, as long as he stays out of the way."

Bren smiled in satisfaction and stepped aside so I could precede him down the plank. "I will protect you," he whispered as I passed. I faced straight ahead, afraid to look his way and encourage his devotion.

The last thing I needed was Bren trying to protect me.

CHAPTER 6: ROVER ISLAND

Neasa hustled us through town toward the largest hill overlooking the harbor. I don't remember much of that trip except the smell of smoked fish and rotting seaweed on the docks and the press of people along the road. I had trouble getting used to walking on land again, and my twisted leg made it worse. I was forced to hop along like a maimed hare.

Bren tried to assist, but I pushed him away and refused to take his arm. He ended up hovering next to me, making encouraging sounds. At that moment, I decided I preferred the old, composed Bren to this new, obsessed one.

Neasa led us to a great hall at the top of the hill. She paused outside. "Stay here," she said and continued past a pair of guards who stood at the entrance. Only Talon accompanied her into the hall.

As we waited under the eaves, I tried to catch my breath while Carrog gave me an encouraging nod. "Don't worry, my friend. We'll be on our way before you know it."

Since our encounter in the ship's cabin—actually, immediately after Carrog took my uncle's money—I had lost my fear of the huge warrior. There is something comforting about knowing where a man stands. It wasn't as if I trusted Carrog—but in this strange city full of Kail killers, his was a friendly face. There was no use letting him know how I felt, though, so I kept my face neutral and ignored him.

A moment later, the door opened and Talon waved for us to enter. He was flanked by a pair of Kail warriors wearing leather armor and matching brown tunics. Seeing two Kail warriors wearing the same colors was enough to make me pause.

"Come along," Talon said. "The Reik will see you tomorrow."

The Reik? I had not expected to be seen by the Reik of Gwyr.

Reik meant "high king" in Kailish. The Reik once ruled all the clans, but now he ruled in exile from Rover Island, across the Inner Sea. It was complicated, as all politics are, but I knew that the Reik was still the most powerful of the Kail clan leaders.

"The Reik … wants to meet with me?"

Talon nodded. "Come along, Olaf, and we'll talk." He waved for us to follow him into the hall.

His sudden friendliness rubbed me wrong. "Are you sure Neasa will let you?" As soon as the words were out of my mouth, I regretted them.

Talon faltered and turned to give me a hard look. "I don't answer to Neasa," he snapped.

"Of course you do!" Carrog chimed in, letting out an evil little laugh. "We all love Neasa, Talon."

The look Talon sent Carrog's way was worse than the one he had given me.

I laid my hand on Talon's shoulder. "I didn't mean anything …"

Talon started to shrug me off, but then stopped himself. "It has been a long journey, Olaf. Come along and let's get reacquainted." He nodded toward Carrog. "You can go your own way until Neasa calls for you." Carrog ignored him and kept pace with Bren at my back, as did the two brown-clad guardsmen.

The hall held several people seated at tables and benches. A raised chair on the opposite end—the Reik's seat—was empty. I took all this in as we turned left to climb the staircase to the second floor.

Because of my twisted leg, climbing stairs always made me feel awkward, but I ascended to the top without incident. The woodwork on the second floor reminded me of the sterncastle deck aboard the *Sea Cow*. I guessed that the same carpenters that built the Macha's vessels had built the Reik's hall.

"This way," Talon called.

I reluctantly pulled my eyes away from the impressive woodwork. Talon scowled at Carrog, who was still following us, and then led us to a door. "You will stay here until the Reik calls for you," Talon said as he opened the door and held it for me.

Bren slipped past me, heading for the wardrobe to unpack my few belongings. Besides the wardrobe along the back wall, the room held a bed, a washstand, and a small table with two stools.

"No need for you to stay," I heard Talon say behind me.

I turned to look.

Talon stood in the doorway, blocking Carrog from entering. Carrog looked ready to argue, or even attack physically, but I waved him off. "We aren't going anywhere, Carrog. You can check on us in the morning." His loyalty to my uncle's money was almost reassuring.

A smile twisted Carrog's face, which didn't improve his appearance, and he nodded. "I'll go and find a pot of ale then."

Talon shut the door before he could even turn away. "Why is he following you like a lost puppy?" he asked. The exasperation on his face matched his tone.

"Stenson silver," I replied as I made my way to the small table and pulled out one of the stools. "You never know when you'll need an ally."

Talon stalked over to the table and took the other stool. "Ally? That one will cut your throat for your purse while you're sleeping."

The vehemence in Talon's voice made me smile. "I think you're right."

Talon had an easygoing nature, but he was easily riled. We had become good friends when we'd traveled together, several months past. At first, I had thought him a rival for Tessa's favor, but he obviously had different tastes.

"So how is it with Neasa?" I asked him now. "Do you have an alliance with her people or is she stringing you along?"

A flash of anger crossed Talon's face, but then suddenly softened. "What happened with Tessa?"

The pain hit as soon as he spoke her name. I knew he would ask me eventually, but I had hoped to avoid the conversation as long as possible. I closed my eyes but then jerked them open again, because that flashing dagger hadn't gone away. Instead, I covered my face with my hands and took a deep breath to compose myself.

Talon was probably one of the few people that I could talk with about Tessa. No matter how painful it was to talk about her death, I felt like I owed him an explanation.

Bren saved me from speaking. He spoke in a soft tone from across the room, but his words cut at my heart. "She died in Kartoba." He paused as if trying to find the words. "Master Olaf has not spoken of it to anyone."

I heard Talon's sudden intake of breath. The room stood quiet for a moment before he spoke. "I'm truly sorry, Olaf. I had no idea. If you want to talk …"

His words hung in the air between us, but I felt no desire to respond. It took an act of will to lower my hands away from my face and look at my old friend. "Do we have an alliance with the Kail?"

Talon exhaled, looking somewhat relieved that I had refrained from speaking of Tessa. "No," he said. "Neasa has pushed for it, but the Reik has not decided."

He suddenly looked weary. It made me wonder about his mission. "Have you been to Kailand, then?"

He nodded with a faraway look in his eyes. "It is different from our homeland. There are more trees than I've ever seen, and it rains every day." He focused upon me again. "The Kail are always at each other's throats. They have feuds that have been raging for generations."

Bren must have finished unpacking, because he approached our table and poured each of us a cup from the clay pitcher sitting on the table and then retreated to the other side of the room. I hadn't even noticed the pitcher. I took a sip. It was a bitter draught—Kailish ale, no doubt.

Talon ignored his cup and kept talking. "There is no way the Kail will ever unite to help us, unless one of the clans conquers the rest."

"Is that why you're here—to help the Reik retake Kailand?"

He shook his head. "That would be the quickest way to unite the rest of the clans *against* us. The only thing they can all agree upon is that the Reik will never rule in Kailand again." He toyed with the corners of his golden blonde hair as he spoke. Talon's hair had grown out since I had seen him. The way his hair fell about his shoulders—and the leather jacket he now wore—made him look more like a barbarian warrior than a member of the Order of the Dog.

His Order was the strongest mercenary company in the Seven Kingdoms, and its captain was the Supreme Commander of all five companies. I wondered what Commander Musk would think of Talon's current appearance.

"Why have you come to Gwyr then, if not to unite the clans?"

Talon took a quick breath, as if preparing himself for an argument. "Neasa thinks that the Reik will help us against the Empire of Jewel, for a price."

"What's the price?"

He seemed surprised that I didn't ask for more information. The questions certainly occurred to me: What can the Reik do without the backing of the clans? Why is Neasa in the middle of this? I could have tried to untangle it all, but at this point, the only thing that mattered to me was getting on with my mission to the east. Maybe Talon would be successful with his mission to the Kail—and maybe not. I just didn't care.

"What's the price?" I repeated when he didn't answer.

Talon pursed his lips and I could tell he was hesitant to say, but finally he answered. "He wants Andamar."

Andamar province was on the southwestern tip of the Empire of Jewel. The heart of the Empire of Jewel—the Imperial city for which the empire was named—was in the east, and the Seven Kingdoms were in the west. Andamar stood between them, its steep and rocky coastline jutting south into the sea. The empire's main trade route cut through the more prosperous provinces north of Andamar, leaving Andamar as a backroads province with few residents.

While it was close to Rover Island, I couldn't imagine why the Reik would have his eyes on the province. "Why?"

"He dreams of establishing a new Kailand in the east to rival the one his ancestors lost." Talon sounded almost apologetic as he explained. "He thinks that Jewel won't care about Andamar, especially if they are too busy fighting the Seven Kingdoms in the west and the Confederation in the east."

"The Eastern Confederation!" My pulse quickened. If hostilities had arisen again between Jewel and the Confederation, my mission was over before I even arrived. I hadn't considered the possibility. "Have they begun fighting the Empire of Jewel again?"

Talon shook his head. "No, but it would be a good thing for the Reik, as well as our homeland, if they did." He leaned in to emphasize his words. "This is the reason the Reik will let you go. I'm sure Neasa is arguing that point with him now."

I sat back and mulled over what he had told me. If the Reik invaded Andamar and I managed to stir the war back up in the east, the pressure would be off my uncle. At the least, the empire would have to divide its forces, which meant the Seven Kingdoms would have a chance of surviving. Unfortunately, my guess was that the Reik would wait for the west and east to be fully engaged in war before he would move into Andamar— so what help would he be before then?

"The Reik won't move into Andamar until after the battle is raging in our homeland."

Talon nodded. "I'm not privy to his thoughts, but Neasa thinks he will wait until the empire is committed elsewhere. If Jewel and the Eastern Confederation renew their fight, it may be enough."

I noticed the earnest look on Talon's face and paused. He had been so carefree in the past, but now he seemed seriously committed to his mission—or was it to Neasa? He spoke of her often, as if dedicated to her. And I remembered his reactions to Carrog when the scarred warrior had teased him about the woman.

"Who is Neasa?" I asked. "How does she have the Reik's ear?"

Talon's face turned red. "She is daughter to the Macha Dryhten."

Well, that explained her influence. The Macha remaining in Kailand had split away from the Reik and had a Dryhten of their own. Officially, he was at odds with the Reik in Gwyr. Obviously, it was a ruse though, if the Dryhten's daughter had the Reik's ear.

"Will that cause problems with the other clans?"

Talon shrugged and gave me a grin. "They're content to ignore it as long as the Reik stays out of Kailand."

I nodded. "Will Neasa's father help invade Andamar, when the time comes?"

"Neasa thinks that all the clans will send warriors. They'll try to claim their own portion of the new land, if only to spite the Reik." He finally reached out to sip his ale, silencing my questions, but he glanced at me over his cup, raising an eyebrow as if daring me to ask him a question while he quenched his thirst.

"Enough about Neasa." Talon set his cup down on the table between us and ran his hand through his long locks. His devilish grin reminded me of the Talon I had met back in the Seven Kingdoms. "We're a pair, aren't we?" His look quickly turned somber though, and I was sure he wanted to ask me about Tessa.

I reached out and grabbed my own cup to stall him. I noticed it shaking in my hand as I pulled it to my lips. I held it there for a long moment, not drinking but hardening my resolve.

"Tessa is dead," I finally said, letting my cup slip back down to the table. "And it was my fault."

It hurt to say the words. I didn't dare look at him, so I focused on my cup, watching a bead of ale slide down the outside rim. I reminded myself that I should feel a sense of relief, because I had spoken the awful words at last.

Growing up an outcast in my own family had not taught me much about friendships. I would not have even met Talon had I not been on a quest to gain my Uncle Olaf's favor. We were very different—and yet, I liked him. I didn't know how he'd react to my news.

Talon reached out and clasped my arm where it sat on the table. "We don't have to talk about it now, Olaf," he said, giving my arm a squeeze before releasing it again. "I'll let you get your rest. We can talk about it sometime later, if you want to." He stood and headed out the door.

Once the door shut, Bren said, "No, Olaf. Tessa's death was Griselda's fault—not yours. I heard what happened."

My anger flared, but it flamed out quickly. While his words had been meant to comfort me, I knew Bren had it wrong. He didn't know everything. He didn't know my part.

"Aunt Griselda wielded the blade," I agreed, "but I caused it!" The words burned as I spoke them, as though they had been smoldering in my heart. "I ordered the coup against the Duke because Tessa was leaving and I wanted to go with her. I did it because I was selfish and too stupid to see what would happen."

"You couldn't know."

I pushed myself up from the table and headed to the single bed, sighing as I flopped down on it with my back to him. That way, I didn't have to close my eyes as I ignored my valet.

Bren got the message and refrained from saying more.

As I lay there, I tried not to think about Tessa and the dagger waiting to foil my sleep. I wondered, as I had for so many nights, how things had turned out the way they had.

I was exhausted, yet I could not sleep. I spent the dark hours fretting over my impending meeting with the Reik.

.

CHAPTER 7: NEGOTIATIONS

Waking up the next morning was a surprise. Somehow, I'd slept through the night without my normal nightmare. I sat up and enjoyed a long stretch before the feelings of guilt hit me.

How could I suddenly sleep? Tessa was still *dead*. I was still to blame.

I heard Bren clear his throat and looked to where he slumped on the floor next to the bed. "You snored all night," he said as he pulled himself to his feet and offered me a fake frown. "I hope you feel better."

Looking at my valet's sleep-glazed eyes, I realized that I did feel better. I felt better than I had in months.

I pulled myself out of bed and headed over to the piss pot in the corner. As I relieved myself, I called over my shoulder to him. "Think you can find us some breakfast?"

I looked over my shoulder to spy Bren straightening his wrinkled coat. He rubbed the sleep from his eyes before replying. "Yes, Master Olaf."

The half-smirk on his face reminded me of our time together in the stables. "Gotta feed the animals before you get to eat," I joked.

Bren laughed as he headed for the door. "I'll see if I can find you some hay." His laugh turned to a startled cry when the door suddenly opened.

Talon stepped in and held the door for Neasa. She entered the room like an empress ascending her throne. Gone was the shabby green tunic. Instead, she wore a long yellow tunic with a green, checkered cloak thrown over her left shoulder and held in place by her thick, leather belt. She had taken the braids out of her hair, which now flowed around her face like a dark cloud. Small bells sewn into the hem of the tunic tinkled as she stopped in the doorway. The transformation was enough to make me gape in astonishment.

Neasa laughed. "Pull up your trousers, Olaf, and let's go to breakfast."

I had finished pissing, but had forgotten what I was doing when she entered. I quickly cinched up my trousers and turned to greet her.

"Neasa, you startled me." I blurted out the first thing that came to mind, my face growing hot. I had never been good at witty banter or awkward situations.

"Come along," she called, and twirled around to lead the way down to the main hall. The bells on her tunic tinkled softly, as if inviting us to follow.

Talon held back a chuckle as he waited for me at the door. "You do make a strong first impression, Olaf." His words reminded me of our first meeting. I had been jealous because Tessa flirted with him and tried to drink myself happy. It had not been one of my better nights.

We walked side-by-side in Neasa's wake with Bren taking up the rear, along with the pair of brown-clad guards that seemed to have been assigned to watch me. It was a different pair of guards than the night before, but they looked just as grim-face as the previous two. I smiled at them over my shoulder and got a pair of frowns in return.

"Don't mess with the guards, Olaf," Talon whispered. He grabbed my shoulder to get me to look ahead as we walked. "There's a much better view up ahead."

I remembered watching Neasa walk away when I first met her on the pier in Kartoba. She had been wearing her shabby green tunic at the time that didn't quite cover everything and I had gotten an eyeful. Now, with her current ensemble, she looked more—elegant—like a lady of one of the great houses in Kartoba. "She cleans up good," I muttered to Talon out of the corner of my mouth.

Neasa chuckled and turned to give me a wink. "I can be dirty when I want."

I missed a step and then tried to recover. "I-I only meant …"

Talon slapped me on the shoulder to get me moving again. "She has many talents, Olaf—but for today, we'll be relying on her power of persuasion."

Neasa nodded back at me as she led us down the stairs to the hall below. "Don't worry, Olaf Stenson. You may get a chance to persuade me, too."

I was relieved to find food being served. Neasa sat us at an isolated table and a pair of servants brought our breakfast. On the *Sea Cow*, my breakfast usually consisted of smoked fish, with maybe some cheese and bread. The platter set before us in the Reik's hall looked like a midday feast in comparison. There was fish and bread, but the bread was fried flat bread with rice and vegetables rolled inside. I had heard of the dish, but had never tried it. Also, there was some type of rice porridge with fruit and nuts and plenty of tea to wash it all down. My stomach rumbled at the sight, and I soon lost myself in the pleasure of eating.

Talon laughed at my exuberance. "The Kail enjoy breakfast," he said, pointing toward a covered crock that sat next to the bread platter. "You should try some of this pepper sauce. It tastes great on everything."

I spread some sauce on my bread roll and took a bite. The sauce blazed such a fiery trail through my mouth that I nearly choked, but it was delicious, so I kept eating.

Talon grinned at me and Neasa let out a chuckle. "Not bad for a first-timer."

My eyes watered, but I took another dab of sauce with my next bite. The stuff was hot, but addicting. I needed a long sip of tea before I could speak. "Good!" I exclaimed as I ate several more of the fried bread rolls smothered in pepper sauce.

Finally, I realized I was the only one still eating. Then it dawned on me that Neasa hadn't eaten at all.

Talon leaned toward me. "Neasa does not eat breakfast. She says it slows her down."

Neasa broke in. "So if you're finished loading your bellies, maybe we can get on with our business." She pushed herself away from the table, and we all quickly stood.

"Will the Reik see us today?" I asked.

Neasa smiled. "We'll go to see him now." She turned and headed for the back of the hall.

My stomach turned over, and the pepper sauce felt like fire in my belly as I followed. Sweat broke out on my forehead. I wiped it away with the back of my coat sleeve. It was not much warmer here than Kartoba, but I was dressed in my full regalia. Back home, I had worked in just a tunic on most days; onboard the ship, I had left off my jacket more often than not. But today, as my uncle's representative, I had dressed to make a good impression.

Thinking about it made me remember how much I hated wearing trousers. I had to fight an impulse to pull at the crotch. That would be the perfect first impression to give the Reik.

When we finally stopped before a door at the back of the hall, I was trying my best not to squirm in my clothes.

A single guard stood next to the doorway, wearing mail over his brown tunic and holding a long spear at the ready. He nodded to Neasa as one of my watchdogs opened the door for her.

"Stay outside," she told the guard as she led us into the room. I looked back at Bren and nodded for him to stay as well.

The room was smaller than I expected, dominated by a wooden table. Two men stood on the opposite side. A single lamp hanging over the middle of the table gave off enough light so that I could see both men clearly as they pored over a pile of maps and old parchments.

The man on the left was obviously the Reik. He was several inches taller than the other man and his wardrobe marked him as important. He was dressed in a long, purple tunic with gold trim that flowed well past his knees and wore a pair of golden rings hanging from his ears. His face was angular and his expression severe, as if he would be a hard man to convince. His balding head ruined the stern effect, though, because what hair he had left stood up in grey tufts along the sides of his head. It looked like he hadn't attempted to tame it in a while.

I tried my best to ignore the spicy breakfast still roiling in my stomach as I looked him in the eye. I bowed low. "My Lord."

To my surprise, the man on the right spoke first. "You are Olaf the Younger?"

He spoke in Imperial, which made my heart pound with panic. Had the Reik sided with the Empire of Jewel after all? I hadn't looked closely at the second man. He wore mail like the guard outside the door, though. I had assumed he was one of the Reik's men. I hazarded a peek past my eyebrows.

The armored man smiled at me. "By all means, relax. I don't stand on ceremony in this room." He definitely looked to be Kailish, with dark, short, spiked hair and their distinctive eagle-eyed look about him. He was much younger than the taller man.

Neasa, standing to my right, spoke. "He understands Kailish, Lord Maedoc."

The warrior nodded, confirming my suspicion that he was the Reik—not the man in purple. I quickly straightened and gave my full attention to the Reik. "Apologies, Lord Maedoc."

The Reik laughed and continued in Kailish. "Padruig looks more the part." The taller man snorted at his words. Lord Maedoc waved for us to join them at the table. "So, let's talk about how you can help me."

His relaxed behavior did not improve my apprehension. My stomach continued to churn as I moved to join the men at the table.

The Reik pointed to a map that lay at the top of the pile on the table. It was a world map showing the Empire of Jewel at the center. "The Imperials think they sit at the center of the world," the Reik remarked.

"Don't we all," Padruig quipped.

Lord Maedoc grinned sideways at the older man. "Gwyr lies at the center of my world, for now." He gave me an appraising look, his dark eyes glinting with mirth ... or perhaps avarice. "Will you help me to expand that view?"

I took a deep breath and thought about my Uncle Olaf. No matter how intimidating the Reik was, I had never met another man that scared me as much as my uncle. The Reik was tame in comparison. That thought helped me to regain my composure. "Will you help the Stensons in their endeavors?"

"You mean, will I help you, young Stenson, please your uncle?" He had been standing back, relaxed. Now he leaned forward to look me over. "I've heard about your uncle. He's a hard man—and not one a sane man would want to be friends with."

Padruig cut in, "The Duke of Kartoba found that out."

I shivered at the name. It was my doing—the Duke's death—but my uncle was seen as the mastermind behind it. Maybe he was. He had sent me there, after all. Maybe he had known what would happen.

"The Duke was another hard man," the Reik conceded. He kept up that appraising stare. "You were in Kartoba when the Duke died, weren't you?"

I didn't know how he was so well-informed, but the Reik controlled much of the sea that surrounded the Seven Kingdoms, so it shouldn't have been such a surprise to me. I took another deep breath, trying not to think about deaths in Kartoba. I nodded. "I was there."

He looked at me for another moment and then said, "You'll do, Olaf the Younger. I think we can help each other."

His words came as another surprise. Why would he suddenly decide that I could help him? I wanted to ask, but I didn't want to sound unsure. I nodded instead. "How do you propose we do that?"

On the map, the Reik pointed to the border between the Empire of Jewel and the Eastern Confederation. "If your goal is to start the fighting up again here, I will support you."

I couldn't tell what he was thinking. The Reik had been a statesman his whole life and I had just barely gotten out of the stables. Still, I knew what he wanted, so I figured there was no use playing dumb. "If I do that, will you invade Andamar?"

The Reik's eyes flashed past my shoulder to Neasa and Talon behind me. He had been bending over the map, but now he stood bolt upright. "You don't play games, I see." He pursed his lips and I could hear one of his feet tapping under the table.

"We could just kill him now," Padruig said, "and Neasa's pet as well." He nodded toward Talon. His severe expression and the pitch of his voice had not changed. He made the statement in the same way another man might have spoken of the weather. I decided I didn't like Padruig.

I guessed that not many people knew of the Reik's plans to invade Andamar. My stomach had started to settle, but now a pang shot through my gut that threatened to double me over. I gritted my teeth and held steady.

Neasa chose to join the conversation at this point. "Would you rather side with the empire, Padruig? Become another advisor in the emperor's court?" The emperor's advisors were no more than high-ranking captives from the lands he had conquered. He was famous for offering the title to rulers who capitulated without a fight, or to those who betrayed their homeland to the empire.

Padruig shot Neasa a nasty look. Still, his voice remained calm when he replied, "I am not the one giving away the Reik's secrets."

Neasa scoffed. "It's not a secret when all of Kailand has heard the rumors." She turned back to the Reik. "Lord Maedoc, you know that the time to act is now. The clans are balanced upon a knife's edge. If we wait too long, we will lose them."

Talon had said the other Kail clans would send warriors to stake their own claim in Andamar. Obviously, the word had already gone out in Kailand. "If we wait for the empire to attack the Seven Kingdoms, it might be too late."

So, it turned out the Reik needed a fight in the east just as much as my uncle did. My stomach started to settle again and I decided to repeat my question. "If I stir up the east, will you invade Andamar?"

The Reik's good humor returned and he flashed me a bright smile. "I shall, and I will help you in your endeavor as well." He turned toward his companion. "Padruig shall accompany you. He will be my eyes and ears, *and my voice* in this matter."

I noticed Neasa stiffen next to me as Padruig actually smiled and said, "Your will, my lord."

Now the Reik turned his smile on Neasa. "I expect you will wish to tag along?"

Neasa bowed her head in acknowledgement. "My birlinn will be close enough to assist if needed."

With a curt nod, the Reik turned back to his map. "Then I suppose you should get to it."

We all headed out of the room, with the exception of Padruig, who remained with his master. I was surprised to see Carrog standing alongside Bren outside the door. The two brown-clad guardsmen had disappeared.

"When do we leave?" Carrog asked.

Neasa swept past, pulling the rest of us in her wake. I had to hurry to keep up as she led the way. The bells tinkling on her tunic sounded loud in the awkward silence. She led us through the hall and out the front door.

Once outside, she whirled around and snapped. "That weasel Padruig! I should have expected him to stick his nose into this."

"It is not surprising," Talon began and then quickly relented when she glared at him.

Carrog shrewdly kept a tight lip and raised an eyebrow in my direction.

Neasa turned her glare on Bren and commanded, "Go and get your master's gear. Meet him at the ship."

He looked to me for confirmation before heading back into the hall. I was impressed that he weathered her foul mood until I nodded agreement. Carrog nodded at me after he left and mouthed, "Good man," as if to confirm his earlier assessment on the *Sea Cow* when Bren first started following me around.

Neasa waited for Bren to re-enter the hall before gifting us all with a frustrated frown. "Padruig cannot be trusted." She turned her attention to Carrog and me. "You must watch him closely throughout your journey."

She hadn't questioned Carrog's presence or the fact that he was accompanying me. I gave the big man a sidelong glance, wondering for whom he truly worked. Himself, I finally decided, and put it out of my head for more important things.

"Don't you belong to the same clan as Padruig?" I asked. Kail clansmen were notoriously loyal to their clan leaders. I would expect them both to be doing the Reik's bidding.

I thought she would shout at me, but instead, her face suddenly calmed and she gave me a tight little smile. "But you can trust me, Olaf Stenson," she said softly. She and Talon exchanged a look I couldn't interpret before she turned and stalked away.

Talon let out a sigh. He combed his hand through his blond locks and shook his head. "Shall we head to your vessel? Who knows how long we'll have until Padruig arrives."

I hadn't expected Neasa to let Talon out of her sight, at least not for the voyage east. "You'll be coming with us?"

He shook his head. "Yes, for now—but not when we sail. I figured you'd have more questions you want answered before it's time to leave."

Carrog laughed. "You don't trust me to set him straight?"

Talon raised an eyebrow at the giant Kail but otherwise ignored his comment. "Shall we?"

We headed back to the *Sea Cow* with Carrog in tow, grinning as if he had won a prize.

Moshe and Mehki met us at the rail and took their normal positions without a word or even a change in expression. Bren's family, in contrast, rushed forward to greet us. Gabriele stopped short and gave me a bashful smile, but Sofie kept coming and wrapped me in a hug while their mother stood back and beamed at me. "Master Olaf," she called out excitedly.

Their greeting, especially Sofie's, was embarrassing. I tried to push Sofie away. She clung even harder, and I realized that she wasn't the little girl she pretended to be. Even though her head only came up to my throat, I could feel her breasts pressed against my belly. Just when that realization hit me, she looked up and gave me an innocent smile—only it wasn't so innocent. She bit at her lower lip and then whispered up at me, "I knew you would come back."

I managed to push her away, feeling like I had done something wrong. Her mouth twisted into a sly grin before she turned and skipped away, swishing her tunic from side to side like a little girl would. I was no longer fooled by the act.

"You're a popular man," Talon said.

I wasn't sure if anyone else had seen through Sofie's act and had no desire to find out. My face was hot, and I knew it would be red with embarrassment. I grunted out a reply and made a quick escape to the sterncastle.

While we waited for Padruig, Talon answered my questions. I didn't learn anything that I hadn't already guessed, and to be honest, I was only half-listening. Sofie had disturbed me. I wasn't sure how to deal with her. I did find out that Neasa was betrothed to the Reik to strengthen the bonds between the Macha Reik and Neasa's father. Talon didn't seem too happy when he delivered that bit of information.

Padruig finally arrived and we readied to set sail. Talon said his goodbyes and headed down the sterncastle ladder just as Padruig came aboard with a pair of mail-clad guards. They passed each other on the main deck, neither man deigning to look at the other. Carrog's group of ruffians still stood at the rails, and they eyed the new Kail guardsmen with disdain.

Carrog stood next to me at the sterncastle rail and let out a chuckle. "It'll be an exciting voyage." He had somehow decided that we were friendly now. His good humor rankled me, but I tried not to let it show. For better or worse, I had paid him and I was stuck with him and his handful of Kail warriors— although I liked it better when he stayed on the main deck.

I scanned the deck below and spied Captain Gregor directing his men. He had once more taken command of the *Sea Cow* and looked no worse for wear from his dunking in the sea. Still, I wondered if his presence below was the true reason that Carrog was on the sterncastle.

Captain Gregor looked my way and scowled. He hadn't liked me before. I was sure Carrog standing next to me didn't improve Gregor's opinion. "Prepare to cast off," he called to his men as he finally turned his attention away.

"Did you have to dunk him?" I asked Carrog with a frown.

Carrog grinned, his puckered eye and the scar on his head making him look like some kind of fiend. "He needed a bath," he growled.

He turned away and headed toward the ladder. I hoped he would round up his men and keep them out of trouble.

CHAPTER 8: GOOD HELP IS HARD TO FIND

I felt almost relieved to be back on the sterncastle deck as we rowed out of Gwyr harbor. Carrog, Captain Gregor, and Padruig were all on the main deck below, sizing each other up. They reminded me of a bunch of women at the town well, trying to decide who had the right to get her water first. I hoped they would just stay down there until we reached the Eastern Confederation.

I turned to survey my domain. Moshe, Mehki, and Bren hovered at my back. Ivan was not far off, giving me that "we need to talk" look. Along the port rail stood my Stenson guardsmen, decked out in their blue coats; they looked as if they weren't sure if they could relax yet. Guard Captain Luther gave me an uncertain nod when he noticed me looking.

The three women stood along the starboard rail, near the steersman at the tail of the ship. Gabriele and Ursala leaned on the rail and watched the shoreline glide past, but Sofie stood with her back to the scenery. Her eyes met mine and she gave me a slow smile.

I quickly turned my attention to Bren, afraid he had seen the exchange. His brow furrowed in confusion. "Do you need me, Olaf?"

"No," I snapped, embarrassed but unwilling to admit it. "Why don't you go visit your family? You don't intend to hover over me for the entire voyage, do you?"

His eyes flicked to my Wolf guards, who would do just that, and then he shrugged and said, "As you wish." I watched him head to the starboard rail, his back stiff, as if I had offended him. I was relieved to see that Sofie had turned away. I sighed when I remembered Ivan. He would not wait long for me to update him on my visit in Gwyr. No use in putting it off. I turned to meet him at my normal spot at the rail.

My conversation with Ivan continued until dark. To my relief, Carrog, Gregor, and Padruig had all stayed below. We were finally making our way east, although Neasa's birlinn still shadowed us. Surprisingly, their presence reassured me as I turned to settle into my pallet for the night. At least no other Kail ships would assault us with Neasa's vessel as an escort. I settled in under the canopy near the stern of the ship, not far from the steersman.

Even at night, one of the Wolf guards stood over me. Tonight it was Mehki. I watched his silhouette in the moonlight as he leaned on the nearest rail. My thoughts no longer revolved around the flashing dagger; instead, I worried about Sofie. I had no idea what to do about the girl, and despite my efforts to sleep, I lay there fretting over her recent advances. I knew it was no longer my imagination. The young girl was playing a game with me. Finally, I gave up and joined Mehki at the rail.

The Katchian nodded at me but said nothing. I had met Mehki and his brother on the march to Kartoba. While we would never be true friends, I felt affection for the brothers and was happy when they were assigned as my protectors. Mehki, in particular, had a sense of humor and an easy-going nature. Still, I didn't have anything to say, so I contented myself with standing at the rail next to him.

We stood in silence for so long that I was startled when Mehki spoke. "The girl will be trouble." He spoke in Imperial, the language of his homeland. It didn't surprise me that he had seen Sofie's antics. With his keen eyes constantly searching for potential danger, he always saw more than I did.

I hadn't spoken to anyone about Sofie, not even Ivan. I took a deep breath to clear my thoughts as I stared at the moon's reflection on the water. I finally turned to Mehki and asked, "What do I do?"

He didn't hesitate to answer. "That family is a weight around your neck. Send them home when next we reach land."

There was no humor in his voice. Mehki was serious. I was sure I saw real concern in his dark eyes.

I realized that, in my moment of weakness, Bren's family had latched onto me. Now I was their benefactor. I could not simply send them home now … yet the look in Mehki's eyes and my own trepidation made me think I should. Finally, I shook my head. "No, I can't do that now."

He grimaced and then shrugged. "My people have a saying: It is better to choose a woman's embrace than a life of lonely wisdom." When he saw the confused look on my face, his humor finally returned. He chuckled and said, "Women control your fate, Olaf. You might as well accept it."

His words struck home. I had tried to please Tessa, and it had led to her death. I had no desire to repeat that experience.

I glared at Mehki, but luckily, it was too dark for him to see. It was not his fault, anyway, that I found myself in this predicament. "Can you keep them away from me?" I snapped, my command edged with desperation.

He laughed louder. "It would be easier to keep the rain from falling." He leaned in close to me. "You are a rich man now, Olaf. It is your fate."

I shook my head and returned to my pallet, where I lay for hours, fretting about Sofie. Mehki's words had only made it worse.

From that evening forward, I tried to avoid Bren's family. When Gabriele brought me my meals, I refused to speak to her, which earned me dark looks from her mother. When Sofie wandered nearby, I turned the other way. I had more important things to worry about than a strange girl who seemed set on ensnaring me.

But it wasn't working. On the small ship, there was no way to avoid the women. I knew I should be making plans with Padruig; instead, I found myself spending my days at the ship's rail, lost in thought. At night, instead of lying awake at night for fear of my dagger dream, now I worried about Sofie and Gabriele and Ursala. Mehki's words kept repeating in my head: "Women control your fate, Olaf." In my twenty years of life, I'd had little experience with women. They still bewildered me. Tessa had seemed different ... but I realized now that I hadn't truly known her, either.

Not a week later, as I lay on my pallet pondering that thought, Sofie took matters into her own hands.

Mehki stood nearby once more, which didn't help clear his words from my head. The memory of Tessa's death kept fighting back to the surface of my thoughts. At the end, she had reached out for her dead husband instead of me. She hadn't even known I was there. I couldn't blame Tessa—but at the same time, it hurt. It made me doubt whether she had ever cared for me.

I had loved Tessa with all my heart, but she had gone on to the Halls of the Dead to join her family, leaving me alone. My Aunt Osha had, in her usual manner, cut to the heart of it. "She was not meant for you, Olaf."

As I lay there, lost in memories, a light touch on my arm nearly sent me hurtling from my bed. I must have cried out, because Mehki stepped away from the rail to peer down at me. He let out a grunt that sounded suspiciously like a chuckle and turned back to his post.

I knew I didn't want to look, but I turned and wasn't surprised to see Sofie kneeling next to me. She wore her normal, too-small tunic. For some reason, the sight made my heart pound. The night was dark, but the steersman's lamp hung near enough that I could see the concerned look on her face.

She must have crawled from her place at the other end of the covered deck. Pulling myself up onto my elbow, I looked over her shoulder to see if any of her family was awake and looking our way. "What are you doing here?" My words came out a harsh whisper, and I found myself shivering from fright or excitement—I wasn't sure which.

She eased herself down next to me. "Why have you been avoiding me, Olaf?" Her voice was soft and husky instead of the high-pitched, little-girl voice she normally used.

I felt my body responding, and I tried to bunch my blanket between us. "Why do you pretend to be a little girl?" I whispered back. "And why are you tempting me?"

"Am I tempting?" She smiled and pulled the blanket open enough to slide in next to me. I turned onto my back away from her as she settled next to my left side. I knew I should push her away—she wasn't Tessa—but my body didn't want to do it. I shivered as her breasts pressed against my ribs and she rubbed her foot down the top of my leg.

I had lain with women before … well, with one woman. One of the serving girls at Stenson House had taken me behind the barn when I was sixteen. I think she wanted to see if my manhood was as twisted as my leg. I guess she passed her findings to the other girls, because it never happened again.

"I told you that you would marry me," Sofie whispered in my ear. "And what else?"

I had no idea what she spoke of. It was hard enough trying to resist the lustful thoughts that boiled through my head as she breathed next to me.

She giggled, "It's my job to cheer you up."

Her hand slid up my leg and found its way under my tunic. There was no hiding my excitement from her then. As she stroked me, she breathed a little sigh into my ear. "Are you happy yet?"

She didn't really need to ask, because it only took a few strokes for me to make a mess of the bed. As I lay there trembling, she kissed me on the cheek. "Don't ignore me anymore, Olaf," she whispered. Her voice was almost stern. "You'll hurt my feelings." She arose quietly and walked back to her bed, leaving my blankets and my thoughts in utter confusion.

I watched Sofie leave with mixed emotions. She definitely was not Tessa, but I was beginning to realize that Tessa had never been mine. She had never gotten over the death of her husband and child. I wasn't sure she would have ever been able to return my feelings, no matter how much I loved her.

Sofie was nothing like Tessa. The young beauty was anything but modest. She was a tease, and she had designs upon me. Mehki's words echoed in my brain: "Women control your fate, Olaf. You might as well accept it."

I closed my eyes and sighed. I had undertaken this journey because of a woman, and now another woman had appeared to complicate my life again. Perhaps Mehki knew what he was saying.

As I lay there contemplating this fact, the more immediate reality suddenly struck me. I had a mess to deal with. I pulled my blankets aside and inspected Sofie's handiwork. The blankets were fine, but my tunic was a sodden mess. It needed cleaning immediately.

Bren, as my valet, typically took care of my clothes—but I had no desire to explain this particular chore to him. I pulled the tunic over my head and quickly pulled on a spare. It was early morning and the deck was quiet as I found my way to the rail with Mehki.

He didn't say a word, but took in the tunic draped over my arm. The look on his face made it plain he was gloating.

"Can you grab me a bucket of seawater?" I was embarrassed to ask, but he was already aware of my predicament.

He gave me a knowing nod and went to fetch the line and bucket. His silence only made it worse.

I spent the rest of the pre-dawn morning scrubbing my tunic and vowing to drop Sofie off at the next port. But even as I made that vow, I knew it was empty.

The next day, Sofie changed her game. When she emerged from the canopy that morning, she wore the trappings of a woman. Gone was the little tunic; in its place, she wore one of Gabriele's blue woolen dresses. Though she didn't wear a coif like her sister, she had tied her hair up instead of having it fall around her shoulders. The dress hugged her curves, and it was immediately apparent to everyone on board that she was no little girl. I knew some of the men had made that discovery already, by the way they'd watched her out of the corner of their eyes. Now they no longer hid their interest.

That morning, when Gabriele brought me my breakfast, she was beaming with pride for her sister. "Did you see Sofie?" she asked. "She's finally decided to grow up." Her eyes glowed, and I had to turn away to hide my shame. Did she know? "We had to hem the dress, but she looks good in it, don't you think?"

What did she expect me to say? Yes, I lust for your sister instead of you? I couldn't face her and handed the plate back before turning to my place at the rail.

Even my usual indifference didn't bother Gabriele that morning. "She'll make someone a good wife, you know," she announced to my back. "Just you see."

I wanted to turn around and scream at her. I wanted to tell her that Sofie intended to be that wife for *me*—but I stayed put and let her go. I had known Gabriele for a long time, and I knew she liked me. She had been kind to me when the voyage started. I didn't have it in my heart to hurt her, and yet I didn't want to lie to her, either. It was all so complicated.

Moshe had taken his brother's place when the dawn came. He rarely spoke, so it surprised me when he joined me at the rail after Gabriele took her leave. It was obvious that the two Wolf guards were brothers—they had the same face—but Moshe was younger, so he lacked the gray in his beard. Moshe also rarely smiled, which made him look more severe, even frightening. I had been around him long enough to be able to detect his moods. Today, he was reflective.

We stared out over the water together while I waited for him to speak. Finally, he took in a deep breath and let it out slowly. "I had a wife once."

These were not the words I'd expected. Moshe spoke little, and mostly about military matters. I looked at him carefully. His body was rigid, just as it looked before a fight.

He ignored me and kept his gaze on the sea. "It was before Katch broke away from the empire, before the Wolf Lord came." They called my uncle "Wolf Lord." As I said before, they are a bit fanatical.

Moshe's voice came out flat and emotionless, but I knew he held his emotions tightly bound. "She was pretty and she knew it, and so did all the other men in my village. I was jealous. I tried to keep her hidden." Now he looked at me with hard eyes. "I wasn't very nice to her. I didn't treat her as a wife should be treated."

It was obvious to me that he knew about Sofie, and I wondered at the meaning of his tale. Did I not treat Sofie well—or was it Gabriele? My Wolf guards were typically tight-lipped, especially Moshe. For them both to speak to me meant they had real concerns.

He took another deep breath. "When the fighting began, I joined my countrymen to fight against the empire and left her behind. I did not think to ask her before I left what she wanted. I did not think she would want to come with me." He fell silent and stared out to sea again. For a moment, I thought his story was done. I was about to ask him why he was sharing this information, but then he continued.

"After the fighting was over, I went home to look for her. During our time apart, I realized my cruelty toward her and wanted to make it right. It was too late. She had moved from my house to the town brothel. She'd had no other choice to survive. And after that, I had no choice but to denounce her."

He hung his head and spoke once more as he stared down at the sea. "I had hidden her away, inciting the lust of my neighbors, and then I abandoned her. I later learned that the first man had forced himself upon her, and after that, she was shunned. She had to make her living at the brothel."

I could see his fingers were white on the rail where he gripped it. I wanted to reach out to him, but because it was Moshe, I held my place.

"I went to see her once, but she was ashamed and wouldn't look at me. She just stood there in the doorway with her head bowed in shame. She asked me but one question: Why hadn't I taken her with me?"

Moshe pushed himself away from the rail with a sudden jerk and turned to me. His eyes looked more haunted than usual. "Tessa was a good woman, and I'm sure you would have been happy—but don't punish the women here for your loss. Pick a sister, Olaf. Treat her well—even if it is just to pass the time." He turned away and resumed his post at my back.

I understood Moshe's point, and I finally understood his dark demeanor. I didn't understand how I had become the villain in this mess. I'd never asked for Gabriele's affection or Sofie's attention, but somehow it fell on me to resolve the situation. It wasn't fair. Yet Moshe was right—I had to choose one sister or set them all ashore, to find their own fates.

Whatever I decided, I would have to make sure everyone knew my choice.

CHAPTER 9: REVELATIONS

That afternoon, I invited Bren to join me for tea. We sat on cushions laid out on the deck, near my place at the rail. Somehow, I felt more comfortable there than anywhere else on the ship, probably because everyone else stayed away and gave me my privacy.

Bren seemed uncomfortable and sat quietly by my side. It dawned on me that Bren was probably the closest thing to a brother that I had. We'd worked together in the stables for several years, before he was elevated to house servant and I was demoted to the pigs. Besides my cousin Decker, he was the only other person that I spent much time with growing up in Stenson House. That was why I had invited him to be my valet, even though he had grown testy since our early years together and our relationship had turned awkward.

I waited until Gabriele brought us both a mug of tea before speaking. As she walked away, I asked him, "What does your sister want from me?"

"Which one?"

A ship at sea is like a village. Everyone knows their neighbor's business. So it was on the *Sea Cow*, although I hadn't realized it.

I choked on my tea.

Bren could be downright annoying with his uptight ways, but we had known each other long enough that he did not stand in awe of me, even though he had sworn his loyalty. It was an odd combination, for I did not doubt his loyalty, but I'm not sure he liked me much.

"What do you mean?" I tried to play dumb, hoping that he didn't know everything that had happened with Sofie.

Bren shook his head. "You haven't changed at bit, Olaf. You don't realize that people watch your every move."

I tried not to panic at his words. Who, besides Mehki, knew of Sofie's visit to my bed? Did Bren know?

I tried to stall. "What do you mean? People didn't watch me when we worked in the stables."

Bren actually got angry at that. "You were watched then to make sure you didn't make trouble," he snapped. "And you are watched now to make sure your every need is fulfilled. You are the lord here, after all."

Was he angry about his sister, or was it something else? I studied him over my mug of tea. His eyes blazed. I could tell he was holding back something that bothered him.

"Who watched me when we worked in the stable? It was just you and me." He looked away, and a sinking feeling entered my gut. It had been just the two of us for all those years, and yet he said I was watched.

He turned back to me, no longer angry. His face told it all.

"*You* watched me? You spied on me in the stable? For whom? Uncle Karl?"

He sat there looking at his hands, as if trying to figure out how to reply. When he looked up again, the anger was back. "How do you think I got promoted to the house? Do you think someone noticed my work with horseshit and said, 'We need to make this one a house servant'?"

I felt hollow, as if my life was a lie. I had hated my cousin Jarad my whole life. I thought he was the enemy—and yet Bren had been by my side the whole time. Even better, I had taken him on as my valet.

Bren spoke softly now and leaned in, trying to look me in the eye. "Olaf, I have dedicated my life to your service. I–I cannot change the past, but I can serve and protect you now." He sounded so earnest.

When I didn't answer, he pushed away from me again and sat up very straight. Prim and proper Bren was back. He slowly set the mug on the deck before him and rose to his feet. Bowing to me, probably for the first time, he said, "Master Olaf, I will understand if you wish to dismiss me."

I looked at the top of his head. His hair had always reminded me of straw, and the stables. It reminded me of our time together when we were just boys. He was the only person I could talk to back then. I remembered when his father died. Had that been the point when he started to spy on me? Did he do it to feed his family?

I realized that I could not hate him. I had used up all my hate on my Cousin Jarad and Uncle Karl. It didn't matter anymore.

"It must be hard to live with such a thing," I said.

Bren trembled but did not speak. He waited for my verdict.

I stood, as gracefully as my twisted leg allowed. "You are my valet, Bren, and your family is still in my service."

The look of relief that passed over his face was eclipsed by the smile that followed. Bren rarely smiled. It made him look younger and more like his sister Gabriele. "You will not regret it, Olaf."

I was surprised by how good it felt. For some reason, despite the long years of deception, I felt closer to Bren than I ever had.

He bent to retrieve our cups from the deck and then turned back to me once more before taking his leave. "As for my sisters …"

I had forgotten that this topic was how our conversation began. "Know that Sofie is not truly my sister. So if you must have a distraction, make it her." He turned and headed away.

Again, these were not the words I'd expected—although, as I thought about it, Bren had always been a realist. Rich men slept with serving girls all the time. I had just never thought of myself as a rich man before.

Watching Bren heading back to his mother, I suddenly wondered whose idea it was for Sofie to visit me and to stop dressing as a child.

It didn't surprise me when Sofie showed up that night— only this time, she didn't skulk to my bed. She walked across to meet me as I prepared to retire. Bren had already set up my pallet and blankets and had made his way back to his family's sleeping space, which was close enough to make me uncomfortable with the whole situation.

I tried to ignore her approach, but Sofie positioned herself between me and my pallet. She gave me a determined look and asked, "Shall I share your bed tonight, Olaf?"

So many thoughts ran through my head at the sight of her that I couldn't immediately answer. She was pretty in the blue dress with her hair pulled up, and I had to admit that I had thought about her coming back to my bed. It bothered me that she had come like this, though—for all the ship to see. I wanted to look over my shoulder to see if her family watched.

I knew Bren's mind on this subject, but what of Ursala and Gabriele? Were they glaring at my back this very moment? Would Gabriele forgive me if I took her sister to my bed? But she wasn't Gabriele's sister after all, was she? Bren had confirmed Sofie's story. Did that make any difference?

Sofie stood before me, patiently waiting. The look on her face was slightly less confident than it had been a moment before.

It suddenly struck me that I had worried about everyone *but* her. Why did she want to do this, really? I took a deep breath and reached out to grab her hand. Her face lit up, but dropped when she realized I didn't lead her to my bed. I took her to the nearby rail instead. The rail was my refuge, a place where I could think—and in this instance, talk.

I dropped her hand, but instead of looking out to sea, I leaned my good hip on the rail and looked down at her. "Why do you want to do this, Sofie?"

To my surprise, she smiled. "I like you, Olaf. Isn't that enough?"

"Did your brother put you up to this?"

Sofie laughed, but I noticed that she tugged nervously on the sides of her dress as she answered. "Bren is not my brother, just as Ursala is not my mother."

"You told me that before, when you played at being a child," I said. "Why don't you tell me now who you really are?"

Her smile slipped a bit. I could tell she didn't want to talk about it, but she squared her shoulders and did so anyway. "They are my family, Olaf. Ursala is my aunt, my mother's sister."

The news came as a surprise. "Then tell me about your mother," I demanded.

Her hands were clenched tightly on the sides of her dress, yet her face showed no turmoil. For a moment, I thought she would bolt. Instead, she took a deep breath and said, "My mother was a whore. And now she is dead."

The words had come out hard and I wanted to pull her into my arms for comfort, but I held back.

"Aunt Ursala took me in," she continued. She looked me in the eye as if daring me to condemn her because of her mother.

"I'm sorry."

"I am not sorry," she said bitterly. "Aunt Ursala took me in. She let me play at being a child long past when I should have been looking for a husband." She jutted her chin out at me, reminding me of her child act. "And by the way … I have decided it will be you."

Did she truly think I would marry her? Perhaps I would. I didn't know yet, but I was certain this was not the typical way to begin a courtship. I wondered if she knew this, coming from the childhood that she'd had.

Suddenly, she reached out to me, beckoning me to take her hand. "Shall we retire?"

She was young and beautiful, and her brazen manner was … almost irresistible. Still, I suppressed my urge to hold her. How could I let go of the memory of Tessa so easily?

Even though the sun had fallen, I knew the whole ship watched us. What would my people think of me? As these thoughts raced through my head, I recognized that my real fear wasn't shame—it was guilt. Did I deserve this? After a lifetime of being shit on and the tragedy of Tessa's death, I feared that I was cursed.

Eventually, it was the look in Sofie's eye that persuaded me. Her life had been just as hard as mine, yet she was still reaching out to me. She was offering the companionship of a kindred soul—and whether I deserved it or not, I knew I would be a fool to refuse. My hand shook as I touched her.

Her grip was strong and her smile lit up the evening as she led me to my bed. "I will make you happy, Olaf."

My head and body agreed with her, but my heart still felt the weight of doubt upon it.

The next day was awkward. The whole ship knew I had taken Sofie as my mistress. When she left my bed in the morning to return to her family, I stayed by the rail and tried to ignore everyone. I wasn't ready to face them—especially Gabriele.

Of course, she would be the first person to approach me. She came with my breakfast, as usual. I debated whether I should ignore her as I heard her approach at my back, but hunger gnawed at my stomach. No use in putting it off. I turned around and looked her in the eye.

To my surprise, she smiled at me. "Master Olaf, you look well refreshed." She bore a tray laden with fruit and smoked fish along with a mug of tea.

Her happy disposition startled me. Did I not just sleep with her sister—who was actually her cousin? Had I only imagined Gabriele's fondness for me? It took an effort of will to keep my hands from shaking as I reached out and took the plate. I nodded my thanks to her, not trusting myself to speak.

She leaned in close. "Olaf, I hope you find your happiness with Sofie."

Women! Could there exist a living thing more baffling? I could not detect any anger in her face or manner, but how could she be happy? Why wasn't she jealous? I had to know. "I don't understand, Gabriele. I thought *you* had feelings for me?"

Her face turned pink, but she didn't look away immediately. Gabriele had always been graceful. She showed great poise as she stood before me. "I am grateful to you, Olaf, for what you have done for my family. I am grateful for the friendship you have shared with my brother, and with me." She gave me a deep curtsy. "We will serve you well in all things."

She held the curtsy for a long moment, and I thought she was finished speaking. She rose again and smiled. "You, and Sofie—you both deserve happiness." Then she walked away.

Even if I didn't understand it, my encounter with Gabriele set my mind at ease. It seemed the matter with these troublesome women was resolved. I put aside my fears and decided to enjoy the rest of the voyage.

In the days that followed, Sofie became my constant companion. She cheered me with her playful wit and her passion. It almost felt as if the curse of my life had been lifted.

CHAPTER 10: NEW YEAR'S DAY

Not long after taking Sofie as my mistress, Captain Gregor came to me to discuss the New Year. We had left Kartoba in late autumn and had reached Rover Island near the beginning of winter. It felt odd to be nearing the New Year and yet still feel the warm sun on my face. But I knew the land in Kartoba would likely be covered in snow.

In my country, New Year's was by far the largest holiday— in fact, it was the only real celebration of the year. Unlike other nations, we did not have feast days for our gods. On the contrary, my people did everything in their power to avoid their notice, fearing the gods would grow jealous of our happiness.

The one exception to this was the New Year's celebration. It was the one day that we did not fear their wrath, and the only time we could let loose and enjoy ourselves. Our ships traditionally made for land to celebrate the New Year.

For the upcoming New Year's holiday, Captain Gregor wanted to stop for a day to celebrate. He knew of a cove along the coast of Andamar with a hamlet where we could pull in and buy supplies.

"Oyvu is a common travel stop," he explained to me. "The village sits on a sheltered cove and caters to trading ships." He had come to the sterncastle on the pretext of inspecting the steersman, but I knew this holiday talk was the true reason for his rare appearance. Prior to the Kail coming aboard, he would have planned the stop without consulting me. Now, he wanted my concurrence, in case our allies disagreed.

"We should arrive in Oyvu the day before New Year's," Captain Gregor said. He stood before me like a debtor before the magistrate. His dunking by Carrog seemed to have taken some of the fight out of him.

I wasn't sure what the sailors, or even my own guardsmen, would do if we didn't stop for the New Year's celebration. I nodded my consent. "Let's make for Oyvu then and plan our celebration."

A smile looked out of place on Gregor's weathered face. I couldn't remember him actually smiling at me before that moment. In fact, he looked so overjoyed that I thought he might try to hug me. He grinned instead and headed back to the main deck, no doubt to pass the word to his crew.

We were two days out from Oyvu when Captain Gregor slowed the *Sea Cow* and signaled to our escorts. Padruig had thrown a fit when he'd heard of our plans to stop at Oyvu. He insisted we call a meeting with Neasa to discuss it. I stood on the main deck with Carrog and Padruig, waiting for Neasa to board. Captain Gregor hovered over my shoulder with my wolf guards and Bren at my back.

Neasa climbed aboard the *Sea Cow* with Talon in tow. She was back in her ragged green tunic, looking more like a beggar than a sea captain except for the sword hanging from her thick leather belt and the way she dominated the deck with her purposeful stride. "What do we need to discuss, here?" she called as she stepped into our circle.

Padruig was the first to speak. He had given up his more regal garb for a brown tunic. It resembled those worn by the Reik's guards in Gwyr, only his was trimmed in fur with a bit of embroidery covering his left breast, presumably his seal of office. He also wore a fur cap, which hid his flyaway grey hair. It made his face look even more angular as he began his objection. "The ship's captain plans to stop for some sort of holiday. I believe we should continue our journey east. We have no time to waste on frivolities."

Neasa arched an eyebrow at Carrog and he quickly explained. "They want to stop in Oyvu to celebrate the New

Year." His tone indicated he did not give the idea his full endorsement. Maybe my silver didn't buy as much of his loyalty as I had thought.

"We will be stopping," I broke in. "It is our custom."

"The Reik has mandated this mission …" Padruig sputtered, but Neasa interrupted him.

"Padruig, would you skip Macha's Feast Day?"

Padruig sneered. "These uplanders have no gods!"

The Seven Kingdoms was mostly hill country. Outsiders called us a variety of names: uplanders, rock hoppers, hill dwellers. It always sounded odd to me, since I was from Kartoba on the relatively flat coast.

"You show your ignorance, Padruig." Neasa let out an irritated sigh. "You have schemed and planned for years. Another day will not matter."

It was clear that Padruig had expected Neasa to support him. She had the birlinn and the men to persuade us to continue our voyage. Without her backing, he had no leverage. His eyes narrowed at her words and I thought I heard his teeth grind together. "The Reik will hear of this," he sputtered as he stalked away.

Neasa smiled at his retreating back and then turned to me. "My birlinn will not approach Oyvu. The villagers would run and hide, and that might ruin your festival." Her eyes flicked to Carrog and then back again. "We will meet up after the New Year."

She turned to leave, but Talon hung back, which made her pause. Talon cleared his throat. "I wish to accompany you, Neasa, but the New Year's …"

She stood with her hands on her hips, lips pursed as she took in his words and hesitant stance. Then her smile returned and she addressed Carrog. "Go, take the birlinn and wait for us, and have them send over my small chest."

Carrog looked at me and then shrugged. "Yes, my captain." So much for twenty-five silver pennies. It was obvious who held his chain.

Neasa smiled at me. "We'll take the cabin."

I shrugged. "Talk to whoever has it now."

It had been bad enough with Padruig aboard, I thought as I headed for the sterncastle. They could fight over the cabin and the captaincy for all I cared. I just hoped that Captain Gregor didn't end up in the sea again.

While a jennet is bigger than a birlinn, it is still just a hunk of wood crowded with people. Even in my self-isolation on the sterncastle, I was aware of what happened below, just as the people below knew what I did above. To my surprise, it was Sofie who kept me informed of Neasa's activities. Sofie told me that Neasa and Talon had taken to the ship's cabin and hadn't emerged since.

"They say she takes a new lover as often as she changes her clothes, and that no one can resist her seductions," Sofie murmured as she lay next to me, the evening before we were to arrive in Oyvu. She was on her side facing me, the blanket covering her hip, but her breasts laid bare for my pleasure. She had learned that I liked breasts. What man didn't?

I rubbed my finger along her nipple, not daring to remind her that I had been unable to resist *her* seductions. What were "they" saying about that? Also, I wondered who these "they" were she spoke of. Sofie rarely left my side now. When did she have a chance to trade gossip? Besides, I was sure that Talon hadn't tried to resist.

"She put that Padruig fellow in his place as soon as she came aboard," Sofie continued. "He was moving out of the cabin before her chest arrived from her ship."

Padruig was a tough customer, but Neasa was betrothed to his master and had more resources along on this trip. I was not surprised that he would capitulate. Still, I remembered Neasa's warning against him outside the Reik's hall. I hoped she didn't push him too far—for Talon's sake, if nothing else. Actually, I liked Neasa better than Padruig. She did have nice breasts— even nicer than Sofie's, although I refrained from mentioning that.

Sofie let out a little sigh, indicating she was finished talking and had something else on her mind. I took the hint.

We pulled into Oyvu the next morning. Another jennet flying a Stenson banner was there ahead of us. The cove was large enough to hold about five ships. A rocky cliff stretched upward on the left as we entered, and the hamlet of Oyvu sat on a sandy beach between the cliff and the sea. A breakwater of large, jagged stones jutted out from the beach to form the cove.

As we dropped anchor, about a ship's length out from the other jennet, a group of small boats cast off from shore and headed our way.

Captain Gregor had been directing his crew from the sterncastle. After the ship dropped anchor, he stepped over to the rail next to me. "They know why we're here," he announced. He sounded happier than ever I'd heard him. "They'll already have prepared a feast."

He nodded toward the other jennet. "There'll be food and drink and women waiting for us ashore." The change in his manner was understandable. I had known many people who only seemed happy as the New Year approached. It was as though they hoarded up all their joy for one night of celebration.

Sofie giggled on my right. Because of her mother's profession, I had thought she might react badly when the captain mentioned women.

As Gregor left for the main deck, she giggled again. "Can you imagine tubby old Captain Gregor bedding a whore? She would have to be made of stout stuff to survive it."

I didn't know what to say. I didn't understand my lover. While I fretted over my life, she seemed to think it all a joke, as though nothing touched her.

Sofie squeezed my hand. "You are too serious, Olaf. Let's enjoy the New Year and forget about the past and the future."

She was right. I bent down and kissed her forehead.

She beamed at me and then pointed toward the water. "Look, the boats are approaching."

We headed down to the main deck to meet the boats. The deck was crowded with sailors and my guardsmen doing the same thing. Only Padruig and his two guards stood, aloof, in the shadow of the sterncastle. Padruig's arms were crossed and his face was a mask of scorn.

The door to the cabin opened and Neasa and Talon emerged. Neasa wore a long tunic like the one she had worn in Gwyr, only this one was a bluish-green and was cut low enough in the front to make any man forget to look any higher. I saw more than one appraising look on the faces around me.

Talon strutted next to her like a man who had just been given his greatest wish. His blond hair flew around his face in the slight breeze and his blue eyes twinkled with satisfaction and joy.

I grabbed Sofie's hand. She looked up and gave me one of her sultry smiles. "They seem happy," she said. The look on her face told me that she was even happier.

"Shall we go ashore?" Neasa called.

The deck shook with the roar of approval.

The other ship was the *Sea Wasp* and her captain was named Bruno. He was a tall, lean fellow with a cheery disposition—or maybe it was the holiday. He met us on the shore as we alighted near Oyvu.

"Welcome, welcome," he called, holding out his arms as if expecting a hug from the women. He wore his blue Stenson captain's coat and had a dark, fashionable goatee.

I instinctively reached up and stroked my own facial hair. I had started growing a goatee when we left Kartoba, but it had not progressed as much as I would have liked. The strands of hair felt finer and silkier than I imagined a man's goatee should feel.

A large canopy had been set up on the beach. Captain Bruno led us there, trying his best to catch Neasa's eye. "We have planned a superb celebration," he announced, leaning toward Neasa, who walked by his side. "We are happy for the company."

We were lucky the other crew had already arrived and had planned a feast—but would there be enough for all? As we approached the canopy, I spied an older Oyvu villager who looked to be in charge. I tossed him a purse of Stenson silver and said, "We are all here to celebrate, my friend. Keep the food and drink flowing."

The man had been frowning when we approached. Now he weighed the purse in his palm and then gave me a welcoming smile. "Welcome, my lord."

The residents of Oyvu reminded me of the Katchians I had known in Haven. Their stature and coloring was similar, but they wore much less in the way of clothing. Instead of the long robes that the Katchians favored, they were covered in little more than a loincloth and a strip of fabric over their breasts. The attire was scandalous by Seven Kingdom standards, but most of the servers were women, so I assumed they were whores as well. In fact, some of them were already wandering off, hand-in-hand, with their chosen sailors, which reinforced that conclusion. Of course, they could have just been exceptionally friendly.

Wooden benches and tables had been set up under the canopy. Sailors from the *Sea Wasp* were lounging, eating, and fondling the servers when we approached. As we moved to join them, Captain Bruno led us to a group of leather chairs arranged to one side. Well, he led Neasa there, and we followed.

They were folding chairs—the kind a rich man might take on a trip—but they looked more comfortable than the wooden benches. Bruno took his seat, ensuring that Neasa sat to his right. I took the chair on his left, with Sofie next to me. My chair was still warm, and I assumed I had poached it from one of Bruno's crew, but I didn't care.

I looked to see where the rest of my charges had gone. Bren had taken up his station behind my seat, even though I'd told him to go and enjoy the day. Mehki stood next to him as one of my ever-present shadows.

I looked for Gabriele and Ursala, to ensure they had found a place at one of the benches. To my relief, Moshe hovered nearby. I had asked the Wolf guards to watch out for them during the celebration, afraid of what might happen with so many drunken sailors present. I hadn't been sure the guards would comply. To no one's surprise, Padruig had chosen to stay on the ship.

One of the half-naked serving girls immediately rushed forward to offer us libations. She handed me a mug filled with what appeared to be beer, but it had no froth to speak of and looked a bit watery. I sniffed at it and was surprised by the sweet smell. "What is it?"

The girl smiled. "It is sonti—rice beer."

"It's good." Captain Bruno tossed back his own mug of sonti and then let out a loud belch. "It goes down easy and don't taste bad coming back up, either." He smacked his lips a couple of times as if appreciating the taste of his burp.

Neasa raised an eyebrow at me from the other side of Bruno. She was probably hoping he would pass out sooner rather than later. I also hoped he would, for his sake. I couldn't imagine Neasa remaining patient with him.

Bruno slapped me on the back. "Come on, lad, bottoms up."

I tilted back my own cup, expecting a bitter brew like the beer from my homeland. To my surprise, the sonti was sweeter and easier to swallow. Actually, it went down a bit too easily. I drained the cup and the serving girl quickly refilled it. It seemed for a moment that she planned to stay close by me, but a look from Sofie sent her scurrying away.

"Not bad," I replied to Bruno. "By the way, I'm Olaf."

"Hah!" Bruno tossed back another mugful. "Like our new Stenson master, huh. Bet you wish you had his silver."

Neasa let out a sudden snort of laughter and Bruno turned his attention back to her.

Sofie leaned into me and whispered, "He won't make it to supper."

"Neither will I, if I drink more of this stuff." Even after saying it, I quickly finished my second mug. My life had changed drastically in the past year, especially after finding Sofie. I felt the need to celebrate life.

"Then drink away, my love," Sofie said. She had been sipping at her own cup, but now she held it up to me in salute and then drained it. "You have trusty men at your back to keep you safe, and," she leaned in and gave me a lingering kiss, "you have someone to celebrate with."

Why not? It was New Year's! The gods were on holiday, so we were free from their jealous attentions until the cock crowed. I had a beautiful woman by my side and plenty of sonti to fill my cup. Why not celebrate? Who knew how my journey would end? I certainly didn't, but I could guess from my past history that it wouldn't be a happy ending. I looked Sofie in the eye and saw a spark of the same fear.

"More sonti," I called.

The rest of the day elapsed in a drunken blur. We drank, we ate, we went and pissed in the water when nature called—well, at least I did—and then drank some more. As anticipated, Bruno didn't make it to the evening meal. He was slumped in his chair as we tore into a feast of goat, rice pudding, and a variety of roasted vegetables that I didn't recognize. The vegetables tasted like dirt, but I ate them anyway, all the while grinning at my companions like a drunken fool.

After supper, we tossed Bruno out of his chair and Bren took his seat instead. He had given up on the dutiful valet routine and was as drunk as the rest of us. He kept raising his mug to "Stenson generosity"—a phrase that had probably never been uttered before, which struck me so funny that I giggled like a little girl every time he said it. I remembered laughing so hard that I almost lost my supper—I'm sure it wasn't the sonti—and then everything became a blur again.

I woke in the wee hours of the morning in my leather chair with my mouth tasting like horse dung. My neck ached from being cocked to one side for too long. I stretched it back and forth to ease the pain and then turned to check on Sofie. She was curled up in her chair next to me with her legs drawn up to her chin and her dark hair in disarray across her face. She breathed deeply, sound asleep.

"More sonti!" Neasa called out. She sat somewhere to my right, and I scanned the crowd as I turned to find her.

Torches still sputtered under the canopy, and a few serving girls still moved about with jugs in hand, but the majority of the crowd was passed out on the sand. Just a few, hard-core drinkers still sat upright. I spied Neasa over Bren's empty chair. He had fallen out of it and lay at our feet, next to Captain Bruno.

"Welcome back," Neasa said. She still sat upright in her chair, even though Talon leaned against her with his head on her shoulder. A serving girl, maybe the same one, poured sonti into her cup.

I held out my hand and the girl handed me a new mug full of the sweet beverage. I remembered dropping my mug earlier and looked down to see several mugs lying in the sand at my feet.

Neasa grinned at me. "See if you can keep your grip on this one."

I held up my mug aloft and then drained it, to show her that I could.

The world did a slow turn and started to blur again. Neasa reached across the empty chair and grabbed my hand before I could drop my cup again. Even with her glassy eyes, she looked more sober than I expected. She glanced behind my chair, where Mehki still watched over me, although he was far enough away that he would not overhear.

"I will not marry the Reik, Olaf," Neasa whispered. She stared at me so hard, it felt as if she had stopped the world in its tracks to impart this wisdom. Her intensity was frightening to behold, and even in my drunken state, I realized she was deadly serious.

"I will not marry the Reik," she repeated through clenched teeth, her eyes boring into my own. "I will sail my own course, Olaf—and it overlaps yours."

She smiled, her teeth glinting white in the torchlight, looking more predatory than friendly. "A raven told me. It sent me a vision. Together," I realized that she still held my hand tight, "you and I will change the world."

I yanked my hand free as a shiver ran up my spine. My people feared the gods—*all* gods. My gods had left us to our own devices on New Year's—but what about Neasa's gods?

The raven was her clan's patron. Had she really seen one in a vision? The thought of any god taking notice of me made me want to run away and hide.

Neasa let out a high-pitched, drunken giggle, and the spell was broken. The world started to spin again. But I felt a chill inside.

***

Blinking back tears from the sunlight streaming through the side of the canopy, I stood and stretched. All my drinking companions had already risen. Most of the sailors had stirred as well, and a steady stream of boats were ferrying them to their respective ships.

I could see the two ship captains standing, side-by-side, near the water's edge. They were an odd couple, with Bruno towering over Gregor's bulk like a pole bean next to a pumpkin. Sofie was nowhere in sight.

I turned to Mehki, who had approached as I stretched. He looked as though he could use some sleep, but said nothing as he took up his shadow position. "Where did Sofie go?"

Mehki nodded toward the ship. "She and the Kail woman took a boat across earlier."

The memory of Neasa's words the previous evening flooded into my head. My chest tightened at the thought of Neasa spending time with Sofie. "Then let's go."

I made it two steps before I was confronted by the old villager in the wrap. He stood in my path and bowed his head. "I hope everything was to your satisfaction, lord?"

I knew he was hoping for more silver, but I had given him the purse I carried from the ship. "Yes, yes." I said. "It was a great celebration and I will recommend your town to all our ships."

The headman knew a dismissal when he heard one. He bowed and stepped aside, but he gave me a sidelong look of disappointment. The look had the desired effect: it made me

84

feel guilty for not paying him more. Truthfully, I had no idea if I had given the man enough money or too much, but it had bothered me my whole life that Stensons were known for being tight with their coin. My uncle had sent plenty of silver along for me to spend on his cause. Why not spend some of it to change that reputation?

I turned back to the man. "I truly do thank your people for your hospitality. Come to my ship before we sail, and I will make sure you are well-compensated." The man's eyes lit up. "Ask for Master Olaf." Then I hurried past, remembering my concern over the women.

Mehki and I boarded the next boat out. It was just large enough for the two of us, a pair of sailors, and the two locals who rowed it. I took up station in the bow and watched the *Sea Cow* grow larger as we approached. In just a few moments, we were scrambling onto the main deck, where I spied Sofie and Neasa chatting outside the captain's cabin.

I imagined Neasa telling Sofie about her vision of the previous evening and hastened over as quickly as my twisted leg would allow. Both women looked up and smiled as I approached.

"About time you woke up," Sofie teased.

"Yes," Neasa joined in. "We nearly ran out of things to talk about." Her smile seemed mocking rather than friendly. "I was just about to tell her about my recent dream."

"We should get settled," I said. I grabbed Sofie by the arm and headed to the sterncastle ladder.

"Maybe later," Neasa called as we headed away.

Sofie looked up at me with a question in her eye.

I loosened my grip and took a careful breath. "Sorry, but that woman gives me the shivers."

Sofie laughed. "Don't worry, brave warrior, I'll protect you." She sauntered ahead of me to the ladder and gave me a playful look over her shoulder before climbing it.

After we reached the upper deck, she took my arm and led me to my favorite spot at the rail. As we stood there, watching the boats going back and forth, I began to breathe easier.

"I don't know why you don't like her," Sofie said. "She appears to think highly of you."

Her words caused me a moment of panic, but I quickly recovered. "Why do you say that?" I was pretty sure my voice sounded normal, although I avoided looking at Sofie for fear of giving away my concern.

"She was telling me that she admired how you presented yourself to the Reik." She hugged my arm, laying her head against it. "She said you would be a great statesman and that she was happy to be working with you."

Those words seemed innocent enough, but I was wary of Neasa's motives, especially after her pronouncement the previous evening. Had it been a coincidence, or had she spoken to Sofie for a purpose? Was she trying to win over my woman? I had no idea, and that bothered me. "Still," I said, "we'll have to keep an eye on her."

Sofie pulled her head from my shoulder and pulled me toward her. She looked up in my face and gave me a pout. "You'd better just keep your eyes on me."

I felt the blood rush to my face and tried to think of what to say. Did she know about Neasa's vision? Had they spoken about it, after all?

Sofie let out a chuckle as she reached up and gave me a kiss. "Men! You are so easy to tease." She nestled under my arm and sighed. "As if you could ever take your eyes off of me."

She was right, of course, on both counts. I exhaled the breath I had been holding and squeezed her close. No matter Neasa's plans for me, little Sofie had captured my heart, and she knew it.

The headman came out to the *Sea Cow* just before we sailed. I gave him another purse of silver, this time sure I had overpaid him for our festivities. He was overjoyed and kept promising eternal friendship between his village and my family. He even presented me with a barrel of sonti as a gift, because I seemed to like it so much.

Once the headman departed and I made my way back to the sterncastle deck, we were ready to get underway. Ivan met me

86

as I settled at the rail. I hadn't noticed him the previous evening, but judging from his prior habits, I figured he had drunk his fill.

"That's the most expensive barrel of sonti ever," he remarked.

"What I do with my uncle's money is my business," I barked, but he only smiled in return.

Ivan always looked as if he had just come off a drinking binge, which was usually the case. Today, he actually looked better than I'd expected. He scratched at his scruffy chin, the whiskers looking more gray than blonde, and broke into laughter. "Not all of us get to sit in leather chairs and drink ourselves into oblivion," he muttered. He actually looked sad that he hadn't joined in. "I did drink with the locals, though. That man you were so generous with has the most clout in the village. He is the vintner, and for him to give you a barrel of his most-prized sonti is a good sign." He reached out and clasped my shoulder. "How you blunder into such lucky situations is beyond me. You must be a natural." He was chuckling as he wandered away.

"Blunder" was an unflattering word, but I knew that he was right. I had *blundered* in Kartoba and caused Tessa's death. I couldn't afford to do so again. The New Year's celebration was over. It was time for me to stop playing at being a statesman. I owed it to my uncle and Sofie and her family, and the rest of the Seven Kingdoms to do this right.

One day out from Oyvu, we met up with Neasa's birlinn. She waved up at me as she left, and Sofie waved back as she stood with me at the rail. "She is so nice," Sophie cooed.

Nice and dangerous, I thought, but kept it to myself.

I was happy as we renewed our voyage east. I enjoyed Sofie's company and I was delighted that Padruig left me alone for much of the voyage. It would have been the happiest time of my life, if it wasn't for Neasa's vision.

I could not get her words out of my head. I fretted over them for the remainder of the voyage. It was almost a relief when we finally sighted Rock Island, which sat at the mouth of the Sea of Pearls. It would be nearing the end of winter back home, but it still felt like summer on the ship.

CHAPTER 11: WELCOME TO GEA

We were now deep in Jewel territory. We anchored just offshore near Rock Island at the entrance to the Sea of Pearls and gathered on the main deck once Neasa came aboard. Padruig, Neasa, and I stood in the shadow of the ship's mast and eyed each other. Padruig and Neasa seemed to be in a contest of wills, staring at each other as if each were daring the other to speak first.

I cleared my throat, and they both turned to me. "Do we enter the Sea of Pearls, or keep on farther east?"

While the Sea of Pearls was hotly contested, the Empire of Jewel held most of the sea's shoreline and dominated the waters with its fleet of galea. Imperial galea were swift battleships. Each was similar to a Birlinn, but larger and with more oars and fighting men.

I knew that, if we entered the Sea of Pearls, we would be at the mercy of the empire's fleet. The alternative was to continue along the coast, past Rock Island, and dock farther east, where the Empire of Jewel held no sway. I didn't have to explain any of this. We had discussed this matter before with no clear consensus.

"There is no need to go into the Sea of Pearls," Neasa began. This was her standard argument. "We should go to Mani-Sama and ask for their aid. They are the most powerful kingdom in the confederation."

The Kingdom of Mani-Sama was the farthest east, but it was the political heart of the Eastern Confederation. Although it would take us longer to sail there, we might be able to avoid the empire's ships. Her argument was valid, but I knew Neasa's real concern. Her birlinn would not be able to follow us into the Sea of Pearls. The Empire of Jewel controlled Rock Island and stopped all Kail ships from passing into the sea. The birlinn could possibly slip by at night, but despite the heavy traffic on the sea, they wouldn't go unnoticed for long.

Padruig was working up to his own standard argument. "The fight is here, Neasa. You and your birlinn can wait for us or go on to Mani-Sama. Either way, we need to land in Suma. That is where we can stir up the conflict anew."

Suma was the western-most kingdom in the confederation and was the only one positioned on the Sea of Pearls. "The Malik of Suma has never stopped fighting the empire. They will welcome us as allies."

"The Malik of Suma is a fool," Neasa cut in. "His obstinacy in continuing his vendetta against the empire has been a burden upon his allies. They will not answer his call to war again so soon. We have to seek out help elsewhere."

"We can create an incident on the Sea of Pearls that will pull the rest of them in," Padruig countered, his voice rising as he tried to drown out his rival. "In Suma, we can make that happen and help stir up the people at the same time. We already have people in Suma who can help."

"We have people in Mani-Sama as well," Neasa retorted, her hands on her hips and a fire starting to burn in her eyes. "We have people in Suma. We have people in Mani-Sama. We have people in Gea. We have people in *all* the coastal kingdoms. That is not an argument."

"What about Gea then?" I asked before they could start shouting again. They both turned their angry faces toward me. I fought the urge to take a step back, instead hardening my expression to match their twin glares.

It helped that I had rehearsed my argument with Ivan. In reality, it was as much his argument as mine. We had come up with it after the last time Neasa and Padruig butted heads. That was a fortnight ago, when we'd pulled into shore as a storm threatened to blow us out to sea.

"Gea stands in the middle, between Suma and Mani-Sama," I explained. "We can send delegations to all three countries at once—and it is not so far up the coast as Mani-Sama."

"But it is not the heart of the Eastern Confederation," Neasa argued. "Aren't you supposed to go to Xiang to take up your post?"

Xiang was the largest port in Mani-Sama. Actually, it was the largest city within the Eastern Confederation, and all the confederation kingdoms had envoys there.

Fortunately, Ivan had anticipated her argument, so I was ready for her. "It is true, the Stenson factor is based in Xiang— but there are Stenson posts in all the kingdoms. We can make our base in Gea and I will send word to the factor of my arrival."

Neasa looked displeased, which suited me fine. I had fretted over her words to me the night of the New Year, losing sleep until I finally decided that I would have none of her raven-induced destiny. I was determined to thwart her at every turn. I was even prepared to agree with Padruig and enter the Sea of Pearls without her, if she refused to see reason.

Padruig spoke up before she did. "Gea is a good choice, Master Olaf. When we land in Gea, I will join you in a delegation to the Malik in Suma. Neasa can continue on to Mani-Sama if she likes."

He sounded so contrite that I almost didn't believe it was he who spoke. Then I saw the smug smile he gave Neasa and wondered if he had argued to sail to Suma just to spite her.

Neasa's eyes flashed with such anger, she looked as though she would hit him. I saw her knuckles turn white where she gripped her sword—but instead of striking out, she took a calming breath. I was relieved to see her hand fall away from her sword as she spoke. "We will wait for dark before passing Rock Island," she said. Then she stalked to the rail, where her ship stood alongside.

I tried to control the shivers that threatened to take control of my body as I watched her go. Neasa was a formidable woman. I hadn't realized how frightening she could be until that moment.

Padruig snorted out a laugh just loud enough for me to hear. "Don't expect her to forget this, Master Olaf. And don't expect her to cooperate, either. Once past Rock Island, she will insist we continue on to Mani-Sama."

He raised an eyebrow as if daring me to argue the point. When I remained silent, he headed back to the ship's cabin.

It was well after nightfall when we approached Rock Island. As we skirted along the shore, the fires from the Imperial fortress on the island were visible. We kept our lanterns shuttered as we slipped past. Still, no one slept that night, and everyone stayed quiet.

The next morning, we could see Rock Island behind us but still had not sighted the shore on the other side. Because the ship's firebox was out from our stealthy night passage, I broke my fast with smoked fish and cold tea. I was tired, but couldn't sleep, so I stayed at my spot by the rail.

Sofie had remained by my side throughout the night, but now that it was light, she kept sighing in an attempt to capture my attention. By mid-morning she lost her subtlety. "Let's go to bed," she said, sidling up next to me. She caressed my arm and gazed up at me.

Her hopeful look weakened my resolve. I reached over and tousled her dark locks. "Go on and get some sleep, sweetheart. I will come along shortly."

She gave me a disappointed frown, but pecked me on the cheek. "As you wish—but don't stay up all day. You'll regret it tonight." Her frown turned into a teasing smirk. "I'll be well-rested by then."

Her words tempted me to follow her right then, but I knew I wouldn't be able to sleep until we were out of danger. Several ships had been sighted during the morning. None seemed intent upon approaching us, but each time the lookout called out a sail on the horizon, I held my breath until he confirmed that it was not heading our way.

"It's not the sails we need to worry about." Ivan appeared by my side almost as soon as Sofie left. As usual, he looked as though he had slept in his tunic and his ever-present ponytail was the only thing keeping his hair from looking worse. "Those ships are traders, and they'll avoid us because of our escort of birlinn."

Ivan scratched at his whiskers. "The Imperial galea don't need a sail when they're this close to shore. We won't see them until they're too close to be avoided. With all their oars, they'll run us down like we're standing still."

I could always count on Ivan to cheer me up. I frowned at him and he flashed a fake smile in return.

"They probably wouldn't look twice at us if it wasn't for the birlinn," I said. "Should we send them on ahead, then?"

Ivan seemed to consider my question and then let out a laugh. "Only if you want to deal with Neasa. Do you think she'll go quietly?"

As usual, he had a good point. I sighed. "Then I guess we wait and hope they don't spot us."

Ivan leaned on the rail next to me and took a swig from a wooden cup, smacking his lips. I was so used to his constant drinking that I hadn't even noticed the cup until then.

We had been at sea since the autumn—almost five months, by my reckoning. He drank like a fish, yet he still had whiskey left. I wondered how much whiskey he had smuggled on board. "Where do you keep that stuff hidden?"

He laughed and tilted the cup toward me so I could see the contents. "I'm saving the last of my whiskey for an emergency," he said with a chortle. "This is the sonti you bought with all that silver."

"Hey, I was saving that!" The barrel I had received from the old vintner in Oyvu was high-quality stuff. I had marked it as my own private barrel, and everyone aboard knew to steer clear of it.

Ivan looked anything but concerned. He took another swig from his cup and let out a loud burp. "Think of it as my payment for keeping you out of trouble."

Had he kept me out of trouble so far? Had he done so in Kartoba? Now that we approached our destination, the thought that I was not prepared for what lay ahead made me tremble with fear. "Am I ready, Ivan?"

He caught my mood, setting his cup on the rail and looking me in the eye. "Olaf, we're never ready. I've seen too many of my mates die to think I know what's going to happen. All we can do is guess, and plan, and hope for the best. And if our time comes, then we make our mates proud."

"Like Rolfe?"

"Aye, like Rolfe."

Rolfe Jaeger had been Ivan's partner in Kartoba. He had died holding off our enemies to give us time to fortify Stenson House.

Like Tessa, he had died because of my mistake.

"But I can't let it happen again, Ivan. I can't lose Sofie like I did Tessa."

Ivan shook his head. "You can't—and yet you have no control over it. So you might." He picked his cup back up and held it out to me, as if offering a toast. "Drinking helps," he said simply as he walked away.

I stared at the cup in front of me for a while. I could be like Ivan and stay drunk. It would dull my worry. I reached out and touched the lip of the cup. It was made of wood, and well-worn. I held my finger there for a moment and then tipped the cup into the sea. I needed my senses crisp, to ensure I made no more mistakes. I owed it to Sofie and everyone else who depended upon me.

When we sighted land, late that evening, I finally felt comfortable enough to head for my bed. Sofie had awakened in time to eat her evening meal, but I had not seen her since. I expected her to be waiting for me—rested and lustful—but she was fast asleep in our blankets when I arrived. As tired as I felt, it was probably a good thing. I pulled off my coat and trousers and slipped into bed beside her.

We skirted the coast for several more days before sighting the port of Gea. We had seen quite a few more ships since passing Rock Island. Even though the Empire of Jewel and the Eastern Confederation had been at war, on and off, for many years, trade still flourished between them. We even spotted an Imperial galea at one point, but they didn't approach us, probably because of the birlinn.

Ivan assured me that they would have reported it. I knew we were likely to run afoul of a squadron of galea if we didn't head to land soon. That had been just days before sighting Gea. I was never so glad to see a set of docks as when we entered that harbor.

The harbor at Gea looked much like the one at Kartoba. I saw fewer jennets than in Kartoba, the majority of the ships being local craft. The local trading ship was called an *uru*; it was distinctive from a jennet because the ship's planks were sewn together rather than nailed and the back of the ship was just as pointed as the front. This was common in the east. To my eye, the Eastern Confederation warships looked similar to Imperial galea as well, only they weren't quite as big. One of them stood just off the docks, where Neasa's ships were moored. I could hear a slow drum beat for the rowers as we passed.

It had seemed prudent to arrive separately, especially since the birlinn would be given a different berth than our trading ship. Neasa had gone ahead, and her birlinn were tied together at the remote wharf as we slowly rowed into the harbor proper.

A jennet wasn't really made for rowing, like a birlinn or galea, but the *Sea Cow* boasted two pairs of long oars, which were enough to get us to the pier. As we approached the docks, I climbed down the ladder from the sterncastle and made my way to stand beside Captain Gregor.

He flashed me a nervous smile, looking a bit awkward in his Stenson blue coat. I could see his hand shake slightly as he gripped his captain's staff. He had become friendlier toward me since the New Year's celebration, but he was still not comfortable pulling into port with the Kail onboard.

"It will be fine," I said. "Padruig is in the cabin and Carrog and his men are up on the sterncastle. No reason for the port inspectors to notice them. Besides," I looked at his crew as they went about the business of tying us up to the dock, "they don't look any worse than your own crew."

Gregor ran his fingers through his gray beard, a sure sign of his nervousness. "There's no mistaking a Kail warrior." He shook himself as the plank was lowered into place. "Let's hope these Gea bastards don't look at the crew too closely."

"Don't worry," I assured him. "The tax collectors are only worried about the cargo and how much silver they can squeeze out of us."

Gregor's eyes lit up and his face softened. "Now tax collectors, I can handle."

A large group of men approached the *Sea Cow* as the sailors were lowering the boards to the dock. "How many inspectors do they usually send?" I asked.

"What?" He looked at the dock and frowned. "Those aren't inspectors."

I spied another group heading in our direction from the northern end of the dock. I pointed them out to Captain Gregor. "What …"

One of our sailor's cried out as the first group of men rushed the plank, weapons now visible in their hands. I heard a sickening crunch of a cudgel hitting the skull of one of our sailors.

"Repel the boarders!" Captain Gregor shouted as he rushed past me with his captain's baton in his fist.

The sailors at the rail, who were unarmed, went down in an instant. Moshe was quicker than Gregor. One moment he stood next to me, and the next he stood at the top of the plank, cutting down attackers with his axe.

Mehki grabbed me by the arm and hustled me back toward the Sterncastle. It happened so quickly, I barely had time to react.

When we reached the sterncastle ladder, I heard a roar that sent a chill up my back. Carrog flew down the ladder like a man possessed. Mehki pushed me hard against the sterncastle bulkhead as Carrog rushed past us. He held me in place as Carrog's men and my Stenson guards followed in his wake.

Carrog screamed a second time as he plowed into the attackers, barely slowing as he knocked them from the boarding plank and into the harbor.

Once the sterncastle ladder was clear, Mehki pushed me forward and we made our way to the safety of the sterncastle deck. He took up station at the top of the ladder, and Bren—whom I had forgotten was with us—stayed by my side, his sword in hand. The sight made me remember my own sword. I hadn't even thought to touch it! My heart was thudding in my chest and I was breathing hard as I berated myself for being so useless.

The fight on the dock was short. After Carrog's fierce charge, the attackers melted away almost as quickly as they had come. Moshe came up the ladder to stand beside his brother, looking no worse than before except for a splash of blood on his mail. A moment later, Ivan arrived next to me. "They knew you were coming," he said.

"Who?" I demanded. "And why would they come after *me*?"

He rubbed at his chin whiskers. "Who knew you were coming?" He already knew the answer. "Your uncle only sent word to the current Eastern Factor." He ducked his head and looked at me past his eyebrows. "The man you are here to replace."

Why would the Eastern Factor attack me? He was a Stenson—right? This kind of thing wasn't supposed to happen.

Ivan shook his head. "We'll see soon enough."

On the dock below, a group of soldiers approached the *Sea Cow*. Carrog and his men came back up onto the sterncastle deck to avoid being spotted. As he passed, Carrog grinned at me. "Tell your uncle how good I fight."

The soldiers waited on the docks as two men came aboard the *Sea Cow*. I headed back down to the main deck to greet them. The soldiers were dressed in lacquered mail, but the two Easterners who came aboard wore traditional Eastern attire: light-colored, baggy trousers under long green coats that looked more like robes. They were short in stature, like my Katchian guards, but not as dark-skinned. Both were clean-shaven and wore yellow caps of office on their heads. They looked like twins, except that one wore a red sash tied around his waist and the other wore a yellow one.

Red Sash stepped forward and spoke to us in Imperial. "What has happened here?"

Captain Gregor, who had survived the fight, waved toward the bodies on the deck, which included some of his downed sailors. "Is this how you greet ships from Kartoba?"

"You are the ship that arrived with the Kail raiders," he snapped back. "Perhaps we should ask *them*."

So much for staggering our arrival times.

Captain Gregor pulled nervously at his beard. "I am Has Gregor, Captain of the *Sea Cow,* and we are here with trade goods from Kartoba."

"I am Sun Shuzi. What goods have you brought to trade?"

I recognized the name. The Sun family ruled Gea. Having a member of the ruling family greet us at the pier didn't seem a good beginning. I had hoped for a more muted arrival. My family traded regularly with the east, and we had a presence in each of the confederation kingdoms. Our trade ships were a common sight.

Captain Gregor kept the smile on his face, but his nervousness increased. He tore at his beard as though it had offended him.

Sun Shuzi eyed us both as the man with the yellow sash leaned over and whispered something in his ear. He waved the other man away and said, "If you are here only to trade, then why were you attacked?"

Captain Gregor turned pale and started to sputter out a reply. I stepped forward to stop him before he could say something stupid. My heart still raced and I had to take a calming breath before replying.

"I am Olaf Stenson, the new Stenson factor in the east," I said. "My uncle hired the Kail to escort my ship to your lands."

I had practiced the argument in case we were discovered, but it sounded pretty weak now, standing before these men and their guards. Of course, that was before we had to explain an attack on our ship. "It looks like he was wise to do so."

Sun Shuzi and his companion both looked skeptical.

Ivan had told me that the simplest lie was the easiest to remember and sell to a skeptical audience. I plowed forward with our fabrication. There was just enough truth in it to make it believable. "My uncle now rules the Stenson family, and he worried over my safety on this voyage." I leaned heavily on my twisted leg and tried my best to look pitiful. "It is my first trip outside the Seven Kingdoms."

"You are the Stenson heir?" Yellow Sash finally joined the conversation.

I nodded and Captain Gregor found his voice. "I am glad to finally see him safely to your kingdom." He visibly shivered and I didn't think it was faked. "Having birlinn shadow you across the Sea of Silence is enough to tempt a man to settle on dry land."

Yellow Sash bowed to me. "I am Cao Wangsun. Welcome to Gea."

Sun Shuzi bowed as well, but not before I saw the annoyed look he shot his companion. I recognized the Cao family name as well. The Cao family ruled in Mani-Sama and considered themselves the rulers of the entire Eastern Confederation. Obviously, Sun Shuzi harbored some resentment—whether for his companion or the Cao family, I wasn't sure.

Cao Wangsun gestured toward Sun Shuzi. "My companion will handle this mess. I invite you to dine at my residence this evening, Factor Olaf." He nodded to me and then departed.

Sun Shuzi had kept his face impassive throughout the exchange, but his eyes shot daggers at Cao Wangsun's back as he departed. When he turned back toward us, his face showed only friendliness. "Shall we discuss what happened?"

I left the discussion to Captain Gregor and stepped over to the ship's rail. The attackers had come and gone so quickly, there were few bodies and no prisoners. Besides the sailor who had been cudgeled, there was only one other wounded sailor, who now sat on the deck holding his arm and being attended to by his mates. I shivered at the sight of a couple of dead attackers floating in the water below.

Who had sent them, and why?

CHAPTER 12: A NEW HOME

I had grown up in Kartoba, the largest port town in the Seven Kingdoms. The town of Gea looked similar, but most of the buildings were wooden instead of stone. The roofs had a distinctive, flaring design that made the houses look as if they were wearing caps.

The docks were busy and crowded now. Where had the crowd been a moment before?

A single wooden fortress stood on a hilltop overlooking the harbor. Just down from the fortress sat several smaller structures, which I assumed belonged to noble families. From there, the buildings became shabbier as they approached the docks.

I guessed that the fortress belonged to the rulers of Gea, and the Cao family owned one of the estates closest to the fortress. I had studied Eastern culture growing up in Stenson House, but I wasn't too confident in what I remembered. I did remember that their names were arranged backwards. That meant "Cao" was actually the family name, and the second name was a title instead of a given name. Easterners only shared their given name with family and friends.

"Wangsun" meant that my host that evening was the grandson of the current ruler in Mani-Sama. That would probably explain Sun Shuzi's annoyance earlier. "Shuzi" meant that he was a younger son of the ruler of Gea. I wasn't totally sure which held the higher rank, but I knew I would have to tread carefully to avoid offending any of my hosts. I couldn't afford to make a mistake, as I had in Kartoba.

As I pondered these thoughts, a flash of blue caught my eye on the dock. A man in a Stenson blue coat approached our ship, pushing his way through the soldiers that still lined the dock.

He huffed and puffed as he came across to the ship's deck. "Master Olaf," he called out between gasps for breath. "Welcome to Gea." He bent over and planted his hands on his knees as he tried to catch his breath.

While the man wore a Stenson blue coat, which marked him as a family hireling, the rest of his outfit looked to be of Eastern origin. He wore light-colored, baggy trousers, a blue sash around his waist and a blue cap atop his short blond hair.

"I am Dolph Ingerson," he said, bowing to me in the Eastern fashion. "I am a clerk from the Stenson factor's office in Gea."

"Is the factor in?" I asked.

He shook his head. "He is at the main office in Xiang."

The Stenson factor to the Eastern Confederation oversaw all the Stenson offices in each of the confederation kingdoms, but he was based in the capital city of Xiang. Dolph looked worried as he answered. "We did not expect you to stop in Gea."

The port of Gea was on the way to Xiang. If they knew I was coming, they would have expected my ship to make landfall here. Was Ivan right? Had my uncle's factor set up the attack? Was this man part of the plot?

"Did you know I was coming?"

I could see Dolph struggle with himself before he finally replied. "No, Master Olaf. I apologize for my lapse."

"Who is in charge of the Stenson office in Gea?"

Dolph looked uncomfortable, but he straightened to his full height and gave me a determined look. "I am tasked with overseeing the office in Factor Einhardt's absence."

I paused to think through this information. Even if Factor Einhardt had planned the attack, it didn't seem as though

Dolph was involved. I nodded. "Good. I will need rooms for me and my companions."

Dolph looked past my shoulder at my Wolf guards and Bren. I caught his eye with my hand and gestured towards the Stenson guardsmen who had taken up position at the main deck rail. "*All* of my companions."

His eyes grew wide. "You are staying here, Master Olaf?" Apparently, he had assumed it was a stopover on my way to Xiang.

"Yes, I would prefer something private rather than rooms at an inn. How large is the Stenson factor office?" I knew we would have an office close to the docks, and probably a warehouse of some type—not that I wanted to sleep in a warehouse.

"The Stenson office is close, Master Olaf, but ..." He paused to settle his thoughts. "Factor Einhardt owns a house on the third tier. It would be large enough, but I don't know ..."

"Is it Master Einhardt's house—or is it a Stenson property?"

My uncle had provided me with the layout of our holding in the east. The Eastern Factor had a house in Xiang, which was provided for him by the family, as well as a room at the factor's office in each of the other kingdoms. My late Uncle Karl was not known for being exceptionally generous. If Factor Einhardt owned a house in Gea, it was likely paid for with Stenson silver one way or another ... and that might be reason enough for him to attack his replacement.

Dolph looked down at his feet rather than answer.

"That settles it, then," I said, catching Bren's eye. "I will go ahead to the factor's house. Please ensure all our people follow and are settled there."

Bren was a smart man. He knew what I meant by *all*. Hopefully, he would find a way for Neasa and Talon to meet us there as well.

I turned back to Dolph. "Take me to my new home."

It wasn't as easy as that. Captain Luther had to assemble the Stenson Guardsmen as escort. Once Sofie realized I was leaving, she wanted to accompany me, and to bring along her mother and sister. Then, of course, Padruig and Carrog insisted upon coming along—with their men. By the time everything was sorted out, I took along the whole lot of them. Bren was left behind to find Neasa, along with Ivan, who was still inspecting our attackers.

Once Sun Shuzi realized I intended to leave for the factor's house, he insisted that the Gea soldiers on the dock should serve as our escort as well. We finally headed out, with a nervous Dolph leading the way followed by the Gea soldiers in their baggy pants and mail. I came next, with Sun Shuzi insisting upon walking by my side. Bren's family and the Kail followed behind my Wolf guards. Finally, my Stenson guards took up the rear, with their blue coats and Stenson banner flying.

We all moved at the snail's pace of the master fool, who stomped along in the center of it all, wondering how he had managed to produce such a spectacle.

People stopped what they were doing as we passed and gawked at us, probably wondering why no one had warned them about the parade.

Factor Einhardt's house was more than large enough for all of my assorted followers and allies. It was nestled on the hillside, along with the other merchant villas, not far from Gea Castle at the top. This reinforced my suspicion that he had paid for it with Stenson silver, and I felt better about seizing it for myself.

Once we'd all made it through the massive front gate, we entered a well-manicured courtyard surrounded on three sides by the wings of the house. The main section was directly opposite the gate, which I took as my quarters. The Stenson guards took one of the side wings, and the Kail were given the other.

The house was staffed with a gardener, a cook, and a housekeeper. The gardener, a wizened old man, took our arrival in stride when we showed up at the gate. Ursala immediately clashed with the Eastern housekeeper, a small, older woman with graying hair and a blue robe cut in the Eastern fashion. I watched them argue, in their respective languages, over the placement of my baggage, mostly just pulling items out of each other's hands and trying to place them in different locations. Although I had studied Eastern dialects, I had no idea what the housekeeper was saying, and Ursala was having a hard time keeping her anger in check.

Sofie grabbed me by the hand to pull me out into the courtyard. "They'll work it out," she whispered. "Let's explore the garden."

I didn't argue. I needed some quiet time to prepare myself for the upcoming dinner with Cao Wangsun.

Sofie and I walked hand-in-hand through the courtyard, where various plants and trees were being cultivated. I didn't recognize most of them. Several had unfamiliar fruit hanging from them. I did recognize a mandarin tree, because of the orange color of the fruit. The cook at Stenson House had kept a mandarin tree in a pot behind the kitchen. He'd moved it into the stable in the winter, but I had never tasted its fruit. He'd counted the tiny orange orbs as if they were silver pieces.

We ended up at a bench that sat along the wall next to the gate. Sofie pulled me down to sit by her side, clutching my hand. She let out a great sigh and said, "So, now our time together has come to an end."

Both her words and the bitter tone in her voice took me by surprise. "What do you mean?"

She had always seemed so happy, flirting and laughing, making me feel like the world was better than I knew it to be. Now she looked down at our hands, which were entwined on the bench between us. "Now, you're in the east, and you have your uncle's mission." She looked up at me, biting her lip, only this time there was no sex appeal in it. "I will not hold you back."

I wanted to hug her or smack her; instead, I tried to reason with her. "When have you ever held me back, Sofie? You make me happy. You're my ..." I didn't know how to finish. We'd had such a good time onboard the *Sea Cow*. I didn't want it to end, but I didn't know what came next, either.

Now she had made me angry by bringing it up. Why couldn't things just stay the same? My body shivered with the sudden emotion of it.

"No, Olaf." She finally released her grip, and my hand started tingling as it fell free. "You have work to do here." Sofie's smile returned, but it was a lie, more forced than real. "I won't be a burden to you." When she stood up, my heart lurched in my chest.

How had this happened so suddenly? It felt like the world had crashed around me. I reached out and grabbed her arm before she could move away. "Sofie, you can't leave me now." My words came out in a rush. A vision of Tessa flashed through my mind. I remembered the look on Tessa's face when she pulled her knife free and sealed her fate. It was the same look.

"I am not leaving you, Olaf." Sofie tried to hold onto her smile. She finally gave up the pretense and let the smile fade. "But it'll never be the same. I can feel it. You'd better get ready for your dinner."

As she walked away, I felt empty. I wanted to reach out and hold her. I should have stopped her—but I knew she was right. It was time for me to take up my uncle's cause. I could no longer hide in her arms. I had less than a season to convince the Eastern Confederation to renew their fight with the Empire of Jewel, and I had no idea where to start.

I would have no time to argue with her, or try to console her. I had no time for thoughts of marriage. Sofie was right to step back from our relationship, and it made me love her even more. I promised myself that I would marry her, once my mission was complete. I promised myself that I would prove her wrong—it would not be the same, it would be better.

Neasa and Talon arrived with Bren and Ivan later that afternoon. Neasa brought along a few of her men, and they moved in with Carrog's Kail. Ursala and the housekeeper had finally resolved their differences, so it seemed safe to meet in my quarters. There was a small dining area just inside that overlooked the courtyard with a wall that slid aside so we could enjoy the view.

We sat huddled around the small, round table to discuss our plans: Neasa, Talon, Padruig, and me. As we began, the old housekeeper toddled in and served us fruit juice. The satisfied smile on her face told me she had won the first round against Ursala.

I told them about my invitation to the Cao estate for dinner. Neasa immediately responded, "I shall accompany you, then."

My mind flashed back to our conversation at the New Year's celebration. Neasa meant to tie herself to me because of her vision. The thought sent a chill through me.

I glanced at Talon, who sat to her right, expecting to see anger. He winked at me instead, which didn't help to settle me down. Next I turned to Padruig, and waited for his inevitable argument with everything Neasa recommended.

Padruig wore his normal, dour expression, but he nodded in agreement. "We need to gather information. Neasa is good at such things."

The conversation was not going as I expected. "But the invitation was to me alone."

Padruig shrugged. "Bringing a companion along is expected." He sneered at my reluctance. "You can't bring a servant along to such an invitation."

I fought an urge to hit him, especially after my recent talk with Sofie. Instead, I reached out and grabbed my cup, sipping at my juice to regain my composure.

Neasa sat back and smiled, letting Padruig carry the argument. Since our awkward encounter during the New Year celebration, Neasa had been on a separate vessel. I had pushed her out of my mind, but could no longer do so. She was a strong woman, and I feared her motives.

Talon joined in on the alliance against me. "She's our ally in this, Olaf. Not only does she clean up nice, but she is smarter than either of us."

That's what I was afraid of.

Neasa finally joined in. "Eastern women dine separately. There will be two sides to this dinner. We can't afford to only hear one of them."

I had forgotten about Eastern dining customs. They were all right, and I knew it. Still, I didn't have to like it. "Then let's prepare." I was already worrying about how Sofie would react once she heard the news.

Neasa stood and stretched. Of course, every eye was upon her as she still wore her too-revealing green tunic. She smiled at me and then said, "Come along, Talon, and help me pick out a dress."

Talon jumped to his feet and gave me a grin. "This is my favorite part!" He hurried after her retreating form.

Padruig pulled my attention back to the table by banging his cup between us. "If you were a smart man, you would send her away with her ships now," he said. The grey in his hair caught in the afternoon light, as if emphasizing his greater experience. He gave a sad shake of his head and stood to leave. "But you won't, will you?"

When I didn't reply, he leaned over the table and glared down at me. "Just remember that it is my master who will triumph in the end. You want to be with us when that happens." He walked stiffly from the room.

I shook my head. Hadn't he just argued for Neasa?

I sat alone and finished the juice. I had to change into my good clothes for dinner, but I was afraid I would run into Sofie, so I sat at the little table and looked out over the courtyard instead. The open area near the front gate was large enough for my half-dozen Stenson guardsmen to form up into two ranks. Captain Luther had them marching in circles. I couldn't guess why he felt it was important for them to do so. Maybe it was just being on dry land again.

I watched them march in the afternoon sun and mulled over my conversation with Sofie. I wanted to be mad at her, but I couldn't. Instead, I was mad at Neasa—or maybe myself. I didn't know why. People called me "Master Olaf" and "Lord" now, but I had no idea what I had done to deserve their respect. It felt like I was still herding pigs.

I spied Neasa crossing back over from her wing. Did she want to gloat—or to press her claim on me? I was surprised that Talon didn't follow her and that she still wore her tunic and carried her dress rather than wearing it.

"Come along, Olaf," she called as she sauntered past. "We have to bathe before our dinner."

"What?"

She stopped and shot me a surprised look. "We are going to dine with Easterners. We have to bathe first, or they'll be offended."

I sniffed at my clothes. I was a little pungent maybe, but still acceptable. I had washed the day before, and I knew Bren would have my best set of clothes clean and ready.

"Didn't they teach you anything in that fancy house you grew up in?" Neasa chided.

Obviously, Talon had told her everything he knew about me. He knew I spoke several languages and had been taught about different cultures while growing up in Stenson House. I wondered if Neasa would be surprised to hear that I also had shoveled shit and managed the pigs.

She stood before me with one hand on her hip and the other holding her clean dress. "If we don't bathe before a formal dinner, they'll make us eat in the barn. I guess that wouldn't bother you."

Okay, so she knew about the shit and pigs, too. She laughed at her own joke and then headed into my apartments. "The bath is in the back." She looked back over her shoulder. "Oh, and I'll need to borrow your maid. I hope you don't mind." She continued on her way. "Come along, now."

I jumped up and scurried after her, but Neasa was moving full speed through my apartments, and my bad leg slowed me down. When I imagined the inconsolable look from Sofie if she spied Neasa strolling through my quarters with dress in hand, I increased my speed.

109

The little dining nook opened onto the common area with doorways leading to various sleeping rooms and a passage at the back that I had not yet explored. Neasa was passing out the back with my entire household in tow. Bren looked back and stopped to wait for me.

"Your bath is ready, Olaf," he said as I approached at a fast scuttle. "But I didn't know the Kail woman was joining you." He tried to sound unaffected, but his voice rose higher than normal and the look in his eye was accusatory.

"I didn't even know I was bathing," I snapped back as I rushed through the doorway.

I heard Moshe chuckle behind me, which caused me to miss a step. I had forgotten about my shadows, and to hear the somber Moshe chuckle was enough to make me pause. I still couldn't keep track of when one, or both, of the guards were at my back. They had a system, but I hadn't bothered to ask.

Moshe actually smiled at me. "It is never dull in your service."

Sarcasm was his brother's gift. Hearing it from Moshe just spurred me back into action. I ignored his comment and hurried through to the back room.

I stopped short at the sight of a huge stone tub set into the floor. A curtain had been drawn across the middle, with its ends hanging in the water. I stood there and watched the steam rise as I heard female voices on the other side of the curtain.

Ursala's voice overpowered the rest as she chastised her daughter. "Gabriele, hurry out of that dress. You don't have much time to bathe."

There was a window on the other side of the curtain, letting light into the room. I could just make out the shadow of Ursala struggling to get Gabriele out of her clothes. I turned away to look at Bren, who grinned at my discomfort.

I had actually seen Gabriele naked before, back at Stenson House, when they pulled out the great wash tub every month and set it up in the breezeway between the kitchen and the servants' quarters. We took turns, the men and women, but Bren and I used to peek when it was the girl's turn to bathe.

From his grin, Bren was probably remembering the same thing. The women always went first. Because we worked in the stables, we were the last to bathe, which meant we had the most opportunity to peek.

Bren started stripping off his clothes. "We better get in before they dirty the water."

Because we always went last, I couldn't remember ever having a bath in water that was clean—or warm, for that matter. That thought and the curtain helped to calm my nerves as I started to undress.

"Come on, boys," I heard Neasa's voice from the tub on the other side. "Show us what you got." She pulled on the curtain and laughed.

Bren was in the water before I could finish undressing. He was laughing, until he saw me struggling with my trousers, and then he jumped back out to help me. "Sorry, Master Olaf." He remembered he was my valet a bit late, but he did look abashed at his lapse.

I tried to wave him away, but he persisted with pulling the trousers off my twisted leg while I hopped around on my good one.

"Having troubles?" Now Gabriele called out from the other side of the curtain. The giggle in her voice caused Bren to grin at me as he finally whipped the trousers free.

I waved him away as I pulled my tunic over my head. When I pulled my head free, I was greeted by Ursala's face, much too close to my own. I jumped back and nearly tripped on my clothes but was caught by Moshe, who was still at my back.

"Do you need help bathing, Lord?" Ursala asked. She was a stout woman, and still fully dressed. Sweat rolled off her face from the steam coming off the water. She looked so sincere that I almost missed the mischievous glint in her eye.

In the Seven Kingdoms, baths were often social or family affairs, and I knew many nobles had their servants wash their bodies. I was sure Ursala had seen all her children naked, even as adults. Maybe she had even washed some rich people's backsides in her past service. She had probably seen me wash myself and change clothes on the ship's deck throughout the later part of our voyage. Still, it was a bit unnerving having her standing so close while I was as naked as the day I was born.

I could feel my face burn, and I hoped she would attribute the color to the steam. "I can wash myself," I managed to get out.

I slipped past her and eased into the hot water, trying my best to ignore her presence. In that moment, it dawned on me that being a rich man wasn't as easy as I had always imagined— or maybe you got used to people watching you all the time. I felt nostalgia for the old days, when everyone used to ignore me.

"Okay, then." I heard Ursala heading back to the other side of the curtain. "Bren, make sure you wash him good, now."

After she had gone, I gave Bren a look to let him know he would do no such thing.

Bren knew me well. He laughed silently and then called out, "Yes, mother."

"So, is he twisted everywhere?" I heard Neasa whisper, none too quietly, on the other side of the curtain, which produced a round of giggling.

I resolved to ignore everyone else in the room, at that point, and to enjoy my first hot bath. The water felt glorious. Unfortunately, my pleasure didn't last long enough. Bren climbed out first and dressed so he could assist me. I soaked as long as I could in the warm water. It seemed a shame to get out before the water grew cold.

When I heard the women rustling around on the other side of the curtain, I knew I could put it off no longer. I made my way out of the tub and allowed Bren to help me dry and get dressed.

Growing up, I had one "good" tunic and a working one. Now, I had more outfits than I knew about. The one Bren helped me into was new. I guessed he had saved it for such an occasion. Blue trousers, coat, tunic, cap, and even blue-dyed leather shoes made up the ensemble. The coat had silver trim on the shoulders and sleeves and a silver wolf's head—my uncle's symbol—embroidered on the chest.

I hated this costume—especially the shoes. I had run around barefoot for most of my life and had only recently taken up the scourge of wearing shoes. I was convinced they were torture devices made up by some past king who wanted to see his people suffer.

Just as I finished dressing, the curtain was pulled aside. I turned and spied a beaming Ursala leading Gabriele by the hand. Her daughter was decked out in her normal blue attire, except she left off the white coif and had braided her honey-colored hair and put it up in a more formal-looking arrangement. She looked lovely, but could not compare to Neasa, who followed her out from behind the curtain.

As Talon had pointed out earlier, Neasa did clean up nice. Instead of dark, Stenson blue, her Eastern-made robe was a lighter blue and had a pair of black ravens embroidered on the chest—a not-so-subtle reminder of her now-covered breast tattoos. She wore a sash of darker blue that matched my Stenson colors.

The outfit was enough to turn every man's head her way, but the crowning touch was her own head. Her hair was done up in the fashion I had seen on the local women. Her dark tresses were all tied up in an elaborate bun held in place by golden pins. A golden chain hung across her forehead with an onyx raven as the centerpiece.

The Eastern housekeeper trailed behind her with a triumphant smile, which answered the question of how Neasa had managed the elaborate headdress. Obviously, the rivalry between the two housekeepers had not dwindled.

"You both look lovely," I finally managed to croak.

Gabriele beamed and Neasa looked as though she had expected such a response.

Neasa passed my servants and approached me. "Shall we go? The litter will be waiting for us." She held out her arm for me to take. The voluptuous sleeve of her robe made the gesture seem more graceful than any I could produce.

Gabriele took up station at Neasa's back, tugging on her own woolen dress as if suddenly embarrassed by it. Behind her, Ursala shot the Eastern housekeeper a sour look.

I tried to put all that out of my head as I took Neasa's arm. "What litter?"

Neasa laughed a high, tinkling laugh. "You can't expect us to walk and get road dust on our newly bathed selves." She patted my arm and pulled me to the doorway. "It is the custom here, Olaf."

Bren walked behind me as we made our way out to the courtyard and the waiting litter. I held my head straight and tried to imitate Neasa's regal stride, but my leg made that impossible, and my eyes kept roving for signs of my absent lover. To my relief, Sofie did not appear to see us off.

CHAPTER 13: POLITICS

Traveling in a litter makes you feel like a king. It was a heady feeling—lounging on cushions while strong men hoisted you down the street—or maybe I was light-headed from being enclosed with Neasa after our bath.

I was still a bit warm, and she smelled of some exotic spice that reminded me of the spearmint that grew wild in the woods outside Kartoba. Neasa seemed to revel in the experience, stretching on the cushions next to me like a cat and giving me a look that I preferred to ignore. Instead, I peered out through a gap in the curtains and watched the scenery go by. The fresh air on my face helped clear my mind.

There weren't many people walking the street, and the houses we passed were more lavish than the one I had borrowed from Factor Einhardt. It seemed like a different town than the one we'd marched through earlier.

"Close the curtain, Olaf," Neasa said. "They'll think you're an oaf from the west."

"They who?" I replied as I pulled the curtain shut. "The streets are empty." The minty smell became stronger with the curtain shut. It made my eyes water.

Neasa reached out and patted my arm. "They are watching, believe me."

I fought the urge to pull away. The litter was wide enough for us to recline side-by-side, but with little room to move otherwise. Besides, I didn't want her to realize how frightened I was of her.

It was hard to admit, but I finally had to: Neasa terrified me. She was pretty and powerful and deadly—and, worst of all, she had decided that we were destined to be together. I hoped that she saw us as allies and nothing more, but I was afraid to ask. My body lay stiffly on the cushions and I stared at the curtain in front of me, waiting for her to pull her hand away.

Instead, she ran her finger down my arm. "Why are you so tense, Olaf?"

When I didn't respond, she finally pulled her hand away and let out a sigh. "I just want to talk."

I peeked at her from the corner of my eye. She looked back at me with a serious expression. I wasn't sure if that was better than her teasing.

"Olaf, we are allies in this. I know that I might have …" She paused as if choosing her words carefully. "I know I startled you during the New Year celebration." She looked contrite, almost sorrowful, with a little frown on her face and a tearful gleam in her eye. "I keep forgetting how spooked you Uplanders get when there is talk of the gods, but I'd had a vivid vision, and I could not keep it to myself."

I didn't want to hear about her vision again. I could feel my chest tighten as soon as she mentioned the gods. Anyone from the Seven Kingdoms would have had the same reaction.

"I'm sorry for springing this on you, but you have had plenty of time to think about it since." She moved to reach for my arm again, but I shied away. Her hand paused, just out of reach. "Know this, Olaf. I will not try to trick you or force you to do anything. We are allies and our destinies are intertwined." Then she lowered her hand to rest it on my arm. "Your enemies are my enemies."

Even through my coat sleeve, her touch sent a thrill through me. It was nothing carnal, but more like a shiver of fear. I suddenly felt as though the gods were watching our every move.

The litter came to an abrupt halt and she pulled her hand free again. "We have arrived."

The litter was lowered, the curtains were opened, and Neasa stepped down. I sat there for a moment and took a deep breath, waiting for the shivers to stop so I could follow her to our dinner.

We were in the open-air courtyard of a massive house. Several servants, dressed in the yellow, baggy trousers and robes of the Cao family, stood waiting for us to arrive. An older man stepped forward from their ranks and gave me a formal bow. "If you will follow me, Master Olaf."

Neasa inclined her head in deference to me and then took up a station to my left. Out of the corner of my eye, I saw Bren and Gabriele step up behind us. Mehki and Moshe and my Stenson guards had also accompanied the litter—a proper escort was expected in the east—but only Bren and Gabriele would accompany us into the hall. The rest—even my Wolf guards—would all remain outside the dining area.

We followed the servant through a large set of double doors and were immediately greeted by Cao Wangsun, who wore formal robes of yellow and green. To my surprise, the hall was empty of other guests. He gave me a nod, not quite as formal as I had expected, and said, "Welcome to my home."

I returned his greeting and fought an urge to watch Neasa's reaction. In the east women, were not permitted to speak in public—and because we were in Cao Wangsun's residence, I didn't want to offend my guest by deferring to her.

Neasa took the initiative anyway. "Cao Wangsun, where are the rest of your guests?"

I expected anger, but to my relief, Cao Wangsun laughed and reached out a hand to escort Neasa to her seat. "Neasa of the Macha Clan, it is a pleasure to greet you, as usual."

Again, this was not what I'd expected. We had bathed and dressed up, and I had expected to have to navigate the intricacies of the Eastern court. Instead, we were greeted by a friendly Cao Wangsun, who obviously knew Neasa well.

I stood rooted in place as he showed Neasa to her seat. Neasa glanced over her shoulder at me. "Come along, Olaf, and meet our ally in the East."

Our host sat her at a small table that stood alone in the middle of the room. A curtain had been drawn behind it so the room didn't look so big, but it was obvious by the way Neasa's voice echoed that the hall was much larger. Once Neasa was seated, Cao Wangsun peered at me. "*Our* ally?"

"Yes," Neasa answered. "Olaf and I are united in our future plans."

He turned back to Neasa. "Another of your—conquests?"

Neasa let out a tinkling laugh. "We are allies, not lovers. Olaf Stenson and I will rule the west before we are through."

It was too much to take in—a relaxed Neasa joking with this Easterner, and telling him that we had an alliance, caught me off guard. In fact, it began to make me angry. Had she been toying with me about the bath? Had she known all along about this intimate dinner?

I was tired of being tricked and being left to guess what everyone else was doing. I was tired of not knowing everything. It had been like that my whole life, starting when my uncle sent me to Kartoba.

The anger began to bubble up within me. It was time for me to take charge again, no matter how much I feared the outcome. I was a Stenson, after all. This time, I would ensure that Sofie was well-protected—even from herself if need be.

I squared my shoulders and stamped over to the little table with as much dignity as my bad leg would allow. "Whether we are allies or not, Master Cao, has yet to be decided." It was hard to keep the tremble out of my voice. I didn't want them to recognize my anger—not yet.

Cao Wangsun waved me to a seat and then took the last one with his back to the door. "As you say."

I sat down but noticed Bren and Gabriele still standing near the entrance, looking uncertain of their role with such an intimate dinner. Their familiar faces gave me strength. "Attend us," I snapped, and they jumped to obey, taking up station behind our chairs.

Neasa flashed her eyes at them and then gave me a look as if questioning the trustworthiness of my servants. I ignored her.

Bren and Gabriele had both proven their loyalty to me. I trusted them more than either of the two sitting at the table with me! Besides, neither of them understood the Imperial that we were speaking.

"I don't suppose that either of you care to explain to me the nature of *our* alliance?"

My anger was still there, helping me to let go of my normal mild manners. I held onto it like a lifeline that sailors used to pull in a drowning man. "It is obvious that you both have met and discussed this at length."

Cao Wangsun looked a bit put out by my manner, but Neasa chuckled. She waited a moment while the house servants arrived with drinks and a course of food. Once they had disappeared back behind the curtain, she spoke. "We have the same goals, Olaf. We intend to crush the Empire of Jewel once and for all and share in the spoils."

I knew that would be easier said than done. Although I was new to the east, I'd had good teachers, and they had pounded it into my head that neither the empire nor the confederation had the power to finish the other. "What has changed to make this possible?" I now asked. "Even if you have made an alliance, will the Eastern Confederation trust the Kail? They won't even let your ships enter port without putting you under guard."

"Gea is overly cautious," Cao Wangsun said. "My family rules the Eastern Confederation, and they will follow our lead in this."

"So you think that the Eastern Confederation will rejoin the fight against the Empire of Jewel with the Kail as allies? Will this be enough?" I figured that, even if every Kail clan participated, they wouldn't have enough ships to transport all the warriors. No, the only way they could defeat the Empire of Jewel was if the empire's armies were gone somewhere else.

This thought reminded me of my conversation with the Reik in Gwyr. He planned to attack the Empire of Jewel—that much I believed. But did he really care whether the Seven Kingdoms survived? Did either of the people seated with me care about *my* homeland?

Talon had told me that he believed they would wait until the empire's armies were busy attacking my homeland. I had a strong suspicion this plan had not changed, which meant that now, they were simply trying to manipulate me into helping them. As these thoughts flashed through my head in an instant, I could feel my anger seething.

I looked at Neasa's pleasant face and had to fight an urge to strike her. She was the one behind this! Now she was trying to keep me off-balance with her talk of "visions." She had Talon wrapped around her little finger, and now she was working on me.

"It will be enough," Cao Wangsun answered, "once Sikk joins our cause."

"What?" His comment astounded me.

The kingdom of Sikk sat in the interior of the confederation. In fact, it sat at the center. It was their holiest place, the remnant of the old Sikk Empire and the seat of the Dai Jun. The Dai dynasty had once ruled the east. Sometime in the distant past, the Dai Jun—who was said to be descended from the gods—had retired to Sikk and left the rest of his lands in the hands of its various princes.

Even today, the Cao family's hold on the Eastern Confederation was tentative. They only truly ruled at the Dai Jun's pleasure. I had been told by my confederation tutor that, if the Dai Jun ever decided to regain his throne, the world would tremble. Under the Dai Jun, the old Sikk Empire had never been defeated.

We sat quietly and ate our first course as I digested this information. I was so distracted by my thoughts that I had no idea what I ate. The food only registered once, when I bit into something so spicy that I had to grab for my wine to put out the fire. That was about the time that the servants brought the second course, and Cao Wangsun decided to break the silence.

"With the Dai Jun's blessing," he announced, "we shall overcome the Empire of Jewel and restore our former glory."

I studied the grandson of the current Cao ruler. He looked to be my age, but he was slight of build, like most Easterners.

He also had a fanatical gleam in his eye, which didn't reassure me. "How does your grandfather feel about bowing down to the Dai Jun?" I asked him.

I couldn't imagine such an old and established ruler being overjoyed about having his power usurped by another—even one as legendary as the Dai Jun.

Cao Wangsun laughed, but the disconcerting gleam remained. "This has nothing to do with the *BaWang*. He can rule in Xiang as he does now, and I will lead our people to victory over all our foes."

"BaWang" meant "over-king." It was the title held by Cao Wangsun's grandfather. Although I didn't doubt his words, Cao Wangsun looked more like a wealthy magistrate than a warrior.

He continued to explain, so I remained quiet and listened.

"The Dai Jun has but one heir, his granddaughter—and she has reached the age for marriage. He has promised an army to her future husband. And that will be me."

He sounded completely sure of himself, so I had to ask. "Why are you so sure that you will be that man?"

He looked affronted by my question and pulled himself up in his seat to try to look down at me. "I am the best match in the Eastern Confederation," he said, his smile returning, "and it is my destiny. Upon my birth, the soothsayers predicted that I would journey to Sikk and lead an army of conquest."

More about the gods and destiny! This talk was enough to make a man run and hide.

"Once I have my army," he went on, "I will conquer the Empire of Jewel and make it my own. If you join my cause, I may let your little group of kingdoms have a share of the spoils." He nodded to Neasa and gave me a patronizing smile. "For Neasa's sake, of course."

He reminded me of too many rich men I had seen throughout my life. They all thought that they were chosen for something greater, as if their power and position were a gift from the gods. Even in the Seven Kingdoms, where we try to avoid the attention of the gods, the rich men—like my now-dead Uncle Karl—thought they were special, somehow chosen for glory. Cao Wangsun seemed no different to me—but perhaps I could use this rich man to help my people.

"I would be glad to join you, Cao Wangsun," I said, trying to sound sincere. "How can I help?"

I truly wanted to know. I had no idea why he would need my help in his endeavor, or even why he told me his plans. That thought made me suddenly nervous, and I glanced around the room, wondering if he had men hidden behind the curtains, ready to strike.

Cao Wangsun smiled. "Your uncle has much silver, yes?"

I should have known. When people looked to my family for help, it was always about the silver. I found myself relaxing after that. Greed, I understood.

The rest of the meal was spent talking about Cao Wangsun's great plans. It turned out that his grandfather, the BaWang, intended for the Dai Jun's army to help bolster his own claim to the leadership of the Confederation. Cao Wangsun didn't see the need to share his upcoming rise to power with the old man. Instead, he had his alliance with Neasa—but he also needed outside funds.

 I smiled and nodded. I promised him the sun and stars, including free rein over my uncle's coffers. By the end of the meal, we were close allies—as far as he knew. Neasa had remained quiet throughout, picking at her food and occasionally peeking sideways at me.

When the evening ended, Cao Wangsun rose and escorted us to the door. "I will leave for Xiang the end of this week, and then travel from there to Sikk." Over dinner, he had confided that his grandfather had recently sent for him to prepare for the journey to Sikk to press his claim.

"Your main post is in Xiang, is it not?" he asked. *Where I had better access to my uncle's silver.* "You both shall accompany me."

Neasa spoke up for the first time since the dinner began. "It would be an honor."

I nodded my agreement as we passed back into the courtyard where our hired litter waited. The sun had fallen during our dinner, and the yard was now lit by lanterns hanging from posts.

As we climbed into our litter, one of the Cao servants lit a small paper lantern that hung from the ceiling inside. Once the curtains were drawn, Neasa watched my face until we were carried out into the street.

"What are you playing at?" she demanded as soon as our litter passed through the gates of the Cao estate.

"Playing?" I stared at the paper lantern that hung between us so I wouldn't have to face her. It was round and yellow, with tiny white snowflakes painted on the sides. The beeswax candle inside gave off a pleasant odor that almost masked her minty perfume. Luckily, her fragrance lost most of its potency over dinner.

"Don't pretend you don't understand me," she said. She sounded perturbed, but I didn't look at her to verify it. "Do you even have the authority to promise him so much silver?"

I watched the smoke rise from the top of the lantern and glide across the ceiling before it drifted out the slit in the curtain. I was still mad at her, and still afraid of her. I wasn't quite sure what to say.

After another moment of watching the smoke, I decided that the direct approach was the easiest. "You accuse me of playing, Neasa," I said, facing her to let her see my anger. "You have been playing with me since the day we met. What do you truly want with *me*? You expect me to believe you saw some *vision,* and that is why I should trust you?"

She opened her mouth, but I didn't give her a chance to reply. "Tell me the truth! Are you waiting for the empire to attack my homeland before you make your move?"

My outburst seemed to surprise her. She leaned back, eyes wide, but then quickly recovered. "Carrog said you had iron in you, but I couldn't see it." She pursed her lips as if trying to decide what to tell me. Finally, she let out a little whisper of a sigh.

"Yes, we planned to wait until the empire attacked the Seven Kingdoms before we struck," she said softly. "But that was before my vision. Whether you believe me or not, Olaf, I told you the truth about that."

She reached out and placed her hand on mine. "My fate is tied to yours; I have seen it. You are my chance to escape a marriage to the Reik and forge my own path."

Her hand was cold. She always seemed so sensual; I had expected more warmth.

"And how does that spoiled rich boy play into our plans?" I asked. "Do you really believe he will win an army and then actually be able to lead it?"

Neasa laughed at that. "Yes, he seems a popinjay. But Cao Wangsun has been tutored by the greatest generals, and he is probably the best swordsman in the east." Her words came as a surprise.

"If you want to save your homeland," she continued, "his plan is our best chance. Without the Dai Jun army, we have no choice but to wait until the Empire of Jewel is busy laying waste to your homeland."

"But you already planned this, before you met me!" I shook my head because I didn't understand. "Why …?" I wasn't quite sure how to ask the question.

Neasa understood my confusion even without the words. "The Reik and Padruig know nothing of my plots with Cao Wangsun. Their plan has always been to stir up trouble in Suma once the empire marches west, to get the empire fighting on two fronts before invading Andamar." She looked a little embarrassed. "Cao Wangsun's plan was always a long shot, but it was the only chance I could see to break away from the Reik."

"So that's why we played at bathing and preparing for a great feast—to keep Padruig in the dark?"

She tossed her head, making her headpiece twinkle in the lantern light. "He still plans to go to Suma. We will tell Padruig that Cao Wangsun insisted we accompany him to Xiang. If you tell the old schemer that you will meet him in Suma as soon as you are able, he will go ahead, and we'll be free of him."

If he believes me, maybe, I thought. But I didn't see the need to voice that. Instead I said, "Then we follow this out and see where it leads us."

She startled me by squeezing my hand. I had forgotten that she held it. "Now that you are involved, I know that it will work out."

I still didn't trust her, but she seemed so sincere that I wanted to. I really saw no other choice, especially in the time that I had. Cao Wangsun's potential army seemed the best option for saving my people.

I nodded my agreement. "Then it seems we are truly allies."

When her face lit up, I almost forgot her nature. But then, when she leaned in for a kiss, I remembered. I pulled my hand free and leaned away from her. "Allies only."

Her lips twitched as if she repressed a smile, or a frown. "Of course."

CHAPTER 14: A PARTING OF WAYS

As soon as we returned from the dinner, I sought out Ivan. I hadn't spoken to him since leaving the *Sea Cow*. I had to admit, I was embarrassed that Sofie had rejected me, and I didn't want to tell him. Still, I had come to rely on his counsel.

I didn't have to look far. Ivan followed me back to the little dining area and said, "Tell me everything."

Once I had finished describing all that had occurred since our last talk, he looked thoughtful for a moment before speaking. "I don't trust them," he finally said. "But you planned to go to Xiang anyway, to take your place as the Eastern Factor. After the attack at the dock, you should do that soon, I'm thinking."

"Did you find anything after I left the dock?"

His face froze—a sure sign that he knew something. "They were hired thugs," he finally replied. "It could have been Factor Einhardt …"

"Who else knew I was coming?"

Ivan shrugged. "The Reik, Padruig, Neasa, Captain Gregor, and anyone in Kartoba when we left port—take your pick. You can't trust *anyone*, Olaf." He gave me a rare smile. "Except me, of course."

I felt relief that he didn't mention Sofie. "Even if we can't trust him, it may be better to leave Einhardt in place and pursue this opportunity," I said. "We are supposed to be finding a way to save my uncle's kingdom."

Ivan pursed his lips as if he was about to say something, then paused before finally speaking. "You were sent to take over as Eastern Factor, Olaf. You cannot leave Einhardt in place—especially now."

He was right, but I wondered what he hadn't said. I studied him for a clue. Ivan always looked the same, and whatever he had been thinking did not reflect in his face. He raised his eyebrows as if to ask what I was looking for.

"Okay. We will deal with Factor Einhardt first, but we will still pursue the deal with Cao Wangsun."

Ivan nodded his agreement—but was there still a glint of something in his eye?

I met with Padruig the next day and he agreed to go ahead to Suma on his own. I promised to catch up to him after my trip to Xiang, although he didn't really seem to care. Most likely, he was in a hurry to set his master's plot in motion and decided not to fight me, or worry about my own part in it. To tell the truth, I thought he wanted to be rid of Neasa more than anything.

So it seemed that I had a plan at last. All should have been well—except for Sofie. She hadn't come to my bed the previous evening and had avoided me since our conversation on the bench. After meeting with Padruig, I began to search for her in the main wing of the house. I didn't get too far before running across Bren.

"She is avoiding you," he said as I entered the sitting room that adjoined our bed chambers.

"What?" I stopped in mid-stride to spy him sitting at a low table drinking a cup of something.

"You're looking for Sofie, aren't you?" I had to hand it to him; he kept the smugness off his face, if not out of his voice. "Why else would you be searching the house with that determined stride?"

I definitely spent too much time with these people. Fighting back a frown, I asked, "Where is she?"

"I already told you—avoiding you."

Bren could be annoying on the best of days, and it was apparent that he wasn't going to make this easy for me. I checked my impatience and took a seat at the table. It was difficult, because the Easterners liked to sit close to the ground—usually on cushions, but not always. The table and chairs in the little dining area I had been using were of western design, probably added by Factor Einhardt when he bought the place. This one was Eastern, which meant I had to throw out my bad leg—the one that refused to bend—and try to catch myself before my ass hit the ground. I'm sure I made it look graceful.

"Bren," I snapped, once my ass hit the cushion, "why is she avoiding me?"

He took a sip from his cup and shrugged. "She didn't tell me, but you might as well accept it for now and not go looking for her. Sofie can be more pig-headed than my mother, and she's good at avoiding people."

"But she promised she wouldn't leave me," I whispered. I'm not sure if I said it to Bren or to myself. I felt a wave a darkness suddenly hovering over me, one that would engulf me if I let it.

"She's not leaving you, Olaf. She just needs some time." He reached out and patted my hand where it sat on the table. It was an awkward gesture for him, which made it that much more effective. "Don't worry. She'll talk to you soon."

"But we're leaving for Xiang in a few days," I said. "Is she going to avoid me on the ship, too?" I knew it would be beyond awkward if I had to sleep alone aboard the *Sea Cow* after carrying on with Sofie for most of the previous voyage.

Bren didn't have an answer, so we sat in silence as I brooded over this latest development.

Two more days passed with no sign of Sofie. Cao Wangsun planned to travel along the coast in an Eastern Confederation warship. It was called a *kojan*, but it was pretty much just a smaller version of an Imperial galea. I planned to follow in the *Sea Cow*, and Neasa with her birlinn. She argued to leave the *Sea Cow* behind, because it was so much slower than the other ships. Padruig had not left for Suma yet, and she worried that he would become suspicious if I left in the *Sea Cow* with my entire household.

"He thinks this is a quick trip to Xiang at the request of Cao Wangsun," she argued. "You told Padruig we would be based in Gea."

She had caught me as I sat brooding in the courtyard on the bench where I had last spoken with Sofie. Neasa stood over me, wearing the blue-green dress that nearly exposed her breasts. It was the same one she had worn in Oyvu at the New Year.

"You should come with me in my birlinn and leave that old tub behind," she said again. She had made the same argument every day since the dinner with Cao Wangsun. She also wanted me to leave my household behind in Gea to ward off Padruig's suspicion.

I feared that she was trying to separate me from my people. Her dress didn't help her cause; it reminded me of Oyvu and her vision. The memory only made me more determined to ignore her advice. "We are allies in this, Neasa," I said, "but I follow my own counsel."

She frowned at me and then stalked away.

All I wanted was to be left in peace until it was time to depart. Well, that wasn't entirely true. What I really wanted was for Sofie to come back to me before we sailed. I kept fretting over the upcoming voyage. Sofie's absence wouldn't feel real to me until we were once more aboard the *Sea Cow*.

The scene kept playing in my head—boarding the ship without Sofie, the crew watching and judging. I shuddered at the thought and tried to banish it from my mind by staring at nothing.

It is an acquired art, staring at nothing. I had perfected it in the woods outside Kartoba when I was tasked with watching the pigs. Sometimes it was the best way to keep my mind off things that I couldn't control.

The next morning, as soon as I rose from my bed, Bren stepped into the room, almost as if he had been waiting for me to stir. "Sofie has asked to see you."

My heart raced at the news. I hurried through my morning ablutions and turned back to Bren, who had laid out an outfit. "Where is she?"

I hadn't noticed that his face did not reflect my excitement. In fact, he looked downright unemotional, even for Bren—as if he held back from telling me bad news. "What's wrong?"

He licked his lips. "She's abed, Olaf. She wants to see you."

Abed? She was young and strong. I had just spoken with her three days before. I tried my best not to panic. I slipped on the tunic that Bren had laid out for me, but left the rest. I couldn't even imagine struggling with my trousers. "Let's go!"

Bren was impeccably dressed, as usual. He eyed my lack of trousers, coat, and shoes with a critical eye but did not comment before turning to lead me from the room. This worried me even more.

The women's quarters were just opposite of ours, so we had to take only a few steps across the main room to get there. I had consciously stayed away because of my last conversation with Bren. Sofie had wanted some time, and though it had pained me to do so, I'd given it to her. Now I kicked myself for not going to see her sooner.

Sofie lay covered by a heavy blanket, her hair disheveled and her forehead shining with sweat. Her mother hovered over her from the opposite side of the bed, and Gabriele stood at her mother's back, looking anxious. They all turned my way when we entered the room.

"Master Olaf," Ursala said. She had been holding a bowl, which she quickly dropped to a small table that stood next to the bed as she hurried around to greet me.

I waved her off and quickly moved to the bedside. Sofie looked haggard, but she gave me a weak smile and said, "Hello, Love."

I dropped down onto my one good knee so that I could be close to her. "Why didn't you call me sooner?"

"I will be okay," she said. "I'm just getting used to the heat." The heavy blanket was sweat-soaked, but I guessed they were trying to break her fever.

I was close enough that I could smell the sickness on her breath. She had recently thrown up, probably into the bowl her mother had quickly hidden.

I didn't know what to say. She had rescued me from a darkness of the mind on our voyage. Now I wanted to rescue her from her sickness. "What is wrong with her?" I asked Ursala.

Sofie reached her hand out from under the blanket, and I took it. "Don't worry about me, Olaf. You need to worry about your trip to Xiang."

Of course she knew about my trip—but how could I go now? "I won't leave you," I finally managed to say.

"Of course you will," she replied. "You came here to save our people, right? To make your uncle proud?" She had been my confidant on the ship. She knew how I felt about my Uncle Olaf, and that I wanted to show him I deserved his trust.

Sofie suddenly grabbed at her stomach and turned away from me. Gabriele rushed to her side and held the bowl while Sofie was sick again. Ursala put her hand on my shoulder and I rose back to my feet.

"What is wrong with her?" I demanded.

Ursala shrugged. "Just a touch of something. Maybe it's the strange food. I'm sure she'll be okay in a few days, but she can't travel tomorrow."

Damn the gods and their jealousy! Because I wanted to keep Sofie close, they were forcing me to leave her behind. I knew I couldn't delay the trip. I had to leave on the morrow. We were travelling with Cao Wangsun, and I couldn't afford to make him suspicious of me.

Ursala twisted her pudgy hands in uncharacteristic nervousness. "I would like to stay with her, Master Olaf?"

Of course, she would have to stay to care for Sofie. And I couldn't leave Sofie and her mother alone. That meant I would have to leave behind Stenson guards as well, to keep them safe.

Suddenly, Sofie's illness was forcing my hand. I would have to adopt Neasa's plan after all.

"You will stay with her," I told Ursala, "and Gabriele, too."

To my surprise, Gabriele balked at the idea. "I am your maid, Olaf. You cannot go unattended because of Sofie's illness."

Ursala nodded her agreement. "It is true, Master Olaf. It would be a poor reflection on our family if we let you go off alone. Gabriele should go to serve you."

"I'll have Bren," I argued.

They both lifted an eyebrow at that, and even Sofie chuckled in her sickbed. "You'll starve," Gabriele muttered loud enough for the room to hear.

I looked to my valet, who shrugged. "It's true, I cannot cook."

"Okay then, Gabriele will come." I shooed them away to kneel once more next to Sofie's bed. "You must get well soon, Sofie."

She smiled and reached for my hand again. "I'll see you upon your return."

With half my household staying behind, I agreed to leave the *Sea Cow* in Gea and ride with Neasa in her birlinn. I also left the majority of my Stenson guardsmen behind to watch over Sofie and her mother. I took only a single pair of guardsmen, mostly because I wanted to keep Ivan with me, along with Bren, Gabriele and my two Wolf guards. Guard Captain Luther had argued to come along, but I refused and made it plain that I left the safety of Sofie and her mother in his hands.

CHAPTER 15: A DEN OF SNAKES

The morning after visiting Sofie in her sickbed, I stood on the deck of Neasa's birlinn and watched the port of Gea shrink in the distance. I had done everything I could for Sofie, but I still felt ill at ease leaving her behind. I had stopped by to see her again the previous evening, but she had been sleeping.

Because of our early departure, I left without waking her. Ursala had seen us off, and she assured me again that Sofie would recover, but it bothered me that I had not said goodbye.

The birlinn was more crowded than the *Sea Cow*. I had a place at the back of the ship, right next to the steersman. The crew had rigged a small tent with a door flap. It was large enough for two, and maybe one more if we wanted to squeeze together and sweat.

After losing sight of Gea, I sat on a bench under the shelter with Gabriele. The rest of my people sat outside, creating a human wall between me and the Kail sailors. I hadn't bothered with trousers because of the heat and pulled off my coat before I entered the shelter. As I settled next to her, Gabriele gave me a strange look.

"What?"

She smiled. "Seeing you dressed like that reminds me of the old days."

The "old days" had been no more than a year before. I had to laugh at her choice of words. "You mean back when I used to smell of pig and owned fewer clothes than you?"

She wrinkled up her nose. "You still smell like a pig."

I had always liked Gabriele. She was one of those girls that had a smile for everyone, even an outcast boy who was treated worse than the servants. It was good to see her smile at me again.

We sat in silence, listening to one of the crewmen calling out the stroke as the birlinn glided through the water. Not being much of a sailor, I had no idea why they were rowing rather than using the sail. Maybe it was faster.

"She's pretty amazing."

I felt sudden guilt. Was she talking about Sofie?

Gabriele, her eyes alight with excitement, was staring across the ship at Neasa, who stood in the bow. Gabriele had always loved adventure—or the thought of it, at least. I could see how she might be drawn to Neasa.

"She's dangerous," I said.

Gabriele nodded. "Yes, but amazing, too."

I motioned toward Neasa. "Would you want to be like her?"

Gabriele suddenly turned shy. She cast her eyes towards the deck at our feet and shook her head. "No, I couldn't."

I wanted to comfort her, but held back. Gabriele was a servant—my servant—and I didn't want her to get any crazy ideas about adventure. Wasn't it bad enough that we were riding in a birlinn with a band of Kail? "You wouldn't want to be, Gabriele. She is a killer—not some prim and proper lady."

Gabriele's face flashed annoyance, which she quickly smothered. "Of course you're right, Master Olaf." She stood and moved to sit outside the shelter with her brother.

I watched her go, holding back a sigh. Women were a mystery to me—except Sofie. I always knew what Sofie wanted from me. At least, I always had known, until she pushed me away. I let out the sigh I had been holding back and closed my eyes. It would be a long voyage without her.

The days were hot, and the nights were not much better. With the birlinn crowded with Kail warriors and my handful of retainer, I felt like a fish in a barrel. I stayed tucked away under my canvas shelter and tried to ignore everyone as we sailed along the coast. Gabriele brought me food, but we didn't talk again. She stayed out with the others, even though I offered her a place within. I was pretty sure she was mad at me.

Luckily, it wasn't a long voyage; within a week, we arrived in Xiang. It felt good to get off the birlinn. I stood on the dock and stretched, surrounded by my small retinue of guards and servants.

The waterfront looked no different than any other, but the surrounding town was much larger than any I had seen before. Gea had been similar in size to my hometown of Kartoba—but Xiang made them both look like fishing villages. This city stretched as far as the eye could see. It consisted of a haphazard arrangement of buildings that reminded me of a loaded net of fish that had been dumped on the dock. That was what it smelled like, as well.

Gabriele wrinkled her nose at me, but maintained her silence.

Neasa walked up as I was shaking my head. "It's enough to make you homesick, no?"

Her skimpy tunic had its normal effect on me, and I concentrated upon her face in an attempt to ignore the rest of her. This didn't help: her face was pretty—prettier than most. She smiled at me, as if acknowledging my observation of her beauty, and I had to turn away.

"Let's just get on with it," I snapped, pretending to survey my people and our few belongings.

After a long, painful pause, Gabriele said, "She's gone."

I allowed myself a glance over my shoulder. Neasa had turned back to her own people to hurry them along. I blew out my breath. "Thank you, Gabriele."

She gave me a stiff bow. "It is my duty."

No respite from that quarter. Growing up in Stenson House, I had daydreamed about having servants and guards of my own. The reality didn't quite match the dream.

It was not long before a courtier approached to show us to our quarters. I led my people, and Neasa brought along Talon, Carrog, and a few other warriors as escort. As usual, the guide walked too fast, and I worried that I would not be able to keep up the pace. Neasa noticed me struggling and called out to the courtier. "Where are we heading?"

The man had to slow down to talk to her, and I breathed a sigh of relief. "Cao Wangsun has a house near the BaWang's palace," the courtier answered. "You are to be his guests."

I felt disappointment at the news. I thought we were going to the BaWang's palace, not shuffled away to another house. Neasa must have felt the same, because she said, "Will Cao Wangsun be staying with us, or will he be with the BaWang?"

The courier cut his eyes at her. "It is not my place to know the plans of my master."

Neasa showed me an annoyed look, clearly unhappy with the situation. "Tell your master that we request an audience with him."

"My duty is to escort you," he replied. He eyed her ratty tunic with obvious distaste, "I will bring you, *my Lady*, to my master's house. One of the servants there *may* do your bidding." He turned back to his task and once more picked up the pace.

Neasa stopped abruptly, causing the rest of us to do the same. It took the courtier a moment to notice, but he finally stopped and turned. He took a step back toward us with a confused look on his face. "The house is this way."

Neasa did not answer, but waited for the man to draw closer. He did so with hesitant steps until he stood before her. "My Lady …"

Neasa cut him off with a voice that could slice through the din of battle. "Tell your master that we will be staying at the Golden Swan, where they endeavor to make their guests feel welcome. He may call upon us there."

The man's face blanched white but she turned on her heels before he could speak. We left him standing in the street and headed back the way we had come.

I waited a moment to speak. "Was that wise?"

Her face was still flushed with anger. "No, perhaps not. But Cao Wangsun needs us more than we need him."

I wasn't so sure of that. I was positive he wanted access to my uncle's wealth, but I knew how prickly noble men could get. "He may not come."

"He'll come." She allowed the anger to dissipate from her face. "The Golden Swan is the most expensive boarding house in Xiang." Now she smiled at me. "You're paying."

The Golden Swan was several blocks from the waterfront—close enough for travelers to find it easily, but far enough away from the smell of the docks. When we entered the porch of the establishment, we were met by an older man with a shaved head dressed in formal, Eastern-style robes. He bowed low and said, "How may I serve you?"

"We need rooms," Neasa replied.

The man looked up at us, his expression unchanged, but I'm sure he was trying to decide whether we could afford to stay there.

Neasa motioned toward me. "This is Olaf Stenson, heir to the Stenson family fortune and new factor in the east."

The man's face still didn't change expression, but he said, "How many rooms do you need?"

We decided upon a suite of two adjoining bedchambers with several smaller, attached rooms. Neasa asked for Gabriele to act as her maidservant, as she had done when we first met with Cao Wangsun "to keep up appearances." After our conversation on Neasa's ship, I didn't want to let Gabriele spend any time with the Kail woman, but couldn't think of a reason to say no. So Gabriele was quartered off of Neasa's bedchamber, and the rest of my people shared a couple of rooms that were attached to my bedchamber. It was all quite cozy.

Neasa, Talon, and I met for dinner that evening in a private dining chamber at the Golden Swan. It was a small enough room that my Wolf guard, who happened to be Moshe that night, was content to stand next to the single entrance rather than at my back. We sat at a small table with three chairs. Bren and Gabriele stood behind me and Neasa, acting as proper servants. I would have invited them to join us in our meal, but I knew they would refuse.

"Will he come?" I asked as soon as we sat down to eat.

"He will," Neasa replied. She was once more decked out like a true lady of the east. I knew that if she had been dressed that way from the start, the uppity courier would have treated her with the utmost respect, and we might be staying somewhere else—somewhere less expensive.

Talon piped up on her left. "He needs you more than you need him, Olaf. Staying here just reminds him of that need."

"Yes," I replied. "It reminds him that I have money that he wants. But does he truly need us?" I was feeling the pressure. If Cao Wangsun abandoned us, I had no other plan to help my uncle.

"He will come," Neasa repeated.

I nodded, not truly convinced, but I saw no need to belabor the point. I suddenly remembered my last conversation with Ivan and blurted, "I need to visit the factor's office while we are here."

"We can go tomorrow," Neasa offered.

"I'll go." I had no need for Neasa getting into my uncle's business. "First thing tomorrow. You'll send word if you hear from Cao Wangsun?"

"Of course." The innocent look on Neasa's face didn't comfort me.

The next morning, I dressed in my best Stenson Blue outfit and headed out to the factor's office with Ivan. I had convinced Bren to stay at the boarding house with Gabriele.

I was a bit nervous about meeting Factor Einhardt. I had stolen his house, after all, even though I was sure he'd paid for it with stolen Stenson silver. I wasn't sure how he would react. Ivan would be there to ensure I didn't say the wrong thing, but we had decided that he would be an observer more than a participant.

I was surprised when Neasa met me at the door, although I shouldn't have been. She was decked out in one of her fancy outfits and greeted me with a smile. "Talon will send word if our guest arrives," she said as she matched steps with me.

To tell the truth, I was a bit relieved by her presence. I imagined that she might help soften the factor up.

"I took the liberty of hiring a litter," she said as we headed out to the porch.

Of course, I had to play the part of a rich man—and of course, I hadn't thought of it. I turned to her and bowed my head in gratitude. "Thank you."

Her face lit up and she tucked her arm into mine. "Let's go have some fun."

Visiting the factor's office didn't sound fun to me. She must have seen the look on my face, because she elaborated with a gleam in her eye. "We are going to look at money, right?"

The ride over was uneventful. My gut churned in anticipation of my meeting with Factor Einhardt. Neasa pretended that she didn't notice and chattered away like we were great friends. I didn't hear a word she said, but strangely enough, her voice helped me to stay calm.

When we arrived at the factor's office, I quickly stepped out of the litter and was surprised to see that Factor Einhardt stood waiting for me.

Einhardt was a typical Stenson factor. He was old. He wore a Stenson Blue coat, trousers and cap, as well as a fashionable gray goatee. And he had a shrewd gleam in his eye. I probably shouldn't have been surprised that he knew I was coming.

Einhardt bowed low, in the Eastern manner, and said, "Master Olaf, welcome to Xiang."

Because of my nerves, I had skipped breakfast that morning. Now I felt a pang in my gut that made me want to run back to the Golden Swan.

Neasa took hold of my left arm. "Master Einhardt," she said in an innocent yet sultry voice, "when do we get to see the silver?"

Einhardt looked a bit put out and yet aroused at the same time. Neasa had that effect on men, and his reaction made me laugh, which melted away my fear.

"Why not?" I said. "Let's start with the strong room."

The meeting went better than I'd expected. I even allowed Einhardt to stay on as my assistant in the Xiang office, to keep Stenson business flowing smoothly. In return, I ignored the fact that he had been stealing money from my family. Although I told him I was keeping the house in Gea and acted as though I thought it was Stenson property to begin with, we both knew the truth. He appeared relieved to get off so lightly.

We left just before the midday meal, and Einhardt walked us out. "Master Olaf, whatever you need," he said with deep respect. He spoke the words to me, but his eyes were on Neasa, where they had been throughout the morning. "I am here to serve."

Once we were back in the litter, Neasa let out a giggle. "I'm not sure if he drooled more over me or your family's silver."

I laughed. "It was the silver—definitely the silver."

Neasa pretended to pout, but then gave me a seductive smile. "The silver *was* exciting to look at." She traced her finger down my arm as the litter started to move. "It will take a while before we arrive at the Golden Swan …"

A shiver ran through me, but I quickly pulled my arm away. "Not that exciting, partner."

The pout came back for a moment, and then she shrugged. "Maybe you weren't looking at the same pile of silver."

I *had* been surprised by the amount of silver, and I'd been even more distracted by her hanging on my arm all morning. Her company had helped me deal with my nervousness, but I was determined to resist her. I loved Sofie—and even if I didn't, Neasa scared me even more when she acted so *friendly*.

When we got back to the Golden Swan, I heard an earful from Ivan. He was not happy that I had decided to keep Einhardt on instead of sending him back home.

"He will be trouble, Olaf, mark my words."

I was still a bit flustered from all of Neasa's attention and let it slide right off of me. "But I have you to keep an eye on him for me, Ivan," I replied.

Ivan gave me that look, as if he wanted to say something again, but the shook his head and took his leave. Eventually, I would have to find out what was bothering him.

CHAPTER 16: ALONG THE RIVER HUANG

Cao Wangsun came to the Golden Swan the next afternoon. Neasa and I met him in our sitting room with Bren and Gabriele attending us. My Wolf guards stood at the door.

Cao Wangsun strode in as if he owned the place. "This *is* nicer than my house," he said.

"And more private," Neasa added. She waved her arm to indicate the room. "No spies hiding behind curtains."

Cao Wangsun chuckled. "You made your point, Neasa—but it would be better if you stayed closer to the palace, in case my grandfather wishes to meet you." He paused and pretended to scan the room before continuing. "In any case, the courier has been punished for his lack of manners. There is no need to stay here." Eastern princes do not apologize to those of lesser rank, but by telling us he had punished the courier, he let us know he was embarrassed by it.

Neasa nodded to show him she understood.

"It might be better if we stayed here," I suggested. I tried to get him to look me in the eye. "My guess is you don't want your grandfather meddling in our plans. If he hears that we are staying at your house …"

Cao Wangsun faced me, his dark eyes burning. "My grandfather already knows you are here."

Neasa joined my argument. "But does he know that we are here with you? Olaf has a point—it would be less suspicious for us to stay here."

The young prince frowned at us, obviously not liking the idea. He stood there, thinking it through, and finally let out a sigh. "The fewer people who know of our alliance, the better—for now." He gave us a reluctant nod. "I will send word when it is time to go north."

"You will take us with you?" Neasa looked surprised. "Westerners cannot enter the Dai Jun's Castle."

"Westerners can travel to Sikk—but as you say, they are forbidden from entering Jungong." His was the smile of a politician, cold and calculating. "It is better for you to follow along. You should be close when I win my army."

I noticed he didn't quite answer her question. "I agree," I said. "We are allies in this, and I want to be there to assist you when you need me."

In truth, I had mixed feelings about going to Sikk. It was a site that few westerners had seen, and I wanted to see it—but the trip meant I would be away from Sofie that much longer. Cao Wangsun was my best hope for helping my uncle. I had no choice now.

Cao Wangsun's eyes lit up and he said, "Now that you mention assistance, I am in need of funds." He wore a long, green robe covered with intricate and colorful stitching of songbirds. With the addition of an equally decorated yellow cap and a bejeweled sword tucked into his yellow sash, he didn't appear needy.

He noticed my scrutiny and said, "I am preparing a site in Gea to house my new army, along with gathering ships for the crossing into Jewel." He tilted his head to one side and watched me out of the corner of his eye. "I don't think my grandfather would approve of the expense."

"Will a chest of Stenson silver be enough?"

A twitch of his eye was his only reaction, but it was enough for me to know I had surprised him with my quick agreement. "It will do." He didn't say "for now," but it was evident in his manner.

I nodded. "You will have it today."

Another eye twitch. I was sure it had not been a coincidence; now I knew how to read him. I held back a smile.

He turned to Neasa next. "My grandfather will not allow your birlinn on the Huang River."

The Huang River ran from Xiang on the coast to the Dai Jun's castle in Sikk. It was a major trade route for the Cao family, not to mention the most direct route to the Dai Jun. As such, the waterway was fiercely protected by the BaWang.

"We will find a way," Neasa said.

We stood there looking at each other for a long moment, and then Cao Wangsun bowed to us. "Prepare yourselves. I will send word when it is time to leave." He waited for us to return the bow and then spun around and left the room.

Neasa grinned at me. "We're going to visit the Dai Jun."

I nodded, but I didn't share her excitement. This was what I had come east to do. Why did I feel unease? Westerners weren't welcome in Sikk—so why did Cao Wangsun insist we come along?

It turned out my family owned several riverboats that were permitted to sail on the Huang River. It was a simple matter of ensuring that at least two such vessels were ready to take us aboard at any time. I say "simple" because it was simple for me. I left it up to Factor Einhardt to ensure the vessels were on standby for my use. While he didn't complain when I made the request, he got so red in the face that I worried that he would collapse.

It was the same day that I told him to send a chest of silver to Cao Wangsun. You would have thought I was asking him to spend his own money. Of course, he had treated the Stenson strong room as his own before my arrival, so maybe he *did* see it that way.

Neasa left a skeleton crew with her ships and sent the rest of her men to a Stenson warehouse close to the riverboats, then gave them strict orders to stay out of sight until we were ready to depart.

I sent Ivan and my other remaining Stenson guard to oversee them at the warehouse. Even with Carrog in charge of her Kail warriors there, I trusted Ivan more than him or any of the Stenson retainers in Xiang.

With our preparations complete, there was nothing to do but wait for a message from Cao Wangsun. It came sooner than I expected. Cao Wangsun would be leaving for Sikk with his grandfather, the BaWang.

The message instructed us to leave the next day, so as not to be caught in the inevitable congestion caused by the royal barge's passing. The final words of the message were, "Bring silver!" I had to chuckle at that. Apparently, one chest of silver had only whetted Cao Wangsun's appetite for more.

The next morning, we arrived at the warehouse just as the sun was rising and made for the pier. Ivan waited on the dock with Factor Einhardt at his side and a score of Stenson guards arrayed behind them. I hadn't expected such a reception. I was especially surprised to see Einhardt and all the guardsmen present. I only faltered for a moment before stepping forward to greet them.

Ivan spoke first. "Master Olaf, the factor feels that you need more protection," he said. He stepped forward and lowered his voice, "Because of the silver." I had directed Einhardt to provide several chests of silver for my trip, but I hadn't anticipated this.

Einhardt stepped up next. "You need sufficient guards for such a large sum." He looked determined and upset. I guessed that he was happy to see me go, but not the silver.

I looked over his shoulder at the guardsmen and wondered how many of them actually were loyal to Einhardt.

Ivan spoke up again. "I agree that we should bring more guardsmen along," he told Einhardt, "but not so many. We don't want to draw that much attention to ourselves."

"How many should we take, then?" I asked.

Ivan gestured behind him, and a handful of guardsmen stepped forward. "I have chosen a group of men to bolster your personal guard on this trip, in deference to Factor Einhardt's concerns."

I trusted Ivan's judgment more than Einhardt's feigned concern. He would have selected the most trustworthy guards to accompany us. I nodded my agreement. "Then it is settled."

Einhardt looked as though he wanted to argue some more, but I held up my hand to forestall him. "It is *settled*, Assistant Factor Einhardt. I'm counting on you to keep everything in order in my absence."

Einhardt puffed out his chest. He would, in effect, be the factor in my absence—and if I didn't return ... I could see the wheels turning behind his shrewd eyes. "As you wish, Factor Olaf."

Ivan dismissed the unchosen guardsmen and started heading toward the first river boat. As I watched them go, I caught the eye of the lone guardsman in their midst that had followed me from Kartoba. He had been in my service for several months. We had traveled together, in close quarters for all that time, and I hadn't bothered to learn his name. He quickly looked away and I suddenly felt ashamed.

"Wait!" I called and they stopped in their tracks. I had been distracted and self-absorbed, the very attributes I had always hated about wealthy men. The look in that guardsman's eyes had reminded me of growing up as "Olaf the Unlucky." I was looked down upon by everyone—including the other servants.

Now I stepped up to Ivan. "Introduce me to my new guardsmen."

If Ivan was surprised, he didn't show it. He called the men to attention and waited for them to line up before me. He started with the guardsman I had recognized. "As you know, this is guardsman Sigwald, who accompanied us from Kartoba." Sigwald was tall and slender, with a shock of blond hair. He wore a goatee with a full mustache that curled at the ends. He looked to be a couple of years older than me and gave me a flustered look as I nodded to him. Now that Ivan had named him, I remembered hearing his name in our time aboard the *Sea Cow*, but I hadn't paid attention at the time.

Ivan had chosen four other guardsmen to accompany us. They did look similar in their blue coats, but I tried to remember their names by focusing on distinguishing features. The first was easy because he was the only Easterner, named Li Wu from Gea. Ivan also introduced Yohann and Ulric, brothers from Highpoint in the Seven Kingdoms. Highpoint men loved their beards, and these two were no exception. Yohann had a full, bushy red beard and a twinkle in his eye. Ulric's beard was black as night and neatly trimmed, and his eyes looked more suspicious. He was also more slender than his stocky, older brother.

The last guardsman was named Rupert. He had such a weak chin that it looked like his goatee was sprouting from his neck. I greeted each of them with a nod and a smile. Then we boarded the waiting riverboat.

The riverboat looked more like a floating warehouse than a ship. It was rectangular in shape with just a slight rounding of the bow in front. Once we crossed the plank, we stood on a wooden deck that made up the top of the vessel and from which we could see quite a ways up the river. A team of mules was being hitched up near the bow, preparing to pull us upriver.

"Welcome aboard, Master Olaf," a man called out as I paused on the deck to watch the mule-hitching process.

I turned and spied an older man, maybe my Uncle Olaf's age. He was nearly bald, tall and thin, and wore a blue tunic that looked like it could use a good wash. He had just come up out of the interior of the vessel and now gestured toward the stairs leading below.

"We have prepared an area for you and your," he paused as if trying to remember the word, "entourage." He pronounced the word with a slight lisp and then smiled in triumph, showing off a gap where his front teeth should have been.

He looked so comical that I had to hold back a smile. "Thank you, Captain."

The man ducked his head in embarrassment. "Just call me Otto." He gestured to the stairs once more. "If Olga hears you call me Captain, I'll get no supper tonight."

I looked back at the mules once more, still curious.

"Don't worry," Otto reassured me, "the boy'll get them hitched soon enough and we'll be on our way." When I turned back toward the man, he had been joined by a young girl. She had blonde hair tied up in a braid and stick-thin arms. She wore a blue tunic to match her father's. I assumed he was her father by the obvious resemblance between the two.

"This here is Louise," Otto said. "She'll take you to your …" Again, he paused as if trying to remember the word. This time it took longer, and he finally frowned and said, "place."

Louise patted him on the arm and then smiled at us. "Come along, then."

As she led us down the stair, she chattered over her shoulder. "Everyone calls me Lulu, but you can call me Louise, if you like."

We reached the bottom in what appeared to be a cargo area. A line of crates had been tied in place along the forward bulkhead, but the majority of the space was taken up by several of Neasa's men, who were sprawled out on the deck, looking bored. A handful of them were playing dice in the corner.

Carrog looked up from the game and quickly stood and approached us. "Neasa," he called in greeting, "we are all tucked away, as you ordered." He gestured to the men around us. "Most are in the other boat, but I kept my best men here."

Neasa waved him away. "Just keep them out of trouble. I'll call for you once we're settled."

Carrog winked at me with his one good eye as he nodded to her and then returned to his game.

Lulu, who had waited for the exchange to end, continued with her tour. She turned to her right and headed toward the stern, leading us through a small doorway with a curtain. "This space is for you and your servants."

Ivan and my new Stenson guardsmen paused at the door. "We will settle on this side of the curtain," Ivan said. His look let me know that none of the Kail would get close enough to slip in unbidden. He pulled the curtain closed.

I looked around my new quarters. It wasn't very deep, but ran the width of the boat. The room had enough deck space for maybe a dozen people to lie down, if they packed in tightly. Bren and Gabriele were there, of course, as were my shadows, Moshe and Mehki.

Neasa and Talon had also followed along and now stood to one side. Neasa gave me a bold stare, hands on her hips, as if daring me to ask her to leave. Talon looked a bit hesitant, as if wondering if she would dismiss him.

Fortunately, Lulu broke the silence before it could get more awkward. "When we carry passengers, we sometimes divide up this area," she said. She moved to the table and grabbed another curtain that had been tied against the wooden bulkhead. "This can be pulled across to split the space in two."

"Yes, we will split the space," I announced. I told Neasa and Talon, "You can have that half." I pointed to the half without a bed.

Talon looked relieved and Neasa disappointed.

Lulu shrugged. "There is bedding along the wall there. You can set it up however you like."

She moved to the side of the boat and pushed a side hatch open, letting in a good deal of light. There was another hatch over on the opposite side of the boat. "These can stay open unless we tell you to close them."

She continued towards the back wall, where a set of wooden stairs led up to the next deck. "The kitchen is through here, and you can get back on the top deck this way, too." She paused and looked thoughtful for a moment. "Although, I would go the other way if my ma's in the kitchen cooking." That sounded ominous. The smile returned to her face as she turned to head up the stairs to the kitchen. "I'll call you for dinner."

Neasa opened the other hatch, letting fresh air flow through. I hadn't noticed how stale the air had been until she did so. She paused and gave me an innocent look. When I didn't respond, she laughed and called to Talon. "Let's go check on the men while they figure out our sleeping arrangements." She led him back through the curtained doorway. Talon gave me an embarrassed looked, but he followed her.

Bren shook his head. "She should sleep out there with her men."

His sister didn't agree. "She is the Dryhten's daughter and she deserves better accommodations." Gabriele moved to the bedding stored under the bench that ran along the wall and started sorting through it. "We have plenty of space here to share with her."

I didn't argue about it. I agreed, in fact, that we had the space—but I could imagine Neasa finding some way to make me regret it.

The boat had just lurched into motion, and I wanted to watch. I headed up the stairs with Bren and Mehki in tow. Moshe must have decided to rest up for the night shift. We passed through the kitchen along the way. I was relieved to see that Lulu's mother, Olga, was not present. We came out on deck near the back of the boat, where Otto was manning a large steering oar.

He nodded at us as we emerged. "Just shoving off," he growled. He pointed toward the bow, where the team of mules on the dock was pulling the boat along. "They'll get us through the channel and then we'll cut loose from there."

"Are those your mules?" I asked.

He shook his head. "We have to pay the locals to get through this channel." He shrugged in resignation. "Old Man Cao has to get his cut."

A boy led the mules along the dock, pulling us through the river channel. I could see another boat being towed just upstream, where the docks gave way to the river bank, and I looked back to see our second river boat being hitched to follow behind us. There was a line of boats being towed ahead of us and a line waiting their turn at the docks. Boys were leading mules back down from upstream.

"They claim that this is the only way to navigate the channel safely," Otto said from behind me. As I turned back to listen, he gestured toward the river to his left. A sandy beach stood on the other side of the channel we were navigating. It rose to

150

form a small island in the mouth of the river dominated by a fort that overlooked the river entrance.

I spied fishing boats in a channel on the other side of the island which appeared to be wider than the one we were on. "We could pole our way through the channel. It's not as deep, but it's passable," Otto said, shaking his head. "I could earn more silvers without having to pay for this passage."

The fort overlooked both channels and had a dock where several smaller ships were moored. Otto saw me looking and nodded. "Those paddleboats will run down anyone who tries to sneak through the other side."

I remembered paddleboats from my Eastern tutor. Instead of oars, they used paddlewheels built into each side of the boat. Several men were needed to turn the wheels. The paddleboats were supposed to be faster than boats with oars, and also easier to maneuver.

"I can't see the paddles," I said.

"They're covered by a wooden screen, except what's under the water," Otto said with a shrug. "They churn up the water pretty good, though. You'll see. They patrol the river between here and Jungong Castle."

By midmorning, we had cast free from the mules and had entered a wider section of the river where the two main channels came together. Now Otto and his two sons—whom he introduced as Steyn and Hans—started to row upriver.

Once we were sailing along smoothly, I headed back down below. In the cargo area, they had opened all the hatches. It was surprisingly light and airy, and cooler than standing on the deck in the sun. Neasa rested near one of the windows talking to Lulu and another woman I assumed was her mother, Olga. Olga had her back to me. She wore her blonde hair in a braid and wore a long blue tunic. She looked to be more stoutly built than her husband.

As I descended the stairs, I saw Lulu tug on her mother's tunic. Olga turned and saw me coming. She had been smiling as she talked with Neasa, but she scowled as soon as she saw me and turned away quickly. By the time I reached Neasa, Olga had exited through the curtain, heading toward the kitchen.

Had I imagined that look?

Lulu smiled at me. "Lunch will be ready soon. I need to go help my mother in the kitchen." She followed her mother through the curtain.

I turned to Neasa. "She didn't seem happy to see me."

Neasa feigned ignorance. "What do you mean?" But the saucy look on her face ruined her effort. She gave up and said in a more serious tone, "Maybe you should ask her."

"I haven't even met her!" I really had no idea why the boat's matron would react in such a way. Her husband and daughter seemed friendly enough, and the sons had pretty much ignored me on the deck earlier. I considered going to the kitchen to ask, but I remembered Lulu's earlier warning about avoiding the kitchen when her mother was cooking. I decided I'd have to find out later.

"It doesn't matter," I said. "She has no reason to dislike me."

Neasa just continued to gaze out the nearest window.

CHAPTER 17: FAMILY AFFAIRS

After a couple of days traveling upriver, we had to moor near the shore because the BaWang's barge had come into view. It was earlier in the evening than our normal stopping time, and I stood on the top deck to watch.

First came a paddle boat like the ones I had seen at the mouth of the river. It wasn't much bigger than our own riverboat, but it moved quickly, leaving twin wakes of heaving water, one on either side, churned up by the mysterious paddle wheels. Several soldiers stood on the paddleboat's deck and eyed us as they passed.

I wondered how many men it took to turn the paddle wheels that quickly. The wooden screens hid the men as well as the wheels from view.

I turned to Otto, who stood near his steering oar just behind me. "How many men are working those wheels?"

"Too many," he said. "I c-couldn't afford to feed them." I had gotten used to his verbal tick over the past couple of days and hardly noticed it anymore.

"You just need to have more sons," I joked.

He shook his head. "Not enough, even then." He nodded back to the other Stenson river boat, which was anchored next to us. "My eldest runs the other boat along with his wife and two of his … brothers."

I had no idea his family was so large. "You have been blessed with many children."

Otto snorted and gave me a look that said otherwise. I thought to press him further, but at that moment, the BaWang's barge came into view.

The barge was huge compared to every other craft that lined the river bank waiting for its passage. I counted ten long oars on the nearest side, and I assumed each oar was manned by a pair of rowers. They pulled the vessel through the water at a quick pace—not as fast as the paddleboat, but faster than any of the riverboats that plied the Huang River.

The deck of the vessel was dominated by a covered platform that boasted sheer curtains for walls. I could barely make out the people lounging behind the curtains as the barge glided past. Cao Wangsun would be somewhere behind that curtain, along with his grandfather, the BaWang.

Another paddleboat trailed behind the barge, ensuring that none of the stalled vessels cast free before the BaWang's barge had passed. As quick as the three vessels were moving, I realized they would arrive at the Dai Jung's castle much sooner than we would. "How long will it take us to reach Sikk?" I asked.

"Weeks," Otto replied. He pointed his thumb at the barge and its escorts, which were so far ahead they were fading from sight. "They will be there a week ahead of us … at least."

So much for a head start! I hoped Cao Wangsun didn't expect us any sooner. I also hoped he would wait until we arrived before scoring his bride-to-be and her army.

Otto looked up at the sky and frowned at the late afternoon clouds, which had started to turn dark purple. "The rains will be coming soon. We might as well stay here for the night."

I had encountered my share of storms on the *Sea Cow* as we'd traveled east, but they were nothing compared to the rainy season on the Huang River. Every evening, it was the same thing—rain so hard we had to shut the hatches in our cabin for fear of sinking.

I heard Bren sigh next to me. He had taken to shadowing my Wolf guard again, although I hoped he would give up on his obsession. This time, he stood next to Moshe, who wore his usual scowl.

"More rain," Bren grumbled.

Otto shrugged as he stepped past us to talk with his sons, who stood under a canopy near the center of the deck.

I turned to Bren. "You wanted to go to sea."

"This isn't the sea," he griped. "It rains so much here, the fish could swim in the air."

We had seen flying fish on the Sea of Silence, but I knew it would do no good to remind him. The rain started falling just as he spoke, and I led the way back down the ladder to our cabin. It was the closest ladder, but I hesitated at the hatch. We would have to pass through the kitchen, and that meant an encounter with Olga.

Olga had not warmed up to me at all. The dirty look she had given me on our first encounter had been the first of many. She never spoke to me—even when I addressed her—but preferred to let her face do the talking. Her face told me that she hated me but didn't supply a reason.

When I hit the bottom of the stair, I attempted to skirt through the boat's kitchen without her noticing. The kitchen was a tiny, hot room with an iron stove and several packed wooden counters and cabinets. Olga stood near the stove with her back to us. She was a good cook, and I could smell the fish stew she prepared for supper. It was one of the dishes she cooked most often, because the fish was free.

I tried slipping around the edge of the room to get to the stairs leading down to our cabin. I only made it two steps before she glanced over her shoulder and her eyes turned cold. Luckily, Lulu was standing next to her and called her attention back to the stove. Lulu was nothing like her mother; she was friendly—chatty, really—and had made it her mission to distract her mother whenever I was nearby. I gave her a nod of gratitude and slid across the room and down the stairs.

I had no idea why Olga disliked me. I couldn't ask her, and I was hesitant to ask Otto or Lulu. The brothers didn't talk much, either; they spent much of their time during the day rowing on deck, and in the evening, they retreated to the stable at the front of the boat. In the confines of the riverboat, I was getting tired of trying to avoid Olga without knowing why.

I entered the safety of the cabin and made my way to the nearest window, which was open only a crack because of the pouring rain. I peered out through the slit and pondered my predicament. Our progress upriver had been slow. The current didn't seem too strong, but it took great effort for Otto and his boys to row us against the tide each day. It now appeared it would be weeks before we reached our destination—and that meant weeks of Olga's angry stares. I had endured much worse growing up in Stenson House, but that part of my life was finally over.

I felt a sudden wave of shame for running from the old woman, which was quickly replaced by anger. My uncle was the richest man in the Seven Kingdoms and Olga worked for him. Why was I running from her? It was time to settle this! I squared my shoulders, determined to go back to the kitchen and have it out with Olga.

I headed for the steps to the kitchen but paused when I noticed Moshe and Bren moving to follow me. Most of the time, I barely noticed their presence at my back. This time, I felt I needed privacy. And besides, I didn't want my bodyguard stepping in if my conversation didn't go well. A vision of a furious Olga wielding a butcher knife popped into my head, and I shook it clear.

"Please stay here," I said. "I need to do something on my own."

Bren looked as though he would argue, but Moshe just nodded and put a restraining hand on my valet. "Don't let her scare you," he muttered.

I guess I shouldn't have been surprised that he had read my mind again. Sometimes it seemed as if he and his brother knew what I was thinking before I did. "Thanks," I replied, not bothering to hide my scowl.

Moshe rewarded me with a rare smile, obviously amused by my discomfort.

I headed back into the kitchen.

Lulu noticed me first and her eyes went wide. Olga glanced over her shoulder when she saw the look on her daughter's face. As expected, her eyes turned cold and her face froze into a scowl. When I headed towards the two, Lulu stepped forward while Olga turned, clutching a knife. Of course it was a coincidence: she had been chopping vegetables or fish for the stew. But the gleam of the blade brought a sudden image of Tessa's death.

The memory hit me like a kick to the groin, and I froze in place. I thought I had purged that memory—Sofie had helped me to overcome it. Sofie. Anger surged through me again at the thought of Sofie left behind, which helped me to shake free of the memory. I stalked two more steps towards Olga and stopped short when Lulu came to meet me.

"Master Olaf," Lulu said, her voice cracking. "Do you need something?" Her whole body was tense as she stood between me and her mother.

The look on her face almost made me back away, but then I looked back at her mother's cold eyes and decided to be direct. "Olga, why do you hate me?" I demanded.

The woman's eyes turned from cold to fire and she stabbed the knife down into the counter. "Why should I hate *Stensons*?" She made my family name sound like a curse. "It only makes it worse that you don't know."

She took a deep breath and blew it out slowly, making an effort to soften the look on her flushed face, but her eyes remained hot. "Ask my husband, if you don't know the cause. It's his story to tell." She turned back to her cooking, showing me her back.

Her unsatisfactory answer left me confused. I considered storming over and demanding an explanation.

"Master Olaf," Lulu squeaked, reminding me of her presence.

Seeing the look on Lulu's young face took some of the fire out of me. She had always been friendly to me and my people. Whatever her mother's problem was, she didn't seem to share it. I suddenly felt bad for the girl, but I was still determined to find an answer. I reached out and patted Lulu on the head before turning and heading to the stairs leading up to her father.

The rain still fell at a fast pace as I stepped out on the deck. There was a small canopy to keep the rain from the hatch, and I spied Otto and his sons huddled under the larger canopy that stood above the center hatch leading down to the cargo hold. It would have been dryer to head back below and come up the other hatch, but I was full of angry determination. I crossed over as quickly as I could, my bad leg forcing me to take careful steps on the wet deck.

Otto was talking with his sons: the two who helped him row our boat plus the brothers who managed the other Stenson riverboat. When we anchored for the evenings, they often tied the boats together and gathered on deck to gossip. I had seen them gather together on previous evenings, but hadn't realized they were all Otto's sons. Along with the brothers was another crewman from the other boat, an Easterner in their employ.

As I scuttled across the deck, they all looked over and Otto called out, "Master Olaf … is there a problem?"

They made room for me under the canopy and also for Lulu, who had followed me from the kitchen. As soon as we arrived, the deck hand from the other boat made a hasty departure, probably realizing that he wanted no part of the conversation. When the brothers started to scatter as well, Lulu called out in a surprisingly clear and commanding voice: "You all need to stay."

Standing under the canopy with Otto and his sons, I suddenly regretted leaving my guard behind. The two brothers from the other boat shared Steyn's husky build. I probably looked like a child compared to the three beefy brothers, and I was soaked from my walk across the deck. The rain had diluted my anger, it was hard to find the words with them all staring at me.

I needn't have worried, because Lulu took charge of the conversation. "Papa, Master Olaf wants to know why mama is

158

mad at him." If it was possible to make the situation more uncomfortable, that did it. The brothers all looked at each other. Hans, the youngest brother, looked angry, but the rest just looked as if they were trying to decide whether to speak or flee.

Otto blew out his breath in a long sigh and gave me an apologetic look. "It is old business," he finally said and then gave me a significant look. "Family bu-business."

The look confused me. Why would I know anything about *his* family business?

Otto looked disappointed and sighed again. "I was once the factor for Kar-kartoba—before your Uncle Karl exiled us to the east."

I was stunned. To have been the factor in Kartoba, Otto would have to be a Stenson relation! "What is your family name?" I asked. I felt bad that I had never wondered before. I'd been so wrapped up in my own concerns that I hadn't bothered to get to know this man.

"We are from the Ehrlich branch of the family."

Ehrlich—I had heard the name before. They had been strong supporters of Jarad Stenson, who had been the head of the family before Uncle Karl. When Jarad died, the Ehrlichs had fallen out of favor and had disappeared from Kartoba. It happened at about the same time that my mother died and I became a glorified servant. I was too young to remember any of the details, but I had heard the rumors when I got older.

"Uncle Karl was a mean old bastard," I said. "I had no idea."

Stenson family politics had been hard on my immediate family as well. The elder Jarad had become the head of the family when my grandfather was murdered by the Duke of Kartoba, and my Uncle Olaf was sent into exile. Uncle Jarad had looked after me and my mother until his own death , which I suspected was a murder at the hands of Uncle Karl. They had said it was a fever—the same fever that killed my mother—but I was sure it had been Karl that killed them both.

Now I understood why Olga might hate Stensons. She didn't know I had been as much a victim of Uncle Karl as the Ehrlich's.

"But why should she be mad at me?" I asked Otto. "Uncle Karl screwed us all."

Hans had been stewing throughout the conversation, but now he broke in. "The avenging hero regains control of the family," he snapped, "righting the wrongs against him and you, but what about *us*?"

He was referring to my Uncle Olaf taking back the family— but Olaf had been exiled even before the Ehrlichs. Like me, Olaf probably had no idea what had happened to the Ehrlichs.

Otto cuffed his youngest son. "Quiet!" Otto was normally so soft-spoken that his sudden action shocked everyone. "Do not embarrass your family name."

Hans was silent. He looked embarrassed.

Otto looked at each of his kids, one at a time. "Remember, we are part of the Stenson family," he said. He pointed at the deck. "This is a Stenson boat, and we are loyal to our own. We are loyal to the family." His speech rang out strong and true, with no trace of his usual stammer.

I was shamed by Otto's fidelity. His loyalty endured, even after being exiled from his home.

He finished by looking at me. "Olga is a hard-headed woman," he explained. "She has held onto this hate for many years on my … behalf. But it is time to put it behind us." He held out his hand.

I took his hand and said, "Nice to finally meet you, cousin." Then I shook hands with each of his sons. Even Hans gave me a smile.

When we were finished, Otto said, "I will speak with Olga."

"No," I replied. "I am heading back that way."

He looked concerned, but I only smiled back at him. "Don't worry, cousin, I won't start a brawl."

Lulu headed back toward the kitchen hatch with me, reaching out to take my hand. "I guess we're cousins, then?"

I remembered some of the female cousins I had to endure at Stenson House, especially Uncle Karl's daughters, and was happy to have found one that I liked. "Yes, I guess we are."

The rain had slowed enough that I didn't try to scramble across the deck this time. As we walked, Lulu confided in me. "Papa wouldn't let us tell you," she said. "Mama was just as mad at him as at you."

"She was mad at me because I didn't know?"

She nodded, "and at him for not letting us tell you."

When we entered the kitchen, Olga stood waiting. Was the look on her face as cold as it had been before? She noticed Lulu holding my hand and frowned.

I pulled free from Lulu and headed toward the opposite doorway, stopping just before I reached the curtain. Lulu now stood next to her mother, who hadn't moved. I gave Olga my best court bow and said, "Thank you for your hospitality, cousin."

Then I headed into my cabin. The shocked look on her face lightened my step.

We continued upriver the next morning. I avoided the kitchen, choosing to pass through the hold on my way to the top deck. I still wasn't sure of the reception I would receive from Olga.

Even with the hatches open, the hold smelled of too many bodies. I felt sorry for the men stuck in there, especially the Kail, who were not allowed on deck during the day for fear the other boatmen would recognize them.

We had been traveling with a group of about a dozen riverboats, but Otto had told me that they would split off when we reached the fork where the Huang and Chen rivers came together. Most of the other boats would be heading up the Chen River into the Sui province, while we would be following the Huang River to the Dai Jun's Palace in Sikk.

As I passed through the hold, Ivan followed me up to the deck. We hadn't spoken for a few days, and especially after my activities the previous day, he was looking for information.

"They are family," I told him as we arrived on deck.

"What?"

"The Ehrlichs are a branch of the Stenson family." I motioned toward the brothers rowing their long oars on either side of the boat. "They are my cousins, and I didn't know it." Ivan didn't look surprised, which made me wonder if he had already known.

"They will be loyal to you then," he said.

I looked at him sideways. "Of course."

He noticed my confusion. "I'm concerned about what happens when we split off from the other riverboats." He led me to the edge of the deck and we looked toward the other riverboats in our flotilla. "Once we reach the split in the river, most of them will be going the other way."

"Yes?" I wasn't sure what he was getting at, but he was making me nervous.

Ivan scratched at his chin, showing his own nervousness. "There will be fewer of us—and there are pirates even on this river," he said. "But mostly, I don't trust Factor Einhardt. He wanted to send along all those Stenson guards for a reason, and I fear leaving them behind won't stop whatever he might have planned."

Ivan hadn't shared his concerns until that moment, and to see him acting nervous made me downright terrified. "You think he would try to stop us?"

He shook his head. "No. I think he will try to kill you to keep you from coming back from Sikk."

"We still have Neasa's men."

Ivan nodded. "And he knows it. The best time to make his move will be after we split from the rest of the boats."

He reached out and gripped my shoulder. "Do me a favor. Keep your Wolf guards close. I would assign the Stenson guardsmen to follow you around as well—if I was sure I could trust them." He turned and headed back down the hatchway.

CHAPTER 18: SUSPICIOUS BEHAVIOR

Four days later, we landed at a town called Fenzhi, which was situated where the river Chen fed into the Huang River. We stopped long enough for Otto to trade for supplies and then headed up the Huang.

Two of the other boats headed upriver with us. As we made our way north of Fenzhi, I stood on the deck under the main canopy with Ivan looking for signs that they might be our enemies. The river ran a bit faster above the fork, and I could hear the Ehlrich brothers grunting with the effort of pulling their oars.

"I've been watching them since we left Xiang," Ivan confided, pointing to one of the boats. "That one is definitely not to be trusted."

"How do you know?"

"Every night on the river, they consistently moored as far from us as possible." He pointed toward the figures on the deck, which were close enough to count but not to see their faces clearly. "They have kept their distance, and the men on deck have changed multiple times during our journey."

I had good eyes, but not that good. "How can you tell?"

He smiled. "When your life depends upon what lies across the battlefield, you learn to look for these things."

It was not a comforting answer. Ivan chuckled as he pointed at the men again. "That one on the right is light on his feet and moves about the boat like he was raised on it—but the one on the left moves as if he would rather be on steady ground."

"Maybe he's new."

Ivan shook his head. "Different men were on deck yesterday, and they have changed more than once. I've counted at least a dozen different men on board—and I haven't noticed any women or children."

That was definitely a bad sign. The riverboats were typically family businesses. The wives and children worked just as hard as the men. Children learned the trade on their parent's boats and then either took over or bought their own. No one could afford to hire the dozen men it required to work a boat on the river.

"What do we do?" I asked.

"Watch them closely, and wait," Ivan said somberly. "If you trust your cousins, you may want to warn them to keep an eye on that boat."

"Why don't we just board them tonight when we moor near the shore?"

"What if I'm wrong?" Ivan raised an eyebrow. "Maybe they're carrying passengers."

I nodded. It would not help our cause to attack a boat of innocents just because Ivan found them suspicious. "What about the other boat?"

Ivan shrugged. "Looks normal to me."

This was the way things seemed to go for me. I resolved one issue, but suddenly found I needed to worry about another. After settling matters with Olga, I had hoped for some peace— and now I had to be concerned about a riverboat full of potential killers who might be waiting for an opportunity to attack us.

Fearing for my safety made me think again of Sofie. When we were together, she had a way of making all my fears fade. I tried to picture her smiling face, but could only remember her pale as she lay in her sickbed while I stole off to Xiang. I missed her intensely. I felt a sudden urge for sonti to dull the pain, but I knew that drowning my sorrows would further endanger me.

Several days passed. No one attacked our boat, and I began to wonder if Ivan had been imagining things. I stood on the deck in the evenings and watched as the boats moored. The riverboats tied up close together, but the boat Ivan had pointed out was always farthest away. While I could see a woman and a couple of young children on the closer boat, I never saw more than a couple of men on the suspicious one.

Even though Ivan had posted a watch on deck every night, I worried about the Stenson guardsmen we had picked up in Xiang. Were they in Factor Einhardt's employ?

I called a meeting in my cabin to discuss my concerns. We met in the evening, just after supper. I sat on the steps leading to the kitchen, while Otto perched nervously at my side and Ivan leaned against the bulkhead next to me. Neasa came strolling in from the hold with Talon and Carrog in tow. Carrog sported his normal, cocky grin while Talon looked uncomfortable trailing behind his lover.

"It is a pleasure to see you, Olaf," Neasa called out as they entered the room. "Why have you called me here?"

It was her cabin as well as mine, and she and Talon spent every evening there. She was playing it up for everyone in the room, to taunt me. She wore a simple tunic, not as short or revealing as the one she preferred on her own ship, and had put her dark hair up in a braid in imitation of Olga's. She had been dressed that way since coming on board. I assumed she was trying to gain Olga as an ally.

I sat back and let Ivan explain his concerns to the group.

Carrog was the first to respond. "So we take them tonight! We have more than enough warriors."

Neasa nodded. "My men are getting restless. They need a little action." She led the other two to the bench on the opposite wall and took a seat. Talon sat next to her, but Carrog continued standing, probably too excited at the prospect of action to sit.

Otto spoke up. "My sons are boatmen … not warriors."

"Don't worry," Neasa said. "My warriors will handle it."

"But we can't just attack them," I said. It bothered me that they had the same initial thought that I'd had. I almost felt embarrassed to share Ivan's words from our earlier conversation. "What if we're wrong? We can't just attack innocent people." I avoided looking in his direction as I said it.

Neasa gave an indifferent shrug, but Carrog was not so easily persuaded. "Why take the chance? If they are a threat, we kill them all and keep the boat. If they're innocent," he smiled at the word, "then we kill them all and sink the boat. Either way, we can share in the spoils."

Spending so much *peaceful* time with Neasa and her men, I had forgotten that they were pirates by trade. So it came as a surprise when Neasa spoke against his plan.

"This isn't the sea, Carrog," she said. She stood and somehow seemed to tower over the giant warrior. "We have to tread more lightly here. Besides," she added, tossing her head as if dismissing him, "the water is too shallow. If we had to sink the boats, they would block the river."

Boats? She had actually considered taking both the other boats and killing all the people on board. Her plan made sense if we were worried about witnesses—which meant she didn't care whether they were innocent or not, even though Ivan had made it plain that we did not suspect the second boat.

Otto caught the implication as well. He stood and visibly shook as he replied, "I don't know the people on the first boat, but the other boat belongs to Master Kong and his family. We have w-worked together for years."

"We won't be killing anybody," I broke in, trying not to let my own anger take control. "Unless they attack us first. We just need to keep a watch on them until we reach Sikk."

Carrog had backed down from Neasa, and now Otto visibly relaxed. Neasa raised one mocking eyebrow. "Well, then, I'll make sure my men are ready—just in case you change your mind."

I took a deep breath to calm myself before replying. "Please pass the word to your men on the other boat and ask them to keep an eye out also. I would also like you to set a watch on the deck in the evening here."

Neasa's eyes darted to Ivan, still leaning on the wall, and back to me. She knew we had a guardsmen watch set since leaving Xiang. Her face didn't betray any of her thoughts as she replied. "*All* my men can be trusted."

She turned and headed back out the curtain to the hold. Carrog gave me a sheepish look before following her out. Talon seemed even more embarrassed. He hadn't spoken at all during the meeting, and he seemed to be conflicted about his role with Neasa. I resolved to try to pull him aside as soon as I could manage it. I needed to figure out what was on his mind.

Several more days passed. Talon clung tightly to Neasa, so I couldn't pull him aside to talk. Tension hung in the air, but nothing happened.

On the fourth day, just before the midday meal, we prepared to enter the first river canal. Ivan and I were up on deck when Otto and his sons began to row toward the right bank of the river. Up ahead, a shack stood on the bank where the channel split. I moved to where Otto steered the craft with his oar. He saw me coming and waved toward the shack.

"It is the gate keeper's post," he called. He continued to roll his oar in the sweeping motion that both propelled and steered the boat.

Two canals flanked the Huang River between Qiang and the Dai Jun's Castle in Sikk. They ran parallel to the river in the places where it was too rough or rocky for the riverboats to navigate the river.

Otto had told me the day before that the boats would be vulnerable here, in the narrow channel of the canals, and also when we had to traverse a slipway farther up river. In those parts of our journey, the boats would be confined and, in the case of the slipway, dependent upon mules for passage.

We had determined that an attack, if it was going to happen, would most likely occur before we reached the slipway. Because the boats had to be dragged through the slipway, everyone would have to disembark. The attackers would probably want to make their move before that happened. When I spoke to Ivan about it, we agreed that an attack on one of the canals seemed the most likely.

I turned to Otto. "What if they try to go first?" We had discussed this as well. We had been leading the way upriver, and the suspicious boat has been at the rear. If they tried to enter the canal first, blocking our progress, we would be trapped.

Ivan answered for him. "If they try to pass us now, then we attack them first." I knew the answer, and we were ready—all the warriors were waiting just below the deck ladders, on both boats, with weapons in hand—but I still hoped it wouldn't come to that.

Otto didn't like the idea either, but he nodded. "They would have no other reason to pass us."

I resisted the urge to look back. I didn't want to make them suspicious by watching. Instead, I studied the canal entrance. The gatekeeper waved to us as we approached, and the wooden canal gate stood open.

As we continued to glide towards the canal entrance, I found myself holding my breath. Once we reached the shack on the riverbank I finally started to relax. "Not this time," I muttered under my breath.

The gatekeeper stood leaning on a rail next to the shack. He waved and called out to us as we passed. I didn't quite get what he said—my Eastern language skills were not quite up to it—so I turned to Otto for a translation.

He gave me a relieved smile. "He says the canal is clear to the next water gate."

I looked back and saw that the suspicious riverboat hadn't moved from its position at the end of the line. I turned to Ivan. "Maybe we were wrong about that boat?"

Ivan shrugged and stomped off toward the ladder, no doubt to pass the word to the men below.

Once we passed through the open water gate, the canal widened enough to accommodate two boats across, but we stayed in single file in case of traffic heading downriver.

"How long till we reach the next water gate?" I asked Otto.

Otto grinned as he swept his oar. "We're making good time now. We'll be there soon enough."

I had learned that the river people moved at their own pace and didn't seem too concerned about the passage of time. "Soon enough" was the normal answer to such questions.

I went and sat on the deck in the shade of the center canopy. Now that the danger seemed to have passed, I took my ease and watched the land pass by. The canal bank was higher than the riverbank and was lined with timbers and mud. Also, the trees had been cut back on both sides of the canal, I guessed to stop fallen trees from blocking the waterway. There was a dirt trail that ran along the right bank of the canal, but it was empty of traffic. The regularity of the scene and the smoothness of our passage now eased my nerves.

I found myself daydreaming. I wondered how Sofie fared back in Gea and wondered if my mission would be successful. If it all turned out okay in the end, would I marry her? She wasn't rich or from a prominent family, but did that really matter? Visions of Sofie and I—married, raising a family, and growing old together—warmed me as I lay back on the deck and relaxed.

I woke to Hans' voice calling to his father. "A tree in the canal!"

I sat up and looked around with blurry eyes. Mehki stood over me, and Bren sat by my side, looking alarmed. I couldn't see the tree from the deck, so I reached out for Mehki to help me stand. He pulled me to my feet.

A huge tree lay across the canal, its wide trunk and large canopy of branches blocking our path. It was far enough away that we had time to stop.

My first thought was, "How could a tree have fallen there?" The canal was well-maintained, and I remembered seeing that the trees had been cleared on both sides. I looked to verify, and the land was still cleared as it was before.

Otto and his sons had stopped rowing and were now dragging their oars in the water to slow the riverboat. As we drew closer, a group of men appeared on the left bank from behind the tree's canopy, and another group emerged from the trees next to the dirt trail on the right.

I felt a sinking feeling in my stomach and turned back to look at the last boat in our flotilla. The deck was covered with armed men now, and it was speeding up to pass the third boat. I pointed back at the attackers and cried out to Otto, "Warn the other boat!" I pushed Bren toward the ladder down to the hold. "Warn the others!"

He hesitated for a moment, looking like he wanted to stay by my side, but then turned and bolted down the ladder. The men on the bank started shouting and an arrow tore through the canopy above to drive into the deck at my feet with a loud smack.

Suddenly, arrows began dropping all around. Mehki pushed forward to shield me, but I heard Steyn cry out to my left and his oar thudded against the side of the boat as it dropped from his hands. In the next instant, I was surrounded by Stenson guardsmen and Ivan was shouting in my ear to get off the deck. The world spun as I was dragged down the ladder into the hold below.

My heart was pounding. Moshe and Bren were holding me up while Ivan shouted into my face. "You have to stay down here!" I nodded my understanding and he raced back up the ladder. The rest of the guardsmen and the Kail warriors were all on deck.

I looked around the empty hold. Blankets, clothing, and other items lay strewn across the deck where the men had scrambled to respond to the attack. The side hatches were still open, but Moshe ran around pulling them closed. While he did that, Mehki took up station at the ladder way. I stood in the middle of the hold with Bren and tried to still my pounding heart.

Despite the clamor of shouting and feet and arrows striking the deck above, the sound of the curtain being drawn from the cabin snapped my head around. Moshe reacted quicker than I, ready to strike whoever came through. Lulu peeked out around the doorframe and her face lit up at the sight of me, but with Moshe's axe poised, she hesitated to move. Gabriele appeared next to her, looking just as frightened.

Moshe gave a quick nod and both women rushed over to stand with Bren and me. Lulu wrapped herself around my waist, burying her face in my chest. "Cousin!" she cried and held on so tightly that I struggled to take a breath.

"We're okay," I said as I stroked her golden hair. I looked to Gabriele, who stood next to her brother, and she gave me a little nod to indicate that she was okay, but her hands were white and shaking as she clasped them together. Bren looked white-faced as well, but determined. He had his sword out and he looked ready to use it. That reminded me of my own sword, which still hung on my belt. Again, I hadn't even thought to draw it.

My mind started working again and I took stock of who was present. Gabriele would have already been in the cabin, but Lulu would have come from the kitchen, where she normally helped her mother cook. I looked back at the curtain, expecting to see Olga, but she didn't appear. "Where is your mother?"

Lulu raised her face from my chest. Tears welled in her eyes as she pointed to the deck above.

I couldn't imagine what had possessed her mother to run up on to the deck into danger, especially since we had so many warriors on board. "Why did she go up?"

Lulu seemed surprised by the question. "My father and brothers are up there." She pulled back from me and gave me a fierce look. "She wouldn't let me go. She told me to go to the cabin."

Olga was neither small nor weak, and we hadn't seen eye-to-eye since I came on board, but I worried about her being on the deck for Lulu's sake. I didn't know what to say, so I patted the young girl on the head.

The boat suddenly shook as it impacted with the bank. Lulu caught me as I lost my balance and saved me from falling. Bren rushed over to the nearest hatchway that faced the right bank and peered out through the crack. "Neasa's men are jumping onto the bank."

I could hear the clashing of weapons now from the bank. Ivan's head appeared from the deck above. "Go to the kitchen ladder," he ordered. "We'll call you up from there if we have to flee."

Moshe hurried through the curtain at the back of the hold and Mehki all but pushed me along in his wake. Bren and the women followed us, but I don't think my Wolf guards cared if they came or not. I dragged my feet for a moment to yell at him, "They stay with us."

He gave me a curt nod but didn't slow as he pushed me through the cabin and up the kitchen stairs. Lulu cried out as we entered the kitchen. Otto lay on the kitchen floor with an arrow sticking out of his shoulder and blood staining his tunic. Lulu rushed to his side as Moshe took up station near the deck ladder and Mehki at the entrance to the cabin.

Lulu and Gabriele hovered over Otto. My cousin was holding the arrow tight with his hand where it pierced his skin as if trying to hold in the blood. Lulu pulled his hand away and held it tight while Gabriele ripped away the tunic surrounding the wound to get a better look.

Otto cried out and his whole body shuddered. "No, leave it," he managed to say through clenched teeth. He looked up at me with a grimace. "Make sure Lulu is safe."

Gabriele cut away a piece of Otto's tunic and wadded it up to press into the wound. She looked up at me. "I don't know what to do besides stop the bleeding." Her face was even whiter than before, but she had a determined look in her eye. "Do we pull it out?"

"No," Mehki called from behind me. "It is in too deep. Stop the blood, and stop the arrow from moving." He understood our language, but didn't speak it well. He spoke in Imperial, so I translated for Gabriele.

She nodded and wrapped another scrap of tunic around the shaft of the arrow and under Otto's arm and across his shoulder. After she was done, she looked at me and then back at Mehki to see if she had done it right.

Mehki nodded.

Otto's breathing had been heavy, but now he let out a long sigh and slumped against the wall.

"Papa!" Lulu leaned over him checking to ensure he still breathed.

"I'm still here." Otto reached out his good arm and patted her on the head. He didn't open his eyes though, and I was concerned with the amount of blood on his tunic.

"It's all we can do," Mehki said. He didn't sound very hopeful.

When I tried to look him in the eye, he looked away and my heart sank. I remembered hearing Steyn cry out on deck, and I feared the worst for him. I had no idea about the rest of Otto's family, but I couldn't bear the thought of Otto dying. He was my cousin, and he didn't deserve to die on my account.

"We take him with us," I announced to my wolf guards. "If we have to go, we will take him with us."

Mehki ignored my words, but Moshe—his younger, more serious brother—scowled at me and said, "We are here to protect *you*, Master Olaf."

"Otto is family!" I snapped back. "He goes."

Mehki continued to ignore me and Moshe just shrugged and went back to watching the deck hatch. I wasn't sure if they would listen, but I saw that Bren had put away his sword and he and his sister stood on either side of Otto, to help him if needed. I nodded my thanks to them and then said to Lulu, "Stay with me if we have to go. Bren and Gabriele will help your father."

She nodded but stayed huddled next to her father's side.

The waiting was unbearable. I had time to think about Steyn, and Otto bleeding on the floor, and all the people I knew up on the deck fighting on my behalf. Was Steyn dead already? Would Otto live? What about Olga, who had rushed onto the deck to the defense of her family?

Neasa, Talon, Ivan, even Carrog—would they survive this fight? Waiting was hard when others were in danger, but all I could do was hope for the best.

The stove still smoldered in the corner and the kitchen was stifling hot with so many people inside, but we dare not open the hatch for air. The oppressive heat only made it worse. My fear mixed with the sweat on my body, and it felt as though my heart would explode with anxiety. It made me wish I was on deck with the rest. At least it would be cooler, and I would know who was alive.

I made a move toward the deck ladder, and Mehki put a hand on my shoulder. "We wait here."

"But what if they're all dead?" Just saying the words doubled my anxiety. It felt like I would jump out of my skin if we didn't do something soon.

Mehki and his brother shared a look and Moshe nodded before heading up the ladder. He cracked open the hatch to peek out. A rush of deliciously cool air entered through the hatch clearing my mind of the panic, and I let out a little sigh.

"Shit!" Moshe cried as he let go the hatch and all but tumbled down the ladder. Before he hit the deck, the boat shuddered from another impact. I heard Otto groan and Lulu cry out as I fell against Mehki.

Somehow, he caught me while calling out to his brother. "What is it?"

Moshe pulled himself to his feet and said, "The other boats." He pointed back to the hold. "We have to get out the other way, now!"

Mehki grabbed me by the collar and pulled me through the doorway leading to the main and hold.

"Wait!" I tried to pull away, but now he had an iron grip on my arm and didn't listen.

"They'll come," he said as he pulled me through the cabin and into the hold. We were met by one of the Stenson guards coming down the ladder.

It was Li Wu, the Stenson guardsman from Gea. "Ivan says to come now. We have to get off the boat."

Sudden suspicion flooded through me. Ivan hadn't trusted all the guardsmen, and Li Wu was the only Easterner in the bunch.

"Come now!" Li Wu called again and then headed back up the ladder.

I jumped as Lulu grabbed my other arm. Then I looked back to see Otto being carried by my servants with Moshe guarding their rear.

Mehki pulled my attention back to him and then let go my arm. "Follow me—closely," he commanded. "Moshe will watch out for the rest."

I had my doubts, but there was no time to argue—and I'll admit that I was too frightened to put up a fight. Mehki headed up the ladder and I followed with Lulu clinging to my coat.

The din of clanging weapons and screaming fighters assaulted my ears. Smoke blew across the deck, clouding my vision and threatening to bring me to my knees.

"This way!" I heard Li Wu shout from across the deck. Mehki gripped my arm again and dragged me across the deck while I hacked and coughed. I could feel the heat of a fire and hear the crackle of the flames on the opposite side of the river boat.

I stumbled into the short rail at the edge of the deck and fell over it and onto the bank below. It was a short fall, and Mehki yanked me back to my feet. Somehow, Lulu had managed to cling to my coat. Now she grabbed my free arm and held on as I tried to survey the scene.

To my relief, it looked as though our fighters had cleared the right bank. Carrog was leading an assault against the remaining attackers, his blue tattoos glowing with sweat as he screamed in defiance. I could see Ivan and a couple of other blue coats in the mix of Kail warriors as well as Hans Ehrlich, Otto's youngest and smallest son, wielding his oar like a giant club.

I looked back for the rest of my party and saw that the tree and the boat were both on fire. Bren and Gabriele appeared out of the smoke, still dragging Otto between them. Somehow, they saw the rail in time and managed to jump over to us, Moshe still on their heels. Otto was heavy, and they fell hard onto the bank. Lulu let go my arm and rushed over to her father's side.

The arrow had broken from the fall, but Otto was somehow still alive and conscious. "I'm okay," he kept saying over and over again as Bren and Gabriele struggled to get him back on his feet.

Moshe got his brother's attention and said, "The boats are all jammed up against the tree, and they're coming across."

"Get away from the bank!" Neasa's shrill voice rang out. She stood in the road next to the canal, her left arm around Talon, leaning on him for support and waving toward us with the sword in her right hand. Carrog and the rest of the fighters were behind her, returning from routing the attackers on this bank of the canal.

"They're crossing over on the boats," Mehki told her as he grabbed my arm again and pulled me toward our fighters in the road.

Ivan and two remaining Stenson guards—Sigwald, his white teeth smiling through his smoke-stained fancy mustache, and Ulric, one of the bearded brothers from Highpoint—stepped forward to surround me with their protection. Ivan nodded to Li Wu, who had led us from the boat, and then looked me over for damage.

"You look well-rested."

Before I could reply, Carrog led a charge against the boats as Neasa and Talon approached. "Let's hope the fire keeps them from crossing." Neasa's tunic was covered in blood. I hoped it was not her own, although she was leaning heavily on Talon.

"What about your men on the other boat?" I asked.

She nodded toward the warriors being led by Carrog. "Most are here, but a few stayed behind to hold off the attackers." She looked tired, or maybe injured. She must have noticed the concern on my face, because she grimaced and pulled herself away from Talon. "I need to go to my men."

Talon tried to hold her back, but she shrugged him off and walked stiffly past me to join her men guarding our position. Talon frowned at me and followed in her wake.

"Stubborn woman," Ivan muttered. Then he turned to me with a question in his eye. "How fast can you run if they break through?"

I looked down at my twisted leg and then gave him an equally twisted scowl. He already knew the answer.

He nodded. "Then you should head for the trees now and look for a safe place of concealment."

Hiding in the kitchen had been nerve-wracking and had nearly broken my resolve; I couldn't stomach the idea of doing it again. I looked around at the bodies on the road, men who had fallen while I hunkered below deck, and gritted my teeth. No matter what happened, I wasn't hiding again. I shook my head no.

To my surprise, Ivan smiled at my reaction. "Well then," he said, "let's prepare for a fight."

He instructed Bren and Gabriele to drag Otto to a safer position behind us. Lulu, of course, went with her father. Ivan asked Bren to stay with them, but he refused, saying that he belonged by my side. Ivan didn't argue. Instead, he asked Li Wu to stay and guard them.

We took up position behind the Kail warriors: Ivan and his two remaining guardsmen in front, a Wolf guard on either side of me, and Bren guarding my rear. Although I was now surrounded by more competent warriors than I would ever be, I finally pulled out my sword. Then, we waited.

Waiting on a battlefield was not something I would recommend. I could smell blood and guts, which brought back the memory of butchering days back at Stenson House. That thought turned my stomach more than the smell.

I thought it would be better when the wind shifted and smoke from the burning river boat blew toward us. Unfortunately, there were also bodies on the boat, and along with the wood smoke, I could smell the nauseatingly sweet scent of burning flesh. I immediately imagined Steyn's body burning on the deck and had to choke back the bile in my throat.

We waited for what seemed like hours, until the boats were burned so completely that no one could cross them. Ivan finally seemed to relax and turned back to me with another rare smile. "I guess we get to live today."

CHAPTER 19: A TEMPORARY SETBACK

The riverboats were a jumble of burnt wood next to the tree that blocked the canal. Luckily, the forth riverboat in our flotilla had survived. It had pulled back from the battle raging around the tree. Once the battle was over, the riverboat pulled to the shore so the crew could check on us.

Carrog had stationed men to watch the road and the canal, and the remainder of the Kail were busy cleaning up the bodies. Talon and Ivan had set up a makeshift hospital on the side of the road where they treated the wounded with the help of Gabriele and Lulu.

Neasa and I, along with Bren and my Wolf guards, went to meet the boat as it pulled to shore. I brought along my remaining Stenson guardsmen, in case it was a trick. As the riverboat approached the bank, one of the men on deck threw a line to Ulric. I recognized the man who had thrown the line; it was one of Otto's sons from our second riverboat. I didn't know his name, but I remembered his face.

As soon as the boat hit the bank, he jumped ashore and called, "Where is my family?"

I pointed to the make-shift hospital at the edge of the trees, and he hurried past us.

Next came another of Otto's sons, but he paused on the bank long enough to help his pregnant wife down from the riverboat before following his brother.

"They are Otto's sons," I explained to Neasa. She snorted at me to let me know that I was not telling her something she didn't already know.

I was surprised she had the energy even for that. She had been wounded during the fight and still had bloodstains on the side of her tunic where the spear had pierced her—but she refused to stay still once her wound had been treated. Her face, normally the hue of a tanned sailor, now looked as if she had never seen the sunlight.

She noticed me looking and grimaced. "If it was going to kill me, it would've done so by now," she snarled. She had a point. And I knew Talon would have never left her side if he thought she was dying.

Two Kail warriors climbed down next and looked a bit shame-faced as they approached Neasa. I listened in as they reported to her. "We held them off until the fire pushed us back," the taller of the two said. They were both smoke-blackened, and the one that had spoken had singed hair and was reddened from the fire on his right side, probably because he was naked except for a loincloth. They smelled like that had just stepped out of a campfire.

"Where is Peredur?"

The taller warrior hung his head, exposing more of his burned scalp. "He fell during the fight." He looked up again and gave her a fierce grin, white teeth shining through his darkened face. "He led the attack on their boat. He was screaming like 'The Fiend' himself. Last I saw, he was wading through them like wheat at the harvest."

Neasa gave him a quick nod of dismissal and the two warriors shuffled past us to greet their companions working in the road.

I wanted to ask Neasa about Peredur. I already knew that Carrog's nickname was "The Fiend," although I hadn't realized his reputation was so great among the rest of Neasa's men. Seeing the look on her face, though, I decided to save the question for a later time. Neasa often seemed just as dangerous

180

as any man to me, but I had never seen her look as grim as she did in that moment.

Finally, Master Kong, the boat's owner, appeared at the rail of the boat and called across to us. "We pulled your friends out of the water," he said.

Master Kong looked old to me, maybe as old as Otto, but it was hard to tell with Easterners. His hair was still black, but his face was lined and his back hunched. He wore the Eastern-style baggy trousers and a light gray coat. His sash was a light shade of red, which told me that his family was from Gea.

A younger version of Master Kong—I guessed his son—was working to moor the boat next to the bank with the help of my Stenson guardsmen. Watching them, I suddenly realized that we had lost everything we'd had onboard.

"Do you have supplies?" I asked. "Food? Canvas for tents?"

Master Kong's face turned from friendly to calculating within the blink of an eye. "What do you have to trade? Stenson silver?"

I instinctively looked toward the smoking wreckage that had been my family's riverboats. There had been plenty of silver aboard, but now it was at the bottom of the canal. The canal wasn't so deep that it couldn't be recovered—but how long would that take?

I glanced back to the Kong riverboat and noticed that the younger Kong had paused in his mooring activities and the elder looked ready to flee if I gave the wrong answer. I heard a chuckle from where Neasa stood beside me. She didn't look amused though. "Do you think you can pull away," she called to the Kongs, "before my warriors gut your little boat?"

Master Kong and his son froze in place. Neasa had a good point, and I had no doubt that she meant it, but I didn't want to threaten Master Kong. I had made a pact with myself that I would change the way my family did business.

I cleared my throat to try to disperse the sudden tension and get all their attention. "Master Kong, have you ever considered working for my family?"

The Kong's had been traveling with us along the river. He obviously knew who I was by his earlier remark about Stenson silver. I hoped the Stenson family reputation hadn't been tarnished too badly by the greed of my deceased Uncle Karl and factors like Jorn Einhardt.

The old riverboat man looked as though he considered my offer, but finally said, "Will I have to work with the Factor in Xiang?"

I had originally planned to let Einhardt keep his job, but I was now convinced he had been the one who planned the attack. His actions had ruined any chance of keeping his position—or his life, if I caught up to him.

"No," I assured him. "You will be working for me or another factor of my choosing. The current Stenson Factor in Xiang will be … retiring as soon as I return to the city."

Eastern faces were hard for me to read, but the smile that Master Kong shot my way left no doubt of his answer. He gestured toward the deck of his riverboat. "My boat is yours, Master Stenson."

"It's Master Olaf," I corrected and then said to the Stenson guards, "Go aboard and see what we can use." Just as I gave the order, Ivan walked up and said, "Once we unload supplies, Master Kong, you will head back downstream and inform the gatekeeper of what has happened?"

Leave it to Ivan to be thinking ahead. We would need help in clearing the wreckage and recovering the silver. The quickest route was back down the canal. Why not load everyone on board and head back downstream?

When I asked Ivan and Neasa that very question, I received scowls from both of them.

Neasa spoke first. "I will not run from these bandits!"

Ivan quickly added, "We will not all fit, anyway, and we dare not leave the wreckage for the bandits to sift through." He was thinking of the silver.

I realized they were both right and nodded in agreement. "Then we gather what supplies we can from Master Kong's riverboat and hunker down until they come back with help?"

"It seems the best plan," Ivan answered.

Neasa nodded. "We should send a few men along for protection," she added. I wasn't sure if she wanted to protect the Kongs or didn't trust them. Either way, it was a good idea.

"I'll send Li Wu," Ivan offered. "He can be trusted and will reinforce that the boat is now under Stenson domain."

"And I'll send Carrog and couple of others along," Neasa offered, giving Ivan a smug look, "in case they need to *protect* something." That was fine with me. I had come to like the giant Kail warrior and even trust him—somewhat.

Once supplies were unloaded, Otto, who was now resting on the side of the road with a massive bandage where the arrow used to be, insisted one of his sons also accompany the Kongs. "We know the river and are known," he said. "He can help with anyone who doubts it is a Stenson venture."

I was actually surprised he had enough strength to speak so many words after his ordeal, especially after learning of the deaths of his wife and two sons. The man was made of stern stuff though, because he looked more defiant than broken. He even seemed to have lost his stutter.

My newly acquired riverboat headed back downriver with Li Wu; Carrog and two of his men; and Walden Ehrlich, Otto's oldest son, who had captained our second riverboat. Walden's pregnant wife accompanied him as well.

Otto's family had suffered from the attack. Besides losing the two riverboats, Otto had lost his wife Olga, his son Steyn, and another son, Bertram, from the second boat.

That evening, I went to check on Otto. When he saw me coming, he shooed away his surviving sons, Koenrad and Hans, who had been hovering over him all afternoon. Lulu still clung to his side as I sat down next to him on the grass. He looked pale, but he had been able to eat and it looked as though the arrow had missed anything vital. I felt bad for what happened and wanted to let him know.

"I am sorry about your family," I started out, but he quickly interrupted me.

"The river gives, and the river takes away," he said. His voice was gruff, but I could see the pain of loss in his eyes.

"Yes, but this wasn't the river."

He waved my words away with the back of his hand. "It doesn't matter the cause, Olaf. The gods will take their due." I winced at his words. He had to be beyond caring if he risked mentioning the gods.

"Papa!" Lulu scolded him with a frightened look on her young face.

Otto let out a harsh chuckle. "Oh, they can take me if they want."

Lulu flashed me a concerned look, as if she expected me to convince him to live. I did feel responsible. He was my cousin, and now his family had suffered great loss because of me. He wouldn't have even been on the river if my Uncle Karl hadn't exiled him …

"You can't die," I blurted at him. "I need you."

Otto looked skeptical. "You need a boatman without a boat?"

"No," I shot back. "I need a new factor in the east, once I dispose of the one that tried to kill me."

"Factor Einhardt did this?"

I nodded. "And you can help me get even. I need a man to replace him—someone who will root out all his corruption. Someone I can trust."

Otto's eyes lit up, but he wasn't ready to admit that he wanted the job. "I can't make any promises, Master Olaf." He pointed his chin toward the bandage on his wounded shoulder. "I might still be heading for the Halls of the Dead."

Lulu smiled at me as she squeezed her father's hand.

"I forbid it," I quipped. "The family still needs you."

As I stood to leave, I could see Otto's spirit return. I hoped he would survive—not just because of my guilt, but because I realized that I truly did need him as factor in the east.

The next morning, the sound of a galloping horse roused me out of my sleep. I had slept in a tent we had offloaded from the riverboat. I sat up quickly at the thundering of the horse's hooves and was surprised to see daylight streaming through the tent opening. Moshe was still snoring in the corner as I rose, but no one else was present. As I approached the tent opening, Mehki pulled it open.

"What's going on?" I asked.

He nodded toward the road from the south and said, "A horseman is here."

Yes, his answer was a deliberate attempt to annoy me. Mehki found me amusing, especially when I was annoyed or flustered.

I ignored his comment and headed to the edge of the camp, where I could see a man dismounting from his steed. A crowd of Neasa's warriors was already there, but they moved aside as I approached.

The rider wore yellow trousers and coat with a green sash. Yellow was the color worn by the BaWang's soldiers. The green sash meant this man was somehow related to the Dai Jun.

I stepped up next to Neasa, who stood waiting to greet the rider. Talon, who was always close by her side, held the horse as the rider approached us. "I have been dispatched north to pass the word of the attack on your riverboats," the rider announced.

"Master Kong reached you, then?" I asked.

He nodded. "He stopped at the river gate to inform us of the attack. He has headed downriver to Fenzhi for supplies." While he was talking, Gabriele stepped forward and handed the man a cup of water. The rider took the cup and downed the contents in one long gulp before turning back to us. "Soldiers from the river gate are on the way behind me." He took the reins from Talon and hoisted himself back into the saddle. "The Dai Jun will hear of this, I assure you."

We moved out of the way to allow him to pass. "Be careful on the road," Neasa said. "Some of the bandits escaped the fight."

The man waved and whipped his horse onto the road heading north and was soon lost to sight.

Once he had gone, the crowd of warriors began to disperse back to their respective duties. Neasa looked me over as if inspecting one of her men. "Sleep well?"

Embarrassed for sleeping late, I gave her a quick nod and headed back to my tent.

Neasa followed as if I had invited her along. "We saved some breakfast," she said. Gabriele, Talon, and Bren followed in our footsteps—along with Mehki, of course.

"That would be nice," I replied. With those words, Gabriele rushed past me to prepare a plate.

Neasa laughed. "Sleep late—have a pretty girl serve your meals—that must be a terrible life." She seemed in high spirits for someone who had lost several men and had been wounded herself. Of course, she was a Kail warrior—so she was probably used to it. Kail women, especially, had to be even more bloodthirsty to earn the respect of the men. I shouldn't have been surprised by her apparent happiness after a fight.

"Who was Peredur?" I asked, watching her from the corner of my eye. It was a dirty trick, but I had no desire to play along with her happy game.

Anger flashed across her face, but she quickly hid it. "He was one of my captains … one of the best."

I instantly felt bad. She was an ally, after all. Even if she could be annoying, I shouldn't have taunted her about her loss.

"But it was a good fight," she snapped, "and he died well." She grabbed my shoulder to halt me in my tracks and spun me around to look me in the eye, suddenly serious. "Who could ask for more than that?"

Her eyes bored into mine for a brief instant. It felt as though I saw her for the first time: a woman among men, fighting to control her own future. She knew she was just as likely to end up dead, like Peredur, as she was to gain the freedom she craved.

She released her grip on me. "Enjoy your breakfast, partner."

My shoulder was sore where she had grabbed me, even though she still walked stiffly from her own wound. I was suddenly glad that she was my ally.

That evening, as the sun was setting, the soldiers from the water gate arrived. Carrog and his two warriors were with them. I must have looked surprised to see him, because Carrog called out to me as he passed.

"I'm no merchant's guard dog, Olaf!" he said, winking at me. "Unless you want me to guard *your* silver. You paid me to stay by your side, after all."

What was it about seeing blood and death that made the Kail so happy? Shouldn't the disastrous battle have had the opposite effect? They were all so cheerful, it made me want to scream. I turned my back to him and returned to my tent. Now that help had arrived, we could start trying to recover the silver. That was worth cheering about.

The soldiers got to work the next day, along with our men, clearing away the burnt wreckage. I met the man in charge of our relief force that next morning at breakfast. His name was Jiang Yin. It turned out that he was a cousin to the Dai Jun and was in charge of the security of the Huang River canal system.

Jiang Yin had been inspecting the lower gate when the attack occurred. It was fortunate for us, because it meant more men were available than otherwise would have been. Even though he wore the uniform of the BaWang, Jiang Yin also spoke with the Dai Jun's authority. He had sent a missive to Fenzhi ordering carpenters and tools to be sent to help clear the canal.

"We won't make much progress without the carpenters, and especially their tools," he explained as we sat before my tent, dining on rice and dried fish for breakfast.

Jiang Yin was tall for an Easterner and wore his long, dark hair tied at the back, topped by an elaborate, yellow-dyed felt cap with a green dragon embroidered on the front. The dragon was the symbol for the Dai family. Except for the cap, he didn't look much different from the majority of the BaWang's yellow-clad soldiers. He was the only one sporting a green sash, which reflected his affiliation with the Dai Jun.

He sat on a rug outside my tent with me and Neasa. Bren sat at my back, playing the dutiful valet, while his sister served our breakfast. Jiang Yin had a valet of his own, who stood just behind him as we ate. His valet looked ready to cut us into little pieces if we so much as looked askance at his master. He alone, among the Easterners, was armored beyond their typical long coats and trousers. He wore a sleeveless hide coat that was painted with green lacquer to match Jiang Yin's sash, as well as a matching green helmet.

Moshe and Mehki were both awake, and they stayed close to me, eyeing Jiang Yin's servant like a pair of hounds ready to pounce on their quarry.

Jiang Yin noticed their attention and remarked, "Your men appear to be on edge."

"No more than yours," I replied.

He looked over his shoulder and then chuckled. "Huai always looks like that."

I envied Jiang Yin's easy manner. While I had gotten used to my Wolf guards—I even liked them now—their constant attention still made me uncomfortable. "My uncle insists upon them," I said.

Jiang Yin smiled. "As does mine, Master Olaf." He spread his arms as if claiming the world around us. "Such is the life of men like us."

Men like *us*? Had he grown up shoveling horse shit or watching pigs root in the forest? I knew the answer just by looking at his too-perfect face and the expensive cut of his clothes. I had to fight back a sudden surge of anger. Rich men like Jiang Yin had shit on me most of my life. How could he compare himself to me?

We finished our meal in silence as I pondered his words. *Was* I just like Jiang Yin? Did I look down on everyone around me because I suddenly had my uncle's wealth at my disposal? I didn't think that was the case—but who would give me a straight answer to my question?

CHAPTER 20: ANOTHER ROAD

As Jiang Yin predicted, we didn't make much progress on clearing the wreckage until the carpenters arrived with their tools. While we waited for them, Jiang Yin sent his men out into the surrounding countryside in search of the bandits—but the marauders had disappeared.

With Jiang Yin's soldiers now taking care of security, Neasa had her warriors concentrated on salvaging the wreckage. A few of her men were good divers, and they were able to get inside the hold of our sunken and burnt riverboats. Before long, they uncovered my uncle's silver; it was now safely tucked away in my tent.

While we waited for Master Kong's riverboat to return, Ivan hounded me about going back to Xiang. "We need to deal with Einhardt," he argued. "The longer we stay here, the more time he has to plan another attack."

I shared his concern. Of course, I regretted my decision to keep Einhardt on—but I was still determined to complete my uncle's mission. "My uncle sent me here for a reason, Ivan," I argued, "I cannot let him down."

Each time I made that argument, Ivan gave me the same look—the one that said he knew something that I didn't. I sensed that he still wanted to tell me, but kept quiet instead. I was afraid to ask—afraid it was something I didn't want to know. My relationship with Ivan became a never-ending game of awkward silences and even more awkard arguments.

About two weeks later, Master Kong finally arrived, along with two more riverboats. They carried supplies, carpenters, and more soldiers. The day the riverboats came, Jiang Yin took his leave of us to continue his inspection tour. He left a contingent of soldiers behind to maintain security at the camp as he headed north toward the next canal gate.

As we watched the boats being unloaded, Ivan tried one last time to convince me to return to Xiang.

"Olaf, it is time to go back," he said. "We must deal with Einhardt so that you can take your proper place as the Eastern Factor."

I had heard the argument many times, yet he seemed especially determined now. "Why didn't you try to talk me into this before we left Xiang?" I asked. "You knew he couldn't be trusted, but you didn't argue about leaving then."

When he went silent again, I finally screwed up the courage to ask: "What aren't you telling me?"

When he didn't reply, I looked up in exasperation, expecting to see the same, stone-faced, awkward expression he usually wore. Instead, Ivan looked concerned. "If you don't go back now, Olaf, I fear it will be too late."

"Too late for what?"

But the awkward look returned and he turned away. "This isn't what your uncle wanted," he muttered as he strode away.

"What do you mean?" I called after him, but he ignored me.

Damn Ivan and his vague mumbling! He knew my uncle better than I did—but I knew he was wrong in this. Uncle Olaf had asked me to stir up trouble in the east. I couldn't complete that mission from the factor's office in Xiang! Going to Sikk was the best way to fulfill this task.

Ivan had spurred me into action. I realized that it was going to take too long to clear the canal, and we had heard that riverboats were waiting upstream. If we traveled a few days up the road, we could probably purchase passage upriver from there.

Two days later, we reached the waiting riverboats. I left it up to Otto to procure us passage to continue our journey.

The rest of the trip to Sikk was uneventful. Otto and Neasa both recovered from their wounds, and Lulu seemed to enjoy working with Gabriele. Before long, Lulu started acting like her old self, often pestering me in the evenings for stories of my Uncle Olaf or the Stenson estate in Kartoba. We arrived in the town of Sikk a week later.

The Huang River ended at a lake surrounded by a ridge of hills. The town of Sikk stood between the lake and the ridge. The Dai Jun's castle dominated the ridge like a giant beast hovering over the town. Otto was standing next to me as we moored near the town. "It is called Jungong, the Dai Jun's castle—but I've heard it called Dragon Castle, too."

It made sense. I could see the castle as a giant dragon perched on the ridge. Also, I knew from my childhood tutors that the Dai Jun was known as the Azule Dragon. This was supposedly because he was descended from the gods and had supernatural powers. I had never seen any real magic—and like my countrymen, I had no desire to meet a god, real or imaginary. A shiver ran up my back at the thought.

"I've never seen the castle up close," Otto said. "We are not allowed to enter Jungong. Only Easterners are allowed entry. It is forbidden for us to even set foot on the ridge."

Another shiver ran up my back as I gazed up at the forbidding castle.

Because of my difficulties with Ivan, Otto and I had spent a great deal of time together since the bandit attack. He seemed content with his new role as my factor, and we had gotten to know each other better. We spoke of many things—but not everything.

"Why did you come here?" he suddenly asked. "You cannot visit the castle."

He must have been wondering for some time. His face looked more serious than I had seen since his wounding. He probably also wondered why I brought along the Kail warriors and so much silver, too.

While I had come to like and trust Otto, I didn't think it wise to let him in on all my plans. "I have always wanted to see it," I finally lied.

I could tell Otto wasn't convinced, but he didn't ask again. A moment later, he left my side and I was alone with my thoughts—or at least, as alone as I could be with a valet and a pair of Wolf guards constantly following me around.

Our hired boats had landed at a dock at the opposite end of the lake. Two riverboats were moored there, waiting to travel south. The boats and dock belonged to my family, along with a small warehouse where we stored cargo—mostly the barrels of salt bound for the Dai Jun's table. Otto obviously knew the place well. He waved to the families on the two boats as we disembarked. The Kail warriors caused quite a stir, with the families crowding the boat decks to watch.

A man came out from the warehouse to meet us. He was dressed in Eastern garb, but his trousers and long coat were Stenson blue in color with a green sash for a belt. "Welcome, Master Olaf!" he called as he came out to greet us.

It irked me that he knew I was coming. Our travel to Sikk was supposed to be a secret. Of course, word of the attack on our riverboats surely made it to Sikk before we could, so I shouldn't have been surprised.

"I am Tang Sheng, head clerk of the warehouse here in Sikk." He bowed to me as I approached.

"Thank you for the welcome," I replied. "I believe you know my factor, Master Ehrlich?"

Tang Sheng obviously knew Otto, but he did not know I had made him a Stenson factor. He bowed to Otto as well. "Factor Otto."

"We will be in town for a little while," I said. "I'm hoping you know of a good place to stay."

Tang Sheng eyed the warriors standing behind me on the dock. "Umm …"

"The warriors can stay here at the warehouse," I added. I counted out the people coming with me in my head. "I will need enough space for ten people—and I hope it will be not too far from here."

Tang Sheng gave me another, deeper bow and blurted out, "My home is yours, Master Olaf."

How much money does a clerk make? I wondered.

"That won't be necessary," Otto said giving me an apologetic look for interrupting. He obviously knew the man. Maybe he knew the house wasn't that big. "We can stay at the Happy Dragon."

Tang Sheng looked up from his bow in relief. "Yes, Factor Otto."

Otto nodded in return. "Please take care of billeting Master Olaf's men. I will arrange his lodging."

Tang Sheng bowed once more to Otto and then moved off to see to the warriors.

Otto leaned in close to me and said, "His house is probably large enough to put you up, but he would have to move his wife and children out to do it."

"I'm sure the Happy Dragon will be fine," I said. It couldn't be any worse than sleeping in the hold of a riverboat, or a ship's deck—and I'd spent many nights in both.

Otto nodded. "It is close to here, and it's respectable."

I decided to leave most of the silver at the warehouse with my Stenson guardsmen, under Ivan's watchful eye. I was happy to leave Ivan behind as well. He had avoided speaking to me since our last awkward conversation.

Bren carried my small trunk, and Gabriele and Lulu brought along supplies. With little fanfare, we headed to the Happy Dragon. It didn't surprise me that Neasa followed along without being asked, even though I planned for her to join us. She didn't say a word, just nodded to Carrog as we left, apparently leaving him in charge of her warriors in our absence.

Sikk didn't look much different than Xiang in size or composition, but one thing was noticeably different. With the Dai Jun's castle hanging over their heads like a brooding dragon, I expected the mood in Sikk to be subdued. Easterners were rather somber—even more serious than my own countrymen, who were known for being grim compared to the Kail. I was surprised by all the smiles and happy greetings as we made our way to the Happy Dragon.

I turned to Otto and asked, "Is this normal?"

He knew what I meant, and gave me a smile of his own. "It's a happy place. It's my favorite part of the trip."

I looked around our group and noticed that everyone had begun to cheer up in response to all the friendly greetings. Even Mehki and Moshe looked cheerful. I found myself beginning to smile as well—until I spied Cao Wangsun standing in the road ahead of us. He was surrounded by a sea of yellow coats, his hangers-on, and he was not smiling.

"Neasa," he called out. "I heard about the attack. I hope you are uninjured."

His voice sounded concerned, but his face did not look it. We stopped in the street as he stepped out before us. "I hope my silver is intact," he said to me in a low voice.

I gave him a slight nod, and he suddenly perked up. "Well, you are here now. Where are you staying?"

"We were heading to the Happy Dragon," Neasa answered.

He nodded. "Good! I shall meet you there later this evening." He turned and continued on his way as though we hadn't even spoken.

"Friendly fellow," I quipped to Neasa.

She gave me a broad smile. "So is the gloomy Olaf finally gone?" She hooked her hand around my arm. "It's about time. I was beginning to get bored with your scowling face."

It was true that I had been avoiding her for most of our trip on the Huang River—but since the bandit attack, I had wanted to give her time to heal. And honestly, I still had no idea how to deal with the woman. I tried to pull my arm free as we continued our journey, but she clutched it and giggled.

"Oh no, Master Olaf! You're not ignoring me in the great city of Sikk." She pulled me along as though we were a happy couple. "I want to go sight-seeing while we're here." She flashed me a devilish grin. "I wonder where they keep their silver?"

Her mood was infectious, and I found myself grinning as we made our way to the inn. But in the back of my mind, I worried about Cao Wangsun's greeting on the road. I understood that he didn't want to let on that we were allied, but I'd felt a coldness from him that hadn't been present at our last meeting.

CHAPTER 21: A CHANCE ENCOUNTER?

The Happy Dragon lived up to its name. The people attending us were all smiles and looked genuinely happy to see us. It was a typical Eastern-style building with a peaked roof, huge columns, and paper-thin walls. In fact, I was pretty sure the walls were made of paper, but I was afraid to touch them for fear of ripping the fabric. Paper was very expensive in the west.

Once Neasa had latched onto me, she refused to let go. She sat by my side throughout dinner, trying her best to be entertaining without actually succeeding. Talon sat on her opposite side, looking dejected. She paid him no mind, which made me feel bad. She had never acted quite this friendly toward me in front of him before. I thought about asking her to leave me alone, but she seemed a bit out of sorts, as if her joviality was forced.

Sikk was far from the ocean. I wondered if that's what made her nervous. "Is it strange for you, being so far from the sea?" I asked, interrupting her latest bad attempt at humor.

Neasa paused with a handful of rice on its way to her mouth. She dropped the rice back on her plate and wiped her hand on the table cloth. We were dining with Talon and Otto, with my servants and Wolf guards hovering in the background, as usual.

Neasa looked around at the rest of our party before replying in a low voice, as if she didn't want to be overheard. "It is strange not being able to smell the sea—not being on the water, really." The smile had slipped from her face as she said it.

"We could have stayed closer to the river."

"It's not the same." She stared at her hand as if inspecting it for stray grains of rice, then tossed her head and snorted out a short laugh. "You are more than you seem, Olaf Stenson."

Suddenly, she rose to her feet and exclaimed, "I'm tired." Without another word, she headed toward her room. Talon quickly jumped up to follow her.

Otto watched her go. "A strong woman, that one," he said. "They're not worth the trouble." He went back to eating his meal.

Remembering how troublesome his late wife had been, I believed Otto knew what he was talking about—although the comment seemed a bit harsh in light of Olga's recent death.

After our dinner conversation, I dreaded facing Neasa the next morning, so I decided to head out into the city early, before she was up. I had never liked sleeping late, anyway. When we worked in the stables, Bren and I would rise before the dawn to feed the animals. When I pulled myself out of bed early the next morning to head into the city, I was not surprised to find Bren already dressed and waiting for me.

"You normally lay abed a bit longer," he remarked as he started to prepare my clothes.

"The black suit today," I told him, and he nodded. I didn't want to stand out in my Stenson blue coat. I told Bren to leave his blue coat behind as well.

We left the Happy Dragon, just the two of us, with my Wolf guards in tow.

"Where are we going?" Bren asked as we slipped out of the inn.

"Does it matter?" To tell the truth, I had no clue. I just felt an urge to get away.

Bren shrugged and walked along beside me. My Wolf guards were our silent shadows as we wandered down the road.

We headed away from the river and toward the Dai Jun's castle, which loomed overhead. The streets of Sikk were cleaner than most, and only a few people were out—probably early morning workers heading for their shops. The street outside the Happy Dragon was topped with crushed rock, to minimize ruts I suspected, with wooden walkways lining both sides. It appeared as though the rocks were swept back into place every night.

I almost felt bad for walking on the roadway, but we stayed in the road to avoid the shop owners as they were setting out their wares for the day. As I had noticed the day before, the people of Sikk seemed happy. They offered polite nods and friendly smiles as we passed, even to my Wolf guards with their impassive faces and deadly-looking axes.

We had barely made it a block from the inn when I heard a voice calling my name.

"Cousin Olaf, wait for me!" It was Lulu, hurrying to catch up to us. She arrived out of breath but with a big smile on her face. "You will need a guide," she exclaimed.

She held out her hand for me to take. Of course, she was wearing her Stenson blue dress, which spoiled my attempt to keep a low profile—but how inconspicuous could I really be with a pair of armed Wolf guards dogging my steps?

"Do you know Sikk well?" I asked.

When I didn't immediately take her hand, she grabbed mine instead and started to lead me down the street. "Of course! I've spent half my life here."

I hadn't thought to ask, but I was glad to have her along. To be honest, I liked Lulu more than I cared to admit. She felt like the little sister I'd never had. "Well, lead on then."

"This is the market district," she said as we walked past various shops. "They mostly sell western goods shipped up from Xiang." She cupped her hand to her mouth in order to whisper to me. "This is where the rich people shop."

While I was technically rich, I had no desire to buy some trinket that I could get cheaper back home. "Where do regular people shop?" I whispered back.

"Hopefully, they buy breakfast somewhere," Bren mumbled, reminding me that we had skipped eating in order to avoid Neasa.

Lulu let out a happy little laugh and turned left at the next street crossing, pulling me along. "Trader Square is this way. It's where the locals go." She winked at Bren. "The meat buns are my favorite."

Meat buns sounded much better than the rice porridge we had eaten for breakfast aboard the riverboat. My mouth began to water as we walked toward Trader Square.

One street over from the market district, the wooden walkways disappeared—and soon after, the crushed rock roadway vanished as well. By the time we reached Trader Square, the road looked no different than anywhere else: dirt with ruts from the trader carts.

Trader Square was a wide open space, but it was already bustling with early morning shoppers. Established stalls occupied the outskirts, but the middle of the square was a hodge-podge of tables, blankets, or carts set up by farmers and traders to sell their wares. It was surprisingly quiet compared to the market in Kartoba, although it was loud enough that I missed what Lulu said as she pulled us into the bustling crowd.

Lulu took a quick left turn as soon as we entered the square and followed the line of stalls to one that pictured a steaming bun on the sign overhead. I could smell roasted pork as soon as we drew close.

An older-looking, Eastern gentleman with a long white mustache hanging down past his chin sat on a stool behind a small table, wearing a greasy apron. He looked at ease and not in much of a hurry as he took coins from the customers waiting in line and called back to a pair of women—one quite young and the other close to his own age—who were pulling buns out of what looked like a giant wooden steam pot.

My mouth watered at the sight and I had to fight an urge to push my way to the front of the crowd. Unfortunately, quite a few people were in line ahead of us, so I resigned to wait my turn.

Just when we were about to step up to the old man at the table, a horn blast sounded behind us. I turned toward the commotion and spied a patch of yellow and green across the square. Everyone else in the square stopped and turned to look as well.

I recognized the yellow group as Cao Wangsun and his gaggle of courtiers. Even from a distance, his swaggering walk was easy to recognize. The green turned out to be a group of soldiers in green-lacquered armor, similar to that worn by Jiang Yin's bodyguard, whom we had met on the canal road.

"It's the princess," Lulu called out to me over the noise. "The Dai Jun's granddaughter."

"And her future husband," I mouthed under my breath.

"Should we go and see what she looks like?" Bren asked.

A crowd began to form around the royal shoppers. The common people of Sikk hoped to catch a glimpse of their princess.

"She looks like a child," said a girl who stood in line behind us. "She is only twelve, after all."

The girl who spoke wore a tattered, Eastern dress that had once been dark green in color, but now looked washed-out. When she turned toward me, I could see a huge purple mark covered her left cheek from just below her eye to the tip of her mouth. It wasn't a bruise, but looked to be a birthmark. The mark was in the shape of a butterfly.

It looked as if a large, purple butterfly had landed on her cheek. This was enough to make me pause, but the really striking part of her appearance was her eyes. The right one was a dark brown, like the eyes of most Easterners—but her left eye was a shade of blue so light in color that it appeared to be almost white.

Her appearance had been enough to startle me. Just as shocking was the fact that she had spoken to me in my own tongue—not Eastern or Imperial, but the western tongue of my homeland!

She laughed at the look on my face and twirled around once, as if showing off her tattered dress. "I am a princess, too! And I just turned sixteen."

The old man sitting at the bun table behind me called out to her as she twirled. I didn't understand what he said, but she called back to him and passed me in line to stand before his table.

Lulu leaned in toward me and whispered, "She is called the Butterfly Princess." Pointing toward her own cheek, she added, "Because of the ..."

"*Princess?*"

Lulu shrugged. "She tells everyone she's a princess, and they all play along."

"How does she know our tongue?"

Lulu called out to the girl, "Princess!"

The beggar girl twirled around and spied Lulu. "Lulu, you're back!" She rushed over and wrapped my cousin in a huge hug.

Lulu gave me a satisfied smile. "I taught her. We're friends."

The Butterfly Princess pulled herself free from Lulu because she had a meat bun in each hand. "You should forget about going to see that boring princess and get some of Ren's meat buns instead. They're the best in Sikk."

I was still so startled by her appearance that I could think of nothing to say.

She leaned in close, as if looking to see if I was daft. "What's wrong—wolf got your tongue?"

The girl was spooky. Why would she say *wolf?* How would a beggar girl in Sikk know of my uncle's sigil? She must have seen the wolf's head on Moshe and Mehki's tunics.

When I continued to stare, she seemed to become self-conscious. She backed away and turned her head sideways so that her dark hair fell across her birth mark. It reminded me of the first time I had met Tessa. She had hidden her ruined cheek in the same manner, with the same head tilt and the same dark hair cascading down the left side of her face.

I had tried so hard to forget Tessa. Now she had come back to haunt me in the form of an Eastern beggar girl.

The Butterfly Princess frowned and addressed Lulu. "Your cousin is no fun," she said as she headed away, tossing one of the buns to a man standing in the crowd who seemed to have appeared out of nowhere. She turned back once and said to me, "Will you come and visit me in my castle? You can bring all your friends." Then she skipped away, followed by the man to whom she had thrown the bun.

It took me a moment to pull myself together. I was still struggling to push the memory of Tessa back down into the recesses of my mind. Finally, I turned to Lulu and asked, "Who is that girl?"

Lulu seemed confused by my question. "She's just someone who lives here," she said. "I've played with her since I was little."

"But where does she live?" I knew that I raised my voice, but it was hard to control my emotions after my brush with Tessa's memory.

Lulu shrugged and looked as if she was beginning to get upset. "I'm not sure. I've only played with her in the streets. She's ... just a street girl."

Bren had remained quiet throughout the encounter, but he now spoke up. "How did she know you were Lulu's cousin?"

Lulu looked as if she were about to cry. "I don't know."

Seeing Lulu's welling eyes calmed my own emotions. I patted her on the shoulder and then took her hand once more. "It doesn't matter," I said. "Let's get some buns and head back to the inn."

The buns were delicious—almost good enough to make me forget about the strange girl. We bought extra and brought them back to the Happy Dragon to share with the rest of our party. Neasa met us at the door to our suite of rooms, looking upset at having been left behind, but she quickly perked up once she bit into a bun. The effect of the food didn't last long.

I considered ignoring her, as I had done on the riverboat, but the look on her face made me feel bad, so I approached her instead. She was kneeling at the low table the Easterners preferred, so I plopped down on a cushion next to her.

"Neasa, I am sorry for leaving without you this morning. I just had to get out and stretch my leg." I smacked my bad leg as a joke, hoping to cheer her up.

"It's not that, Olaf." She looked more worried than angry, which frightened me. She looked down at her hands, rubbing the tips of her fingers together as she continued speaking. "I had another vision last night."

My stomach clenched into a knot. Gods and visions were always bad news! My first thought was to get up and leave before she could share details of her vision. Instead, I tried to play it off. "We all have bad dreams, Neasa. If you ignore them, they'll fade away."

"This wasn't a dream, Olaf. It was a *vision*, sent from my ancestor."

"The raven again?"

She nodded. "You were in a dark place, alone—and I could not come to your aid."

I shivered, not wanting to hear any more, but I couldn't pull myself away.

"An angry dragon guarded your cage." She finally raised her chin and looked me in the eye. "But I also saw you standing before the very same dragon, and I was by your side." She shook her head. "I'm not sure which one is real."

"Neither was *real*," I snapped. "They are just nightmares. You need to forget about them."

I wished I could forget them, too. The Dai Jun was known as the Azure Dragon. Was he the dragon from her vision? I shook myself to clear the thought.

"We should leave now," Neasa said, "before the Dai Jun notices you are here." She turned back to the table and picked up her tea cup to take a sip. I noticed that her hand was shaking.

We both knew it was too late for that. The Dai Jun would have heard of the attack on our riverboats, which means he knew I was in Sikk. Cao Wangsun had known the moment we arrived in town, and I assumed the Dai Jun knew as well. It was definitely too late to run away now.

"I am here to help my uncle, Neasa, and to help my people survive. I can't run away because you had a vision."

Neasa paused and gave me a quizzical smile. "Do you remember the first time we met?"

It had been on the docks of Kartoba, when I had accompanied Talon to find passage on a Kail ship. She had been fierce-looking and alluring, dressed in her tattered green tunic that left little to the imagination. I would probably never forget that encounter.

"You looked like a pathetic boy next to Talon that day. I remembered thinking, 'What is this crippled boy doing with such a beautiful warrior?' "

I looked to where Talon was standing across the room, having a conversation with Bren. Neasa must have asked him to leave us alone, because he normally stayed by her side. He had changed since that day on the docks. We were still friends, but he seemed less sure of himself and more worried about Neasa. I knew he had fallen hard for her, and I worried that it would not end well for him.

Neasa's initial assessment of me wasn't a surprise. People had always treated me like shit before my Uncle Olaf took control of the Stenson family. Now, they only respected me for his money. Why Neasa chose to remind me of it now, I had no idea—but hearing her first impression of me didn't improve my mood.

Neasa noticed where I was looking. "Talon is a beautiful man and a good warrior, but I think I may have been blinded by his looks that day." She leaned her shoulder into mine for a brief moment and then pulled away. "I didn't see you for what you are."

Watching Talon glance nervously over his shoulder toward us as she said the words angered me. She obviously wanted something from me and was trying to win me the same way she had won Talon.

"And what am I to you now, Neasa?" I asked. I was pretty sure I kept the anger out of my voice, but equally sure that my face showed it. I looked straight ahead as I waited for her reply.

She let out a little laugh as she rose from the floor to look down at me. "My *partner*, of course."

I bit off a bitter reply and watched her slink over to Talon and put her arm around his shoulder. The look of relief on his face made my stomach churn.

I contemplated getting up and going over to give her a piece of my mind, but a commotion at the door drew my attention. Cao Wangsun rushed in with just a pair of his followers in attendance. He quickly scanned the room and spied me seated at the low table. He looked angry as he strode over toward my table, and he was intercepted by Moshe's axe before he could get close. Moshe called out as he moved to intercept Cao Wangsun, and Mehki appeared from my room where he had been napping, quicker than I would have imagined.

Cao Wangsun stopped short, in sudden surprise at the axe barring his path. His two shadows quickly pulled out their swords as well, but he waved them away and took a step back from my Wolf guards. "What have you done, Stenson?"

I had no idea what had set him off, but it couldn't be good. I motioned for Bren to help me to my feet, and he pulled me up off the floor. "I have no idea what you're talking about."

Cao Wangsun stared at me like I was an idiot, then he took a calming breath before explaining. "The Dai Jun has ordered you to Jungong."

"What?" Neasa stepped over to stand next to me with Talon glued to her side. "I thought westerners weren't allowed to visit the Dai Jun's castle."

Otto had been sitting quietly on a small stool in the corner of the room. Now he suddenly cut into the conversation. "Westerners have gone to the castle before—but not to be welcomed," he said. All eyes turned to him. "People who are condemned—westerners included—are sent to be hung from Jungong's walls. It is called the Walk of Death."

"It is my vision!" Neasa whispered fiercely, her voice full of concern. "You must leave Sikk."

My heart pounded as I fought to control my rising panic. *Walk of Death?* What *had* I done?

Ever worried about my well-being, Cao Wangsun asked, "What about my silver?"

The concerned look on his face actually helped me push the panic away. I let out a sudden burst of laughter, which made everyone in the room look at me as if I had lost my mind.

"The silver will be there whether I'm dead or alive," I told Cao Wangsun. "And where can I run? The river is probably still blocked, and even if it isn't, no one would stop the Dai Jun from killing me, even in Xiang."

They all knew I was right. In that moment, I hated being right. I wanted to run.

"Besides," I continued, addressing Neasa, "according to your 'vision' I'm just as likely to stand before the Dai Jun as I am to be killed by him."

Neasa reluctantly nodded her agreement.

"Well then, it seems as if I have no choice but to accept the Dai Jun's summons." I asked Cao Wangsun, "When will he send for me?"

Just then, a knock sounded on the door and Cao Wangsun let out an exasperated breath. "Now," he said.

My bowels churned at the sound of that knock, and my first thought was to not embarrass myself by soiling my trousers. I briefly thought about hiding in my room, at least long enough to find the chamber pot.

Cao Wangsun had the same thought. He looked around for a way out and spied the doors leading to the sleeping rooms. "They can't know I'm here."

Neasa stepped past my Wolf guards and took him by the hand. "You can wait in my room," she said, leading him to the door. Cao Wangsun entered with his two followers, but Neasa closed the door behind him and stayed outside.

Turning to me, she said, "I will go with you."

I shook my head as I tried to keep from shivering with the fear that gripped me. "No, there's no reason to put you in danger."

"But my vision …"

"If this is the Walk of Death," I broke in, "I will walk it alone."

The room erupted as each of my companions voiced their disagreement.

The knock sounded a second time and a familiar voice called out in Imperial from the other side of the door. "Master Olaf, you must come with me." It was Jiang Yin, the commander we had met at the camp on the river canal.

Quiet descended upon the room and everyone looked at me. I took a deep breath and then nodded to my Wolf guards. "Let them in." Then I noticed the defiant look in their eyes and added, "And don't try to fight them."

Moshe moved to open the door but then came back to stand with his brother between me and the doorway. Bren— and, to my surprise, Talon—also took up station with them.

Jiang Yin stepped into the room. He now wore the green armor that I had spied on the Dai Jun's guards earlier. I could see a group of green-clad guardsmen outside the door with Jiang Yin's bodyguard, Huai, at the front.

Jiang Yin waved for them to stay outside. He made a quick scan of the room, taking note of my group of protectors in the middle. Otto was still sitting in his corner, and Gabriele and Lulu stood in the opposite corner, just outside the door to Neasa's room.

"You're missing a few," he said.

Neasa spoke up at my side. "The rest of our men are staying down by the river."

Jiang Yin smiled. "That's fortunate." He nodded toward the defenders between us. "Will you tell them to stand aside?"

I found my voice, although it came out a bit more high-pitched than I would have liked. "What do you want with me?"

Jiang Yin gave me a formal bow and said, "The Dai Jun requests your presence at Jungong."

"I thought westerners weren't allowed there."

Jiang Yin shrugged. "I don't question the Dai Jun's orders," he said, his voice turned suddenly harsh, "and neither does anyone else."

"We will come with him," Neasa said.

Jiang Yin tossed his head to the side as if to say he didn't care. "I am to take Olaf Stenson to Jungong. What you do does not concern me."

I turned to Neasa and said, loud enough for everyone else to hear, "I will go with them. Don't do anything stupid."

I was surprised by how calm I sounded, because my heart was racing and my bowels still threatened to embarrass me. I stepped forward and pushed my way through Moshe and Mehki, patting each of them on the shoulder as I did so. "Please look after my people."

Once I was past my guards, Jiang Yin stepped aside and motioned for me to precede him out the door. I was immediately surrounded by the green-clad guards and ushered out of the inn.

CHAPTER 22: THE DAI JUN

More people were on the streets than there had been earlier—although I didn't see many of them while surrounded by the Dai Jun's soldiers. As we walked along—at a reasonable pace, thankfully—Jiang Yin chatted with me.

"My cousin suddenly took an interest in you," he said, glancing at me to watch my reaction. "I wonder why?"

His too-perfect features made me want to punch him. Maybe it was because he always seemed so smug. "I have no idea," I said, concentrating on staying calm. I tried to change the subject. "I thought you were in command of the canal forts?"

To my disgust, Jiang Yin's musical laugh perfectly matched his appearance. "I go where I'm needed," he said. Then he continued his questions as if I hadn't spoken. "Did you attack someone?"

"No."

"Steal?"

"No."

"Did you disparage the Dai Jun in public?"

"No! I've only been in town since yesterday."

Jiang Yin grinned, obviously having fun with my distress. "You didn't ogle the princess in the market this morning, did you?" I said nothing, but it didn't deter him. "You know, the princess is already betrothed to the BaWang's grandson."

That was quick. Cao Wangsun must have been more charming with girls than he was with his allies.

When I remained quiet, Jiang Yin let out a sigh. "You were more entertaining on the canal road. But no matter, you'll talk once we reach Jungong." He stayed quiet after that.

As we marched along, I wracked my brain trying to figure out why the Dai Jun had sent for me. I hoped he just wanted to meet me, but I could see no reason for that. The Stenson family was rich in the west, but not so much in the Eastern Confederation. In the east, the Dai Jun had much more wealth, as did the BaWang.

I could think of no reason for the Dai Jun to be interested in me except for my dealings with Cao Wangsun—but if he knew of Cao Wangsun's plans, why didn't he call for Neasa as well? Had the BaWang's grandson betrayed me? With such dark thoughts swirling through my head, I didn't look up until we had left the town behind.

The sudden absence of noise finally caught my attention and pulled me out of my thoughts. We were marching along a paved roadway that headed up the rocky hillside towards the fortress, Jungong. The sound of the crowds had faded away, and now I could hear only the crunch of the soldier's boots on the roadway.

Jiang Yin noticed and said, "So you have joined us again." He waved at the castle growing before us on the ridge ahead. "Here is a sight that few of your countrymen have seen," he said, giving me one of his smug smiles, "and none have lived to tell of it. This is the heart of the world."

Jungong stood on the tallest hill overlooking the city of Sikk. From the front, it looked impenetrable, its massive walls jutting from a rocky cliff face. Several Eastern-style peaked roofs were visible above the walls of the fortress. The building took up the whole hillside.

As we drew closer, I could see that the road circled around to the right side of the fortress, where it ended at a stone terrace surrounded by a low stone wall. A steep set of stairs connected the terrace to the fortress above.

As we drew closer, grim-faced guards dressed in the Dai Jun's green lined the roadway and the entrance to the terrace. It was clear that we'd been expected, because the guards blocking the entrance to the terrace stepped aside as we approached. We stopped on the terrace, which had a barracks running along the back side and was large enough to fit my family's estate in Kartoba twice over.

Jiang Yin waved at the guards around us, and they all peeled away except for Huai, who stayed at my back. "Catch your breath," Jiang Yin cautioned, nodding toward the stairs ahead. "It is a long climb."

The stairs rose at a crazily steep angle, and my leg already ached from the march up the hill. One of the guards came over with a ladle of water and offered it to me. I took it gratefully and quenched my thirst.

Jiang Yin pointed to the castle wall above. "See the men hanging up there?"

I saw several corpses dangling from the walls above.

"They are the pirates that attacked your riverboats," he said, pausing to give me a meaningful look. "Maybe you will meet them soon?" He seemed determined to get every bit of pleasure from my fear. We headed for the stairs. Huai pushed me from behind when I didn't move quickly enough.

The climb to the top seemed to take an eternity. I could really only bend my left leg, so I had to take one step at a time, clutching the stair rail for support. Jiang Yin had started out leading the way, but he got tired of stopping to look back, so he finally just let me lead. It took all my concentration to keep climbing, and I hardly realized we were near the top until Jiang Yin spoke.

"Nice breeze," he said to Huai as we drew close to the fortress gate. "You can hardly smell the corpses."

Actually, the walls were high enough that I didn't smell a thing. The Dai Jun's cousin had mentioned death just to taunt me. I wondered if this was a hint of the Dai Jun's personality as well.

Jiang Yin stepped past me to lead the way into the fortress.

I was exhausted from the climb, and my good leg was shaking so badly that I had trouble standing. We stopped just inside the gate, and Jiang Yin said to Huai, "Wait here until I send for you."

Stone benches had been built into the inside wall, and I gratefully sank onto the nearest one. Huai hovered next to me like a dog awaiting his master's orders. More guards patrolled here at the gate, but none of them offered me a drink of water. They did stare at me though, as if they had never seen a westerner before—or a cripple. I rested my face in my hands and waited.

I had no idea how much time passed. I knew it was well past midday, because my stomach started growling instead of threatening to betray me. I rested long enough for my leg to stop shaking and for the fear of what was to come to creep back into my mind.

Jiang Yin finally returned with another man in tow. The second man was bald and dressed in a long, formal robe— green of course. He motioned toward me and said, "Come with me."

When I stood up, he looked me over and pointed at the knife at my belt that the guards hadn't bothered to take. I had left my sword behind at the inn. "Remove that," he commanded.

I placed the knife on the bench. He nodded and led me into the Dai Jun's fortress.

I expected the interior to be stone, like the outer walls, but the inside looked much like any other Eastern building, with wooden columns and paper thin walls.

We walked through a building, out into a courtyard, and across to a gate that led to another courtyard and yet another building. This building appeared taller than the rest and was made of huge wooden columns painted green. A large panel— depicting a green dragon wrapped around the world— hung over the entrance.

The bald man stopped just inside the entrance and said, "You must kneel in the presence of the Dai Jun. Do not stand, even if he motions you forward."

I wondered if the man had even noticed my bad leg. Kneeling was not an easy task when one of your legs doesn't bends properly. "I will do my best," I said.

He glanced down at my leg but didn't look sympathetic. "Crawl, if you need to."

We entered the green building and turned to the right through a pair of wooden columns to enter another chamber. The bald man stopped in the entrance and pushed me to the floor as he announced my arrival in the Eastern language. I threw my bad leg straight behind me and landed hard on my hands and left knee.

"That will be all, Nei-chien."

I assumed it was the Dai Jun who had spoken, but I wasn't sure if I was supposed to look up or keep staring at the floor. "You may rise," the man said, and I raised my head to hazard a peek. He was speaking in Imperial, I assumed for my benefit.

In the relatively small room, I had a clear view of the Dai Jun sitting on an elaborately carved chair on a raised dais. He was old, with a long white beard, and wore a green and yellow robe with a matching hat that looked like a tiny tower on his head. I tried to read his face, but it was impossible to tell what he was thinking.

"I said, you may rise," the Dai Jun repeated.

I looked back at the doorway for guidance, but the bald man had left. He had told me to not stand in the Dai Jun's presence, and yet now the Dai Jun was telling me to rise. Was this a test?

I looked back toward the Dai Jun just in time to see him give a nod to the pair of guards who stood on either side of the doorway. They stepped forward and pulled me to my feet, and then moved back to their positions near the door.

Now that I was on my feet, I noticed the other occupant on the dais. Sitting on a small stool to the right of the Dai Jun was a young girl.

For a moment, I wasn't sure of my eyes. The dais was close enough that I could have reached it in a few strides, but the room was lit by high windows that faced the east, and she sat in the shadow of the Dai Jun's elaborate chair. It was not until she leaned forward and I recognized the birthmark on her cheek that I was sure.

It was the Butterfly Princess that I had met in the market square earlier that morning.

"Welcome, Master Olaf," she said in my own tongue.

The Dai Jun gave her an annoyed look and said, "Speak Imperial."

She smiled up at him and said in Imperial, "Yes, grandfather."

The shock of hearing those words almost knocked me back to my knees. The Butterfly Princess *was* an actual princess. Here she was, sitting next to the Dai Jun, looking just as comfortable as she had in the marketplace. Of course, she was now wearing a fancy dress—yellow with little green dragons embroidered on it—instead of the tattered one she'd worn earlier, and her hair was wound up in a bun with a golden dragon pendant hanging on her forehead. If not for the birthmark, I wouldn't have recognized her.

I'm sure I stared with my mouth agape, because the princess let out a tinkling laugh. "Welcome to Jungong, Master Olaf," she said in Imperial.

The Dai Jun's annoyed look quickly faded as he smiled fondly at his granddaughter before turning his attention back to me. "Yes, Master Olaf," he said. "Welcome to my palace."

I should have returned the greeting, but I was still speechless from seeing the beggar girl sitting next to the Dai Jun. He didn't appear to notice my rudeness as he continued to speak. "My granddaughter persuaded me to meet with you—but, to be honest, we would have met eventually."

Why would that be? Was it because of Cao Wangsun? I was confused, and I didn't like the feeling. With all the questions begging for attention in my head, one jumped forward and I blurted it out without thinking. "How is she your granddaughter?" I asked. "I saw your granddaughter with Cao Wangsun in the market this morning."

The Dai Jun nodded. "Yes, the *gongzhu*—the princess is my cousin's daughter. She is the one betrothed to Cao Wangsun."

"Then?" I pointed to the Butterfly Princess at his side.

"She is my real granddaughter."

That didn't clear up anything for me. I had no idea what was going on, but I suddenly realized that if the Dai Jun was sharing this information with me, I was never going to leave Jungong. The realization left a leaden feeling in my gut. He was going to kill me.

I would not be able to help my Uncle Olaf against the Empire of Jewel, I realized. And I would never see Sofie again.

The Dai Jun explained. "When my granddaughter was born, I had a dream. I dreamed that the Lion of the West would come and take her away. He would come to claim his place as ruler of the world."

More dreams! I hated gods and dreams—and what was it with lions? My friend Amon, the mule handler I had met along the road to Kartoba, had called me a lion. That was when I had first fallen in love with Tessa. When Amon noticed me mooning over Tessa, he had told me to "stop acting like a sheep and be a lion. A strong lion has his pick of the females."

Amon's words came back to me because of the Dai Jun's talk of lions. Was it a coincidence? Of course, Amon had been talking about women—not world domination

"I don't understand," I said. "I am no lion, and I have no desire to rule the world."

The Dai Jun didn't look convinced. "Then why have you come?"

Was it possible he didn't know about my partnership with Cao Wangsun? I tried to think of a good reason for my visit.

"I understand you are looking for an army?" the Dai Jun offered, not waiting for a reply. "Is it not so you can conquer the world? Or do you need an army to save your family from the Black Order?"

He obviously knew everything. So why did he question me? Why bring me to his palace that no westerner has ever walked away from? Was I such a big a threat to him—because of some crazy dream?

The Dai Jun rose from his chair and looked down at me from his dais. "I am the Dai Jun, descended from the dragon that made the world," he said. " I can see the future in my dreams. I saw this in my dream: the Lion of the West will attempt to usurp the dragon's throne."

"Grandfather!" The Butterfly Princess had jumped to her feet and now clutched his arm, as if to hold him back.

He ignored her and motioned for the guards to come forward, commanding, "Take him to the cellar."

The guards rushed forward and grabbed me from either side. They dragged me out of the room, where my bald guide stood waiting. He shook his head sadly before turning and leading the way. This time, they did not go at an easy pace, but dragged me along by the arms.

I can't say that I resisted. I felt limp in their grip, like the life had gone out of me while my mind was trying to grasp what had just happened. Before I knew it, I was standing alone in a dark cell watching the light of a single lamp fade down the long passageway through the iron bars of the window.

I'd gotten a glimpse of the cell before the lamp went away. It was small with stone walls and a hard, dirt floor. The door was made of solid wood with an iron-bar window. There was a pile of straw in the corner to the right of the door and a hole in the floor in the opposite corner. I hoped I would not be in the cell long enough to need these facilities, but I knew that was wishful thinking.

I reached out in the dark and took a hesitant step until my hand touched the stone wall, and then walked along the wall until I reached the corner with the straw. I leaned down and could smell that the straw was fresh. I sighed aloud and lowered myself to the floor and crawled onto the make-shift bed. *How did I end up here?*

Sitting on that straw in the dark, I had visions of rotting away in that little cell, forgotten by my captors. I had no illusions that I would be rescued. Cao Wangsun had his princess, and supposedly the army to go with it. He might miss my silver, but not enough to speak up for me.

I imagined Neasa would forget about me as well, no matter how much she touted her vaunted raven-inspired visions. I worried more for the rest of my companions. What would become of Bren and Gabriele? Otto and Lulu? Ivan and his men? Even Moshi and Mehki?

Most of all, I wondered if I would ever see Sofie again. With me out of the way, would Factor Einhardt have them all killed to protect his position? It wasn't until that moment, sitting in the dark cell, that I realized what it meant to have people count on you.

I was wrong about rotting away—at least, physically. My jailers brought me food twice a day and changed my straw weekly. At least that's what they told me the first time they came into my cell to rake up the old straw and lay out the new. I wasn't sure why they bothered. It almost made things worse.

Day after day, I paced my cell, counting out the steps from one wall to the next—ten steps, turn, ten steps, turn—as I waited for my captors to show up with their precious light. I thought I had gotten over Tessa's death and the despair it had caused, but sitting in that dark cell, as the weeks went by, brought it all back. My only light was the flashing dagger of my vision. The death dagger that had taken my first love returned to me as if it had never truly left.

I couldn't say how long I was in that cell before I received a visitor. I was pacing my cell, trying to keep the dagger-dream from taking me away, when the lamp light approached. I froze in place. It seemed too soon for my next meal, and it wasn't time for my bedding change. I felt the urge to hide, but I had nowhere to go, so I waited at the door to see if death had finally come for me.

I had to shade my eyes from the piercing beam of that single lamp. As I waited for my eyes to adjust, my heart thudded with anxiety. When I finally looked through the barred window, I saw the Butterfly Princess looking back at me.

The purple butterfly on her cheek looked darker than normal in the lamplight, but her left eye shone like a cat's. My first instinct was to back away from the door and try to hide in my straw, but I held my ground and waited to see why she had come.

After a long moment of staring at each other, she spoke. "I had to wait until grandfather's anger cooled before I could come to see you."

I still wasn't sure why the Dai Jun was angry with me. How can a dream cause such anger? As she said the words, I suddenly realized that I didn't care. He was mad, and I was in a cell—did there have to be a reason? Isn't that how the world had always worked for me?

I had no more control over my destiny now than when I'd herded pigs for my Uncle Karl. All I knew for sure was that there was a shiny dagger waiting for me at the end of my journey. Not the same dagger that took Tessa—oh no, she was with her family now, and I would go to Halls of the Dead alone. Would I see my mother there? Would I even recognize her?

The Butterfly Princess cleared her throat, interrupting my dark thoughts. "I have had a vision as well, Olaf Stenson. I share my grandfather's gift."

I didn't think I could sink any lower, but her words pushed me toward a deeper pit of despair. *Please, save me from all these visions!* But I had no god to pray to for succor. Even now, I feared to name my gods, in case they took notice of me and decided to make things worse.

Despite my silence—or possibly because of it—she continued. "Our son shall be the Lion of the West, Olaf. It is our son who will inherit my grandfather's place in this world."

I had been staring at nothing as she spoke, but now I looked at her face. She still reminded me of Tessa, with her marked cheek and dark hair, but she lacked the aura of tragedy that surrounded my memories of Tessa. She gave me an encouraging look, as if willing me to speak.

How could I have a child with this girl? I was locked in her grandfather's cell! I hardly knew her, and besides—I suddenly remembered—Sofie still waited for me in Gea. Sofie's face suddenly appeared before my eyes, as if my memory of her had waited for this moment. I remembered her face: dark hair, but not as dark as this strange princess standing at my cell door, and a round face that always smiled. Then I remembered her as she lay in her sickbed, the day I left on my journey.

Sofie still waited for me—I was sure of it. This strange princess would never take her place.

"Your grandfather will never let me out, Princess," I said, my voice sounding strange to me after being silent for so long. "He will never agree to what you say." *I will never agree.*

She shook her head. "He *will* speak with you again."

Hope flared within me again, but when I looked at the Butterfly Princess' face, it sputtered out. Was she toying with me? Was she using me—like all the rest?

"He will call for me again?" I finally managed to ask between trembling lips.

She tossed her head. Then, still smiling, she disappeared down the passageway. Watching her leave sparked my anger and I shouted at her retreating form, "I don't believe in visions! I will not marry you because of some dream!"

The darkness descended like a blanket, smothering the hope that had tried to come back to life in my heart. I began to frantically pace my cell, trying to hold back my dagger vision. That dagger never brought me light, only more darkness. I struggled to keep it out of my head—ten steps, turn, ten steps, turn—only I miscounted and slammed my good foot into the wall.

With the pain came the sudden vision of Sofie's face. I remembered every detail now. I held fast to that memory like a drowning man holds a lifeline.

CHAPTER 23: THE AGREEMENT

The Butterfly Princess did not come back, but the next time my jailers came to change my bedding, they stripped me down as well. They took away my coat, trousers, and shoes and left me with just my tunic. I was surprised by the color of my clothes. I had forgotten that I wore my black outfit to the market the morning of my arrest. The black reminded me of my Uncle Olaf and his fledgling kingdom. I had come to the east to help him save it.

"Why are you taking my clothes?" I asked my captors, but they ignored my question, leaving me once more in the dark but with fewer clothes and even less hope. Had the Dai Jun heard of his granddaughter's visit? Was this his punishment?

I shivered and huddled in the straw to stay warm. without my coat and trousers, I couldn't stay warm enough. Pacing the room would help, I knew, but I couldn't seem to find the energy to do it. I clung to the image of Sofie's face. It was the only thing that kept me from giving up. I had promised Sofie that I would come back for her.

When the guards brought my next meal, I refused to leave my corner. They never seemed to care if I ate anyway.

"Master Olaf." My jailers had not spoken to me since that first visit. They had always worked in silence.

I lifted my head from the straw to spy the bald-headed man who had first escorted me to see the Dai Jun. At first, I wondered if he was really there.

"Master Olaf," he repeated. "You must get dressed."

I sat up in the straw and saw that he had my clothes. "Why are you here? Is this some kind of game?"

The bald-headed man let out an exasperated sigh and motioned toward the doorway. In rushed a group of servants carrying lamps. A pair of men pulled me from the straw and dragged me to the center of my cell. The room was lit so brightly now that I was blinded as they pulled my tunic from me and splashed cold water on my body. The shock of it took my breath away. Hands poked and scrubbed at me. I felt someone cutting at my hair. I had always kept it short, but it had grown long in that cell. Finally, I felt a new tunic being pulled over my head and hands tugging on my trousers and coat. When I stepped back into my shoes, I felt like I had been reborn.

My eyes finally adjusted enough that I could squint and make out the bald-headed servant standing before me. "Come," he said. "It is time to see the Dai Jun."

My heart leaped from my chest, not at the prospect of seeing the Dai Jun, but because I was finally leaving that dark cell. The bald man led me out of the cellar and back into the main castle. This time, I walked on my own instead of being dragged.

We ended up back at the same little room where I had met the Dai Jun before. To my surprise, I wasn't winded when we arrived. All that pacing in my cell must have kept me better conditioned than I would have thought.

This time, when I entered the audience room, I dropped to the floor without being pushed. Even looking at the stone floor, my eyes watered from the sunlight streaming through the high windows. It must have been morning outside.

"That will be all Nei-chien." I heard the bald man's footfalls fade as he left the room. My ears seemed to have become more sensitive during my captivity.

I was surprised by how calm I felt. The last time I had been in this chamber, it had felt as though I would explode from the fear and anxiety. This time, I just wanted to get it over with.

Whatever the Dai Jun had in store for me, I was ready to face it.

I counted out several heartbeats as I stared at the floor until the Dai Jun spoke again. "You may rise."

I struggled to my feet—clumsily, but without assistance—and faced the dais.

This time, the Dai Jun sat alone; the Butterfly Princess was nowhere to be seen. He looked the same as he had before—same white beard, same green and yellow robe with a funny-looking, matching hat. We watched each other for what seemed like several minutes, but I couldn't be sure. My sense of time was still somewhat skewed.

The Dai Jun spoke again. "My grandfather's grandfather's grandfather was the one who retired to Sikk."

This was not exactly what I expected him to say, but I could feel the sunlight streaming through the windows above as it bathed my skin. It felt glorious. I hoped he would talk forever.

"He had a dream, you see. We who are descended from dragons pay heed to our dreams, because they are sent from the dragon that created the world."

He paused as if expecting a reply, but when none came, he continued. "He dreamed that a wolf would swallow the world. At that time, his greatest general was the leader of the Wolf Legion. Because of that dream, he sent the Wolf Legion to the farthest corner of his empire and then created a new legion to hunt it down. That is how the Black Order came to be, and that is why it has been pursuing the Wolf ever since."

I assumed he meant the Order of the Wolf, my uncle's old mercenary company. "But the Order of the Wolf was destroyed over a season ago. The Black Order destroyed them in Katch."

"Yes, but your uncle has raised the wolf banner again in the west." He pointed out my clothes, black and silver for my uncle's kingdom. "And you even wear it here," he said, leaning forward to emphasize his words, "in *my* hall."

"Is that why you put me in that cellar?"

"The Lion of the West shall rise—that I have seen." He shook his head, suddenly looking even older. "My granddaughter is the last of my line. She has the Dragon's Gift. My granddaughter has convinced me to not fear my vision. My ancestor feared his vision, and what has become of it?"

I waited for him to deliver the rest of his cryptic explanation. "My granddaughter convinced me that the Lion will correct what was wrought by my ancestor's fear." He took a deep breath and let it out. "She has convinced me that *her* vision shows the future for our family."

I remembered the vision she had told me about in my cell. Our son would be the Lion of the West and would inherit her grandfather's place in the world. Did the old man truly believe that?

"I hardly know your granddaughter," I began.

He cut me off by slashing his hand in the air. "You will marry my true granddaughter, Master Olaf," he said with great certainty. "You will marry her—and I will give you an army to save your homeland."

I closed my eyes and saw Sofie's face as it had appeared to me in my cell. I had promised that I would marry her. She had saved me from myself more than once, and I had told her that she would one day be my wife. How would she react if I came back to Gea already wed?

The Dai Jun's voice cut through my thoughts. "Cao Wangsun is betrothed to my cousin's daughter, but he will get no army. If you want your army, my granddaughter's vision is the price."

He knew why I had come, and he knew I had no choice—because he left me no choice. "You leave here as my granddaughter's consort, or you will never leave."

The thought of returning to that dark cell sent a shiver through me. Was I weak for fearing to go back into the dark? If I agreed to his terms, I would have an army to fight for my uncle and our homeland.

Even as I tried to come up with reasons to not let this happen, I knew I had no choice. As I nodded my head in agreement, the vision of Sofie's face disappeared.

The bald-headed servant took me to a suite of rooms in the adjacent building—apparently, this was to be my upgraded cell, because green-clad guards stood outside the door. I was just as much a prisoner of the Dai Jun's will as ever.

As I entered the sitting room, I was surprised by familiar faces. Bren and Gabriele; Otto and Lulu; and my two Wolf guards were all there to greet me.

"What are you doing here?" I cried. I could feel tears coming to my eyes. I hadn't realized how much I missed them all.

"We couldn't leave you, Master Olaf," Bren answered for the group.

"But what about the Walk of Death? What made you think I would ever come back?"

Bren took me by the arm and led me to a small table with a pair of chairs. I was relieved to see western-style furniture. I'd had my fill of sitting on the floor. He helped me lower myself into one of the chairs before answering, "We are your *household*, Olaf. Where would we go without you?"

My eyes blurred as I let the tears flow. It was such a relief to be back among my people! They *were* my people, I realized finally.

Gabriele brought me a cup of tea, and I had to fight the urge to hug her. Who knew how she would react to that? When my tears finally had abated, I looked at my companions. My Wolf guards stood next to the doorway leading out to the hall, looking more vigilant than usual. Gabriele, Lulu, and Otto sat on a padded bench across the room, trying unsuccessfully not to stare at me. Bren stood attentively at my back, as if waiting for me to give him an order.

I turned to Bren and asked, "Where are the rest of my people?"

"Your guardsmen and the Kail are camped at the bottom of the hill," he replied. "The Dai Jun's guards wouldn't let them come."

The Kail? Did that mean Neasa was still here? I wasn't sure how long I had been in that cell, but I guessed it had been a couple of months, at least. "What season is this?"

224

Otto spoke up next. "It is nearly harvest season. You have been in the Dai Jun's palace through the end of summer."

Most of the year gone! Had the Empire of Jewel already marched against the Seven Kingdoms? Would procuring an army from the Dai Jun make a difference now? "Is there any word on the Empire of Jewel?" I asked.

Otto shrugged. "We were camped outside until yesterday, but I have not heard anything about Jewel or the Seven Kingdoms."

I wished Ivan had come along. He would know what was happening outside of Sikk.

Lulu and Gabriele had been sitting quietly on the stool next to Otto. Now Lulu stood and came over to my table. "They told us that you are marrying a princess," she said. She stopped at the far edge of the table and peered up into my face. "You don't look so good for someone getting married soon."

They had cut my hair in the cell but had not touched my beard. I could tell it had grown out some. It probably looked unkempt.

"I could use a bath and a shave," I acknowledged.

Gabriele jumped off the bench and bustled over to grab Lulu by the arm. "We shall prepare a bath for you, Master Olaf!" I had never seen her so eager. Did I look that bad?

After the girls left the room, I motioned for Bren to take a seat at the table beside me. "We're alone, Bren. Come, sit with me."

While waiting for my bath, Bren and Otto caught me up on our little group. Once I had been taken away by the soldiers, Bren and my Wolf guards had followed behind to see where they took me. They were stopped by the guards at the foot of the hill, and Moshe had headed back to the warehouse to inform Ivan and my guardsmen of what had happened. They all came back and made camp just out of the reach of the guard post on the road. The next day, Neasa showed up with all her warriors and joined them.

When the Dai Jun's guards realized they had no intention of leaving, Jiang Yin came and talked to them. He told them that I had been imprisoned and they should leave, but they all refused. Over time, Neasa's men built up the camp into several wooden buildings, with the help of the silver that I had brought to Sikk. The locals started calling the place *waicun*—the "foreign village"—when they came to sell food and supplies.

For some reason, the Dai Jun's soldiers didn't make them leave, so they stayed in their wooden houses and waited for word of my fate. Yesterday, Jiang Yin had come back and told them I was marrying a princess. Then he had led my servants up to the castle.

I was touched by their dedication, and a little surprised at Neasa's fidelity. At last, my bath was ready and I went to wash away that dark cell from my soul.

I stayed in the tub so long that my whole body felt shriveled up. Gabriele and Lulu brought hot water more times than I could count, but the water was still cold by the time I got out. I didn't bother to dress—I no longer cared who saw me naked. Even Gabriele's red face had no effect. My time in the cellar had changed me that much, at least. I had no more time for embarrassment.

I lay on the bed in my room while the girls took away the bath. Just lying on a bed cushion felt like an incomparable luxury. When they had finished tidying up, Gabriele stood next to the bed. "Master Olaf, would you like anything else?"

Lying there naked—with Gabriele standing before me, red-faced with embarrassment—reminded me that I had not slept with a woman since leaving Gea. Gabriele had once had feelings for me, before I slept with Sofie. Did she still?

I looked her over. She was taller and slimmer than Sofie, and she had a pretty face. I remembered spying on her, and the other serving girls, in the bath when we worked together at Stenson House. She had always been nice to me, even then.

If I asked her to join me in my bed now, would she refuse? I felt my body stirring at the thought. Then I rolled away from her.

"No, that will be all."

Sofie was the one I loved. Sofie, not Gabriele—and definitely not some spoiled princess who seemed to think I was her personal stud horse.

As Gabriele was leaving the room, she started to close the door behind her. The room descended into darkness and that evil dagger flashed before my eyes. I jumped up with a sudden urge to pace. "No!" I called out, trying to hold back my panic. "Leave it open."

Gabriele paused in the doorway, giving me a startled look.

"Leave it open," I said again, this time trying to sound normal, "and light a lamp before you go."

Gabriele did as I bid. When she left me alone, she left the door cracked open. I lay back on the bed and tried to regain the peace I had felt from my bath. It took a long time coming, but I finally fell asleep for what felt like the first time in ages.

I awoke some time later to the sound of voices. At first, I wasn't sure where I was. I knew I wasn't in that dark cell, because there was light.

I rolled over and saw the lamp that Gabriele had left on a small table next to the cracked open door. I had no idea how much time had passed, but I figured I had lain on the bed in the afternoon, and it must now be night. I wrapped a blanket around my naked body and headed toward the doorway.

As I drew closer, I recognized one of the voices as Gabriele's. She was speaking in our native language.

"I tell you, he's different," she said, sounding a bit distressed. "He was scary in the room earlier, after his bath. The way he looked at me ..."

"We don't know what happened to him while we waited outside," Bren answered.

"You don't think they hurt him? Tortured him?"

There was a pause before Bren replied. "I don't know, but something must have happened for him to go from solitary confinement to marrying a princess."

"Mother won't like that," Gabriele said, sounding as though the idea made her happy.

"No." Bren didn't sound happy at all. "He was supposed to marry Sofie."

"That was mother's plan, not his, or Sofie's." Gabriele sounded distressed again. "Isn't it enough that he made us his household servants?"

"Not enough for mother," Bren replied harshly. "You know how she is."

Ursala had been overbearing at times, but I'd had no idea that she schemed behind my back. She always seemed so willing to serve. Of course, when we first started our journey, I had been lost in my dagger dream. After that, I had found Sofie.

Had Ursala put Sofie up to seducing me? I didn't want to believe that. No! But Gabriele had said that it wasn't Sofie's plan.

Gabriele let out a disgusted snort. "Yes, I know. Mother is never happy. But when Olaf returns with a wife, she will have to settle for being his housekeeper. It is better than she deserves."

Bren was quiet for a long time, but finally replied in a small voice, "But she's going to take it out on me."

It sounded as though one of them moved toward the other. Then I heard Gabriele say in a tender voice, "No, she won't, Bren. I won't let her."

I slipped back to my bed and lay there, wide awake. According to the things Bren had said about his mother as we grew up, working together in the stable, Ursala had always been a bitter woman. She was never happy with her lot. I'd always thought Bren was the strong one, leading his family despite his mother's poor influence. I realized now that I had been mistaken. Ursala still dominated him—and Gabriele was stronger than I had realized.

I thought back to my conversation with Bren on the deck of the *Sea Cow*, back before Sofie became my mistress. I had asked him about his sisters, and he told me to pursue Sofie as a lover instead of Gabriele, because she was not his true sister. Had

Ursala told him to encourage my lust for Sofie? Could I still trust him?

My happiness upon being reunited with my servants faded as I pondered all this. Were they loyal to me, or to my family status? I sighed as I stared up at the ceiling. Life had been simpler in the cell.

The next day, Cao Wangsun came to visit me. I was surprised to see that he came alone—or at least, he left his entourage in the hallway as he entered my suite. He was dressed in a long, Eastern-style robe, yellow with green birds embroidered upon it. He also wore a yellow hat adorned with pearls that looked almost as silly as the Dai Jun's hat. It perched atop his head like a tiny fortress upon a hill.

Once Gabriele opened the door for him, he stalked into the room and approached the small table where I sat.

"What have you done, Olaf?" he demanded. For him to leave off any honorific to my name let me know the depth of his distress. "I thought we were allies!"

I had been sipping tea and speaking with Otto about the details of him taking on the Eastern Factor position. Otto gave me a quick nod and moved away from the table. Cao Wangsun didn't even seem to notice, he was so intent upon glaring at me.

"Allies?"

"Yes," he replied. "You were supposed to help me fund my rise to power! But now ..."

It was apparent he knew about my upcoming marriage. Did he also know about the army the Dai Jun had promised me? "Do you need more silver?" I asked, trying to keep my face passive.

"No, you western barbarian," he snapped. "I want my army!"

"Well, I'm sure if you appeal to the Dai Jun—the same way you appealed on my behalf while I was in the cellar—he will listen."

Cao Wangsun's eye twitched when I mentioned the cellar, and my question was answered. He had *not* tried to help me when I was imprisoned. "Of course I spoke on your behalf," he stuttered out, barely able to keep his face from betraying him.

"Then I will speak for you as you have done for me," I said with great seriousness. He knew what I meant. I could tell by the look that crossed his face.

He stood before me, probably trying to figure out how to salvage the situation. Watching him, I realized that I had no hatred for the man. In fact, I almost felt sorry for him. I knew how it felt to be pushed around by others—although in his case, he normally did the pushing.

"Neasa tells me that you are the best swordsman in the east," I said, "and that you were tutored by your grandfather's generals."

He looked surprised and then a bit puffed-up. "Of course. That is why I should be leading the Dai Jun's army."

"I believe you should," I agreed and saw his eye twitch again. "I don't think you have to marry a princess to lead an army—do you?"

He gave me a suspicious look as he shook his head.

"And marrying a princess does not mean you are qualified to lead an army, either," I continued. "I think we should continue our partnership, Cao Wangsun. And I think we can both still get what we want."

He took a deep breath, and then bowed his head to me. "It is as you say, Master Olaf."

CHAPTER 24: FINALLY MARRIED

My wedding took place within a week of my leaving the cellar. With my bride being the Dai Jun's granddaughter, I expected to wait for an elaborate ceremony to be planned, with many guests and public decrees. Instead, it was a more sedate affair.

Although the Butterfly Princess was a familiar character in Sikk, it was a well-kept secret that she was the Dai Jun's granddaughter. It seemed our wedding would be a secret as well.

It was traditional in the east, as it was in my country, for family members to witness the wedding. The only family I had available were Otto and Lulu. They were cousins, after all, if not closely related. I decided to take them along when we headed to the ceremony.

My head pounded as we prepared to leave, thanks to Bren and Otto insisting that we celebrate the day before. Apparently, it was also a tradition for the groom's male friends to send him off with a splitting headache on his wedding day. Growing up with no friends, I had never participated in this ritual before.

We were led from my rooms across to the green building where I had initially met with the Dai Jun, which I had learned was the inner palace. We passed the little meeting room with the raised dais and headed down a long hall with a set of double doors at the end. The doors were golden with a pair of writhing green dragons painted on the panels. Only the Dai Jun's family was allowed within; my servants and Wolf guards would have to remain outside.

The inner chamber was not as large as I had expected. It was relatively bare, compared to the rest of the palace, with no windows and only small lamps hanging from hooks on the bare walls. On the wall opposite the doors was a small table with a green dragon statue as the centerpiece. Various plates and candles and scraps of paper were scattered around it.

The Butterfly Princess stood before the shrine facing toward me with a nervous smile upon her face. She wore a plain green gown embroidered with yellow butterflies and had her hair pulled up with the same golden dragon pendant hanging on her forehead as she had worn before. She was pretty, even with the birthmark.

The Dai Jun stood next to her as several other people filed into the room. I recognized Jiang Yin, whom I had met previously, but I also noticed several others, including a young girl I assumed was the princess Cao Wangsun was betrothed to marry. Otto, Lulu, and I—all dressed in Stenson Blue—looked like a small pool of water surrounded by a large, green meadow.

One of the relatives stepped forward and bowed to me. He was thin with a pinched face and had dark locks streaked with gray. I didn't know the man, but he looked like an older version of Jiang Yin. He even looked down his nose at me with the same expression of disdain. "I am Jiang Qui," he said. "Welcome to our family sanctuary." The look on his face didn't match his words.

I bowed in return and said, "I am honored."

He moved gracefully to one side while motioning for me to approach the shrine. "We welcome your union with our beloved gongzhu, Dai Ling." He said the words in such a way that everyone in the room knew he didn't mean a bit of it. I ignored his tone though, being somewhat surprised to finally learn my bride's name. I had thought of her as the Butterfly Princess from the start. I'd never even thought to ask about her actual name.

I stepped past him to approach the shrine next to Dai Ling. In the west, the marriage ceremony was pretty simple. While clasping hands, the couple pledges to be united; their promise is witnessed by their families, and then they are bound together at the wrist to symbolize that bond. I knew that the Eastern ceremony was similar, except the couple exchanged gifts rather than being bound.

I stopped before the green dragon shrine and faced Dai Ling. I felt numb. Actually, I had felt numb since the day I was released from my cell. On that day, I had agreed to this marriage—but only to get an army to help my uncle, and to end my imprisonment. I had resolved to go through with this wedding, but then to be a husband in name only. Now I found it hard to maintain my resolve when my head ached from too much sonti and the Butterfly Princess stood before me with that shy smile.

The Dai Jun moved to stand before the shrine facing us. He reached out and took each of us by the right hand. He drew our hands together. "Before our ancestors, do you pledge loyalty to each other above all others?"

"Yes," Dai Ling answered immediately.

Sofie's face flashed before my eyes, and I promised myself that I would keep her in my heart, no matter what words I spoke that day. "Yes," I finally replied.

The Dai Jun nodded and stepped aside so that we stood alone before the dragon shrine. Dai Ling reached into her robe with her free hand and pulled out a golden pin made into the shape of a lion with green emeralds for eyes. She reached over and pinned it to my coat over my left breast. "With this gift I pledge myself to you."

Her touch was light on my chest, but it broke through my numbness and my chest suddenly felt tight. My hand shook as I reached into my coat to pull out my gift. The golden lion pin looked to be a delicate and costly piece, which made my own gift look all the poorer for it.

I had nothing of real value to give my future bride. I had never owned jewelry, not even a ring. My clothes had been bought for me and my sword given to me by a friend. I had nothing else of value. When I had discussed this with Otto and Lulu two days before, Lulu pulled a simple silver necklace from around her neck and offered it to me.

Otto sucked in a breath when she did so and looked a bit distressed.

Lulu patted him on the arm and held the necklace out to me. It was a Stenson silver piece on a small silver chain. "It is my good luck charm," she said. "I hope it brings you luck in your marriage."

Otto found his tongue and explained the significance. "When your Uncle Karl stripped me of my factor title and exiled my family to the east, I professed my loyalty to him and pointed out my years of loyal service." He shook his head at the memory. "Your uncle tossed me that coin as 'payment for my service,' and sent me east."

"I can't take this," I had protested.

Otto held up his hand and said, "You have welcomed me back into the family, Olaf. This silver piece has lost its significance."

I took the little silver necklace out of my coat and reached across to place it around Dai Ling's neck. I had to let go of her hand to do it, but quickly clasped her hand once more as I said, "With this gift, I pledge myself to you."

The necklace looked small and tarnished next to the bright yellow butterflies on her dress and the golden dragon on her forehead, but she fingered the silver coin as if it were a treasure and gave me a happy grin. "I will cherish it always, my husband."

"It is done," Jiang Qui called out and stepped up to stand next to the Dai Jun. "Now, we should finish the rest of our business here."

What other business? Dai Ling stepped away from the shrine, pulling me with her to stand next to Otto and Lulu. "Welcome to our family," Lulu said in an excited voice as she reached out to hug my new wife. They clung together for a heartbeat. I had forgotten that they were already friends.

I turned back to watch the Dai Jun and Jiang Qui face each other before the family shrine. They began a rapid exchange in Eastern. Jiang Qui looked belligerent while the Dai Jun seemed unruffled. I turned back to my new wife and asked, "What is this business they are discussing?"

The Butterfly Princess took my arm and told me in a lowered voice, "My grandfather is abdicating his position as the head of the family. He is turning over Jungong and the kingdom of Sikk to his cousin, Jiang Qui."

"What!" I took a step toward the pair and called out, "What about my army?"

The Dai Jun gave me an annoyed look and Jiang Qui looked as though he wanted to kill me. "This has nothing to do with you, barbarian," the future king of Sikk growled. He motioned toward Jiang Yin, whom I was now sure was his son. "Escort them to their chambers."

Jiang Yin bowed to his father and stepped out of the crowd of family members to lead us from the room. In the hallway outside, he said, "Enjoy your privileged status while you can, Master Olaf." He gave Dai Ling a sidelong look when he said it.

He led my party, which now included my new wife—who clung to my arm as though she was afraid I would try to escape—back down the hallway to our rooms. I hardly noticed my surroundings, as my mind was awhirl with what I had just heard.

How could the Dai Jun give me an army if he was no longer the Dai Jun? Had he given up his position and power just so he could marry off his unpopular granddaughter? I had a sinking feeling that I had just married a woman I hardly knew—and for no reason at all.

When we arrived at my rooms, I was surprised to see a group of green-clad servants waiting for us. Two women and a man who looked somewhat familiar to me. The man wore the same long, green coat and baggy pants as the servants we had passed in the hallway, but he was older than most and his face looked a bit weatherworn, as if he had spent years outdoors.

"Who are these people?" I snapped, still fuming over the Dai Jun's abdication.

"These are my body servants," Dai Ling replied. Then she inclined her head toward the lone male servant, "and my *shiwei*—my bodyguard." I remembered where I had seen the man before. He was the one she had tossed the bun to in the market, the first time I met her.

Dai Ling finally let go of my arm and stepped toward the two women. They immediately embraced her and spoke what I assumed were words of congratulations. Dai Ling turned back to me. "I shall prepare for you, my husband."

Her maids began leading her towards my bedchamber and a lump suddenly formed in my throat. I had no intention of consummating our marriage—not today or any day! I didn't even know if I would get my promised army out of the deal. "Wait," I called out feebly.

Lulu giggled and joined the group of women. Gabriele gave me a teasing grin as she joined the others. "It is tradition, Master Olaf." They all disappeared into my bedchamber to prepare my bride for our wedding night.

I was left staring at the other men standing in the common room. Moshe and Mehki had taken up station near the door, and then ignored me, as usual—although Mehki did have a slight grin on his face. Dai Ling's bodyguard stood outside the door to my chamber, looking rather intimidating. Otto and Bren took seats at the nearest table. It happened to be the table where we had sat the previous day, and still held a pitcher of sonti and several cups. Bren lifted one of the cups to his nose and sniffed at it. He gave me a sympathetic look and raised the cup to me. "Sonti?"

My first impulse was to grab the pitcher and down what was left in it, and then to ask for more. The whole situation seemed to be unraveling. If I was married to the Dai Jun's granddaughter—a girl nobody knew was his granddaughter—and he just abdicated his title, what did I have? Certainly not an army to save my uncle! I probably didn't even have a safe way back out of Jongong for me and my people.

Judging by the way Jiang Yin and his father had acted toward me, I doubted that they would let me leave. What was the Dai Jun thinking?

I took a seat at the table but refrained from picking up a cup. I needed to have a level head when I was called to "do my duty" with my new bride. I needed a clear head so that I could resist doing anything besides demanding an explanation from her. If she didn't know why her grandfather did what he did, then it was time to break out the sonti and drown myself in it.

We sat waiting, hearing the occasional bout of giggles come from my sleeping chamber, but saying nothing ourselves. I stared at the far wall, trying to keep from worrying over our situation. Finally, the door opened and the women emerged, except for Dai Ling. They lined both sides of the doorway and Gabriele said, "Your bride awaits you, Master Olaf."

I stood and faced them. I could see the lamplight in the room beyond, but not Dai Ling. I assumed she waited for me on the bed in the back corner of the room. I tried not to think of it as I stumped my way toward the doorway. The happy smiles on Gabriele and Lulu's faces felt like a betrayal—especially Gabriele's smile, because she knew I loved Sofie.

Just as I stepped between the two lines of women, Bren called out from behind me, "Do you need my assistance, Master Olaf?"

The girls burst into giggles around me. I knew what he meant—he typically helped me disrobe for the evening, especially to take my trousers off my bad leg. Still, my face burned at the sudden giggling and I shook my head as I stepped into the bedchamber. The doors closed softly behind me, shutting out everyone but me and my new bride.

Dai Ling sat on the edge of the bed wearing a white linen gown. From the light of the single lamp that stood on the table next to me, I could see that it was sheer enough that her nipples were visible through the fabric and short enough that my face remained hot as I stood near the doorway and dared not take another step.

"Husband," she said in my native language, "I await you."

237

Somehow, it didn't feel right talking to her as if she were a native of my country. It almost seemed disrespectful to Sofie. I switched to Imperial when I answered her. "Dai Ling, we have much to discuss."

She frowned—either at my answer or because I spoke Imperial, I wasn't sure which. She patted the bed next to her. "We are newly married, Olaf. The talking can wait until later, yes?" The hopeful smile she sent my way, coupled with the little tilt of her head that almost hid her butterfly birthmark behind her long dark hair, weakened my resolve.

I steeled myself with a deep breath and stepped closer. "I did not marry you because of your dream, Princess. I married you because of your grandfather's promise of an army." I let her see my anger. "How will he give me an army if he is no longer the Dai Jun?"

"There is only one Dai Jun," Dai Ling replied. "Jiang Qui will never bear that title. He is not a direct descendant of the dragon." She stood and took a slow step toward me. "I am the last of that blood, and our children will inherit my grandfather's place in this world."

"What children?" I snapped. "We will never have children, Butterfly Princess. I married you for an army that will never be mine. As it stands, I will probably never see the air outside this keep again. I doubt Jiang Qui will let me traipse about Sikk like a beggar—or you either, going forward."

She grabbed at her neck, and I realized that she still wore the silver necklace I had given her. She clasped the silver coin tight as she answered. "You will have your army, and I my son. I have seen it." She took another step toward me. "Trust my grandfather in this."

"Trust your grandfather? The man who threw me in a cell and forced me to marry you?"

She winced at my words, and I almost felt sorry for her. She took another step forward and reached out to touch my arm. "We are married now, Olaf. I will be a good wife to you."

Her touch made me shiver and I quickly shrugged her off. "You can have the bed," I said. I stumped over to the opposite corner to the floor pad where Bren normally slept. I slumped down on the pad and looked away from her so that I wouldn't be tempted by the sight of her in that gown.

I heard her sigh and move back to sit on the bed. "The Moon Festival will happen in two days' time," she said quietly. "During the festival, we will go to the square in Sikk to announce our wedding and my grandfather's abdication. You will see the light of day again outside this palace. You will have your army. And we will never come back."

I heard the bed rustle as she lay down among the covers. "And I shall have your son, my husband."

I knew the Eastern Moon Festival took place in the fall. A whole year had passed since I'd left the harbor in Kartoba. Now I had a wife I never asked for, and I still had no army to help my uncle.

I slept in my clothes that night, huddled on Bren's bedding. I lay there for a long time, listening to Dai Ling breathing and holding the vision of Sofie's face tightly in my mind.

Just as Dai Ling had said, two days later, we prepared to leave the palace to attend the Moon Festival in the Sikk market square. As we stood side-by-side, surrounded by our attendants, anyone watching would assume we were a happy, newly-married couple. Dai Ling wore a Stenson Blue dress with golden butterflies embroidered upon it and a white lion's head over her left breast. In fact, all her attendants now wore clothing with the same white lion symbol. I knew it was because of her vision, but I refused to comment upon it.

She tucked her hand into my arm as we made our way out of our apartment and into the hallway. At Dai Ling's insistence, Bren carried my clothes chest and Gabriele carried her bundle. Her two serving girls also carried bundles. Dai Ling had insisted that we were not going to return, but I doubted that Jiang Qui would let us go so easily.

A group of about a dozen guards in the Dai Jun's green armor surrounded us and escorted us out of the palace. We made a slow procession down the steep stairway to the terrace below in deference to my afflicted leg. Dai Ling clung firmly to my arm to give me support, which made me want to shrug her off, but I didn't want to lose my balance.

When we made it to the bottom of the stairs, another group of guardsmen, led by Jiang Yin, surrounded our party as we made our way down the hill toward town.

"How many guards do they need?" I muttered to Dai Ling, who still clung to my arm. I doubted my two Wolf guards and her bodyguard, even with Bren's help, could fight their way clear of the first level of guards, let alone the double layer.

"The ones who escorted us out of the palace are *nei-chang*," she explained. They are from the inner palace and are loyal to my grandfather. The others are the *wai-chang*. They are the terrace guards and are loyal to Jiang Yin."

So the palace guards were there to protect us from the terrace guards—or at least, to protect the princess. It made me feel a little better, but I was still confused. "I thought Jiang Qui had control of the palace now?"

Dai Ling squeezed my arm with her hand and said, "I told you, there is only one Dai Jun. The nei-chang are loyal to the blood of the dragon."

My Eastern Confederation tutor had not prepared me for visiting Jongong or the intricacies of the Dai Jun's court. I felt lucky that my new wife knew what was going on. I stopped asking questions and made my way down the hillside road towards the town of Sikk. I could see some buildings, part of the way down, that hadn't been there when I was dragged up the hill months before.

"Is that your camp?" I asked Bren, who was walking beside me.

Bren nodded. "It is Waicun. Your people should be waiting for us there."

As we drew near the encampment, a banner was raised by the inhabitants. It was Stenson blue dominated by a roaring white lion, like the one on Dai Ling's breast. A cheer rose from within the encampment, and Jiang Yin pulled our party to a sudden stop.

Out of the encampment marched my Stenson guardsmen, carrying the lion banner. They were surrounded by a group of Kail warriors and followed by a crowd of locals. I could see Neasa next to Ivan at the head of my guardsmen and Carrog leading the Kail warriors.

Jiang Yin tried to approach, but Dai Ling's palace guards blocked his path. He stopped and called out to me, "Tell your people to clear the road ahead."

"Why?" I called back. Maybe it was finally being out of Jungong, but I was feeling suddenly defiant.

Even through the screen of nei-chang guardsmen, I could see the look of consternation on Jiang Yin's face. His guards did outnumber our guards, but with the addition of my Stenson guardsmen and Kail warriors, it was probably pretty even. Maybe this was how we were going to stay out of Jongong, but I couldn't see how we were going to escape Sikk with the handful of guardsmen and Kail warriors against a whole country.

Dai Ling turned to her bodyguard and said something to him in Eastern. The man nodded and called out a command. Immediately, the palace guards started marching forward again. I could see the hesitation in Jiang Yin's face. He wanted to order his men to stop us, but he didn't want to start a fight on the way to the festival. He called out a command, and his men parted to let us through.

Dai Ling smiled at me with excitement.

"What do we gain by annoying Jiang Yin?" I asked. "Once this festival is finished, they will take us back to the palace by force if need be." Of course, I had started it with my flippant answer to Jiang Yin, but now I began to worry about my people. Was it wise dragging my guardsmen and the Kail into our troubles?

Dai Ling tilted her head and peered at me with her light-blue eye. I'll admit, that eye made me uncomfortable. "I have seen what is to come," she said. "Trust in my vision."

Gods and visions are what I trusted least, but I held my tongue as we united with my people from the camp. Ivan

241

saluted me with an uncharacteristic grin on his face, and Neasa actually seemed relieved to see me. She, and her men, looked to be dressed for battle. She wore her normal green tunic, but had covered it with a studded leather vest and had her hair pulled up in a braid. She stepped before me and looked Dai Ling up and down before saying, "Thought you could get rid of me by hiding in the fortress? We are partners, are we not?"

"That we are," I replied, finding that I had a hard time keeping a grin off my face. I turned to look at Ivan and my guardsmen, and was surprised to see more men in Stenson blue than I remembered. At least a score of men were lined up behind Ivan wearing Stenson guardsmen uniforms. I looked to Ivan for an answer. "I don't remember this many guards."

Ivan shrugged, finally losing his grin and reverting to his typical more serious expression. "It seemed prudent to do a little recruiting," he said. He nodded to the lion banner held by one of the guardsmen. "The banner was not my idea, though." He raised an eyebrow at me, letting me know he expected an explanation in the near future.

So did I—but for now, we needed to finish our journey to the market square. My Stenson guardsmen fell in behind us as the nei-chang led us to the market square. Neasa and Talon followed along, but the rest of the Kail warriors stayed behind at the little settlement. "They will hold it, in case we need a place to fall back to," Neasa explained. "It may look like a hodgepodge of buildings, but we built the place with defense in mind."

I looked back and saw Carrog wave from the line of Kail. Even the sight of his ugly face reassured me, and I had no doubt he would be a hard one to dislodge if Neasa told him to hold the place. I felt a little better as we continued our procession to the square. I would rather make a stand at Waicun than go back to the cellar.

My heart felt lighter than it should have as we made our way to the square. Just having all my companions back made me feel like anything was possible.

As we marched through town, the noise grew louder. The square was overflowing with people, but the crowd opened for us as we approached. In the center stood a raised platform surrounded by green-clad guards. I guessed they were more of Jiang Yin's men, but couldn't really tell.

On the opposite side from where we had entered the square, there was also a group of yellow-clad soldiers. In the middle of the platform stood the Dai Jun and Jiang Qui. The Dai Jun stood alone, but Jiang Qui was accompanied by the princess that was betrothed to Cao Wangsun. Cao Wangsun stood next to his future bride, and an older man formally dressed in yellow stood next to him. I assumed this was his grandfather, the BaWang.

It appeared obvious, from the way they were positioned, that the Dai Jun was alone and the rest of the party was there to support Jiang Qui.

As we approached the platform, the guardsmen parted to let Dai Ling through. I tried to stop and stay with my people, but she kept hold of my arm, and I ended up ascending the platform at her side. Moshe and Mehki pushed their way through as well, thanks to a nod from the Dai Jun to the guardsmen surrounding the platform. Maybe these guards were on our side after all.

Once we made it to the Dai Jun's side, he stepped forward and raised his hands and the crowd quickly fell silent. As he spoke, Dai Ling leaned in close to me in order to translate.

"Tonight, the roundest moon can be seen in the sky," he intoned. "It is time for reunions, a time for families to gather and share their blessings with each other."

The crowd cheered and he waited for the sound to subside before continuing.

"During this time of reunion and family, I want to share my family with you, and to share my blessings as well." He motioned for Dai Ling to step forward. She held my arm so tightly that I had no choice but to join her next to her grandfather. Of course, it meant she continued to translate for me as he spoke.

"You all recognize the girl known as Hudie Gongzhu, the Butterfly Princess." I could hear a low murmur pass through the crowd. "She is my true granddaughter, Dai Ling, heir to the dragon's blood."

The crowd fell silent People looked at each other in disbelief.

"And here is her consort, the White Lion of the West, Olaf Stenson." The crowd remained silent except for a shout of support from my Stenson guardsmen. I could see people beginning to whisper behind their hands.

It seemed that I had a new nickname, and a banner. I wondered what the Dai Jun hoped to accomplish with them. Would giving me a fancy name convince his cousin to let me leave? Did they think I would give in to Dai Ling's vision if they made me look the part?

The silence of the crowd was worrying. Jiang Qui stepped forward to stand beside us with the BaWang next to him. He didn't speak, but nodded to the Dai Jun.

The Dai Jun scanned the crowd one last time before he spoke again. "As I have reunited with my true family on this Moon Festival, I have decided it is time to share my blessings with my extended family." He motioned toward Jiang Qui. "My cousin, Jiang Qui, has been loyal and faithful to me. It is time for him to be rewarded for it."

Jiang Qui stepped forward so that he stood alone before the crowd. "As of today," the Dai Jun announced, "I step aside for my cousin and name him Jiang Jun—head of the Jiang family and ruler of Sikk."

Jiang Qui turned and gave the Dai Jun an annoyed look. I guessed he had expected to inherit the Dai Jun title. The crowd let out a low moan as they realized their beloved Dai Jun was retiring. Then they started to shout and finally chant. "Dai Jun! Dai Jun!"

Jiang Qui was raising his hands for quiet, but they ignored him and kept chanting, "Dai Jun! Dai Jun! Dai Jun!"

The Dai Jun raised his hands and the crowd fell silent again. "I leave Sikk in the care of Jiang Jun as I travel west with my granddaughter and her consort." It sounded as though the entire crowd drew in their breath at the same time. "The blood of the dragon lives in my granddaughter, your beloved Butterfly Princess. I will follow her and her consort to their destiny."

I stared at Dai Ling as she translated. She smiled back at me and said, "Now you will have your army."

The crowd went wild and soon a new chant rose, slowly gaining strength until it filled the square and the town beyond. "Hudie Gongzhu! Hudie Gongzhu! Hudie Gongzhu!"

The Dai Jun leaned toward us and said, "Now is the time for us to leave."

He led us past Jiang Qui, who stood fuming with disbelief, and into the crowd. His palace guards surrounded us and led us through the crowded square, along with my Stenson guardsmen. The crowd pressed us on all sides, screaming their love and devotion to my new wife.

As we pushed through the crowd, the nei-chang raised another standard next to the white lion. It was orange with a green dragon—the Dai Jun's banner. The crowd cheered even louder. When they raised a third standard—a green flag with a golden butterfly—I could no longer hear myself think.

CHAPTER 25: NEW PLANS

We headed back to Waicun to join up with Neasa's men. I was surprised to see new construction next to the western-style encampment. A huge pavilion tent was being erected, surrounded by several smaller tents. Many more of the Dai Jun's guardsmen were there to keep the crowds at bay. The noise was still deafening as we entered the guarded area.

Carrog ran up to us the moment as we arrived, looking more excited than I had ever seen him. "We're gonna have a fight!" he shouted. "Those Imperial bastards don't know what's coming."

The Dai Jun motioned toward his massive tent, which was being erected. "It's not done yet. Is there somewhere we can talk?"

I looked at Neasa and she nodded. "This way."

She led us to a hall in the encampment large enough for us all to gather on benches around a long, rough-hewn table. At one end sat the Dai Jun, accompanied by a guardsman I assumed was his captain and the bald-headed servant who had escorted me in the palace. Dai Ling sat next to him with her bodyguard standing at her back. I sat next to her with my Wolf guards behind me. Neasa, Talon, and Ivan filled the remainder of the table. Carrog stood nearby, but did not take a seat.

After I introduced my companions, the Dai Jun began. "I have given up my place in Sikk in order to follow my granddaughter's vision, Olaf Stenson—and I have given you the army I promised."

It had all happened so fast, that I was still trying to figure everything out. While I gathered my thoughts, Neasa spoke up. "An army of shopkeepers and farmers won't topple the Empire of Jewel."

The Dai Jun grinned at her. "I have heard of you, Neasa Dark Thunder—and your captain, Carrog the Fiend. You are famous on the Sea of Silence for your savagery." Why hadn't I heard Neasa's nickname before? Was there a story behind it?

Neasa scowled at the Dai Jun but waited for him to give an answer.

He shrugged and said, "My people will fight if I wish it—but I also have an army coming from Sui in the north."

Sui was the northernmost territory of the Eastern Confederation and was the home of various tribes who were in constant conflict. They were said to be the most war-loving people in the eastern kingdoms, but they mostly fought among themselves. The Dai Jun turned to the guardsman seated next to him. "When will your people arrive?"

The guardsman shrugged. "Any day."

Any day? How could that be? An army from Sui would have to march a long distance to get here. They would have had to have been marching for more than a month already, and to have been preparing long before that. I would have been in my dark cell when the Dai Jun called for that army. In fact, he must have planned it before he tossed me in that cell.

The Dai Jun was watching me closely as I wrapped my mind around this information. When I worked it out and looked up at him, he gave me a slight nod. "The Sui are loyal to the dragon's blood. They will be the backbone of your army, just as they were the backbone of my ancestor's armies."

He had planned to help all along—even while letting me rot in that cell? Had it all been a test? What would he have done if I'd killed myself in that hole? What if I'd gone crazy?

The whole thing made me so angry that I couldn't move or talk. It took all my strength to stop myself from screaming. My body shook as I tried to hold it in. I gripped the edge of the tabletop so tightly that my fists ached.

When Dai Ling placed her hand on my right fist, I wanted to push her away—to lash out at her. I wanted to do anything besides sit there, frozen in place. The room had become quiet now and all eyes were on us, sensing the tension.

The Dai Jun watched me boil for a moment before he spoke again. "I lied to you when we first met. I had a dream when my granddaughter was born, but in my dream, she was a happy butterfly, fluttering around Sikk without a care in the world. So I let her be that butterfly. I let her have her freedom."

He paused and smoothed his long, white beard as if uncertain of what to say next. "Before you came, I had another dream; a lion arrived during the Moon Festival and stole her heart, and taught her pain and sadness. The lion took away her freedom and made her his bride."

"Grandfather!" Dai Ling called out, but he silenced her with an upraised hand.

"We cannot avoid our destinies, Olaf Stenson—neither you nor I, nor my granddaughter." He shook his head. "But I tried, for her sake. Even after I made the arrangements to fulfill my granddaughter's vision, I tried to change it. I locked you away and hoped that you would perish."

I heard Neasa suck in a breath, but the room stayed silent. "But you would not quit! You paced that cell like a caged lion. Finally, she convinced me that I could not change your role." He spread his hands toward me, as he observed the rage on my face

"I don't ask for your forgiveness," he said with finality. "I have followed my granddaughter's vision. I gave you what I promised. My time is done—but I will stay by her side until this has ended."

Until this has ended—what did that mean? The old man who sat before me looked as though he didn't regret a thing, and my dislike for him grew. He was like all the rich men I had hated my whole life, selfish and unrepentant.

I finally pulled myself together and shook Dai Ling's hand loose from my own. "I don't care about your vision, or her vision, or …" I cut my eyes at Neasa, "*anyone's* vision. All I care about is getting back to Gea, and then leading this army west to save my uncle."

I stood and stared down at the Dai Jun and his granddaughter. "I am done being manipulated. Once this has ended, all of you can find another toy to play with." I stomped from the room, shaking with fury.

Bren and Gabriele were waiting outside for me. They accompanied me to one of the wooden buildings, but I sent them away. After all, they had tried to manipulate me too—hadn't they?

I sat in that building with just my Wolf guards for company. Once my anger had cooled, I brooded over everything that had happened.

Had it been so bad being Olaf the Unlucky and watching the pigs? If things had stayed that way, I would still have my little room in the servants' quarters where I could hide from everything. What did I have now? I was still being shit on, but now it was by more powerful people. That didn't seem like a great improvement.

Everyone I knew *wanted* something from me. Even my own servants tried to manipulate me. I had been fooling myself into thinking I had some control over my life. In fact, I now realized, I had no idea what I was doing or why. I dropped my head into my hands and gave in to my anguish, my body lurching with sobs.

I heard a chuckle behind me and jerked my head upright. Mehki tried to quiet his younger brother, but Moshe kept laughing. His usually dour face had been transformed by his mirth into a mirror of his normally cheerful older brother. It was a shock to see, and I found myself staring back at him.

He finally stopped laughing long enough to speak. "How do you *do* it, Olaf?"

"Leave him alone," Mehki admonished.

Moshe ignored his brother. "How do you keep falling into shit and coming out smelling like honey?"

I didn't know what to say. My Wolf guards were normally just silent shadows. Yes, they did occasionally comment on my behavior, but usually they didn't judge my decisions. For Moshe to speak up like this—especially when I was so upset—came as a shock.

Moshe didn't move from his place by the doorway as he continued to talk. "If I had your luck, I would be married, probably with children. Instead, I'm standing here watching you hang your head."

I remembered his story, about leaving his wife behind. He had lost her because of his pride and jealousy. He'd told me the story back when I was conflicted over my feelings for Sofie.

But why was he *laughing* at me now?

"Don't you know, Olaf?" Moshe continued. "Most people don't get second chances, or third chances, or more." He shook his head while his brother gave me an apologetic look. "You have a wife, and a mistress, and several people who want to help you. Your worst problem is that you don't realize how lucky you are."

Mehki finally cut him off. "Enough, Moshe. We are here to guard the boy and keep him safe. Let him figure it out on his own." He stared hard at his younger brother until Moshe nodded at him. In a moment, his face had returned to its normal expression of stony detachment.

Mehki gave me a nod. "Your uncle bade us to keep you from harm, Olaf. We will do our best, for his sake." Then he fell silent as well. They stood by the doorway as still as two statues.

Moshe had let his feelings be known, but what about Mehki? He always seemed so happy next to his younger brother. Did he share his brother's feelings about me? Did he think I was just a spoiled rich man—no, a spoiled, rich *boy*? He had called me a boy! Is that how my uncle saw me as well?

The look on Mehki's face reminded me of how I felt about my uncle. My uncle's father had been the head of the Stenson family, but had been killed by the Duke of Kartoba. Uncle Olaf had been sent into exile, but he returned and won himself a kingdom. He was the toughest man I knew.

I shook my head and took a few deep breaths. I needed to find a way to take control of my life. I wanted to make my uncle proud, but I wanted to do it on my own instead of being manipulated by everyone around me. I needed to find a way to control my destiny without throwing a fit like a spoiled, rich boy.

I stood and made my way to the doorway. I paused as I passed my guards and gave them a nod. "Thank you," I said. Then I headed back to confront my future—the way my uncle would.

The army from Sui arrived two days later. We had been in a standoff with the new Jiang Jun. His troops were stationed between our encampment and Jungong. He wanted the Dai Jun and Dai Ling to return to the palace. He was even willing to let me leave, but only if they complied.

Unfortunately for him, the palace guardsmen had all remained loyal to the Dai Jun and his granddaughter, and the crowds had not subsided since the Moon Festival. In fact, we now had hundreds of men and women coming forward to pledge themselves to Dai Ling and our march west. My new bride was more popular than I had realized.

When we discussed our growing army of common folk, the Dai Jun said that he already had an army, and it was up to me and Dai Ling to deal with these volunteers. Ivan and my guardsmen—with the help of Dai Ling's bodyguard, Talon, and Carrog—started sorting through the people and trying to organize the men who insisted upon being in Dai Ling's army.

The bodyguard's name was Liu De. He was a native of Sui, as were all of the Dai Jun's palace guardsmen. Apparently, the original Dai Jun had conquered the tribes of Sui and became their *kehan*, or supreme king. They had sworn loyalty to his bloodline and had provided warriors for his conquering armies. Later, they had become guardsmen for his palace.

When the Sui army arrived, Jiang Jun retreated to his newly acquired castle on the hill and we controlled the town of Sikk. The day after this occurred, the BaWang descended from Jungong to visit our encampment. I was eating breakfast in the hall in Waicun when a runner came to let me know of the BaWang's visit.

I headed over to the Dai Jun's Pavilion with Dai Ling and Neasa in tow. To my surprise, the women got along much better than I had anticipated, probably because of Dai Ling's sunny disposition.

When we arrived, the Dai Jun was waiting for us, seated on a chair that looked suspiciously like the one from the room in Jungong where I had first met him. He had a pair of stools on one side for Dai Ling and I to sit on, and Neasa stood next to us, along with my Wolf guards. The three banners hung at our backs—with the Dai Jun's in the center, of course. All his talk of following Dai Ling and me to our destiny seemed to be forgotten. He acted as though it was *his* campaign now, not ours, or mine.

"Why has the BaWang come now, grandfather?" Dai Ling asked.

The Dai Jun gave her a smug little smile. "He has recognized that Jiang Jun is not the power he had anticipated."

"And he is worried about what you might do with your army," Neasa said in a voice that was low but loud enough so that we all heard.

The Dai Jun preened upon his chair but otherwise ignored her comment. "The BaWang hoped to use my cousin to further his own ambitions," he said. He shook his head in mock consternation, obviously enjoying the drama. "I suspect he is here to shower us with his good will."

The bald servant led the BaWang into the pavilion. He was accompanied by Cao Wangsun, but the rest of his yellow-clad attendants were stopped at the tent opening by the Dai Jun's guards. The BaWang wore a long yellow robe and matching sash and a hat that made the Dai Jun's monstrosity look pale in comparison. He appeared to be of an age with the Dai Jun, except his beard wasn't quite as long. He held himself with the same air of smugness as my benefactor. Cao Wangsun, in contrast, look as though he didn't want to be there. He glanced nervously between me and Neasa, probably worried that one of us would reveal our past partnership.

"Dai Jun!" the BaWang called out in an annoyingly false-happy voice. "I am your servant."

He dropped to his knees at the appropriate distance and waited for the Dai Jun to acknowledge him. Cao Wangsun dropped down beside him but said nothing.

The Dai Jun looked over at me and raised one eyebrow as if showing off. He waited long enough for the pause to feel awkward before replying. "Why have you come, Cao Fan?"

The BaWang looked up, his face a neutral mask. The Dai Jun had not addressed him by his title. In fact, he had not even given him a title but had called him by his given name. For Eastern nobility, this was insulting—but not even the BaWang would dare confront the Dai Jun over it, especially with his army of Sui warriors at hand.

The Dai Jun had not given him permission to rise, so the BaWang stayed on his knees as he answered. "I have come, Great Kehan, to ask what you plan to do with your army of Sui warriors."

His use of the title *Kehan* was telling. Dai Ling had explained her grandfather's relationship with the Sui to me earlier. The Dai Jun was the benevolent ruler of the Eastern Confederation, content to sit in Jungong and leave the kingdoms to themselves—but the Kehan was the war-leader of the Sui, the conqueror who made the world tremble when he raised his banner.

"I go where I will," the Dai Jun answered. "It is not for you to question."

The BaWang bowed his head in acknowledgment of the rebuke. What had he hoped to gain by coming? He had already sided with Jiang Qui at the Moon Festival. Was he worried the Dai Jun would seize his kingdom and his title as recompense?

"I go west, Cao BaWang," the Dai Jun said. I wondered if he actually felt sorry for the man, although it was hard to imagine pity from the man who had thrown me into his cellar to see if I would crack. "My granddaughter wishes it, so I go west to Jewel and beyond."

"You will not pass through my kingdom?" The BaWang hazarded the question, not daring to raise his head. Was that hope I heard in his voice? "You do not require my warriors?"

To my surprise, the Dai Jun gave me a sidelong look, a question in his eyes. Did he actually care what *I* wanted, or did he expect me to be swept along in his wake?

I had resolved to not be manipulated. I had resolved to follow my uncle's example of courage. I cleared my throat. "I will march to Gea before heading west." The Dai Jun already knew that was my plan. He also knew I went to recover the woman I loved—a woman who wasn't his granddaughter.

"There you have it," the Dai Jun said. "I will march west, to Jewel, and my granddaughter's consort will also march west by way of Gea and the sea."

Now he looked directly at me. "Do *you* require assistance from this man?" He was putting me on the spot, testing me again to see what I would do.

I had assumed we would all march to Gea and then west. It now appeared that, despite his talk of supporting his granddaughter, the Dai Jun's only thought was to attack his hereditary enemy, the Empire of Jewel.

Of course! It suddenly dawned on me that this was what I had come east to do. I wanted to re-ignite the fighting between Jewel and the Eastern Confederation. He had to know that, too. Was he actually trying to help me?

I looked at the BaWang, who was still kneeling but now looking at me to see what I would say. Cao Wangsun hadn't uttered a word or even lifted his head up from the floor. Was he still worried that his grandfather would find out about his scheming? Cao Wangsun had agreed to be my general at our last meeting. Neasa said he had been trained for it.

As I realized what I should do, I felt a flash of something— was it excitement or maliciousness?—when I imagined how the room would react.

"I leave it to my general to decide what he needs," I said. I saw Cao Wangsun's shoulders slump as I called out his name. "Cao Wangsun, you will decide how your grandfather can support our effort."

Feeling smug, I looked to the Dai Jun to see his reaction and caught the tail-end of a look between him and the BaWang. Neither of them had been surprised. The Dai Jun had told me before that he knew of my plans with Cao Wangsun. Had the BaWang known, as well? Had they somehow anticipated what I would do?

They were both much wiser in the ways of politics than I would ever be. Frustration gripped me, but I fought to keep it off my face.

Dai Ling reached over and squeezed my arm, which made me feel worse. She was a sweet girl, but she had grown up in Jungong and had a keen understanding of Eastern politics. The fact that we still slept in separate beds, and that I continued to rebuke her attempts to seduce me, only made her sympathy feel worse.

Cao Wangsun finally looked up, appearing more ecstatic than distressed. The BaWang, who knelt beside him, looked rather proud of himself. It was hard to tell because of their practiced, emotion-free faces, but I had a sinking feeling I had been manipulated again.

I pulled free of Dai Ling and stood. "I leave it to you, then." I tried to sound unconcerned, but I was pretty sure they saw my distress. "Stay here and let me know what happens," I hissed at my wife. Then I left the tent with Neasa close behind.

Bren waited for me just outside. I snapped at him, "Call all my people together now, in the meeting hall."

He looked startled and began to ask, "Who—"

"Everyone!" I answered. "Otto, Talon, Ivan." I looked back at Neasa who was still following me. "And Carrog."

Bren gave me a quick nod and turned to rush away. "And make sure none of my wife's people are there," I called after him.

Once he was off, I led Neasa to the hall. "You can trust Dai Ling," she said. "She will support you for the sake of your future children."

Not for my own sake? Neasa would know better than I; she and Dai Ling had become cozy in a short period of time. "Maybe," I said, "but she is his granddaughter, and I don't trust him or his people."

"Do you trust anyone?"

I paused to look at her. Neasa still wore her leather vest and had her dark hair pulled up in a braid. She looked like the Kail war-leader of her reputation—not the ship's captain nor the Dryhten's daughter. It seemed her persona changed with each new outfit.

"Why do they call you Dark Thunder?"

For a brief moment, her face took on a menacing look, but then it passed into a smile. "You're avoiding the question."

"So are you," I shot back. She stood there smiling at me until I finally spoke again. "For some reason, I do trust you— Neasa *Dark Thunder*."

Her smile brightened. "I told you, it was my vision—"

"I trust *you*, Neasa—not your vision. I have no use for visions or gods."

She shrugged. "That's good enough, partner. Let's go and talk to *your* people."

I filled everyone in on the Dai Jun's plan to march west to Jewel while we headed to Gea. We talked about building our army along the way. Talon and Carrog were tasked with keeping an eye on Cao Wangsun. I asked Ivan to continue recruiting Stenson guardsmen, but only men he felt sure he could trust.

Neasa offered to send some of her men downriver back to Xiang to have her Birlinn meet us in Gea, and to spread the word among the Kail that were loyal to her. I asked Otto to provide a riverboat for them. He also insisted upon traveling with them to take up his position as factor to the Eastern Confederation. I had Ivan assign a contingent of Stenson guardsmen to escort him.

256

The meeting was quick, as I wanted to finish before Dai Ling returned. Afterwards, I felt better than when I left the Dai Jun's pavilion.

We were doing something, finally. I hoped I had people I could trust behind me.

CHAPTER 26: GOING HOME

Otto left for Xiang the next day. He insisted that Lulu stay behind with Gabriele. She had been working with Gabriele for some time, and he felt that she would be safer traveling with me and the army. Also, if Factor Einhardt resisted being replaced, Otto didn't want to worry about his daughter's safety.

Ivan sent Sigwald with a contingent of Stenson guardsmen to protect Otto on his journey. Sigwald deserved the promotion. He had been with me since Kartoba.

We began our march to Gea later that week. The Dai Jun agreed to stay in Sikk for another couple of weeks to ensure Jiang Jun wouldn't pursue us. Then he would march to Jewel. I was a bit surprised that Dai Ling didn't stay with him, but she had professed her loyalty to me and stayed by my side. This was good, because I wasn't sure her people would remain with us unless she was there.

Our army had grown, partly due to a contingent of yellow-clad troops that Cao Wangsun had wrangled from his grandfather, but also because of the people from Sikk who had pledged themselves to Dai Ling. Unfortunately, there were too many of us now to go by river, so we had to march to our destination.

Dai Ling had procured—I assumed from her grandfather—a four-wheeled carriage that we used as transport. Her shiwei sat in the front with the carriage driver, and my Wolf guards rode on a bench on the tail end of the carriage. Our servants followed in one of the mule carts that carried our baggage—

well, it was mostly Dai Ling's baggage. I still had just the single clothes chest and what was left of my uncle's silver.

Besides our personal guards, our carriage was surrounded by about a score of her nei-chang guardsmen, mounted on horseback. Not to be outdone, Ivan had procured horses for an equal amount of Stenson guardsmen, so that they could stay close as well. I didn't yet trust the nei-chang, even though they appeared to be loyal to Dai Ling. Ivan gave command of the Stenson horsemen to Li Wu, the Eastern guardsman who had joined up with us in Xiang.

Our army really looked more like a traveling circus than an army to me, with the yellow, green, and blue uniforms, various banners flying, and the myriad of carts, mules, and people tagging along. Maybe that was what armies always looked like, but I had no experience with such things. Luckily, Cao Wangsun seemed to have everything in hand as we began our journey.

The first day's march was a disappointment. It seemed we spent more time sitting in the carriage and waiting for the army to march than we did actually moving. It was frustrating, because I was finally heading back to Gea, and Sofie—but we hardly seemed to move at all. Of course, sitting in that carriage with Dai Ling made me feel worse. She was upset over leaving her grandfather—and probably distraught over my stubbornness in the bedroom.

If my days of suffering through that ride were bad, the nights were even worse. We had a pavilion—not as big as the Dai Jun's—that Dai Ling's people set up every night. After the march, we met with the leaders of the army, ate dinner, and then retired for the evening. Once we were alone, Dai Ling continued her attempts to lure me to her bed. She was hard to resist. She had a seemingly endless supply of provocative bed clothes. But I had resolved to deny her dream. I wanted nothing to do with whatever her dragon ancestor-god had in store for me.

Sometimes at night, while I lay on my pad across the tent from her, I wondered if I was the biggest fool ever. A pretty girl desired to sleep with me, and I continued to resist her. On those nights, I held the memory of Sofie in my heart. I kept reminding myself that each day, I was drawing closer to my real love.

The days and nights continued their familiar pattern as we made our slow way across the countryside toward Gea. Each night, when we met with Cao Wangsun, he reported more people joining our army. News traveled ahead of us, and people came from all around, flocking to Dai Ling's butterfly banner.

When I met with Ivan, he told me that his recruitment of Stenson guardsmen was progressing well. He was being choosy, so we didn't have nearly as many men marching under our lion banner, but he assured me these men would be loyal if the time came that we needed them. I hoped he was right. My fear was that Dai Ling would eventually tire of my bedroom resistance and leave me to march alone.

The march to Gea seemed to last a lifetime, but finally, we neared our goal. When we made camp the night before we were to arrive, I was beside myself with excitement. I could barely sit still as I met with the council.

As usual, Cao Wangsun gave a report on the army. When we had left Sikk, the army consisted of one thousand soldiers that Cao Wangsun had borrowed from his grandfather, plus a couple of hundred nei-chang guardsmen and not even a hundred trained men under my banner. The multitude of people who had followed us from Sikk had been organized into the army—not to mention all the people that had joined us on the march.

Now, Cao Wangsun's thousand yellow-clad soldiers were dwarfed by the rest of the army. The number of fighting men was nearly ten thousand strong. True, most of them were half-trained and under-equipped, but they were full of fire at the prospect of Sikk rising to its former glory. I now had more than a thousand Stenson guardsmen among their ranks.

It seemed like a lot of men to me, but Cao Wangsun never seemed satisfied. "We will need more troops than this," he said every night as he ended his report.

Dai Ling seemed as good-natured as ever, but the closer we got to Gea, the more distracted she became. She suddenly looked up when Cao Wangsun finished his report and said, "If we need more soldiers, Cao Wangsun, ask your grandfather to send them."

The BaWang had promised to send more troops once he reached Xiang, but none had joined us on the march, and none seemed to be waiting for us in Gea, either. Everyone figured that the BaWang was biding his time and waiting for us to leave the Eastern Confederation so he could consolidate his power. Nobody mentioned it in our meetings, though, in deference to Cao Wangsun's honor.

Cao Wangsun had avoided the subject, as well. Now he looked embarrassed. "Yes, princess, I will do so."

It was not like Dai Ling to make anyone uncomfortable, and all eyes were on her as he replied. She seemed startled by the attention and suddenly rose from her chair. "I shall retire now," she announced. She didn't even give me her normal, hopeful look as she made her way to the curtain that separated our sleeping quarters from the rest of the pavilion.

Everyone rose when she did and started making their way out of the tent. Only Ivan remained. Sitting across the table from me, he let out a sigh and looked me over as if trying to decide how to begin whatever it was he had to say.

"What is *wrong*, Ivan?" I demanded. Ever since our talk at the camp on the river, he had seemed more tight-lipped than usual. Was he finally ready to tell me what was bothering him?

Ivan scratched at his dirty blond whiskers, looking solemn.

"Are we out of sonti?" I asked, attempting to be funny.

He shook his head and licked his lips before finally speaking. "I have come to like you, Olaf."

His statement surprised me, but I remained silent to see what else he had to say.

"Despite your poor judgement and inexperience, you have come far—farther than I would have expected." He looked down at his hands. It looked as though he wanted to reach for a cup. "But that's the problem."

"What?" I didn't understand what he was trying to say. Yes, I was inexperienced, and had definitely made mistakes—but we were now heading back home with an army to help my uncle. "I have accomplished what my uncle asked. We will march home with an army, and the Dai Jun will attack Jewel. I did everything he asked."

He nodded in agreement. "Yes, but that is not what your uncle truly wanted."

"What?"

His blue eyes were clearer than I had seen before. "Your uncle asked me to keep you safe, Olaf. You were supposed to come east and be safe—not go rushing back into danger."

"I don't understand." Uncle Olaf sent me as his envoy and had trusted me to pursue his interests in the east. Ivan had helped me the whole way.

"Think about it, Olaf. He sent you east with a handful of guardsmen and a small group of servants. He gave you control of your family's business in the Eastern Confederation. Do you think he ever expected you to accomplish anything? He just wanted you to survive." He shook his head. "He was my old order mate, and he asked me to *keep* you in the east."

My mind couldn't grasp what he was saying. "But he said … we have an army." I stared at the old mercenary-turned-guardsman, my long-time confidante. "You helped me."

He sighed and shook his head. "It's too late, Olaf. The Dark Order has already marched."

"What?" It couldn't be too late! I had finally done what my uncle had asked. I'd sat in a dark cell for months, and married a princess to complete my mission. It could *not* be too late! I felt like the world had turned on its side.

"A couple of days ago, I had Ulric ride ahead," Ivan explained. "He returned just before our meeting. The Dark Order has marched west. There is no way we'll beat them to your uncle."

"How does Ulric know? Who did he talk to?" I had a sinking feeling in my gut, even as I tried to refute what he was saying.

"He met with Captain Luther and that Stenson clerk in Gea. Olaf, it is too late. You need to stay here in Gea. Stay safe, as your uncle wanted."

"How do I know that's what he wanted?" I pushed to my feet and stared down at him. "How do I know you aren't lying to me, Ivan? I thought you were my friend."

Ivan didn't rise. His face remained set in his normal, unreadable expression. "You have a wife here, and your family business. You are consort to a princess. You could have your own kingdom here. Stay and be happy."

"Why are you telling me this now, Ivan?" I trembled as I stood before him. "Why now? Why not before we left for Sikk? I could have been happy then, together with Sofie, in Gea."

Ivan's expression finally broke and he lowered his eyes to the table. "Go to your wife, Olaf. Make her happy. Establish a kingdom and stay with her here and live." He pushed himself up from the table and turned away without looking back at me.

Something wasn't right. I had spent too much time with Ivan to be fooled. "What aren't you telling me?" I called out—but he left the tent without answering.

Something wasn't right. I knew it in my bones. Ivan had not told me everything. Was my uncle already dead? Had the Seven Kingdoms been laid to waste while I languished in that cell?

Everyone had left now except my Wolf guards and servants. Moshe and Mehki looked impassive, as usual, but Bren and Gabriele looked as if they expected me to burst into flames at any minute. They were right to be concerned.

I watched the curtain that Dai Ling had passed through. Ivan had told me to make her happy and stay in the east—but that was not what I wanted. I wanted to see Sofie and my uncle again. I wanted to save my homeland. I couldn't even think about facing Dai Ling in that moment. Another night with her and another day in that damned carriage would be more than I could bear.

"We will be in Gea tomorrow," Bren tried to console me.

"No," I said. "We will go now." I needed to get to Gea and see Sofie. I needed to find out for myself what was going on.

"Get me a horse!" I shouted at him. "I'm leaving for Gea."

Bren looked close to panic. "I'll get Ivan."

"No! Bren, if you are as loyal as you say, you will get me a horse. Secure mounts for yourself and Moshe and Mehki, too. We will leave for Gea at once."

"I am loyal, Olaf." Bren looked suddenly grim-faced but determined. "I am your valet. Meet me at the horse picket and the horses will be waiting." He hurried from the room.

Moshe and Mehki didn't say a word, but they began to pick up their belongings. Gabriele looked white-faced. "Do not say anything to anyone, Gabriele," I warned her. "Not even Lulu."

I could tell she wanted to argue, but she nodded instead. "Yes, Master Olaf."

We left the pavilion and headed to the picket. Bren was waiting, as was Li Wu and his group of mounted guardsmen. Bren apologized as soon as I arrived. "He would not let me take the horses unless I told him why."

I looked a Li Wu. I had barely spoken to him since meeting him in Xiang months before, but he was sworn to my service. "I am going to Gea," I said. "You cannot tell anyone."

He nodded and then gave me a smile. "I cannot tell anyone if I am riding with you, Master Olaf. We are your guards, after all."

I didn't have time to argue, and actually, I would feel safer with the escort. We mounted up and headed out of the camp.

That ride through the night was a blur. No one spoke. I was lost in my thoughts, and the rest caught my mood.

I felt torn—excited to finally see Sofie again, but dreading the news I would hear of my uncle and his kingdom. We pushed the horses as hard as we could, alternating between a trot and canter, until we finally came within sight of Gea. It was early morning when we spotted firelight in the distance. Once sighted, I could no longer contain my impatience, and I galloped my exhausted horse forward.

The lights turned out to be torches set on the walls of Gea. I knew it was a walled town, but I hadn't really left the harbor district on my last visit. I slowed my horse as we approached the mud-brick wall, taken aback by the closed gates

The sun was just beginning to rise, but we approached the city from the north, so the wall was still dark except for the torchlight. We reined in our horses and looked up at the archery tower over the gate. A man called down at us in Eastern.

I turned to Li Wu to translate, glad that he had insisted upon accompanying us.

"He asks who we are."

I hadn't thought past getting to Gea and seeing Sofie. I hadn't even thought about the city wall, nor considered that the gates would be closed. I sat before the gate now and tried to think through what to say.

I wasn't sure how friendly the ruler of Gea would be to us. He was just as much a king as the BaWang, and I had no idea if he would bow before Dai Ling without her grandfather present. Should I even tell him who I was?

"Ask him if they have heard that the Butterfly Princess and her consort are approaching."

Li Wu relayed my question, and the man immediately responded.

"He says that they have heard and are eagerly awaiting her arrival."

I glanced at Li Wu's red sash. He was from Gea. He would know if they were being truthful—wouldn't he? "Will your people welcome us?" I asked him.

Li Wu grinned at my question. "She is of the dragon blood. All of the world will welcome her."

I had my doubts about the whole world, but I believed he was right about Gea. Still, I had no desire to be hampered by protocols if they knew who I was. I wanted to get into the city and go to the house where I had left Sofie and my guardsmen.

"Tell them that we are here on behalf of the Butterfly Princess's consort and wish to enter the city to prepare for his arrival."

265

Li Wu called this up to the tower. When they responded, he translated. "The gate will be opened shortly, Master Olaf. They will allow us to enter, but the guard captain would like to speak with us before we enter the city."

I nodded and then fretted as we waited for the gates to open. Hopefully, only the one guard captain would question us, and then let us on our way. I dreaded the thought of being passed from one officer to another, waiting to be allowed entry.

A pair of wooden doors behind the metal gate opened first, and a group of guardsmen wearing red uniforms stood just on the other side of the gate. One of them—presumably the guard captain, because he had a bigger hat—stepped up to the gate and spoke in Imperial, recognizing that I was from the west. "What news do you bring of the Hudie Gongzhu and her consort?"

They had heard about my wife. It still surprised me that no one questioned how she suddenly appeared as the Dai Jun's heir. "They are a day's march to the north and should be here by nightfall."

The captain nodded. "General Cao had already sent us that word, but his messenger said nothing of *your* arrival."

Of course, Cao Wangsun had sent messengers ahead of the army. I hadn't even thought to ask him if they had returned with any word from the west. Had he known of the Black Order marching from Jewel, but said nothing? I pushed that from my mind and replied, "My master left people here on his last visit, and he asked that I check on them before he arrives."

"Yes," the guard captain said. "We heard he is the heir to the Stenson trading family. A rich man from the west. He was here in the summer before traveling to Sikk."

So they knew all about me, too. I shouldn't have been surprised. News traveled fast—especially big news like the Dai Jun and his granddaughter visiting from Sikk. They probably knew about my twisted leg, as well. I stayed up on my horse, hoping they would not ask us to dismount. "Will you allow us to enter Gea, to carry out our master's bidding?"

The guard captain looked us over one more time and then nodded. He called up to the tower above, and the metal gate began to rise. "I will provide an escort to ensure you don't get lost trying to find the proper residence in Gea."

And to keep tabs on us, I imagined—but that was fine, as long as I arrived at my destination.

We entered the gate and traversed a short tunnel to the inner gate, which stood open. The ride through the tunnel, even though it was wide enough for several horses abreast, was scary. The walls were filled with arrow slits, and men looked down on us from above as we passed through. I would hate to be an army trying to break into the city through that narrow passage. Once we passed through the gatehouse, a handful of Gea guardsmen on horseback were waiting to escort us.

The guard captain with the large hat had followed us. He now mounted a waiting horse. "Your master has a house upon the hill overlooking Gea," he said. "I will escort you there."

Now I was getting worried. Did all the Gea guards know about me and where I had left my people? How fast had the news traveled back from Sikk? I guessed I should have realized that news would travel faster than a slow-moving army.

The guard squad headed through the streets of Gea toward the hill where I had confiscated Factor Einhardt's house. It was a good thing the guardsmen led the way, because I probably would have taken a few wrong turns trying to find the place. I doubted Bren or my Wolf guards would have fared any better with their memory of the town. So much had happened since we'd been here.

Few people were on the roads so early, and we traveled quickly to the hill. Still, time seemed to stand still. Maybe it was my heart thudding in my chest at the thought of reuniting with Sofie.

I recognized the house when we approached and could barely contain my excitement. The guard captain reined up in front of the gate and waited. I wasn't sure why he waited. I wanted him to leave so I could hop off my horse and rush into the place looking for my love.

"Thank you for your assistance," I said, hoping he would take that as a dismissal.

He nodded but said nothing.

I turned my horse and nudged him toward Li Wu with a questioning look.

"You must pay him," Li Wu explained. "The rich merchants pay for an escort through the city. They aren't paid much by Sun Wang," Li Wu looked somewhat embarrassed. "That is why I joined your guardsmen, Master Olaf."

"You were a Gea guardsman before?"

Li Wu nodded.

"What is the going rate?" I asked.

Li Wu turned to the guard captain and had a quick conversation in Eastern and the turned back to me. "A silver apiece, and two for the guard captain."

It was a hefty price for a quick jaunt through the city, but I pulled the silver out of my purse and handed the coins to Li Wu. While he paid the guardsmen, I dismounted and stumped over to the gate to pound on it. While I waited for a response, I called back up to Li Wu.

"Why don't you have him show you the way to the Stenson warehouse near the water? There should be enough space there for all of you. I'll call if I need you." From what I remembered, the house was probably big enough to house them all, but I wanted privacy for my reunion with Sofie.

Li Wu nodded, and I tossed him a purse with more silver for the next "toll."

They waited until the gate opened before leaving. Li Wu saluted me as he rode off. I stood before the gate with Bren and my Wolf guards, looking into the face of a startled Stenson guardsman.

"Master Olaf!" he cried out.

"Yes," I replied with a huge smile on my face. "I'm back."

I recognized the guardsman, but couldn't recall his name. Actually, I had never bothered to learn it. As I stood there, I wished I had paid more attention to my men back then.

He pulled the gate farther open, looking rather startled—or perhaps frightened. "I'll get Captain Luther," he stammered as he rushed away.

I traded a look with Bren, who shrugged, as we walked through the gate. I could hear the sounds of people stirring as we walked across the courtyard. Before we could make it half-way, Captain Luther rushed out of the side building, where the guardsmen were staying, followed closely by the rest of the guards who had stayed behind in Gea. They formed a hasty line and stood to attention as Captain Luther approached me.

"Master Olaf, it is good to see you!" Even though the captain smiled, the look on his face set off an alarm in my head. Before I could question him, I spied Ursala emerging from the main house with a bundle in her arms. She approached me slowly with a solemn gait that made the hair stick up on the back of my neck.

I called out, "Where is Sofie?"

The courtyard fell suddenly quiet and no one wanted to meet my eye. I felt sick.

Ursala stopped before me. "Here is Sofie—your daughter," she said.

The words froze me in my tracks and I looked at the bundle she had been carrying and realized it was a baby. "Daughter?"

So many images flashed through my mind in that instant that I couldn't describe any of them, but the last image that burned the rest away was the image of Sofie's face that I had held close for so long.

"Where is *my* Sofie?" I knew the answer from the look on Ursala's face, and I could feel my world start to crumble before she spoke.

"It was a hard labor …"

I didn't hear the rest. Sofie had been pregnant when I left. She had been pregnant, but she hadn't told me, so that I would do my duty to my uncle instead of staying with her. I could picture it in my head: Sofie pushing me away, telling me to go and do my duty, while she stayed behind to have my child.

Had she imagined a happy reunion—me coming home to her loving arms and our new child?

Ursala was still talking, but I had no idea what she was saying. She tried to push the child into my arms, but I stepped back as if stung. I couldn't accept what was happening. I needed to get away.

I turned and fled.

The next thing I remembered was sitting in a tavern and drinking sonti. I had no memory of how I got there, but the sonti helped with the pain, so I kept drinking.

CHAPTER 27: BE THE LION

I woke up convinced that someone had used my head as a drum. Something still pounded away behind my eyes, and I didn't dare open them for fear that my head might explode. I felt the bed move, and wondered if it was from the sonti, but then I felt soft skin rub against my arm.

Sofie? No, it couldn't be Sofie. *Sofie was dead!* The realization brought back all the pain I had tried to drink away. My eyes flashed open of their own accord.

Light seared into my eyeballs and I groaned as I rolled away from whoever shared my bed. It had to be a whore from the tavern, I thought. I tried to get my eyes to focus.

"How are you feeling, my love?" Dai Ling's happy voice hit me like a charging lion, and I froze in place, too stunned by her voice to respond or think straight. My stomach turned over and I stumbled out of bed looking for a pot to puke in. As I threw up on the rug, I realized that I recognized the pattern. I was in our pavilion.

"How do you feel, husband?"

I stared at the mess I had made on the rug. How did I get here? I had been in Gea and Dai Ling had been a day away.

The loss of Sofie suddenly hit me again, and I stumbled for the corner where my pad should lay, but it wasn't there.

"Come back to bed, Olaf," Dai Ling called. "You need to recover."

I finally turned and looked at my wife. She lay on her side facing me, naked. Her hair fell across her face, obscuring her birthmark. Once I looked, she stretched like a happy cat and gave me a satisfied smile. By her look, I guessed that she had finally gotten what she wanted from me—but if she had, I had no memory of it.

"Sofie is dead," I whispered.

She knew I loved Sofie. Had she even planned this? Did she wait for me to drink myself stupid so she could finally claim her prize?

Dai Ling nodded and tossed her hair away from her face, revealing her birthmark and her intimidating seer's eye. "That girl was not meant for you, Olaf. I am your wife."

I didn't know what to say. I had avoided her for Sofie's sake, and to spite her dragon's blood- inspired visions of the future. I realized in that moment that I was no *lion*, maybe a housecat—or a dog. Dogs were obedient, right? They came running back, no matter how many times you kicked them. Seeing Dai Ling lying there, basking in her triumph, was too much to bear on top of Sofie's loss.

My anger boiled to the surface. "You have won," I shouted at her. "I am you lapdog to do with as you please. Train me to be a good boy, and maybe I'll get a treat." I felt the tears flowing, but I didn't care anymore.

The smile slipped from her face and she moved to the edge of the bed, covering herself with a blanket as she rose to approach me. "Olaf," she said, reaching out to me, but I backed away, not daring to let her touch me for fear I might melt away.

I was tempted to let it happen. Mehki had once told me that my fate was tied to women. Why not this one? Did it really matter anymore? Then I noticed that, even as she reached for me with the one hand, the other went to her belly. Could she be pregnant already? I knew it only took one time, but it was too early to know, wasn't it? Or did her vision tell her that, as well?

The gesture hardened my resolve again, and I pulled away from her. "You have what you want, Dai Ling. Now leave me in peace."

She pulled her hand back with a stricken look on her face. "I am your wife."

"And I am a dream you once had that I never shared. My dream died while I was locked away in your grandfather's cellar. She died here, alone, without me."

The look on her face made me hate myself for those words. I hardened my heart and turned away. "All I need from you is an army." I made myself walk toward the exit, fighting the urge to turn back. I was finished being a dog. If Dai Ling wanted a lion, she would have one.

Bren waited for me outside our sleeping area. He didn't say a word as he helped me dress.

"What day is it?" I asked my valet.

"You were drunk for two days," he replied. "The army arrived yesterday evening and we managed to carry you back to your pavilion."

I turned and eyed my Wolf guards, but they looked as impassive as ever. "I'm not sure I should thank you."

Bren just looked at me for a moment and then said, "I am sorry, Olaf."

His words threatened to bring back the tears, but I had resolved to be a lion. "Go fetch Ivan and Cao Wangsun," I snarled.

To my Wolf guards, I added, "Not a damn word."

I tried to eat something before everyone arrived, although I wasn't sure my stomach would allow it. Lulu brought me breakfast, instead of Gabriele. When I gave her a quizzical look, she said, "Gabriele has gone to see ..."

I knew what she was going to say. She looked embarrassed and scurried away.

Neasa and Talon arrived, along with Ivan and Cao Wangsun. They all gave me sympathetic looks, but waited for me to speak. Just as we were about to begin, Dai Ling emerged from behind the curtain to our sleeping quarters and took her place by my side. Neither of us looked at each other as we discussed our plans.

Gea had opened its gates for my wife and Sun Wang had pledged his support. Also, Neasa's men who had gone ahead of the army had passed the word, and several Kail birlinn had arrived in Gea to support her. She also got word that Reik Maedoc had sailed for Andamar once he got word of the Dai Jun's march on Jewel.

"Where do we go from here?" I asked.

Cao Wangsun spoke first. "Sun Wang has offered his fleet, and there are several other ships in Gea to transport a portion of our army across to the western shore."

"How many?"

He shrugged. "Maybe half, but the first wave can secure a position in Malar and hold it until the rest arrive. It would be quicker than marching overland, and with The Dai Jun marching against Jewel itself, I wouldn't expect much resistance."

We had a map on the table before us. Malar was the Imperial province that sat adjacent to Gea and straddled the strait that led into the Sea of Pearls. The capital of Jewel was north of us and dominated the western shore of the Sea of Pearls. It would be a straight march west from Sikk for the Dai Jun, but we would have to march up the east coast of the Sea of Pearls to get there.

Cao Wangsun was right. It would be quicker to sail across the strait, past Rock Island, to the western shore. This was fine with me, since I had no intention of marching north to the City of Jewel.

I had to march west, to try to catch the Black Order. My uncle was all I had left. I couldn't let him down.

"Who goes first?"

Neasa spoke up. "My Kail warriors are impatient for a fight. We will be in the vanguard." I had no idea how many birlinn had arrived to join her, but I appreciated their aggression. It matched my own.

I looked to Cao Wangsun, and he, in turn, looked at my wife before replying. "We each have a thousand men under our banner, Master Olaf, but mine are better trained. I should go with the vanguard and help establish our position. I will take half of your wife's forces with me. You can follow with your thousand men and the other half." He looked to Ivan, who nodded.

"Okay," I said. "How soon can we start?"

"I will go with the vanguard as well," Dai Ling suddenly announced. We looked at each other for the first time since our encounter in the bed chamber. She seemed more determined than I had seen before. "Even in Malar, people will flock to my banner if I am there."

She may have been right, but I wondered if she decided she wanted a break from me because of my cruel words. I didn't blame her, and I welcomed it as well.

I just nodded. "That makes sense." I turned back to Cao Wangsun, "How soon can you leave?"

"Within the week." He leaned over and traced his finger along the coast of Gea on the map. "You should march to the nearest shore, while we sail along the coast. That way, once we land across the strait, the ships will have a shorter distance to travel to ferry your men over."

Ivan spoke up. "How many soldiers should we expect in this part of Malar? I assume Jewel maintains several garrisons along the border with Gea."

Cao Wangsun shook his head. "The border between Malar and Gea has been peaceful for some time. Most of the past fighting was farther north, between Suma and Jewel proper." He pointed at several points along the Malar border. "We have word that these garrisons have marched north in response to the Dai Jun's advance on Jewel—and of course, the Malik of Suma has supported the Dai Jun in the attack."

Ivan gave me a nod. "It sounds like there should be little resistance. We should be able to march right through the border."

"Even if we leave in a week," Cao Wangsun pointed out. "The ships will make better time to the straits. You should march as soon as possible to meet us there."

"Then we shall leave tomorrow," I said. "My troops and half of my wife's. We will meet the returning boats at the straits."

The army had just arrived at the city of Gea. I expected some kind of resistance, but nobody else spoke. When I stood from the table, everyone stood with me. Without another word, I swept out of the tent.

I spent the day wandering through the camp, trying to keep my mind off of Sofie's death and my resultant tryst with Dai Ling. Ivan could have handled all the details for our march, but I accompanied him as he made the arrangements. I didn't want to go back to the pavilion—I couldn't face Dai Ling again.

She had been trying her best to seduce me since we married, but had never been mean or cruel to me, as I had been to her that morning. I knew that I owed her an apology, but couldn't bring myself to do it. I had to be that damn lion she had dreamed about—not for her sake, but for my own. I had to keep my anger burning hot so that I could keep marching forward to save my uncle.

I made it back to the pavilion in time for the evening meal with Dai Ling. We ate in silence. When we retired to the sleeping area, I noticed that my sleeping pad was back in the corner. Once Bren assisted me with removing my clothes, I headed for the corner. As usual, Dai Ling's handmaids undressed her before leaving us alone.

The lone lamp left burning near the curtain was the only light. I had insisted that a lamp remain lit every night since my stay in the cellar. Since that time, the darkness had played tricks on my mind.

As I lay on my pad, I stared at the lamp across the room and waited for Dai Ling to fall asleep. I could hear her toss in the bed for a while before she finally quieted down. Afterward, I hazarded a look toward her bed and was shocked to see her staring at me.

"I could march with you to the coast, husband, instead of sailing with Cao Wangsun—if you wished it." She looked rather sad when she spoke, and I wanted to reach out to her to make her feel better. Instead, I rolled onto my back.

"I think it is best this way," I replied, not too kindly.

She let out a great sigh and I heard her roll away. "It will be as you wish." The tone of her voice sent a shiver down my back, as if she had invoked another of her visions.

Our breakfast the next morning was just as silent as the evening meal had been. When I finished, I stood and cleared my throat. "I will see you across the water."

Dai Ling only shrugged in response, not meeting my eyes. She looked so sad sitting there that I almost reached out to her again, but stopped myself. I had married her under duress. She was not Sofie, or Tessa, even. I had no room left in my heart to feel anything for her. I had to save my uncle.

My portion of our army marched west. I rode near the front with my mounted guardsmen, leaving the carriage for my servants, which now included Ursala and the daughter that I had no intention of acknowledging.

We met no resistance at the border with Malar, so we kept marching west. We set a fast pace, hoping to reach the coast as soon as possible. Each day, I rode my horse at the front of the army and said little to anyone.

Sofie's death still weighed heavily on me. Her face had kept that death dagger away, but now it was back again. I rode for hours staring at nothing in an attempt to keep my dark thoughts at bay. At night, I stared at the single lamp in my tent until my eyes finally fell closed. Then I dreamed of that dagger, and Tessa's death—only sometimes the face was Tessa's and sometimes it was Sofie's. I would awaken in a cold sweat and stare at the lamp until it started all over again.

Like my early voyage on the *Sea Cow*, the days rolled past without my knowledge. Only brief glimpses of what occurred around me broke through my dazed mind. One was after the first day of marching, when Ursala tried to present Sofie's child to me. I looked down at the babe's face and had to fight an urge to throttle it for the death it had caused. I turned away and ordered the baby taken from my sight. Wasn't that part of

Ursala's plan? She had wanted to snare me with Sofie, and now with Sofie's child?

The next moment of total clarity was when we finally reached the coast. We had been marching for several weeks when we topped a rise to look down upon a sandy beach, where several boats waited offshore.

I turned to Li Wu, who rode by my side. "Call for Ivan."

He looked startled by my words, probably because I hadn't truly spoken to him since leaving Gea, but he quickly turned his horse to call for Ivan. When Ivan came marching up, it felt as though I looked at him through a long tunnel. I had to shake my head a couple of times to properly focus my eyes.

"How soon can we get loaded on the boats?"

Ivan looked up at me, searching my face as if to see if I was really there. "Are you back with us, Olaf?"

"How soon can we cross?"

He glanced down at the beach and then back at the army behind us. "We will make camp on the sand and begin loading first thing in the morning. It might take most of the night getting prepared to load."

I looked around. It was late afternoon. Night or day didn't matter to me, but I realized Ivan was right, and we should prepare for the morrow. I nodded down at him. "Make it happen."

He stayed next to me as I dismounted my horse. When I gave him a questioning look, he said, "The order has already been given, Olaf."

He reached out to me, but then pulled his hand back. "How are you feeling?" He had been with me on the *Sea Cow*. He probably wondered if I would come back to myself now, as I had done then. I wasn't sure. This time, there was no Sofie to help me.

I realized that I had pushed Dai Ling away because I couldn't stand the thought of another woman that I loved dying. The realization didn't make me any happier, nor did the thought of meeting back up with my estranged wife on the opposite shore. I resolved to keep my mind as clear as possible moving forward. If I was going to save my uncle, I had to keep my wits about me.

I gave Ivan a fake smile. "I am ready to march to Haven, Ivan. We are going to save our home."

Ivan wasn't fooled by my smile, but he nodded at me. "They are setting up your tent, Olaf. Try to get some rest before morning … if you can."

"Rest," I scoffed. "I will rest once I am with my uncle in Haven."

Ivan didn't say anything else. He hurried away to see to our troops.

I was surprised the next morning to see the *Sea Cow* was one of the ships waiting to ferry us across. When I came aboard, Captain Gregor smiled my way, but I ignored him. I headed straight for the ladder to the stern castle and took up my position at the rail.

For a brief moment, it felt like I had never left Kartoba. I remembered standing at that rail as we set sail more than a year before. Sofie had been alive then, and I had no idea that my servants conspired to ensnare me.

I looked over my shoulder at Bren, who stood as stone-faced as my Wolf guards and as still as a statue. At the beginning of our journey, he had been running barefoot on the deck, enjoying his first experience onboard a ship. Had he changed for the better? Had I changed at all?

I mentally shook myself, trying to drive the thought from my mind. I had changed, and I was determined to save my uncle or die trying. It was all I had left.

It took two days to cross the strait. This time, we didn't worry about passing Rock Island, which guarded the entrance to the Sea of Pearls. Our fleet was too large for the patrol craft there to challenge.

It was late on the second afternoon when we spied the far bank. The ship captains headed for the spot where the first half of our army had landed. As I watched our approach from the rail, I saw fewer tents than I'd expected. A lone birlinn approached from the beach. The *Sea Cow* flew my white lion banner, so the birlinn headed straight toward us.

As it drew near, I recognized Neasa on the birlinn and hurried down the ladder to meet her as she crossed over. "She has left," Neasa called out as I approached.

"What? Who has left?"

"Your wife, the Butterfly Princess. She has marched north to join her grandfather in Jewel."

My mind flashed back to the last words Dai Ling had said to me and the look upon her face. She had offered to march with me, but I'd turned her down. She had said, "It will be as you wish." Had she planned this, or seen it in her vision?

I reached for Bren for support. I felt my dagger vision start to take hold, and then my head flew to the side and my vision cleared. Neasa stood before me, her left hand on her hip and the right poised to slap me again.

"Snap out of it, Olaf! Now's not the time."

I was shocked by her action. I turned to look at my Wolf guards, who had done nothing to stop her from striking me. My face burned. Surprisingly, normally dour Moshe was the one who smiled back at me as if to say, "About time."

"Who's left?" I finally managed to ask, rubbing my cheek.

"My warriors are still here," Neasa said. "Cao Wangsun left with the princess."

No surprise there. I turned to Ivan, who had also travelled aboard the *Sea Cow*. "What about my wife's army? Will they stay with us once they learn she's left?"

"You are still determined to go west?" Ivan asked. He knew my answer, so I just stared at him until he nodded. "Okay, then," he said. "We land our guardsmen first and raise her standard up as if she's still here."

"I'm sure at least the officers will realize she is gone, along with half our army."

Ivan shook his head. "The Nei-chang traveled with her and took the best that we had. The ones who are left are the newest recruits—barely trained and relatively clueless."

I shook my head at our predicament. "Maybe we're better off leaving them here."

Neasa shook her head. "They are bodies. We can train them as we march west."

Her words struck me as strange. I tried to figure out what she meant. "Why are you still here?" I asked. "You could take your birlinn to Andamar and join in the Kail invasion."

For a moment, she looked as though she was going to slap me again. Instead, she smiled and said, "I little bird told me to stay."

I looked past her to the raven banner flying on the mast of her birlinn and repressed a shudder. More visions? I was afraid to ask.

We landed the men as Ivan had suggested. After further council with Ivan and Neasa, I addressed the troops that evening. I told them that the first army had marched ahead to clear a path and that we were going to follow. We heard no complaints from the troops.

We marched out the next morning.

CHAPTER 28: A DESPERATE MARCH

The march west was a blur. I tried my best to stay focused, but spent much of the time looking out at the countryside as I rode along.

Ivan, Talon, Neasa, and Carrog took care of training the recruits as we marched. We had maybe five thousand fighting men, and just as many women and children tagging along, as if we were on a holiday. Dai Ling had been right, though. As we marched through Malar, more people flocked to her banner.

The Empire of Jewel took up a large area of land, but the western part, through which we marched, was not as heavily populated as the heart around the Sea of Pearls. We passed several towns, but didn't stop to fight.

All my people knew why we marched, and where. We pushed hard, day after day, week after week, to reach Haven before it was too late.

Once we passed out of Malar and into the province of Naga, we saw signs of the Black Order that had passed before us. A marching army of that size left a noticeable trail. The width of the trail, trampled from so many marching feet, worried me. Did we have enough men to even make a difference?

Ivan talked to the people that we encountered and kept me abreast of our progress. Originally, we were several months behind the Black Order. As we traveled, we were catching up to them, because we were smaller and traveling faster. I had no idea if we would reach them in time to make a difference.

About a month into the march, Ivan came to me to let me know that the men were grumbling. We had marched quickly, for long days and short nights. My army was getting tired. They were starting to realize that the Butterfly Princess had not gone this way.

Somehow, the word had gotten out—probably from the new recruits we picked up in Malar—that Dai Ling had gone to Jewel. Also, it was getting colder. It was early winter, and we weren't prepared for the cold weather.

We had a conference in my tent that evening to discuss our options. There was no table, as it would have taken up too much space and too much time to set up at the end of each long march. We sat on cushions in a circle. Ivan was the first to speak.

"We have gained on the Black Order, Olaf, but it is going to get cold soon. We should probably look for a town to stay for the winter."

"Do you think the Black Order will stop for the winter?" I asked.

He shook his head. "They have been stripping supplies from the towns as they pass. They won't stop until they reach their destination."

Talon nodded his agreement. "Yes, they have left little for us to forage. We are already on reduced rations. We need to stop for a while, to regain our strength."

"And what happens to Haven and the rest of the Seven Kingdoms if we do that?"

Ivan shook his head. "More than likely, the battle will be over before we get there."

He paused to let me think about the impact of that statement before he offered options. "It is not too late to turn back. We could turn south and join the Kail in their attack on Andamar. I'm sure we can find a town in that direction that has not been plundered."

"No!" Neasa shouted, beating me to it. "Our destiny is to the west. I will follow Olaf through the winter, if need be." The fanatical look in her eye probably matched my own. It made me stop and wonder why she was so determined. Was it just to avoid marrying the Reik? Was there something more to her latest raven vision? That look in her eye almost made me reconsider my own determination.

Ivan sighed. "Okay, but you probably need to address the men again, Olaf, to keep them moving forward."

"What am I supposed to say?" I knew my own mind, sort of. I knew that I would not stop until I saw my uncle. Maybe if I saw him again, that death dagger in my nightmares would leave me for good. But how could I explain that? If I told them the basis for my obsession, it would probably drive them away.

"I will speak to the men," Neasa announced. All eyes turned to her. "They know me, don't they? I've been training them. Besides, I know how to get men fired up." That last was said with a sly smile, and none of us argued the point.

"Yes, speak to them," I said, not wanting to think any more about what motivated her. As long as she didn't try to slip into my bed, I would take all the help she would give me. "We march again at first light."

I didn't listen to Neasa's speech to the men, but the next morning, we marched out again, heading west.

Despite Neasa's encouragement, we were slowly losing our army. The terrain we passed through was changing from heavily wooded to sparsely wooded, and finally to a rocky plain. Once we passed out of the trees, more and more of our men and their families disappeared in the night.

The core remained: Neasa's men, the guardsmen that Ivan had been recruiting, and a hardcore group of mostly Sikk men who were determined to fight under the golden butterfly banner whether my wife was present or not. We had also picked up a few men as we passed through Jewel, mostly those disgruntled by the passing Imperial army.

By the time we arrived at the river that marked the border of Katch, the last Imperial province before reaching Haven, our army was a lean but determined force. It had turned cold. We saw our first flutters of snowfall as we crossed the river.

I had been in Katch before, with my uncle. We had ridden to a town called Uris to parley with a representative for the Katchian king. Uris was still a little way to the northwest, but it seemed close compared to how far we had come. I remembered that meeting. The King of Katch had demanded my uncle's support against the Empire of Jewel, and my uncle had refused. I just hoped that Katch had held out long enough for us to reach my uncle in time.

We followed the Imperial army's tracks through Katch. Within a week, we arrived at the capital city of Azule—or what was left of it. The city had stone walls, but we could see where they had been breached in several places. The gates were torn and broken. A haze hung over the city, from where the buildings had been razed. The area was trampled and littered with weapons and the dead. The smell of rotting flesh and wood smoke permeated the air.

A small camp of people had formed next to the ruined city, where several people were digging through the battlefield, either looking for lost family members or pillaging the corpses. The army was silent as we looked over the carnage. One of the scouts grabbed a man out of the camp and brought him over to where I sat on my horse. Ivan and Neasa came up to listen to what he had to say.

"What happened here?" I asked the man. He was older, with a long robe and beard like a typical Katchian. He hands were covered with blood and he had a cloth wrapped around his nose and mouth.

"The Black Order." He lifted the cloth to spit on the ground as he said the name. "They came and slaughtered everyone."

"Where did they go?" Ivan asked.

The man turned and pointed to the northwest, towards the Seven Kingdoms. "They went to fight the Wolf Lord," he said.

We were still several weeks from Haven. Would we get there in time?

"How long ago did they leave here?"

The old man pointed again. "They left for Uris maybe a month ago. Uris fell, and then they marched west."

So Uris had fallen as well. There was nothing else between Azule and Haven except dry grassland.

"Do you know if Haven still stands?"

He shrugged. "Many people fled to the Wolf Lord when the Black Order arrived. If it does not stand, there will be more dead there than there are here."

I looked over the ruined city, which was much bigger than my uncle's fort, and tried not to think about his fate. "We have to go!"

"Who are you?" the old man asked. He wouldn't recognize any of our banners, and he probably wondered if we came to help or hinder the invaders.

"I am Olaf Stenson," I said. "Nephew to the Wolf Baron."

He looked up at the banners flying overhead—the golden butterfly, white lion, and black raven—and then back toward my army. We probably looked none-too-impressive after our prolonged march, but to my surprise, he smiled.

"The wolf cub comes to join his uncle," he said. He gestured back toward the camp. "We have some food and the weapons we pulled from the dead. Maybe some of our men will join you."

"Thank you," I said, "but we must hurry."

"We will take the food," Ivan quickly cut in, "and the men and weapons." He looked up at me, not quite in challenge. "We can make camp nearby tonight before continuing."

It was midday, and I didn't want to stop, but Ivan was right. The men were tired and hungry. I nodded in agreement.

It began to snow a bit harder as we left Azule the next morning. A few days later, we passed a burnt-out Uris. Fewer corpses littered the streets, probably because most of the remaining Katchians had fled to my uncle's keep after the fall of Azule.

I remembered the grasslands around Uris from my last trip there, but now the grass was brown and a light layer of snow covered everything. At our current pace, we were maybe a week's march away from Haven.

I was beginning to get nervous. We sent mounted scouts out ahead to see if my uncle's keep still stood. Each hour that passed, as we waited for their return, seemed like an eternity.

When the pair of scouts came back two days later, they brought word that my uncle's keep still held. The Black Order's army besieged it, but it stood. The scouts reported that the attacking army looked to be approximately twenty thousand men—mostly foot soldiers, but they had more than a thousand mounted troops as well.

They had built a fortified camp outside the keep and had siege machines that threw stones at the walls. I had never seen the banners of the Black Order. I'd heard about them through my uncle's men and later the Dai Jun. The scouts told me the army flew a banner that looked similar to the Dai Jun's, only the dragon was black instead of green. That made sense, if the Black Order had been sent out by a Dai Jun of the past.

CHAPTER 29: HEART'S DESIRE

Four days later, I looked at the black dragon banner with my own eyes. The land was flat, but in the distance I could see the walls of Haven with my uncle's wolf's head banner still flying from the keep.

By comparison, the surrounding army looked enormous.

As Ivan and his officers called out orders to our own army, I spied a group of horsemen heading in our direction from the Imperial army. We had no more than a hundred mounted men, because most of our horses were used for carrying supplies. Over the course of our journey, Li Wu had become the leader of our mounted troops. He left a couple of mounted guardsmen with me but took the rest out to meet the enemy.

I quickly dismounted. Although I had ridden across Jewel to get there, I had no desire to try to fight on horseback. I handed off my mount to one of the Stenson guards and stumped over to where Ivan stood. He was watching the approaching horsemen through a glass.

"Their scouts have been watching us since yesterday, but I'm sure they're coming over to see who we are and why we're here." He lowered the glass and frowned at me. "I'm wondering myself, Olaf. We can't do anything against an army of that size."

I ignored him, but held out my hand for the glass. He handed it over, and I put it to my eye. The horsemen heading our way weren't enough to do more than talk, so I looked past them to the camp and fortress beyond. I could see the wooden machines throwing stones at the fortress walls and hear the crack of the impact. The walls were higher than when I had left, but in several spots, the stones had cracked from the pounding.

My uncle's keep still looked intact behind the walls, and from the battlement I could see his wolf's head banner flying along with several others—hawk, dog, rat, and snake—which meant all the free orders were present. I also saw banners for other kingdoms: Highpoint's fortress banner, and the horse head of Cree among others. That meant that the Seven Kingdoms had sent all their military strength to hold back the Black Order. If the Imperial army won here, they won my entire homeland.

"All the free orders are there," Ivan said, "along with whatever armies the kingdoms could throw together."

I looked over at him as he rubbed at his chin. "Highpoint's the only one that'll do any good. That means they may have six thousand real fighting men behind those walls—enough to hold them for a time, maybe, but not to attack."

He gave me a serious look. "Once the Black Order realizes how many men we have, they will leave a small force to keep them bottled up and send the rest to take care of us." He shook his head. "Your uncle won't be able to help us, Olaf. We should withdraw now before it's too late."

There was no way that I would leave after getting this close. Ivan knew, by the look on my face. "At least send the women and children away," he said. "Send them back to Uris with an armed guard to keep them safe. There are enough walls left standing to provide a little protection, at least."

I nodded. "You handle it, Ivan. Send a few of our guardsmen that you trust with the men from Azule. They know the area."

Wu Li and his horsemen had met the enemy riders and now were escorting them back toward us. Ivan shook his head and spoke slowly. "I should have died a long time ago, Olaf. I'm not afraid of death—but that is what we are facing here." He gave me a sardonic smile. "If we're going to attack, we need to do it soon, before our men realize it."

Then he said under his breath, "I'd rather die than face your uncle anyway." I knew what he was talking about. He had failed in his mission to keep me safely in the east.

Ivan sent out the order for the women and children to leave for Uris while we waited for the enemy's messengers. I felt a brief pang of guilt as I thought of Gabriele and Lulu, and even Ursala. They had traveled with me across Jewel and now I sent them away, trying to keep them out of danger. I hoped they made it to a safe place, but I couldn't dwell on their fate.

I had finally made it back to Haven, and I was determined to strike a blow against the Black Order.

As the enemy riders approached, most of them were held back, but one rode forward, surrounded by Li Wu's men. He rode up next to where I stood with Ivan, surrounded by guardsmen.

"Who are you, and why have you come," the man demanded. He wore black-lacquered armor with a matching helmet that was topped with horsehair.

I figured it wouldn't hurt to try a little misdirection. "We are from Jewel. The Dai Jun in the east has marched against the capital. The emperor demands that you return."

The black-clad messenger looked up at the banners flying overhead. "I do not recognize your insignia. You are not from the empire."

I smiled up at him. "Okay then, we are here to ensure you leave."

His returning smile held no mirth. "You should have brought a bigger hammer." He turned his horse and headed back to his men.

"Once the women are away," I told Ivan, "give the order to march."

He nodded and moved away. I stood there, staring at the field before us. The ground had a thin layer of snow, but it was more a brown slush than white. The army across the way outnumbered us by more than I cared to think. It didn't matter, though. The only living person who still mattered to me was in the keep on the other side. Either I was going to get there, or I'd die trying.

Neasa walked up next to me and surveyed the terrain. "I told you about this day."

"What do you mean?"

She was dressed for war in her leather and braids and had added a shield to her sword.

She smiled at me and then pointed toward the enemy camp. "I told you I saw it. We would stand side-by-side before a dragon."

I still didn't understand the woman. "Is this the kingdom your vision showed you?"

She threw back her head and laughed. "It is what has come to pass, partner. At least I'm not marrying that old bastard Maedoc, and my father can stop worrying about what I'll do with my life." She slapped me on the shoulder and turned back to gather our army.

I saw that they were forming up in ranks. My blue banner flew from the middle above relatively ordered ranks of blue-clad guardsmen—more than I had ever seen in one place. On my right were Neasa's forces, brightly colored Kail warriors of all shapes and colors. They were deadly-looking fighters. On the left was the golden butterfly standard with a mishmash of men with various weapons, but their ranks looked as ordered as the guardsmen, after so many days and nights of training along the way from Sikk. Li Wu's horsemen were behind me, ready to advance before the infantry.

Neasa headed over to her warriors and I approached the front of the Stenson blue ranks, flanked by my Wolf guards. I stopped next to Ivan.

"You should be on horseback, Olaf, near the back," he said. He wanted me positioned so I could escape if things went as he expected. He probably also knew that I wouldn't listen.

My heart was suddenly filled with pride. I hadn't felt that way since as long as I could remember, but standing before that army made my heart swell. I forgot about everything else as I pulled out my sword and held it over my head. "For Haven!" I shouted.

The army was quiet, so I shouted it again, "For Haven!"

Upon the third try, the men started responding. Before long, the whole army was shouting, "Haven! Haven! Haven!"

As we began to move forward, it felt as though I marched on a cloud. I took a deep, shuddering breath. So this was what it felt like! After all this time, I finally felt alive. At last, I had a purpose beyond surviving.

As we marched forward, Li Wu's horsemen screened our advance, but finally, the enemy encampment started to stir. I heard horns sound in the distance as they began to form up to meet us. Ivan grinned at me, "They did not fortify this side of the camp. They will have to march out to meet us if they don't want us in their baggage." He shrugged. "They'll still crush us, but maybe we can take a few with us—enough to make this worth it."

After riding for so long, I had a hard time keeping up with the marching army. In fact, Ivan soon outdistanced me, and I began to fall back within the ranks, limping as fast as my crippled leg would allow. The army parted and marched around me, except for my Wolf guards and Bren, and a group of guardsmen who had obviously been assigned to protect me. Ulric, the surviving brother from Highpoint I had met in Xiang, led this bodyguard.

"Make them slow down!" I shouted at him, suddenly realizing Ivan's strategy for keeping me out of the fighting. Ivan knew I would insist upon marching with the army, so now they marched around me. By the time we met the enemy, I would be in the last rank.

Ulric just nodded and smiled and kept on marching beside me.

I picked up my pace, my bad leg protesting the increase in speed. I was probably in the center of the ranks now and determined to slide no further. For the next few minutes, I could think of nothing besides keeping up the pace. My leg ached and threatened to dump me on the ground with every step, and I took gasping breaths from the effort.

The ground was already rumbling from all the marching feet, but then it felt like the earth itself shook, and I heard the thunder of hooves. I was too far back to see, but I heard a crash and the screaming of men and horses.

The men around me slowed. Now I had no trouble keeping up as I continued to push forward.

Suddenly, I stopped short against the guardsman in front of me, and the clashing of weapons grew closer. I could see the men pressing forward around me, but my guardsmen kept an area clear so that I was not crowded. Mehki and Moshe stood just ahead on either side, and Bren stood at my back. Moshe turned to me and said, "They are coming."

A line of attackers were pushing their way through our ranks. Several horsemen led the way, but they had lost their momentum and were being pulled from their horses as they tried to keep moving forward. One horseman headed toward us, and Moshe stepped forward before he could get close and hit the horse between the eyes with his axe. It dropped to the ground and the rider was crushed underneath its weight. I heard the animal scream and saw it kick the air as we passed.

Before I knew it, we were in the midst of the fight. Moshe and Mehki swung their deadly axes as if they had been born with them. They cut through man after man as the enemy pushed against us. My blood was pumping, and it felt like I could run all the way back to Sikk without stopping—but that was the last place I wanted to be.

I couldn't see my uncle's keep ahead of us, but I kept its image in my mind's eye as I swung my sword at anyone that got close.

The men we fought were not wearing black-lacquered armor like the messenger, but I could see the black dragon banner just ahead as we tried to advance against them. Men streamed around us as we fought. I found myself in the middle of the army again.

A horn sounded, and the enemy stopped pushing forward and began to back away from our line. The men around me shouted and cheered.

I pushed my way forward until I once again stood at the front of the army. Ivan was nowhere in sight, but I looked to the left and saw Neasa with Carrog by her side. Once they saw me, they exchanged words and then Carrog headed my way with a group of Kail warriors.

"Ho, Olaf!" he called as he approached. "They are trying to break through your men in the middle. The fools think you are the toughest nut to crack." He smacked his chest with his huge axe and let out a cry that would do any beast proud. "Let's show them a thing or two."

"Fiend! Fiend!" his men cried out in response to the call.

Carrog laughed and then winked at me with his good eye. "Now they will send the real fighters." Just as he said it, another horn sounded, and the black-clad warriors began to advance against us.

Carrog lifted his axe above his head and his men took up the cry again. "Fiend! Fiend!" He looked down at me one more time and said, "Let me show you how it's done." He rushed forward against the black line with his men screaming at his back. The guardsmen around me caught their excitement and followed. I found myself moving to follow, my blood pumping. Moshe and Mehki easily passed me, but they kept close as we rushed towards the enemy.

My ears were filled with screaming and the ringing of weapons, and my eyes with flying blood and men pressing close together. It felt like I was watching the chaos through someone else's eyes. Men fell all around, but I still moved forward with the help of my Wolf guards.

Suddenly, I saw Mehki spin sideways with a surprised look on his face. His axe fell from his hands as he toppled. Then Bren was next to me, swinging his sword like a madman and screaming like one of the Kail.

I heard drums suddenly begin to pound and a new set of horns sounded in the distance. A moment later, men were shouting all through our ranks. Then a man to my right cried out, "They are coming out from the fort!"

My heart surged at the news. My uncle was coming! I would see him again!

A sudden line of pain seared through my side and I looked down in disbelief at the blood that began to soak through my blue coat. Where had it come from?

Moshe pushed me aside and cut down my attacker, who fell at my feet, his black lacquered helmet bouncing off the bloody snow.

Bren yelled in my ear, "Come away, Olaf! You need to come away."

I could feel the warm blood flowing down my side and the searing pain of the wound, but his words had no effect because a figure caught my eye across the battlefield.

She was standing there in the middle of the bloody field looking at me. My heart soared.

Sofie gestured for me to come to her, and all the pain of the world melted away. I took a step forward and looked down in surprise at my right leg that had somehow grown straight again.

I thought I heard Bren call my name again, but then Sofie stepped forward and held her hand out to me. "Come away, Love."

When I took her hand, the frantic feeling that had been with me as long as I could remember disappeared. I was flooded with a sense of peace that I had never felt before.

Sofie smiled at me, her hand warm in mine.

"I have been waiting for you."

EPILOGUE: CRY UNCLE

I looked over the battlefield from the top of my shattered walls and wondered how I still lived. I should have died years ago, in one battle or another, like the rest of my lost company. But still I live, sitting here looking over another field of death.

I was sure it would happen this time—sure I would finally find my rest. Who would have expected an army of strangers to show up and turn the tide of battle for me and my fledgling kingdom, to save all the Seven Kingdoms?

A group of riders approached from the burnt-out remains of the enemy encampment. The black dragon flag had flown above that camp. It was the banner of the Black Order, who had sworn to destroy the Free Orders and the Seven Kingdoms. Somehow, it was almost disappointing that they had been defeated. Who would I fight now? Why was I still here?

The riders stopped before the walls and the leader called up to me, "They are coming!"

It was my nephew, Jarad. Somehow, he had survived weeks of fighting at the head of his cavalry troop. He was vain and stupid, but I had to admit that he knew how to fight on horseback. Too bad he was the wrong nephew—or should I say, the wrong relative. I had sent my one true nephew east to keep him safe.

Osha had been standing at my back, but now she stepped forward and placed her hand on my shoulder. She knew my mind better than anyone. She knew that I lamented my survival, but somehow she still loved me, fool woman.

"You should go down and meet them, Olaf." She was always reminding me of what I should do, and she was usually right.

I nodded and headed down the stairs to the main gate, or what was left of it. Musk waited for me at the bottom of the stairs. He was the supreme commander of the Free Orders. If he hadn't come to Haven against the council's wishes, I wouldn't be alive, either.

Musk gave me a wave as I arrived. "Let's go see who these saviors are." He sounded as boisterous as usual, but he looked tired. We were all tired.

I nodded and led the way out the gate.

My men had cleared the bodies away from the path. My Wolf guards surrounded us as we headed toward the group of strangers who had come to our aid. Most of my troops were Katchian now. For some reason, they had adopted me as their own. I had no idea why, besides their king being a royal ass who had fled with as much gold as he could carry once the Black Order arrived at his doorstep. I should have killed him when I first met him.

Among the strangers approaching us was a big man with a terrible scar cutting across his face. The scar was obviously old, and the man was obviously a Kail, as was the woman walking beside him dressed out for battle. The group included several other women, which was surprising. The other women were dressed in a familiar blue. Finally, I spotted two men carrying a stretcher. Even from that short distance, I could tell one of them was a Katchian—a Wolf guard?

Kail warriors? Wolf guards? Who *were* these people?

I stepped forward, waving my own guards away so I could see more clearly.

As the party stopped before me, I had a sinking feeling in the pit of my stomach. I knew that Wolf guard. He shouldn't be here!

He averted his eyes as he stepped forward with the other litter-bearer to set the body before me. "I am sorry, Wolf Lord," the man said in Imperial. He knew he had failed me.

I didn't want to look. The gods couldn't be that cruel. This was *my* time to die!

I felt Osha squeeze my arm as she stepped up beside me. She had seen worse, and I had stopped trying to protect her from such things. She dropped to her knees next to the litter. "Oh, Olaf!"

With her words, my heart felt heavier than I could ever remember, but I forced myself to look down upon my nephew. The fool had a smile on his face. How could he have died happy when he should have been safe in the Eastern Confederation with all the silver he would ever need?

I felt the hot tears coursing down my cheeks before I realized that I cried. He looked just like my sister with that silly grin on his face. I hadn't thought of her for years until I met him, a little over a year ago, and now I was reminded of her again.

The other litter-bearer wore a Stenson blue coat. He spoke from the other side of the body. "Baron Stenson, we have served your nephew, and have brought him back to you." He looked so young and earnest. I remembered him from Kartoba, when I sent my namesake east. What did he expect from me now?

He waved towards the odd pair of Kail warriors. "These are the allies who fought by his side, along with the Eastern army that he brought here to fight for you."

The Kail woman stepped forward. "I am Neasa Dark Thunder—your nephew's greatest friend and ally."

I wiped the tears from my eyes and growled at her. "You are Kail."

She nodded. "But my destiny is here—maybe with you, maybe not." She looked toward the other three women in the group as if to say they would decide.

This woman was no weeping maid. How had Olaf found such a woman? What good did it do him, and what did I care what she did now? I was supposed to be dead, and my nephew should have been alive and safe. She could have my kingdom as far as I was concerned. I had no use for it now.

The three other women, all dressed in Stenson Blue, stepped forward. Two were younger, but the one in the middle was quite a bit older. She carried a baby, which she now held out to me. "Master Stenson, here is Sofie, your nephew's child."

The girl looked up at me with my nephew's eyes, my sister's eyes. Oh, the gods are cruel!

Osha jumped up and reached for the child. The woman handed her over, rather reluctantly. The babe reached up and grabbed Osha's nose and then smiled.

Osha turned to me. "Olaf, you still have a family." She clutched the baby to her chest, but walked over so she was close to me.

I held out my hand, and the girl grabbed my little finger and held it tight. I let out a long sigh as I looked down at the last of my blood line.

It wasn't time to die. I had to train yet another grub.

ABOUT THE AUTHOR

Freddie Silva has been writing Fantasy and Science Fiction Stories since 1993. He has always had a passion for history, religion, and mythology. He strives to use elements from these interests in his writing. You can visit the author's web site at www.freddiesilva.com.

Printed in Great Britain
by Amazon